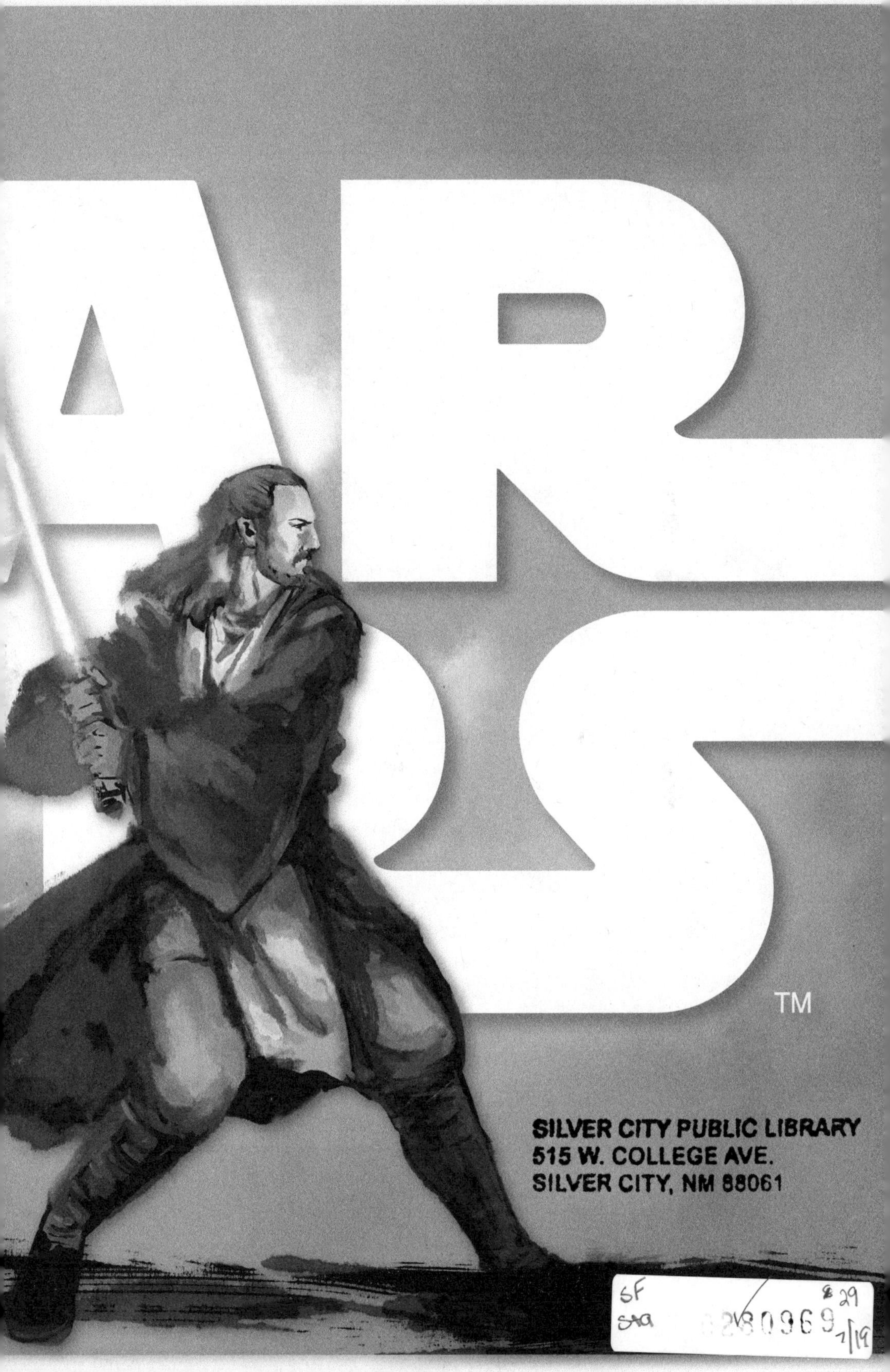
TM

By Claudia Gray

STAR WARS
Star Wars: Lost Stars
Star Wars: Bloodline
Star Wars: Leia, Princess of Alderaan
Star Wars: Master & Apprentice

EVERNIGHT
Evernight
Stargazer
Hourglass
Afterlife
Balthazar

SPELLCASTER
Spellcaster
The First Midnight Spell
Steadfast
Sorceress

FIREBIRD
A Thousand Pieces of You
Ten Thousand Skies Above You
A Million Worlds with You

CONSTELLATION
Defy the Stars
Defy the Worlds
Defy the Fates

MASTER
&APPRENTICE

MASTER
&APPRENTICE

CLAUDIA GRAY

DEL REY
NEW YORK

Published in the United States by Del Rey,
an imprint of Random House, a division of
Penguin Random House LLC, New York.

DEL REY and the HOUSE colophon are registered
trademarks of Penguin Random House LLC.

Hardback ISBN 978-0-525-61937-6
International edition ISBN 978-1-9848-1954-3
Ebook ISBN 978-0-525-61938-3

Printed in the United States of America on acid-free paper

randomhousebooks.com

2 4 6 8 9 7 5 3 1

First Edition

Book design by Elizabeth A. D. Eno

THE DEL REY

STAR WARS

TIMELINE

MASTER & APPRENTICE

 THE PHANTOM MENACE

 ATTACK OF THE CLONES

THE CLONE WARS (TV SERIES)

DARK DISCIPLE

III REVENGE OF THE SITH

CATALYST: A ROGUE ONE NOVEL
LORDS OF THE SITH
TARKIN

SOLO

THRAWN
A NEW DAWN
THRAWN: ALLIANCES
THRAWN: TREASON

REBELS (TV SERIES)

ROGUE ONE

Prophecy in dreams is possible through the illumination
of the active intellect over our soul.
—Ibn Rushd, also known as Averroes

A long time ago in a galaxy far, far away. . . .

MASTER
&APPRENTICE

It is a time of peace. The GALACTIC REPUBLIC, which has governed for thousands of years, has provided prosperity to many worlds and opportunity to most. Only a few shadows of conflict darken the galaxy—and these are handled by the JEDI KNIGHTS, the guardians of peace and justice throughout the Republic.

One of those conflicts arises on the planet Teth, a source of corruption that threatens many nearby systems. The Jedi Council sends QUI-GON JINN and his young Padawan to investigate. But the criminal element on Teth has chosen not to cooperate . . .

CHAPTER ONE

———————— ⚜ ————————

There is no emotion—there is peace.
There is no ignorance—there is knowledge.
There is no passion—there is serenity.
There is no chaos—there is harmony.

Whoever wrote the Jedi Code, thought Qui-Gon Jinn, *never had to deal with the Hutts.*

He ran through the stone passageway of the Hutt compound, the sound of blaster bolts echoing behind him, flashes of red lighting up the darkness like heat lightning. His pursuers would round the bend soon and have a clear shot, which made it a very good time to dash through the nearest door.

"Obi-Wan!" he called. "To the left!"

"Yes, Master," panted Obi-Wan, who was only steps behind Qui-Gon.

Is he winded already? Qui-Gon thought as they dashed down a staircase that would lead to the outer, more modern area of the Hutt compound. Their escape thus far had included no more than a three-minute run—and of course, scaling a twenty-meter wall. But in the proper meditative state that shouldn't have been difficult.

Obi-Wan hasn't perfected meditation in combat, Qui-Gon reminded himself as his Padawan's steps echoed behind his on the long staircase. *By his age, I was able to—*

Qui-Gon stopped himself. Comparisons between his training and Obi-Wan's weren't constructive. Each individual had a different path to the Force. What he needed to be concentrating on was their path out of here.

The darkness surrounding them was pierced below by light streaming in through an open doorway. Qui-Gon grabbed his lightsaber and activated it, illuminating the stairwell. Obi-Wan did the same, only a second behind him, and in time for them to run out of the stairwell into what turned out to be a very large, very crowded room.

Specifically, one of the Hutts' spice-hookah dens.

Heavy, sweet smoke fogged the air. Musicians played atop various floating platforms, which hovered at different heights above the spice-addled denizens below. From his gilded dais, Wanbo the Hutt sucked in enough smoke to fill all three of his lungs. Nobody was alert enough to immediately notice the two Jedi Knights who'd appeared above them.

But lightsabers tended to attract attention.

"Apa hoohah gardo!" Wanbo croaked, dazedly gesturing with his tail. One of his Gamorrean guards squealed and waddled to intercept them at the foot of the stairs. This concerned Qui-Gon far less than the heavy thudding of half a dozen human guards on the steps, only seconds behind, and two more Gamorreans at the door.

"Jump!" Qui-Gon called. With that he leapt across the room to land on one of the band platforms, currently occupied by the horn section. The Kitonak stumbled back in alarm, and one of them toppled from the edge of the platform into the filthy, pillowed moat that surrounded

Wanbo. She landed atop a Trandoshan, who hissed in protest, but most of the dazed group hardly seemed to notice.

He glanced back. Obi-Wan's jump had taken him to the platform where a Shawda Ubb was playing the Growdi harmonique. Unfortunately, this was a sterner species of musician. While the Shawda Ubb kept two steady limbs on the harmonique, he lashed out with another, then spat at Obi-Wan.

Poison, Qui-Gon thought with horror, but Obi-Wan dodged easily. His Padawan's reflexes were sharp. If Obi-Wan lacked serenity in battle, he didn't lack instincts.

As the human guards appeared at the stairs, Qui-Gon called, "Handle that door!" With that he stamped the platform control, sending it zooming toward the guards. Amid the fray, he called upon the deep quietness within, the soul of the universe that always listened, always answered.

Without consciously thinking, or aiming, Qui-Gon brought his lightsaber up, over, aside—blocking every blaster bolt. They fired faster, but it made no difference; he could sense each shot before it happened. His confidence was not shared by the Kitonak musicians, the rest of whom jumped from the platform. Good—that way he could concentrate on only his own safety and his Padawan's. Of course, Obi-Wan could take care of himself.

Or so Qui-Gon thought for the remaining two seconds before Obi-Wan swooped down over the door controls and stabbed them with his lightsaber, heat melting the controls from within.

Blast it! Qui-Gon thought. "I meant, take care of the *guards* at the door!"

"You could've said so!" Obi-Wan shouted.

Which was true. *Always with the specific instructions! Must he be so literal?* But this made little difference with two Gamorreans still between them and their best escape route. Worse, the control panel appeared to govern not only the door but also the floating platforms, which went haywire. Qui-Gon stumbled as his platform tilted sharply to the left, yet he retained his balance. Barely. One blaster bolt seared past him to blow a smoking chunk from the wall. Even that one miss was too many—

No time for hypotheticals, Qui-Gon reminded himself. *There is no past, no future. Only now.*

Obi-Wan did not appear to be trying to calm himself. He looked anything *but* calm, jumping down from his platform moments before it sent the Shawda Ubb and the Growdi into the wall with a musical crash. Yet he handily slashed through the ax of one Gamorrean and the arm of another, which sent the first squealing off in terror.

This finally pierced the haze of spice and stupidity in Wanbo the Hutt's head. *"Hopa! Kickeeyuna Jedi killee!"* The Gamorreans at the stairs began thumping down, no doubt to seize Qui-Gon when he fell from his crazily off-kilter platform.

"Master?" Obi-Wan called. "Are you all right?"

"Just get us a ship if you can!"

With a nod, Obi-Wan obeyed, dashing out of the spice den into the labyrinthine Hutt palace of Teth.

Qui-Gon gripped the edge of the platform as it careened toward Wanbo again. A few of the people below had begun to chortle at the spectacle of a Jedi clinging onto a band floater. *Well, let them laugh— better that they remain distracted,* he thought as he flicked on a tracker unit at his belt.

His hover platform whizzed toward a counterpart that remained mostly stationary, where a Kitonak huddled with his Kloo horn over his head. Qui-Gon jumped to that platform, a meter lower, roughly in the center of the room. From there, he could steady himself to leap again, up and over—

To land on his feet on the dais behind Wanbo, his lightsaber poised only centimeters from the Hutt's fleshy throat.

"Ap-xmai nudchan!" Wanbo attempted to turn—not easy for Hutts—but Qui-Gon brought the lightsaber closer. The heat of the blade must've been palpable even through that thick skin, because Wanbo went still. The human guards and the Gamorreans did as well.

Most of the spice addicts sat up, finally interested in what was going on, though at least one woman on the floor continued to stare at the ceiling, her mouth open in an intoxicated smile. The last two platforms crashed into walls and fell, leaving no casualties that Qui-Gon could see.

Wanbo remained silent, waiting to take his cues from his captor. Without his majordomo, Wanbo had no idea how to handle any crisis whatsoever.

"Now that I have your attention," Qui-Gon said, "I'd like to discuss my departure from this palace."

"Chuba, jah-jee bargon," Wanbo said sulkily, which more or less translated as "Fine. I'm ready to see the last of you."

"The feeling is mutual. Now, I'm taking this dais to the compound's hangar." Fortunately, these things often could be raised or lowered between floors, the better to allow Hutts to remain motionless. To the room, Qui-Gon announced, "My ship will be waiting for me there. Wanbo should make a very good shield for any bolts you plan to fire."

"Stuka Jedi poonoo juliminmee?" Wanbo muttered. Since when do Jedi take hostages?

It wasn't the kind of thing Jedi usually did. Not the kind of maneuver Qui-Gon liked to employ. Definitely not something the Jedi Council would be glad to hear about when he and Obi-Wan returned to Coruscant. But Qui-Gon tailored his tactics to his opponents. Against the Hutts—whose massive wealth had been derived solely through the misery of other beings—he felt free to do whatever it took to survive.

"Since now, it appears," Qui-Gon said lightly. With that, he stamped on the controls, and the floor panels shifted from beneath them. Wanbo's small arms twitched as the platform descended from his spice den into his compound's hangar. Glancing upward, Qui-Gon could see several beings staring down at this spectacle, wide-eyed.

Then he returned his attention to the hangar—and saw Obi-Wan surrounded by five human guards, well-trained ones, to judge by their fighting stances. Although his Padawan still held his lightsaber ready, he could not simultaneously move forward to the ships and defend himself. Obi-Wan met Qui-Gon's eyes only for a moment, then looked away.

Standing nearby was Thurible, Wanbo's human majordomo, his hands clasped in front of him, his smile relaxed.

"Master Jinn," he said in his cultured, polite voice. "How lucky we are to have both Jedi together at once."

Obi-Wan tensed, no doubt preparing for battle. Qui-Gon merely smiled. "Very lucky," he said to Thurible. He kept the lightsaber at Wanbo's throat. "Especially as my tracker unit has been broadcasting for—oh, quite a while now. The Jedi Council can't take part directly, of course—but they'll be able to review everything that's happened so far. And everything that will happen. It feels almost as though they're actually here."

Thurible's smile briefly flickered. The Gamorrean guards shuffled nervously on their clawed feet. As soon as Qui-Gon had discovered the duplicate shipment logs in the Teth records, Wanbo's forces had attacked. Thurible had planned for this contingency from the very beginning, and his plan had been set into action as soon as they realized the fake records weren't fooling anyone. The original scheme must've been to report the two Jedi "missing under unknown circumstances," in order to cover up their assassination. But not even the Hutts were brazen enough to openly kill Jedi Knights.

In only an instant Thurible had regained his calm. "It appears you have taken my employer hostage. I, in turn, have taken your student hostage. We seem to be at an impasse, do we not?"

Instead of fighting his way out, Qui-Gon would have to bargain. With the Hutts.

It was all Qui-Gon could do not to groan.

An hour later, Qui-Gon sat in the majordomo's office, calmly sipping tea.

"These misunderstandings are so unfortunate," said Thurible, slowly pacing the curved stone wall of the office, like a pilgrim meditating upon a path. He radiated a calm confidence, more like another Jedi than a crime lord's right-hand man. "We've had security problems in the past. The guards . . . well, they let their vigilance slip into paranoia, from time to time."

"Indeed." Qui-Gon raised his eyebrow. "What reason could you have for paranoia here on Teth? The Hutts hold sole control here."

"You might be surprised," Thurible said. "The balance of power shifts constantly. None of us can afford to take anything for granted."

A Hutt's majordomo was almost always a flunky, a hapless warm body who ran interference with local officials, simpered and flattered others in power, and exercised no independent authority at all. The average term of employment for a majordomo lasted, as far as Qui-Gon could figure, a few months. So did the average majordomo's life expectancy. Sooner or later—usually sooner—they either took bribes, got crossed, and were executed for cause . . . or were murdered for no cause whatsoever when the Hutt in question lost his temper.

Thurible was different. Wanbo the Hutt held his position only because of nepotism; he was unfit to lead a cartel, due to both his tiny brain and his enormous spice habit. Through what Qui-Gon assumed to be sheer luck, Wanbo had hired an individual as intelligent, cunning, and amoral as the mightiest of the Hutts. Thurible dressed like a poet or an artist—albeit a wealthy one—and spoke with more polish than an aristocrat of Coruscant. Yet everyone in the sector knew that Thurible was the real power on Teth.

Though, of course, the majordomo was too smart to say so himself.

Obi-Wan had been released to save Wanbo, and vice versa. The only way for Thurible to do this and save face was to pretend the attack had been spontaneous. Until they got off this planet, it would be wisest to play along.

But if Thurible believed he had the upper hand over Qui-Gon now, he was very much mistaken.

"Again, I apologize for the terrible misunderstanding," Thurible said smoothly. His long, burnt-orange caftan trailed just above the floor, revealing flashes of his bare feet as he continued to pace. "Rest assured, the guards will be appropriately disciplined—yet kept alive, in deference to the customs of the Jedi."

"I'm pleased to hear it." Qui-Gon took another sip of his tea before adding, "There's no need for this unfortunate misunderstanding to eclipse the rest of our journey here."

Thurible smiled and bowed, black curls falling around his face. "You are generosity itself."

"So I'm told," Qui-Gon said, his voice dry. "I'm also still highly interested in precisely what's happening with agricultural shipments through the Triellus trade route. Especially given that the records of shipping in the nearby systems appear to be . . . highly inaccurate."

The sudden shift to the offensive didn't make Thurible blink. "We, too, are curious about this. To have so many ships going astray, so suddenly—it's alarming for the Republic, I'm sure."

"*Alarming* may be too strong a word. But these disappearances are disruptive, and the Republic will ultimately take whatever measures are necessary to protect the shipments."

Thurible inclined his head again, though the obsequious tone had left his voice as he replied, "How good it is to know that the Republic protects its many citizens so well."

Of course Qui-Gon knew that the Hutts had been capturing and seizing these shipments, selling the foodstuffs to struggling independent planets of the Outer Rim. And Thurible knew that Qui-Gon knew. But as long as Qui-Gon could make the Hutts stop—at least for now—there was no point in a direct challenge. It would only lead to bloodshed, at the end of which the Republic would remain triumphant and strong. The Hutts would scramble and scurry through months of infighting, at the end of which a new set of crime lords would emerge to behave in exactly the same way.

"Sometimes," Qui-Gon murmured, "it feels as though nothing in the galaxy will ever change."

Thurible straightened, obviously unsure what to make of the shift in topic. Folding his hands together, he furrowed his dark brows. "Do you truly think so, Jedi?"

There had been a time when Qui-Gon believed great, transformative change was possible. That these changes had been foreseen millennia ago by the Jedi mystics. How young he'd been. How innocent, how optimistic.

Time had taught him better.

"Nothing remains static," Qui-Gon said, "but sentient beings will always remain the same."

Thurible shook his head no. "Changes come when we least expect them—but they do come." He was more on guard now than he had been when Qui-Gon had his lightsaber to Wanbo's neck. His dark eyes searched Qui-Gon's for something unguessable. "Who knows what transformations we may yet live to see?"

CHAPTER TWO

"Nice place, Alderaan," said Rahara Wick as the *Meryx* flew away from the planet. "Beautiful. Serene."

"Not to mention *unsuspecting*," Pax Maripher added with relish. "I like that in a planet."

"Good. Because it's the last place I want to run into any problems."

"Why?" Pax frowned at her. "We'd face far harsher penalties virtually anywhere else."

Rahara crossed her arms. "Yeah, but on Alderaan we couldn't bribe our way out of it."

"They are *appallingly* moral, aren't they? No place for you and me." Pax smiled mischievously. Sometimes he liked to pretend they were far more criminal than they actually were.

Rahara, on the other hand, sometimes liked to pretend they weren't criminal at all. After all, they hurt no one. They took nothing of any value from the worlds they visited. Just rocks.

But one planet's rock was another planet's jewel.

Take Alderaan, for instance. Its archipelago continent was practically carpeted with a fine, whitish stone that was most often used as gravel. But take that stone to Rodia—show it to Rodians, whose eyes detected some wavelengths humans didn't—and it became spectacular, iridescent, glittering. It became precious.

Millennia ago, back in the days of legend, when the Sith still governed so much of the galaxy, gemstones had been traded freely. But flooding the market with a precious commodity tended to destroy the commodity's value. Sometimes it led to widespread looting or illicit mining on worlds whose ordinary stone was extraordinary elsewhere. An influx of such jewels could even collapse a planetary economy. So strict rules had been put in place to regulate, and even ban, the trading of most gems.

She and Pax were simply . . . pretending those rules didn't exist. They couldn't crash an entire world's economy, not just the two of them. As Pax had said to her, when he first hired her as a copilot and analyst, *Who would notice if we took what little could fit in the* Meryx's *hold? Who would be the poorer? No one. So why shouldn't we be the richer?*

Rahara didn't see why not. It wasn't like they were *real* crooks.

But it was something she had to tell herself, time and time again.

They were in some ways an unlikely pair: Rahara had grown up rough, to put it lightly, and taught herself everything she knew, while Pax had been educated by droids with memory banks containing endless data, droids with absolutely nothing else to do. She was tall, with golden skin and straight, blue-black hair that fell to her waist. Pax was a few centimeters shorter, with wiry hair that sprang up from his head as though he'd been electrocuted, and a complexion so pale that strangers sometimes asked if he was from a planet where the population lived underground. His clothes were of the finest quality, but disheveled, and hung slightly on his skinny frame; Rahara wore plain black working garb she bought on the cheap from spaceport stalls, which could be made to look local almost anywhere with the addition of a simple cape or hood. They were both human; that was where the similarities ended.

Most people write us off as an absentminded scholar and his low-class pilot, Rahara thought. That was fine by her. The important thing was that they be written off. Overlooked. Forgotten.

She'd spent her childhood being monitored. Being controlled. Rahara would never allow that to happen again.

Pax pulled the lever that sent the *Meryx* into hyperspace. As the viewscreens turned blue with wavering light, Rahara rose from her seat. "I'm going to check the spectrometer."

"No need to bother just yet," Pax said in his crisp Coruscanti accent. "We won't be heading to Rodia for weeks." It was important not to travel directly between the stones' source and the market; that left a trail.

"Might as well." In truth, silences between her and Pax had become . . . awkward, lately. Better to have something to do.

Rahara went to the ladder and clambered down into the heart of the *Meryx*. In most *Gozanti*-class freighters, this space would be an ordinary cargo hold, stark bare metal and not that much light.

In the *Meryx*, however, the entire space glowed golden. And at its heart lay thousands of kilograms of gemstones.

She would've been impressed by Pax's scanner-blocking field no matter what. But he hadn't only created the technology; he'd also made it beautiful. Beauty mattered to Pax, she knew. Whether or not he'd ever admit it, that was the real reason he stole jewels rather than other, easier, more lucrative cargo. He just liked *looking* at them.

But Pax Maripher would never admit he did anything for sentimental reasons.

Pulling her hair into a ponytail, Rahara stripped off the robe that had helped her pass unnoticed through Aldera. She stepped to the scanner-blocking field's controls, which were fiendishly complicated; she'd been working with Pax for a pretty long while now, and still she needed to review them every time. (Pax didn't understand what people meant by *user-friendly*. Either you were smart enough to use his tech, or you weren't.) Once ready, she pushed her sleeves back to her elbows, and then punched in the commands that took the field down—a flood of brightening light, followed by darkness—for just a split second. That was enough time for her to grab a large handful of their haul. When she was only centimeters clear, the field reenergized with a blinding flare. Blinking, Rahara congratulated herself on not getting singed this time.

"You know," Pax said from the ladder behind her, "we've made what is known as a clean getaway. You can turn the field off."

"You say that every time. And every time, I tell you I need to practice operating the field in tighter time frames."

"I would've thought you'd have it by now."

Carrying the gems, Rahara stalked over to the other side of the hold, where the spectrometer bench sat. "I would've thought you'd have learned how to interact with other human beings by now, instead of suggesting everyone in the galaxy is a moron, besides you. Looks like we're both disappointed."

She lay the stones on the bench and began separating them by size and probable quality. Rahara had first been put to work sorting minerals when she was only nine years old; to her, this was almost automatic.

"Rahara," Pax said more quietly. "I'm sorry if I hurt you. I meant it as a joke."

He hadn't hurt her, merely irritated her, but that was bad enough. Sometimes she got weary of a partner who acted more like a protocol droid than a human being—even if he *did* have a good excuse. "Do you see anybody laughing?"

"I do not. Obviously my understanding of humor requires refinement."

That, of course, made her chuckle. Pax was funniest when he didn't try.

"We ought to talk," Pax said as Rahara strapped on her magnifying goggles. "About our next destination."

"Gamorr, right?" Which would be disgusting, but at least they could call on their fresh memories of Alderaan to get them through weeks of dredging fetid swamps. "Sooooo excited about that."

"You're being sarcastic. Let me assure you that this lack of enthusiasm is entirely mutual. The thing is, I've been thinking." Pax leaned closer, peering down his long nose at the white gravel on the bench. "We can collect Gamorrean coral anytime. But what if we went after something rarer? Rather more valuable?"

"Like what? Mustafar fire diamonds?" Rahara had never been to Mustafar, but from what she'd heard it would make working on Gamorr seem like a journey to paradise.

"Nothing so dangerous." He half turned to face her as he said, "Kyber crystals."

"*Kyber*? Are you *nuts*?" Rahara pushed her goggles atop her head, the better to look him in the eyes. "The Jedi police Kyber trading like . . . like . . . well, more closely than anything we've ever traded. Or anything we ever *should* trade."

"Yet a black market still exists—as well as certain industrial applications. And if no industry will buy from us, and the markets in question are rather too black for our comfort, well, we could alert the Jedi to a new trove of kyber. Make some friends. It could come in handy someday, having friends among the Jedi."

That made more sense. Still—"Kyber isn't found in that many places. The Jedi control those areas. Are you seriously suggesting we try to steal from them?"

Pax scoffed. "Please. I'm not suicidal. I'm *daring*. I'm also the person who might just have found a completely undiscovered kyber source—on the moon of a perfectly safe world, even. No guards, no danger, a pleasant climate, and, if my analysis is correct, a *very* large number of kyber crystals."

Rahara had seen Pax combing through various planetary scans for hours on end—all public information, yet too minute and dense for most people to search through without already knowing what they were looking for. But he saw more than others did.

She said, "I knew there was a reason I put up with you."

A grin spread across Pax's face. "Then let's hunt some kyber."

Traveling home proved awkward. Obi-Wan was obviously hoping to avoid talking about what had gone wrong during the firefight on Teth—no wonder, for someone so young.

In many ways, Obi-Wan was so mature for his age, so steady, that Qui-Gon sometimes forgot he was just seventeen years old. Only in moments like this, as they sat side by side in the cockpit of the *Rainhawk*-class shuttle, did Qui-Gon realize how gawky his Padawan still was, how both the past child and the future man could be glimpsed in his face.

As always during those moments, Qui-Gon felt a pang of guilt. Obi-Wan had such potential. Such promise.

He deserved a Master who could bring it out in him.

They'd been an uneasy match from the start, with misunderstandings and emotional swings. That in itself wasn't unusual. Qui-Gon sometimes questioned why Padawans were transferred from the crèche to their Masters in the middle of most species' adolescence—exactly when *every* change became more difficult. (He, like Dooku and Yoda and Yoda's old Master before him, had taken a younger Padawan; Obi-Wan had become his apprentice at thirteen. This had not helped.) Qui-Gon had talked things through with fellow Masters such as Mace Windu and Depa Billaba, even Yoda, all of whom assured Qui-Gon that the initial months were almost always rough. "Worry you should, if conflict arises not," Yoda had intoned. "Then growing enough, your Padawan cannot be." Had Qui-Gon's first months with Dooku been so different?

But he had forged a powerful bond with Dooku well before they'd been together for a year. Most Masters and apprentices did. Yes, Rael had helped at first, but he and Dooku would've come together regardless. It was Dooku who had guided Qui-Gon through the ancient Jedi prophecies, igniting interests in ancient history and linguistics that would long survive his fervent belief in the mystics' foresight. Besides that, they'd shared so many personality traits: self-reliance, skepticism, and a reluctance to take the Council's word as sacred.

The characteristics he and Dooku had in common were, almost entirely, the ones for which he and Obi-Wan were exact opposites.

Qui-Gon believed in dealing with each situation on its own merits; Obi-Wan wanted procedures to follow. Qui-Gon valued flexibility, which Obi-Wan seemed to think of as sloppiness. Qui-Gon had learned to get on better with the Council over time, but had always retained his independence. Obi-Wan still thought he had to obey the Council in every particular, at all times, and was horrified every time Qui-Gon deviated from standard protocols in the slightest.

None of this made Obi-Wan a bad candidate to become a Jedi Knight. Many Jedi Knights—some of the best—thought and acted along the same lines. But it made him an awkward match for Qui-Gon. Years into their partnership, they still remained out of sync. Had the situation been more dire today—if the threat in the Hutt palace had been more serious—that gap in their mutual understanding could well have gotten them killed.

How do I fix this? Qui-Gon wondered. *Can I? Obi-Wan deserves no less.*

"I'm sorry about before, Master," Obi-Wan finally said. "I should've understood what you meant by getting the door—and letting myself get caught stealing a ship—"

"Obi-Wan. The fault was mine." Qui-Gon lay one broad hand on Obi-Wan's shoulder. "First I gave you unclear instructions." *And a better Master could've taught his Padawan to understand his battle instincts by now.* "And I knew you probably wouldn't be able to get a ship all by yourself—it was worth a try, that's all. You're not to blame."

Most Padawans would be relieved to be off the hook. Obi-Wan only frowned. "I can do better."

Qui-Gon sighed. "We both can. Now let's get home."

On the planet Pijal, beneath a blazing sunset, the race was on.

"C'mon!" shouted Rael Averross, urging his mount onward—toward a wide gash in the ground, deep and stony. The varactyl chirruped as it sprang forward, crossing the chasm in one bound. As its heavy, clawed feet thudded onto the grass, Averross laughed out loud. "There we go," he cried in his thick Ringo Vindan accent. "That's it!"

Varactyls had been imported from Utapau some decades ago by the Iltan clan, to give themselves an edge in the Grand Hunt. By now those original creatures had been bred into streamlined, swift, crimson-feathered varactyls unique to Pijal. Someday, Averross figured, the rest of the galaxy would discover the Pijal varactyls, and after that no one would ever race fathiers again. For the time being, however, these creatures—their speed, the sheer joy of riding them—belonged to Pijal alone.

Averross sighted the finish beacon and silently directed his varactyl toward it; the beast responded instantly, accelerating with every bit of its strength to reach the end as fast as possible. Varactyls loved speed for its own sake, and Averross thought they even understood the difference between winning and losing. His mount trilled its battle cry as it dashed past the line, skidding to a stop so fast its claws cut sharp lines in the loamy ground. With a grin, Averross reached into the gear basket and grabbed a large stick of mollusk jerky—a Pijal "delicacy" he couldn't stand. The varactyl appreciated the stuff more, chewing with relish.

Other riders reached the line, shouting their congratulations and friendly taunts as they did so. Averross hopped to the ground as they began leading their varactyls back to the palace stables. He shook his head ruefully just after he landed. Next to him, Captain Deren—stoic as ever—asked, "Is there a problem?"

"Just wonderin' why my knees are rude enough to age along with the rest of me."

"You could get synthetic replacements—"

"No big deal. You know what they say about gettin' old—it beats the alternative." Averross tried to remember that. Force knew he'd seen too many people fall before their time. If sometimes, in the morning, he looked at himself in the mirror and wondered who that graying old geezer was . . . well, that was just proof he wasn't dead yet. And he intended to live his remaining life to the fullest.

Once they reached the stables, the servant boys took the varactyls' reins from the riders and walked the beasts off for dust baths and feed.

Deren and some of the other soldiers went back to their barracks afterward, but Averross led the larger group to the nearest cantina. It wasn't exactly palatial—a muddy hole carved out of a dingy rock, which smelled a fair bit like the Wookiee bartender—but that was one reason Averross liked the place. The customers gave a cheer of welcome as he strode in, and the hostess—Selbie, who had blond hair, a saucy smile, and large breasts—gave him a warm smile as she took his long cloak.

The rider closest to Averross leaned in and muttered, "The two of you back on, then?"

"Maybe." Averross didn't indulge in female companionship often. When people found out about it, they got distracted. Made a fuss. It wasn't often worth it. But . . . it had been a while, and Selbie was decently close to his own age, and she had the bawdiest sense of humor of anyone he'd ever met.

Why not? he figured. Might as well see if she was game. He gestured toward Selbie, and she lit up as she began moving toward him.

"Hey," grunted a gigantic Chagrian who was obviously already drunk. His grayish-blue hand clutched Selbie's elbow. "*I* was talking to her. I was getting somewhere!"

"The blazes you were," Selbie retorted. "Get along, then. You've had enough."

"Throwing me out, now? For *that*?" With his free hand, he gestured vaguely in Averross's direction. "Muddy boots, unshaved face, no manners—*that's* what you like? Believe me, I could keep you in better style."

"You must be new here." Selbie pulled herself free. "Nobody *keeps* me. I keep myself."

"Give me a chance, girl." The Chagrian tried to pull Selbie closer, but she tugged herself free of his drunken grasp. This only made him angrier. "Who do you think you are? Turning down the likes of me when you're *trash*! Nothing but trash!"

It was obvious Selbie didn't care what insults the Chagrian hurled at her. But that didn't mean Averross shouldn't step in.

Besides—he'd enjoy it.

"Hey. You," he said to the Chagrian. "Get out before I take you out."

The Chagrian's chest swelled. If he couldn't get himself a woman, he seemed to think a fight would be the next best thing. "Take me out, heh? And how do you think you'll do that?"

In a blink Averross's hand went to his belt, seizing his weapon. His lightsaber blazed into life, its blue glow illuminating the entire room. The Chagrian froze as the cantina fell silent. Averross grinned. "Bet I could manage."

"Jedi," muttered the Chagrian. Already he was shuffling backward toward the door, head bowed. "I didn't know—you—you don't look like a Jedi."

"Huh," Averross said. "I always figured other Jedi don't look like *me*."

"I'll report you." The Chagrian shook his horns, as close as he could get to being threatening now. "Jedi or not, you're answerable to the law. The authorities will hear about this!"

Selbie had her hands on her hips and looked like she'd never had so much fun. "Welcome to Pijal! Until our princess grows up, we're ruled by a regent." She gestured grandly to Averross. "Meet our lord regent."

The Chagrian backed out of the cantina, to laughter and jeers from the others. The music started up again, and Averross switched off his lightsaber as he turned back to Selbie with a smile.

But that was when the holoscreen behind the bar lit up, its borders red.

The grin faded from Averross's face even before the image sharpened to reveal a warehouse outside the capital city, smoldering in the last stages of a fire. If Princess Fanry was watching this—and surely she was—it would terrify her. He'd have to get back to her immediately. *Do these monsters even think about the people they hurt?*

While firefighting droids wheeled about, extinguishing the blaze, a label appeared at the top of the holoscreen: SUSPECTED OPPOSITION ACTIVITY.

"Halin Azucca," he muttered. "I'll send her to hell."

CHAPTER THREE

     ✦

"*G*et the door!" *Why didn't I understand what Qui-Gon meant? The guards were the problem, not the door controls, and if I'd been calm I would've seen that—though of course he could've just said exactly what he meant, and then—*

I must keep my mind on the present. The future does not exist; the past has ceased to be. Only the present is real.

Obi-Wan forced his attention back to the Rainhawk's controls. At least nobody could criticize his flying; there, the tasks were concrete, predictable, known. As he set the course for Coruscant, he ventured, "Did you gain any further insight about Thurible, when you two spoke?"

Qui-Gon shook his head, a rueful smile on his lips. "Hardly. That one reveals almost nothing while hinting at almost everything. Not a bad way to develop a reputation for inscrutability."

You'd know about being inscrutable, Obi-Wan thought. "Thurible's tactics make no logical sense."

"Oh, I'm sure they do." Qui-Gon rose to his feet. In the small Rain-hawk cockpit, his height and broad shoulders made it seem as though the ship could hardly contain him. "The problem is, we can't judge another's logic until we know his ultimate objective, and Thurible's remains hidden."

"Master? Are you going to your cabin?"

"I wish to meditate," Qui-Gon replied. "Don't worry, Obi-Wan. I won't leave you to fly the ship the entire time. I know how you dislike it."

Obi-Wan laughed at his Master's sarcasm. As Qui-Gon well knew, Obi-Wan *loved* flying. "I believe I can bear the burden."

Qui-Gon's low chuckle was his only farewell as he walked back toward his small cabin, leaving Obi-Wan alone.

See? He's joking around with you. He wouldn't joke around if he was truly disappointed in your performance on Teth.

Yet there had been so many disappointments. So many shortcomings. The fault could not be Qui-Gon's; he was the Master, and Obi-Wan was but the student. Even though Qui-Gon Jinn could be contradictory, mysterious, vague. Despite the fact that he sometimes did the exact opposite of what the Temple leaders would've counseled. If Qui-Gon was, well, *unorthodox,* his Padawan's job was to gain understanding of that and adjust to it accordingly.

In theory. In fact, Obi-Wan still could not predict when and how his Master would ignore the rules. Rarely did he understand why. And as he grew older, he became more and more frustrated with Qui-Gon's renegade nature.

Rules are rules for a reason, Obi-Wan thought as he stared out at the wavering, electric-blue light of hyperspace. *They're not arbitrary. The Jedi rules exist to steer us toward the greater good, and to reduce uncertainty.*

Better yet, rules could be memorized. They could be written down, studied, made certain. They were the opposite of the archaic mystical writings Qui-Gon seemed to value more than any other texts of the Order. Obi-Wan preferred certainty when it could be had.

Most frustrating of all: Qui-Gon's methods *worked,* most of the time. Whatever changeable madness he steered by, it steered him well.

Which meant there was something important about being a Jedi that Obi-Wan didn't yet understand.

By the Force, I'm brilliant.

Modesty was not a virtue where Pax had grown up, which might be why he'd never acquired it. In his opinion modesty sounded boring.

Obviously I am not the first to study the potential of kyber crystals, Pax reasoned as he prepared to take the *Meryx* out of hyperspace. *However, almost all such studies will have been conducted by the Jedi. Any results that could create an ever greater market for kyber would not have been shared openly. Yet possessing the crystals is not illegal on any world I've ever heard of.*

This might have been simply because Pax never much bothered finding out what was "legal" or "illegal" on every single world, details details, blah blah blah. That was Rahara's department. She was a worrier, that one. Then again, who could blame her?

"Almost there?" Rahara asked cheerfully as she returned to the cockpit. Her silky black hair was tied back from her face, which was aesthetically pleasing.

"You know perfectly well that we're almost there."

She leaned back in her chair, resting her feet on the console—a liberty Pax would've allowed for no one else. "And *you* know that pleasant conversation sometimes begins with everyone affirming what they already know."

"I was brought up to believe that directness is a virtue."

Rahara sighed. "You were brought up by *protocol droids.* They're not exactly experts at normal human communication. But you could get the knack of it, if you'd practice."

"Waste of time," Pax said.

Her lips pursed, but she said nothing else. On the whole, Pax felt he should be relieved.

He liked Rahara more than he liked just about any other biological life-form he'd known. When he'd taken her on several months ago, he'd known she was a perfect fit for the work he did, but hadn't realized how easy she would be to get along with. Nor how pleasant it would be to talk with her, or hear her laugh. It had taken him a while to recognize that the energy between them had shifted from co-workers to friends—and then from friends to something more. One evening, as they'd shared a bottle of wine, it had seemed as though things might . . . as though they might get out of hand.

So Pax had taken that opportunity to explain that, really, human emotions were short-lived and fallible, and no basis for rational people to interact. Rationality was the only thing that really mattered, wasn't it?

To judge by Rahara's reaction that night, she didn't agree. But they continued on as before, albeit with a few more awkward pauses. Pax felt he should be satisfied with that.

Surely, eventually, he would be.

He grinned as he put his hands on the controls and said to her, "Now allow me to present to you the happily obscure world of Pijal."

The *Meryx* slipped out of hyperdrive at standard approach distance, revealing a planet dominated by abundant blue oceans, ringed with broad green-and-gold islands at its equator and tropics. To his surprise, ancient planetary shield generators orbited Pijal, which meant a few other vessels were also hanging back, waiting for landing clearance. In Pax's opinion, a planetary shield that ancient was probably too weak to keep out any ship larger than a *Theta*-class shuttle; probably the wait for landing clearance was a mere formality.

Anyway, Pax didn't need to go to Pijal itself. Instead he gestured at its darkly verdant moon. "Behold what I believe to be the single best source of kyber in the entire galaxy."

Rahara stared out at the scene before them, her face expressionless.

"You might show some enthusiasm," Pax suggested. "Or at least interest."

She said nothing, only rose to her feet. Not once did she glance toward Pax.

Had he violated some unknown social etiquette rules? The 3PO protocol units who'd raised him had taught him how to recite etiquette rules for a thousand different planets . . . but very little about how to put them into practice. Sentients' behavior was rarely clear-cut, often complex, and invariably *nothing* like the simulations. Pax mostly responded to this by ignoring etiquette altogether. Yet he also knew that, when he ignored the rules, Rahara's feelings could be hurt. She was the last person in the galaxy he would wish to hurt.

He ventured, "Ah, of course I'm aware, *highly* aware, that I could never have analyzed the planetary data if not for your preliminary analysis of the mineralogical tables—a brilliant calculus for the data—"

"You didn't say Czerka ships would be here." Rahara's voice was dull and flat.

How had he missed it? Pax inwardly cursed himself as he picked out the Czerka Corporation cruiser *Leverage,* long and bulky, probably capable of carrying ten thousand souls. Other Czerka ships showed up on scans, indicating that the company did considerable work on Pijal and its moon. "I didn't know. I'm sorry."

"Of course you didn't know," she said. Her dark eyes stared at the ship as though it were an enemy; in some senses, he supposed, it was. "You didn't check. You can't know unless you check."

Pax didn't feel it necessary to check for the presence of Czerka Corporation in *every single* system, regardless of what Rahara had endured in her youth. However, this was a subject to raise at another time, when she wasn't pale and trembling, and Czerka wasn't represented by a ship large enough to haul away a reasonably large percentage of an entire asteroid belt in its cargo hold. Doing his best to speak gently, he said only, "If you'd rather we left, there are other jewels in the galaxy."

"No. I don't see why Czerka should get to keep me from a major score." Rahara pushed up her sleeves, a gesture that usually meant she was strengthening her resolve. With a sidelong look at him she added, "Besides, if you flew away without checking for the kyber, you wouldn't be able to *stand* it."

"I salute both your courage and your compassion for my base nature. To the moon we go."

Pax steered the *Meryx* in that direction, pretending not to notice the way Rahara stared at the Czerka vessel until it had all but vanished in the distant night.

CHAPTER FOUR

"Strange, the Hutts' behavior is." Master Yoda scratched his chin, tiny clawed hand stroking the few white whiskers there. "Yet important, I feel, it is not."

"I concur." Mace Windu leaned back in his chair. "They're petty criminals who try to appear more powerful than they are. Attacking you was a dangerous gambit, but one that fits into their general pattern of behavior."

Qui-Gon wasn't entirely sure he agreed, but he let it lie. If the Hutts were going to create more trouble, the rest of the galaxy would find out soon enough. Besides, when it came to the Jedi Council, he knew he had to choose his battles.

He chose a great many of them—though fewer, in recent years, than he once had.

As ever, after a mission, Qui-Gon had been summoned to the Jedi Council's chambers for his report. It was nighttime—later than the Council usually met, at least for ordinary business—and the darkness around them was illuminated by the cyclone of Coruscanti traffic and ships' lights. Yet here, within this room, a sense of serenity prevailed. Qui-Gon relished the contrast.

Master Billaba leaned forward, studying her datapad with a frown on her face. "It worries me, this misunderstanding between you and your Padawan. This isn't the first time you've reported such difficulties."

Qui-Gon bowed his head slightly. "It worries me as well. Obi-Wan is strong in the Force, and eager to do his duty. The failure must be mine. Fundamentally, I fear, we are a mismatch. I've been unable to adapt my teaching methods to his needs, despite my best efforts."

Yoda cocked his head. "Adapt he must as well. Cooperation is learned not through individual effort. Only together can you progress."

Agreeing to that proposition—sensible though it was—would mean shifting some of the blame onto Obi-Wan, which Qui-Gon preferred not to do. He simply remained quiet. The Jedi Council had a habit of assuming that silence equaled agreement; Qui-Gon had found this habit useful, from time to time.

Regardless, he expected the Council to eventually ask him if he wanted them to reassign Obi-Wan's training to another Master. He'd known before this meeting began that they might even ask the question tonight, but he still wasn't sure what he would say. The suspense seemed worse than he would've anticipated, maybe because he didn't know what he wanted to answer . . .

. . . or because the silence in the room had lasted a suspiciously long period of time.

Qui-Gon focused his attention back on the Masters surrounding him. They were exchanging glances in what seemed to be anticipation. He straightened. "Have you another mission for us?" Maybe they intended to test him and Obi-Wan one more time before any decision about reassignment would be made.

"Yes, another task for you we have." Yoda's ears lowered, a sign of deep intent. "Consider it carefully, you must."

Mace Windu drew himself upright and folded his hands together in a formal gesture of respect. "You may not have heard that Master Dapatian intends to retire from the Council, effective next month."

Qui-Gon glanced at Poli Dapatian, a Master of great renown . . . so much so that Qui-Gon had failed to note, in recent years, how aged he had become. "That is our loss."

"We hope it will also be our gain," Mace replied. "Qui-Gon Jinn, we hereby offer you a seat on the Jedi Council."

Had he misheard? No, he hadn't. Qui-Gon slowly gazed around the circle, taking in the expressions of each Council member in turn. Some of them looked amused, others pleased. A few of them, Yoda included, appeared more rueful than not. But they were serious.

"I admit—you've surprised me," Qui-Gon finally said.

"I imagine so," Mace said drily. "A few years ago, we would've been astonished to learn we would ever consider this. But in the time since, we've all changed. We've grown. Which means the possibilities have changed as well."

Qui-Gon took a moment to collect himself. Without any warning, one of the turning points of his life had arrived. Everything he said and did in the next days would be of great consequence. "You've argued with my methods often as not, or perhaps you'd say I've argued with yours."

"Truth, this is," Yoda said.

Depa Billaba gave Yoda a look Qui-Gon couldn't interpret. "It's also true that the Jedi Council needs more perspectives."

Is the Council actually making sense? Qui-Gon hoped none of them had picked up on that thought.

Mace nodded. "Yes, Qui-Gon, we've disagreed often. Butted heads, even. But you've always acted with respect for the Council's authority, without compromising your inner convictions. This shows a great gift for—"

"Diplomacy?" Qui-Gon asked.

Mace replied, "I was going to say *balance*."

It was a delicate line to walk, one Qui-Gon had stumbled over on many occasions. But those occasions had become rarer as the years went on. He'd learned how to handle the Council well enough. Now, it seemed, the Council had become ready to hear him in return.

Qui-Gon had never imagined sitting on the Jedi Council itself, at least not since he was a youngling. Dooku had chuckled once, early in Qui-Gon's training, when they spoke of the Council. *"You have your own mind, my Padawan,"* he'd said. *"The Council doesn't always respond well to that."* Given how many times Qui-Gon had clashed with the Council—from his earliest days as a Jedi Knight up to six weeks ago—he'd always assumed that he would never ascend to the heights of the Order.

But now it could happen. *Would* happen. He'd be able to weigh in on the Council's decisions, and perhaps create some of the change he wanted to see. It was the greatest opportunity of his life.

"You honor me," Qui-Gon said. "I ask for some time to meditate upon this before I accept." Of course he would take the seat on the Council. But in doing so, he wanted to more fully reflect upon how this would change him, and the breadth of the important role he would assume.

"Very wise," said Depa. "Most of those asked to join the Council do the same, myself included. If someone didn't—well, I'd think maybe he didn't know what he was getting into."

Laughter went around the room. Amusement bubbled within Poli Dapatian's respirator mask. Depa Billaba's grin was infectious, and Qui-Gon realized he was smiling back at her. Although the Council had never been hostile to him, this was the first time Qui-Gon had felt a deeper camaraderie—the friendliness of equals. Already Teth and the Hutts seemed like a problem from years ago. The future shone so boldly that it threatened to eclipse the present.

Steady, he told himself. *Even an invitation to the Jedi Council mustn't go to your head.*

"Consider carefully, you must," said Yoda, the only member of the Council who remained gravely serious. "No hasty answer should you give."

"Of course," Qui-Gon said. Hadn't he just indicated that he intended to do exactly that?

Before he could think more on it, Mace said, "In some ways, this invitation comes at an opportune time. This change could, potentially, resolve other problems."

Only then did it hit Qui-Gon: If he took a seat on the Council, then Obi-Wan would be transferred to another Master.

It wasn't *forbidden* for a Jedi on the Council to train a Padawan learner; one of Qui-Gon's crèche-mates had become the Padawan of Master Dapatian, back in the day. Exceptions had been made during times of crisis as well, when everyone needed to take on extra duties. But such exceptions were rare. Serving on the Council required a great deal of time, concentration, and commitment. Balancing that commitment with the equally sacred task of training a Padawan—well, it would be a difficult situation, one potentially unfair to both Master and student. Only those who had served on the Council for a long time, and had adjusted to its demands, contemplated such a step.

"I see what you mean," Qui-Gon said. "Perhaps it would be for the best. But I must think upon it."

"Of course," Depa said warmly. Yoda nodded, clutching his gimer stick and saying nothing.

Mace Windu rose from his chair to put his hand on Qui-Gon's shoulder. "We will of course keep this invitation private unless and until you choose to join us. At this point, the only person outside this room who knows of it is Chancellor Kaj herself. But if you need to discuss it with Padawan Kenobi, or any other friends, you may feel free to do so, as long as they will promise to be discreet."

"Understood."

Qui-Gon walked out of the Council Chamber into the Temple in a strange state of mind. He couldn't call it a daze, because this was in some ways the exact opposite. Every detail of his surroundings struck him with fresh vividness, whether it was the colorful patterns of inlaid marble beneath his feet or the scarlet trim on a young Jedi Knight's gown. It was as though the invitation to join the Council had given him new eyes. A new way of seeing the world, one that he would no doubt spend the rest of his life learning to comprehend.

The Council, he said to himself. *By the Force, the Council.*

Perhaps another Jedi might have given way to elation, or even the temptation of pride. Qui-Gon Jinn was made of sterner stuff. Besides, he couldn't bring himself to feel entirely happy when he considered the question of Obi-Wan.

He'd already come to believe that they were mismatched as teacher and student. The main reason Qui-Gon hadn't asked for a transfer before was that he knew Obi-Wan would be hurt by it, and would blame himself. The Council's invitation would allow the transfer to be impersonal, merely practical. Obi-Wan could then be reassigned to a teacher who would serve him better.

Why, then, did the idea fill Qui-Gon with such a profound sense of loss?

The planet Pijal had a pleasantly warm climate, one that led to lush green hills in summertime, vineyards with the potential to produce top-class wines, and tall, slender conifers that waved slightly in the breeze. It was lovely. Everyone said so. Her Serene Highness, the Crown Princess Fanry, had no reason to doubt them.

But she would've preferred being able to compare for herself.

"They say Naboo is lovely," she said to Regent Averross. She kicked her feet back and forth beneath her throne; even now that she was almost fourteen, her feet didn't quite touch the ground. Her red hair was tucked beneath her ivory-colored scarf, only a few loose curls hinting at the blaze beneath. "Toydaria's not supposed to be so pretty, but I'm curious about it. And Alderaan. That's supposed to be the most beautiful planet of the Core Worlds. Naboo has a queen about my age, and Toydaria a king only a few years older—and there's a crown princess on Alderaan, isn't there? Breha? We could have a sort of summit. Something like, 'the next generation of galactic leaders.' "

"Delightfully put," said Meritt Col, the sector supervisor for Czerka Corporation. Czerka had been doing business on Pijal for so many centuries that their supervisors inevitably had places at court. Col wore it more easily than most. "As a slogan, it's catchy, punchy, inspiring. You could do well on one of Czerka's advertising planets—if you gave up the throne, that is." Col laughed at her own joke.

Fanry managed a smile, but no more. Like she would ever give up her throne, for anyone or anything, much less to come up with ad copy for Czerka.

The lord regent paid no attention to Col. Instead he gave Fanry a look. "No time for a vacation," Averross said. He sat, not in one of the many fine chairs, but in the stone curve beneath one of the tall, pink-tinted windows in the throne room, thumping one of his heavy boots against the carved scrollwork. To Fanry, Averross always seemed like a varactyl kept in an enclosure too small for it—uncomfortable, restless, eager to run. "And you know it."

"I didn't say *vacation*. I said a *summit*."

"And you didn't *mean* either one of 'em," he retorted. "C'mon, Fanry. Why do you think you're dyin' to travel all of a sudden?"

Fanry suppressed a groan. Having a Jedi for a regent—even an un-orthodox Jedi, even one who seemed determined to behave more like a vagrant than a nobleman—meant going on a constant quest for self-knowledge. Personally she felt she knew herself quite well, thank you very much, but she also knew this line of questioning wouldn't end until she'd provided an answer.

"The treaty," she said. "It's so close. It's a big responsibility."

"Exactly. Of course you want to escape." He grinned at her, easy and knowing, as he lit a Chandrilan cigarra. "But you've never hidden from a fight once, in all the time I've known you—not even when you were hardly more than a baby. You may get scared, but you don't run scared."

She nodded, once again taking the measure of the man who had run her planet—and her life—since she was six years old. His face must've been handsome once, Fanry mused, before he was old as rocks. (She thought he might even be *fifty*.) Although his once-black hair was now shot through with gray, and wrinkles on his cheeks hinted at long-ago laughter, he carried himself like someone much younger. Like the warrior he had once been. Rael Averross had lived through things she would never experience and could hardly imagine.

But not even he could understand the full responsibility of the crown of Pijal.

Col cleared her throat. "If I may, Your Serene Highness—I've just gotten word that the group from the head office has arrived. Shall we greet them?"

Fanry couldn't think of anything she less wanted to do than go through court formalities with anyone from the head office of Czerka Corporation—even though the company's power was nearly as great as the Galactic Senate's. But it had to be done. She nodded toward Rael and allowed him to lead the way toward the Grand Hall of the palace. The hem of her silky gown rustled against the tiled floor as they went. Her servant girl Cady had wanted to hem it shorter, but Fanry insisted it wouldn't be necessary. Oh, when would she ever grow taller?

Just before she and Rael reached the giant doors of the hall, they burst open, pushed so hard that they slammed against the wall despite their massive weight. A guard halted what would clearly have been a desperate run, panting and wide-eyed.

"What is it?" Rael demanded. Already his hand was on his lightsaber, ready to defend her. Fanry wondered why she didn't feel safer.

"The moon," the guard said. "Halin Azucca. The Opposition. Again. And it's worse this time."

"Aw, hell." Rael dashed toward the hall and its giant viewscreen, with Fanry only a few steps behind. Her heart pounded as she grabbed up her long skirts, the better to run faster.

When they entered the hall, Fanry didn't even bother looking for the Czerka representatives, or for her other guards, or for anyone else. She could only stare at the scene projected there, no doubt from one of their satellites: one of the main factories on the moon, or what had been a main factory, before it exploded. Debris lay around the smoldering remains as electrical sparks blinked within the crushed machinery.

It had seemed so *funny*, at first, the idea of the Opposition as dangerous terrorists. Nobody was laughing any longer.

Captain Deren, the head of her guard, stood directly before the screen, his expression grave. "That factory had few defenses to speak of. Perhaps we should've expected this. At least no one was killed."

"That factory made nutritional supplements. We 'should've expected' Halin Azucca and her Opposition thugs would take it out?" Rael folded his arms, visibly calming himself. "I guess no matter how little credit we give her, it's too much. You're sure nobody got killed?"

"The factory was empty at that hour," Deren confirmed. He stood a head taller than Rael Averross, who was not a short man, and his deep voice rumbled like a groundquake. "So far, our attackers have been careful to spare lives."

"They may not be for much longer," Fanry said. Her blue eyes remained focused on the destruction. A shiver ran along her skin.

"This situation appears more serious than we had been given to believe," said one of the Czerka muckety-mucks, his hands folded together in what was meant to pass as a gesture of respect. "If the unrest on Pijal and its moon is increasing, we must question the wisdom of further investments by the Czerka Corporation."

Fanry startled and glanced at Deren. Before either of them could speak, Meritt Col stepped in. "The unrest hasn't lasted long. The new treaty and the coronation will change everything. Besides, Czerka must not lose its position at the hub of the new hyperspace corridor."

"Of course not," Fanry said. How many people in the galaxy had ever seen a top Czerka official back down?

"We get it," Rael added. "It's scary. But Czerka's not going to get scared off that easy, right? Trust me. We're gonna get to the bottom of this."

"With all due respect," said Meritt Col, "how can we be sure of that, when you've failed to find the perpetrators so far? I believe in our work here on Pijal, but we need a far more thorough investigation than we've had so far."

"We'll have help." Rael straightened. For a moment, Fanry thought, he almost looked troubled. But his usual lazy smile came back as he turned to a nearby communications officer and ordered, "Open a channel to Coruscant. To the Jedi Council."

CHAPTER FIVE

———————◈———————

The duties of a Padawan varied greatly. Certain kinds of instruction were universal—meditation, lightsaber training—and were studied both in groups at the Temple and privately with one's Master. But those Masters ranged widely in talents and temperament, which meant that the assignments they gave were diverse, too.

Obi-Wan's crèche-mate Prie, for instance, had been partnered with a Master who was expert in two things: forming Force-bonds with animals and unarmed combat. So Prie spent most of her time on undeveloped worlds, protecting new settlements from both wild animals and would-be marauders. Once she had even ridden a horned beast two meters high.

Meanwhile, his friend Jape studied with a Master who specialized in astrophysics. When he wasn't in the Grand Orbital Observatory of Coruscant, he was flying around the galaxy to explore unique and interesting phenomena. He'd sent Obi-Wan images from fabulously multicolored nebulae, and from a point just shy of a black hole's event horizon.

And what did Obi-Wan get? Trips to the Archives.

He sat in one of the high-level carrels, his work illuminated by hovering candledroids. From his vantage point, Obi-Wan could scan nearly the entire lower level of the Jedi Archives. Jocasta Nu sat at her desk, patiently reviewing some file or other; a handful of younglings struggled through a dense historical holo, probably for a class project. Otherwise, the Archives were deserted. Most Jedi had better things to do with their spare time, which meant having better things for their Padawans to do in *their* spare time.

Qui-Gon's interest in ancient languages wouldn't have been annoying on its own—at least, not as annoying—but what really irritated Obi-Wan was the reason for this fascination.

Nobody puts much stock in the old prophecies any longer, Obi-Wan thought sullenly as he looked over yet more Old Alderaanian. *These are only things that may never happen. If they ever* do *come to pass, then they were truly foretold, and none of our actions can influence them in any way.*

So why does Qui-Gon insist on studying them?

It would be one thing if Qui-Gon were among the Temple scholars, someone whose entire career had been spent researching antiquity. Obi-Wan at least would've known what he was getting into. But in virtually every other way, Qui-Gon Jinn was a realist, plainspoken and practical, almost to a fault.

"What use are ideals if we cannot fit them to the universe as we find it?" Qui-Gon had once asked him. *"If our beliefs tell us one thing, and the needs of real people tell us another, can there be any question of which we should listen to?"* This all sounded very lofty when Qui-Gon said it, but in actuality it meant things like, *It's okay to "borrow" a spaceship from criminals if you* really *need it,* or *If I can win this tribe's independence in a game of chance, then it's worth selling my Padawan's best robe for chips to get into the game.*

No, Qui-Gon's interests were generally anything but academic. He just had these two hobbies: ancient languages and ancient prophecies. Two *intensely boring* hobbies, both of which seemed to require a lot of research support from an apprentice.

Obi-Wan caught himself just before his annoyance would've turned into anger. It wasn't his job to dictate his Master's hobbies and interests. It was his job to support them, and if that meant digging up more antiquated scrolls and holocrons, so be it.

Later that evening, in Qui-Gon's quarters, Obi-Wan dared to say, "So far as I can tell, Master, the prophecies seem . . . extremely vague."

Qui-Gon looked up from the records Obi-Wan had brought him. His long, grayish-brown hair fell loose down his back, a sign that he intended to go to sleep soon. But he had never failed to respond to Obi-Wan's curiosity. "You've learned Old Alderaanian?"

"Not exactly—but I've picked up enough to make some sense of what I'm collecting." Obi-Wan tugged nervously at his Padawan braid, then stopped as he caught himself at it. It was a bad habit he hoped to break. "One of these prophecies says something about 'She who will be born to darkness will give birth to darkness.' It gives no hint at all as to who that is, or what kind of darkness this is, or when it will happen. Or 'When the kyber that is not kyber shines forth, the time of prophecy will be at hand.' How can there be a prophecy about the *time* of prophecy? Then there's this one—" He tapped on the side of the holocron of prophecy, which Qui-Gon had taken from the Archives for at least the dozenth time in his apprenticeship. " 'When the righteous lose the light, evil once dead shall return.' That's so vague it could refer to anything or anyone! And then the whole 'Chosen One' nonsense—"

"Your doubts are understandable, my Padawan," Qui-Gon said. His tone became dry as he continued, "Certainly they are shared by most Jedi today, including the Council. But I'd warn you not to dismiss this as mere 'nonsense.' "

Obi-Wan folded his arms. "Why shouldn't I?" When he caught the irritated glint in Qui-Gon's eyes, he hastily added, "I don't mean to be sarcastic; I really want to know. Why should we listen to these prophecies? Master Yoda has always taught that looking into the future is uncertain at best."

To Obi-Wan's surprise, Qui-Gon slowly nodded. "The answer to your question is . . . complex. Give me a moment to gather my thoughts, so I can give you the reply you deserve."

He was pleased to have at least challenged his Master this far. There were few things Qui-Gon loved more than a good question. Sometimes Obi-Wan thought that if he just never stopped asking questions, his whole apprenticeship would've gone much more smoothly.

Qui-Gon closed his eyes, perhaps entering a light meditative state. Obi-Wan would have to bide his time.

It wasn't unpleasant to wait in his Master's quarters. They were small and simple, as all Jedi residences were, and yet this room could not be mistaken for anyone else's but Qui-Gon Jinn's. It was individual in a way few things in the Temple were, reflecting its inhabitant's personality. Qui-Gon had a habit of picking up odds and ends on many of the various planets they visited—a bit of driftwood here, a soft woven blanket there. Over time, these mementos had formed quite a collection. Obi-Wan knew the wind chimes were from Gatalenta, the smooth meditation stones were from Ryloth, and the tea set with its delicate jade-green cups had been given to Qui-Gon by some Bivall as a thank-you gift after he'd helped rescue their stranded ship.

And those were just from the adventures Obi-Wan had been around for. As his eyes traveled around the room, picking out unfamiliar objects on shelves and in corners, he realized anew just how many places Qui-Gon had been, how many things he'd done. No matter how unorthodox Qui-Gon was, Obi-Wan knew he was lucky to have such a Master. He just had to find a way to make Qui-Gon feel lucky to have *him*.

"Do you believe," Qui-Gon said at last, "that studying the prophecies is a way of divining the future?"

Obi-Wan wondered if this was a trick question. "Isn't that the definition of a prophecy? A prediction about what's to come?"

"In some senses. But prophecies are also about the present. The ancient Jedi mystics were attempting to look into the future, but they were rooted in their own time—as we all are." Qui-Gon settled back into his chair and motioned for Obi-Wan to sit as well. "They could only predict the future through the prism of their own experience. So by studying their words, their warnings, we learn more about their ways than any history holo could ever teach us. And by asking ourselves how *we* interpret these prophecies, we discover our own fears, hopes, and limitations."

Being a Padawan was reminder enough of his hopes and limitations, in Obi-Wan's opinion, but he knew better than to say so. "You mean, you don't take the prophecies literally."

"Once, when I was younger—" Qui-Gon shrugged. "But no. I don't. However, I also don't assume they're meaningless, like most Jedi these days. Learning what the ancient mystics believed ties us to our history."

"The Jedi don't have such mystics anymore," Obi-Wan pointed out. "We're meant to put aside visions of the future, because we can't know whether they'll come to pass. Master Yoda even says such visions can bring a Jedi to darkness."

"Yes, seeking to know the future can be a form of control, which can lead to the dark side," Qui-Gon said in his deep, resonant voice. From his tone, Obi-Wan knew his Master had heard all this from Yoda many times before. "And learning the forms of lightsaber combat is a way of preparing for violence. Violence, too, can lead to the dark side. We are entrusted with great diplomatic power, which means we exert influence over entire systems—"

"I understand what you mean," Obi-Wan said. "Many paths can lead to the dark side."

"As Jedi, we possess power that average beings do not, and never will. Holding power over other beings will always require us to be vigilant against the darkness within us. Our ability to sometimes glimpse potential futures is no more or less dangerous than any of our other talents."

Obi-Wan decided to keep pushing. Qui-Gon respected challenge . . . to a point. "The mystics of old sought to know the events of centuries and millennia to come. Is that not arrogance? An unwillingness to accept the natural flow of the Force? We may see their writings in a more metaphorical light, but they didn't. They truly thought they were divining what would come to pass."

"I don't set myself up as judge of the ancient mystics, and neither should you." Qui-Gon wasn't going to share any more than that, apparently. Already he'd turned his attention back to the records Obi-Wan had brought him. "You've done good work here. This should provide me with reading for several days." A glint of humor shone in his blue eyes. "In other words, you're safe from the Archives for a while. Go spend time with your friends."

Obi-Wan grinned. "Thank you, Master." He rose to leave, then paused. "But . . . how many more Archive trips do you think I'll have to make?" This prophecy project had been going on for two years now; surely even Qui-Gon didn't mean to investigate them indefinitely.

Qui-Gon froze, cup halfway to his lips. The expression on his face was difficult to read—realization, perhaps, and dismay.

"Master? I didn't mean to complain about the Archives."

"Don't worry about that," Qui-Gon said. His eyes didn't meet Obi-Wan's. "We'll talk later. About many things."

Somewhat cryptic, Obi-Wan thought, but for Qui-Gon that was nothing new. "Good night, then."

"Good night."

Obi-Wan hurried toward the lower levels, hoping it was still early enough for him to pick up a game of dejarik, maybe. Something nagged at him about the final moments of his conversation with Qui-Gon. Obviously his Master was keeping some kind of secret.

But it couldn't be anything to do with Obi-Wan himself. If it were, his Master would've told him.

"You're frightened," said Master Dooku.

Qui-Gon Jinn, twelve years old, knelt in front of his new Master. Only yesterday, Dooku had chosen him as Padawan. He'd spent his last night in the younglings' crèche laughing with his friends, imagining all the adventures he would have, and practicing with his lightsaber in the sparring room until Master Yaddle ordered him to bed.

But this morning, he'd had to pack his few possessions in a small bundle and leave the crèche where he'd lived as long as he could remember. He'd been given the traditional Padawan haircut for humans and no longer looked like the boy he'd always seen in his reflection; instead he'd become a gangly, awkward stranger. And he'd come here to Master Dooku's quarters to present himself to the individual who would decide if he was worthy to be a Jedi Knight—or not worthy.

"Well?" Dooku raised one eyebrow. He seemed to stand three meters tall, looming over Qui-Gon like an obsidian wall. "Have you no response to my observation?"

I'm not afraid. The denial surfaced in Qui-Gon's mind. It was what he wanted to say, because it was what he wanted to be true.

But it *wasn't* true. Surely a Padawan wasn't supposed to lie to his new Master.

Qui-Gon admitted, "I am, Master."

"Why should you fear me?" Dooku said in his deepest, most intimidating voice, as though answering his own question.

Think, Qui-Gon told himself. His fear was so obvious, so all-encompassing, that he could hardly understand where it came from. But he needed to find the truth within that fear.

Finally he said, "I'm afraid of not becoming a Jedi, but that doesn't make me afraid of you, Master. I'm afraid of failing. Of not being worthy."

"Of yourself," Dooku said. "Of a future other than the one you want."

"Yes." Qui-Gon's fear deepened. Surely Master Dooku would realize he'd made a mistake, choosing someone so cowardly as Padawan.

But then Dooku said, "Very wise." When Qui-Gon looked up in surprise, his Master smiled—a distant smile, but a genuine one. "Most young apprentices would deny their fear. If they admitted it, they would almost certainly lack the self-knowledge you have shown."

I got it right? Qui-Gon's amazement must've shown on his face, because Dooku shook his head in tolerant amusement.

"You proved yourself honest today," Dooku said, gesturing for Qui-Gon to rise to his feet. "You demonstrated insight. And you convinced me of your intelligence."

"Intelligence?" Qui-Gon straightened. Standing up only helped so much with his sense of intimidation; his head was at Dooku's elbow level.

"Yes, my Padawan." Dooku's amusement had a feline quality to it—sly and self-contained. "Anyone who begins to journey farther along the path of the Force *should* be afraid. The dangers are many. The struggle is eternal."

Qui-Gon wasn't entirely sure what Master Dooku meant by "the struggle," but he assumed it was something about always doing his best. That was the sort of thing the crèche masters always talked about.

Before he could ask, Dooku gestured for Qui-Gon to follow him. "Come. There are many sections of our Temple that younglings never visit. Understanding our Temple more completely will help you better understand the Jedi Order."

The promise of finally seeing the whole Temple pushed every question out of Qui-Gon's brain. He grinned at Dooku for the first time. "Yes, Master."

Together they walked throughout the Temple—not all of it, because it was too large for anyone to see the whole of it in a day—but the most important parts, the ones Qui-Gon had always been most curious to see. Dooku showed him the Padawans' sparring dojo, and let him take a look at the one for full Jedi Knights. He finally saw the Great Assembly Room, reserved for those rare times when virtually the entire Order met. Various meditation chambers were . . . well, not exciting, but at least of interest. Probably most other Padawans wouldn't have found the arboretum thrilling, either, but Qui-Gon spent long minutes wandering through the trees, flowers, and ferns of a thousand different worlds while Dooku patiently watched.

At day's end, Master Dooku finally brought Qui-Gon to their last stop, the Jedi Archives. The new chief archivist, a woman named Jocasta Nu, welcomed Dooku with a familiarity that suggested they were friends. As she ushered them deeper into the vast, chambered room, she said, "It's been a while since we've seen you."

"My interests change, from time to time," Dooku replied. Qui-Gon wondered why Jocasta Nu frowned at that.

They examined several holocrons of various eras, not to really study them—simply for Qui-Gon to learn his way around. His eye was caught by a particularly old one, so ancient its shape was unlike any of the others. He walked toward it and put one hand on its golden surface. "What is this one about?" he asked. "What centuries does it cover?"

After he spoke he turned back to Dooku for the answer, and was shocked by the expression on his Master's face. Dooku stared at the holocron almost as if . . .

As if it were an enemy, Qui-Gon thought. But that made no sense.

Dooku said, "That is a holocron of Jedi prophecies."

"Prophecies?" Qui-Gon had never heard of this before. "There are Jedi prophets?"

"Not any longer. The ancient mystics sought undue knowledge of the future. It led them down dangerous paths. Those drawn too deeply into them were often . . . were tempted by the dark side."

Qui-Gon whispered, "The dark side?" He knew it was a thing all beings carried within them, a part of himself he would learn to guard against—the crèche masters had taught him all that. But it still sounded a little like some kind of ghost or monster, a mysterious thing that would leap out from the shadows to get you when you weren't looking.

"That is why we study prophecy no longer." Abruptly, Dooku turned and began walking away, which meant Qui-Gon had to follow.

"Master?" he ventured as he hurried to catch up. "Just wanting to know the future can lead you to the dark side?"

"It takes more than that," Dooku said. His dark eyes were unreadable.

CHAPTER SIX

---⊛---

Many Jedi went on retreat for deeper contemplation, but the Temple possessed its own reserves of tranquility. Chambers on the higher levels had translucent windows open to the sunlight, where one could drink in the heat and radiance and utter quiet. On a lower level, a meditation path wove its way through a maze of stonework, inviting the mind to focus. Sensory deprivation pods for various species could be filled and sealed, for those who wanted to all but shed their physical forms and become pure spirit.

Qui-Gon, however, felt steadiest when anchored to life. So he'd gone to the Temple gardens.

He knelt beside a Felucian fern and stroked two fingers along its delicate blue-green fronds. They sprang back slightly from his touch— a sign of sensitivity, and therefore health. Breathing in deeply, he took in the soft green scent, imagining the oxygen flowing through his body.

Through the Force, he reached out to the plant. Its presence was a delicate thing, conscious of nothing but peace.

(The same could not be said of all plants. Qui-Gon still remembered the first time he'd come across a tree that was strong with the dark side; the shock had been tremendous. Master Dooku had shaken his head ruefully and said, "Darkness is a part of nature, too, Qui-Gon. Equally as fundamental as the light. Always remember this.")

I ought to have been one of the Temple gardeners, Qui-Gon thought. It was a thought he'd had before, though usually one that rose from frustration with the Jedi Council.

His comm unit buzzed, and Master Billaba's voice came through the unit. *"Master Jinn, do I disturb you?"*

"Not at all." The Council had spoken to him only yesterday. Were they already impatient for an answer? "How may I help you?"

"There is a mission for you and your Padawan." Qui-Gon frowned, but before he could reply, Billaba continued, *"The timing is perhaps not ideal, but you've been requested."*

"You've sparked my curiosity. Am I correct in assuming you won't be giving me any more details until my Padawan and I show up for duty?"

Billaba's amusement shone through her voice. *"You're learning the Council's ways, Master Jinn."*

Force forbid, he thought—an automatic response, one born from the many conflicts he'd had with the Jedi Council in the past. That kind of thinking would have to change. "We'll be in the Council Chambers as soon as possible."

"Not the Council Chambers," she said, more somber now. *"Chancellor Kaj's office."*

Chancellor Kirames Kaj had led the Senate for many years, and undoubtedly could've gone on for many more. Her light touch and congenial demeanor made her popular among both senators and the public at large. The easygoing nature that made the Togrutan chancellor so well liked also made her, quite possibly, the least power-hungry individual ever to occupy the office. Instead of running for reelection, she'd announced that next year she'd return to Shili and found an academy for the arts.

To judge by the surroundings, Kaj's mind was already more on her future than her past. Various tribute wreaths, holos, and trophies decorated every shelf and wall, each testament to another banquet or reception held in her honor. It seemed that not a single planet in the Republic wanted to miss honoring the chancellor upon her retirement.

"Master Jinn," Kaj said, taking a seat behind her broad desk, "a pleasure to see you again."

"The pleasure is mine." He meant this, more or less. As politicians went, Kirames Kaj was quite endurable.

"And your Padawan here, the name was—Kenobi, yes?" Kaj beamed. "How very good to meet you."

"Thank you, Chancellor." Obi-Wan hesitated, clearly wanting to say something else but not knowing what would be appropriate.

Kaj absently stroked one of her head-tails as one of the aide droids brought up a holo, which filled the room. It portrayed a vast spacescape, one that took in a sizable section of the Inner Rim, as well as the chief enemy of hyperspace traffic through that area, the Byrnum Maw. Glowing at the heart of it—leading directly through the maw—was a thick blue line marking a path with which Qui-Gon was unfamiliar. The line was labeled PIJAL HYPERSPACE CORRIDOR. A small trademark symbol beneath this label indicated that the corridor was protected by the ships and sensors of the Czerka Corporation, just like pretty much every other tricky hyperspace route.

"They've found a path through the maw," Qui-Gon surmised. "That's been a goal for—what, decades?"

"More like centuries." Kaj gestured along the length of the hyperspace corridor. "Since a star went nebula and disrupted the old routes. But scientists have determined that two hyperspace anchors—one on the planet Pijal, and one on its moon—could together generate a field capable of stabilizing a central section of the maw. With that stabilized, several traffic pathways become possible. The worlds on those routes have been left behind, shut out of progress, for far too long. Now that can all change."

Qui-Gon nodded. "Your request for our help suggests that something threatens the new corridor."

"Indeed."

The chancellor's aide droid swiftly magnified the holo to show the planet around which this hyperspace corridor bent. Info cubes floating near it indicated that Pijal was a temperate planet with numerous mountain ranges and caves—a small population for a place that had a relatively benign climate—and that its moon was nearly as large as Pijal itself. It was this moon to which the chancellor pointed.

"Pijal is only now emerging from hundreds of years of isolationism," Kaj said. "But terrorism is threatening all their progress. A lunar dissident group known as the Opposition is sabotaging the mining and agricultural efforts there. Bombing Czerka vessels. Doing anything and everything they can to undermine stability on Pijal."

"Toward what end?" Obi-Wan asked. Then his eyes went wide as he realized he'd dared to question the chancellor of the Republic. Qui-Gon stifled a smile.

Kaj—not the sort to mind being spoken to by a Padawan—simply shrugged. "You'll have to make sense of this one, because no one else has been able to. You see, the Opposition didn't begin as a terrorist group. Apparently they were originally a . . . a performance art troupe."

Neither Qui-Gon nor Obi-Wan said anything for a long moment. Finally Qui-Gon managed, "You're serious."

"The galaxy is big and strange," Kaj said with a sigh. "Anyway, the Opposition would put on these political plays or erect vaguely rude statues overnight, that sort of thing. Their leader, a woman named Halin Azucca, apparently specialized in interpretive dance before she got into explosives. There wasn't any one ideology at work in the Opposition, other than wanting to change the status quo and some vague talk about more representation for lunar citizens. But after the potential for the hyperspace corridor became clear, the Opposition became angrier. Bolder. They started bombing places—originally purely symbolic targets. Their violence has increased as the hyperspace corridor's activation gets closer. In the past month they've gone after important government buildings, Czerka structures, even some of the temples. No lives have been lost yet, but it's only a matter of time. And if the Opposition decides to target the hyperspace corridor itself, the damage could be tremendous."

Qui-Gon asked, "What exactly does the Opposition want?"

"It's a bit mysterious, honestly. They issued big pronouncements at first, sometimes in verse. But when the attacks became more violent, Halin Azucca took the Opposition underground. They're getting worse and worse, threatening the planet's stability and the treaty ceremony itself. Pijal's leadership thinks that a third party should come in—someone neutral, with a fresh perspective—and help flush out the Opposition."

"Pijal's leadership—I believe they have a crown princess?" Qui-Gon said.

"Not exactly," Kaj replied. "Eight years ago, the throne was inherited by Crown Princess Fanry, then only six. Her regent has ruled since then, and has negotiated the Governance Treaty—which will change the monarchy from absolute to constitutional, with a representational parliament that will handle most government business. The treaty will also end Pijal's isolationism and allow legally binding agreements with offworlders, such as the Republic officials in charge of the new corridor. Princess Fanry is due to sign the treaty on her fourteenth birthday, only several days from now. They've got all sorts of festivities planned—concerts, rallies, even something called the Grand Hunt. However, the dissident attacks have increased in frequency and severity the closer we get to the signing. So I don't know how many parties they'll get to enjoy."

"So the dissidents want to keep the treaty from being signed," Obi-Wan said, finally daring to speak again. Unfortunately, he was also making assumptions.

"Possibly," Qui-Gon said, "But there are other explanations. They may simply see this as a vulnerable time for the government, and therefore an opportune moment to strike."

"It has the potential to get messy," Kaj admitted. "The hyperspace lane can't be opened until the treaty is signed, and it appears that these Opposition dissidents may try to stop that from happening. We need you to go to Pijal, help prevent any loss of life, and see to it that the Governance Treaty is signed on the appointed day. If possible, we'd also like you to bring the Opposition members to justice. If we leave that for Pijal's government to clean up later, all right, fine. But for the good of both Pijal and many, many neighboring systems, the hyperspace corridor must be opened. The Governance Treaty must be signed."

Important. Challenging. The sort of mission Qui-Gon might've expected to be assigned at any time. Any time, that is, except this one.

Keeping his voice neutral, Qui-Gon asked, "Chancellor, may I ask why we were chosen for this mission?"

"You've been requested specifically, and of course we thought it best that someone familiar with one of the principals should go—"

"I've never been to Pijal." Qui-Gon didn't mind interrupting even the chancellor, when the chancellor kept failing to get to the point.

Whether consciously or unconsciously, Kaj took the hint. "You see, when the princess inherited the throne as a small child, obviously a regent was needed to rule for her. However, infighting in the court meant that no potential Pijali candidate for regent was acceptable to all parties. Therefore a Jedi Knight was sent to take this position—an acquaintance of yours, Rael Averross." The chancellor glanced from Qui-Gon to Obi-Wan and back again. "I realize Averross is something of a, shall we say, controversial figure among the Jedi. But he is a friend, isn't he?"

"We were good friends long ago," Qui-Gon said. He wasn't entirely sure what they were now. "Controversial" was putting it lightly.

"Well, Averross asked for you specifically. I realize the timing isn't ideal, Master Jinn," Kaj said, "what with your having just been asked to

join the Jedi Council. It's a big step, and no doubt you'd prefer to concentrate—"

Damn, damn, damn. Qui-Gon closed his eyes for one moment. It
blocked nothing; the wave of shock that went through Obi-Wan was
so great it could be felt through the Force. Qui-Gon hadn't thought
Kirames Kaj would mention the Jedi Council invitation. It seemed
possible the soon-retiring chancellor of the Republic might not even
have taken much note of information about a new Council member.

But she had. Now not only did Obi-Wan know, but he'd also found
out from someone else. Qui-Gon had well and truly blown it.

*How can I presume to serve well upon the Council when I'm failing as
a Master?*

CHAPTER SEVEN

O bi-Wan felt as though he couldn't speak, couldn't hear. He was
aware of nothing but his own breath and pulse. The shock he felt
numbed him to anything else, except a sense of shame.

Qui-Gon's eyes met his for one instant—long enough for Obi-Wan
to see the pain in his Master's eyes. It didn't help, seeing that Qui-Gon
knew he'd done wrong. It just made it worse.

When Chancellor Kaj ended the official meeting, Obi-Wan immediately rose and headed for the door. Briefly he paused there, waiting
to follow his Master according to custom, but Kaj instead beckoned
Qui-Gon back to her. "Oh, listen, can I ask for some advice? It's a personal thing—I want to give Master Yoda some sort of gift when I leave,
a kind of thank-you for all the work we've done together, but he's *so*
hard to shop for—"

Qui-Gon was stuck, which meant Obi-Wan was free to do what he
wanted most: leave.

Figuring out what to do afterward . . . that was the difficult part.

He wouldn't even tell *me he'd no longer be my Master? I wasn't even worth informing?*

Obi-Wan stopped himself. He opened his eyes, taking in the serene interior of one of the Temple's meditation chambers: glassy blue spherical walls, soft cushions on the floor on which to sit or lie, gentle chimes in the background. Peaceful, soothing, and absolutely useless to Obi-Wan in his current state of mind. If he couldn't calm his mood through meditation here, he couldn't do it anywhere.

Anger sometimes refused to leave the soul except through the body.

By this time it was late at night—after the younglings' curfew, after all official meetings, when most of the few Jedi who roamed the halls belonged to nocturnal species. Obi-Wan's footsteps echoed through the vaulted hallways, unnaturally loud in the silence of the Temple. He wondered if he felt conspicuous because of that sound, or because he didn't have any idea how much others knew.

Had he been the last to discover that his Master was leaving him without so much as a word? Or would he have to explain to everyone why he was a seventeen-year-old Padawan in search of a new Master? He'd never even heard of that before. Was he the first disposable Padawan in the ten-thousand-year history of the Jedi?

Obi-Wan caught himself. That couldn't be true. At least, it *probably* wasn't true. But there was no point in painting his situation as worse than it was. It was already bad enough.

His path took him along the tunnel that led through the aquatic levels of the Temple, where the Jedi and Padawans from waterworlds lived and trained, at least part-time. Rippling lines of blue light illuminated the arched, translucent ceiling, through which he could make out the forms of two younglings—a Mon Calamari and a Selkath—swimming overhead. Were they out after curfew, or did diurnal cycles run differently on the aquatic levels?

There was still so much Obi-Wan hadn't discovered about the Temple, about the Jedi. At the moment it felt as though he might not even get the chance to learn.

Finally he reached the Padawans' dojo. Here, younger Jedi could train and practice together, both to spend time with friends and to learn from their peers. *Able to teach one another much, Padawans are,* Yoda had explained, *and far more able are they when their Masters watch not.*

He paced the length of the hexagonal floor, centering himself as best he could before finally drawing his lightsaber from his belt. Its hum filled the silence, and his grip instinctively strengthened in response to its faint vibration. Breathing in deeply, Obi-Wan assumed battle stance and began the cadences.

The basic cadences were where everyone began. The primary moves, key defenses, potential attacks. Obi-Wan had become very strong in the starter cadences over the years; like most Padawans, he'd expected to be shown other forms of combat, to choose another one to train in and begin establishing his individual expertise.

Qui-Gon still kept Obi-Wan practicing the basics.

Why? We've had misunderstandings in combat, but he can't argue with my fighting technique. Obi-Wan slashed through the air, spun his lightsaber, relished the way its hum warped with every movement. *I've never let him down there, at least.*

As he practiced, memories of past battles, past successes, cleared the fog of resentment from Obi-Wan's mind. The future intruded little on his thoughts, and when it did he imagined potential Masters watching him practice, being impressed, and resolving to do better by this Padawan than—

"Very good." Qui-Gon's rich voice echoed through the dojo. "You're even faster than I realized."

Obi-Wan managed to stop in place without flinching or betraying surprise. He held his lightsaber poised horizontally across his chest, its blue light casting everything beyond it, including Qui-Gon, in black and white. "This is the Padawans' dojo," Obi-Wan said.

"I was once a Padawan, you know." Qui-Gon stepped farther into the dojo, looking up into its vaulted ceiling, where various hand marks and footprints testified to Padawans practicing more athletic styles of lightsaber combat.

"I didn't mean that you wouldn't know where it was."

Qui-Gon raised an eyebrow. "You meant, what am I doing here, where I don't belong?"

He seemed so . . . calm. Even amused. Whatever generosity Obi-Wan had tried to feel toward his Master weakened. "I wasn't asking a question, actually."

The unspoken rebuke flowed around Qui-Gon like water. Qui-Gon Jinn might be an imperfect, unorthodox Jedi in many ways, but Obi-Wan had to envy his Master's ease. Instead of either arguing with Obi-Wan about his right to be there or just walking out, Qui-Gon said, "I wanted to apologize for this morning. That's not the way you should've learned about my invitation to the Council. I'd debated telling you, but thought I should wait until I'd made my final decision."

Obi-Wan bit back a bitter laugh. "Are you seriously considering declining? Were you ever? I doubt it."

Qui-Gon sighed. "Fair enough. Your reaction is understandable. But I have reservations. Concerns that I must resolve within myself before I can commit to a position of such responsibility."

"Concerns you wouldn't dream of discussing with me."

That comment finally pierced Qui-Gon's damnable calm. There was an edge to his voice as he said, "I suspected you would be too upset to discuss this rationally. Apparently I was correct."

"I thought you said my reaction was understandable," Obi-Wan shot back. "So why does it disqualify me from hearing the truth?"

Qui-Gon put his hands on his broad belt, the way he did when he was beginning to withdraw into himself. ". . . we should discuss this at another time. Neither of us is his best self at the present."

Even through his mood, Obi-Wan knew Qui-Gon was right about that much. But he couldn't stand to drop it so easily. "I've been asking myself why you've never trained me past the basic cadences." He twirled his lightsaber, brought it down into a lower stance. "You can't have thought my skill was inadequate. So why not move on? But now I think I know the answer."

"Enlighten me," Qui-Gon said drily.

"Because you decided a long time ago that you'd get rid of me one way or another. That we wouldn't work as Master and Padawan, so why bother planning ahead? Why even try? You knew it would be up to someone else to finish my training." Obi-Wan flicked his lightsaber off. "You turned out to be a prophet after all, Master."

Qui-Gon remained silent so long that Obi-Wan first thought he'd won the debate. Finally he replied, "I kept you in the basics for a reason, Obi-Wan. And if you'd ever understood why, you might have understood me well enough for us to excel as master and apprentice. As it is—I suppose the Force sometimes ensures things turn out for the best."

His Master walked out. For a long time, Obi-Wan remained in the dojo, battling his darker emotions, and wondering all over again why Qui-Gon Jinn was such a mystery.

Dully he told himself, *It's like Qui-Gon said. It's for the best.*

But it didn't feel like it.

There were some things Averross had never gotten to like about Pijal, even after eight years on this planet. Luckily, the food wasn't one of them. These people knew how to eat.

"You've invited the Jedi?" Czerka Sector Supervisor Meritt Col raised an eyebrow as she motioned to the server to bring her another serving of the shaak. The raised outline of the server's tracking chip was barely visible on top of her left hand—a few millimeters of metal that marked her enslavement. They dined in style at the palace. "Of course help is needed, but private security companies could be called in."

"Hired guns won't care about anything but their paycheck," Rael Averross said, picking up his shaak leg by the bone. Sauce dripped down his fingers. "Won't see anything their procedures haven't trained them to see. But a Jedi Knight? A Jedi can sort through this in a fifth of the time some mercenary would take."

Averross sat at one head of the dark wooden table with its gold inlay; Princess Fanry sat at the other, the candledroid chandelier catching the iridescent threads in the scarf wrapped around her hair. Supervisor Col sat at his right hand in her usual starchy white uniform. Palace etiquette declared that the seat next to Fanry was the one of higher honor—but Averross never had given a damn about etiquette. Besides, this meal was more than a formal banquet. It was a business meeting, just one of the endless tasks Averross undertook so Fanry wouldn't have to.

But Fanry—while remaining poised and charming, as a princess must—was obviously listening to him very carefully. She was doing exactly as he'd taught her to do: Always listen. Always learn. Always dig out more layers beneath court protocol.

He smiled to himself and thought, *Atta girl.*

Supervisor Col was smiling, too, but she remained unimpressed. "That prompts the question, Lord Regent—if a Jedi can solve this problem so simply, why haven't *you* handled it?"

"Because the situation needs . . . fresh eyes." Averross took another deep quaff of lunar wine, in the hope it would blunt the edges of what he had to say. He didn't like admitting his weaknesses at any time, least of all when it came to protecting Fanry. "I've lived on Pijal for eight years now, Supervisor. Not just that—I've lived in the *royal palace.* The princess's problems have been my problems. Her world's been my world. My view's the view from a castle window, and you know as well as I do—that view doesn't show you everything. Somebody new is gonna pick up on things I won't."

But there was so much about Pijal that an outsider could never fully understand. As much as Averross looked forward to Fanry's coronation, he could hardly imagine his life after that. He figured Fanry would ask him to stay on as an adviser, and he badly wanted to accept. But he also knew the Council would insist upon his doing something new to prove he wasn't overly attached to any one place, any one mission. Averross agreed with that general principle—but his work here on Pijal was different. He felt like he was doing real good. Like he mattered. And his knowledge of the planet meant he had more to offer here than anywhere else.

Of course, the Council would never admit that, passel of bureaucrats that they were.

If staying on Pijal meant leaving the Jedi . . . Averross didn't have a damn clue what he'd choose.

Supervisor Col nodded thoughtfully, though her dark eyes still betrayed suspicion. Averross knew she'd been a supervisor for more than two decades, gaining authority over commerce in more and more systems over the years. She was careful, canny, controlled. "I take your point, Lord Regent. Yet we at Czerka are concerned that a new Jedi won't understand our arrangements on this planet. Even you took a while to perceive the . . . correctness of what we do here."

"When I was young and naïve," Averross said with a grin. "Well. Maybe not that naïve."

He'd also been in the kind of pain that warped your mind—the kind you never got over, no matter how hard you tried—but that wasn't something Meritt Col needed to know.

Col smiled politely but pursued her point. "What if the Order sends someone else 'young and naïve'?"

"I've requested someone specific. The sharpest Jedi I've ever worked with. He'd never let us down." It felt so good, Averross thought, actually knowing who to trust. "I'm surer of Qui-Gon Jinn than any other person I know."

Late at night, Qui-Gon remained awake in his quarters, a datapad providing the only light.

He'd gone over this record before. Right after it happened, Qui-Gon had watched it repeatedly, as had others in the Jedi Order. Ultimately, the Council had vindicated Rael Averross.

Qui-Gon had never been sure it was the right decision.

The cargo freighter *Advent* had been ferrying foodstuffs to a system suffering from desperate famine, with Rael Averross and his Padawan supervising. Worries about pirate activity in that sector meant every external sensor was checked constantly.

This took attention away from internal problems, and kept anyone from recognizing the real danger: a bloody, violent mutiny.

Standard procedures for a mutiny aboard such a freighter would've called for the Jedi on board to prioritize retaking the bridge. From the bridge, all other ship functions could be taken under control and help from other Republic vessels could've been summoned.

Rael had other ideas. According to the reports of the official hearing, he'd suspected the mutineers might make a deal with the pirates—arms and assistance in return for the food supplies. With pirate help, the mutineers would've been much more difficult to defeat, and a threat to any Republic ships that came to the rescue. So Rael had taken his Padawan to the main cargo bay, to seize that area first.

Jedi could override protocols at their judgment, so long as they remained within their mandate for that mission. Rael's decision might not have attracted any notice, if not for the tragedy that followed.

Qui-Gon watched the *Advent* footage of the moment the mutineers stormed the main cargo bay, slaughtering loyal crewmembers right and left with the aid of reprogrammed droids. Even the screams of the dying didn't stop them—but the sight of two lightsabers did.

Into the fray leapt Averross and his Padawan, a Tholothian in the first year of her training. (*Nim Pianna*, Qui-Gon reminded himself. *Her name was Nim Pianna. She was more than just his Padawan.*) Despite her youth, she braced herself for combat, igniting her green lightsaber simultaneously with Rael's blue blade. Together they fought as smoothly as though they were two parts of one being, displaying the kind of unity a Master and Padawan were meant to have.

The kind Qui-Gon had never managed to build with Obi-Wan—

Qui-Gon's regrets were pushed into the back of his mind as the true horror began to unfold on-screen. Rael and Pianna were fighting their way across an elevated platform some twenty meters above the bay floor. Pianna jumped toward one of the droids, not realizing it had been equipped with a slicer dart. The silvery dart jabbed into her temple—a perfect hit—and Pianna stumbled to the side. Her eyes clouded over, the eerie sign of a brain and body temporarily enslaved by nanotechnology.

The next events played out in mere seconds, but to Qui-Gon they seemed to stretch into slow motion. They always had, no matter how many times he saw this, no matter how well he knew what happened next.

Rael glimpsed his Padawan.

Pianna raised her lightsaber and charged him.

Briefly, Rael hesitated.

A decision was made.

"Master Averross had to prioritize saving the hostages over saving his Padawan," Mace Windu had declared in the official Council statement. "Lightsaber duels, while very rare, are also deadly. He could not save her and still have enough time to save the *Advent*. Averross chose to prioritize the ship's safety above his apprentice's. That is the choice she would have wanted him to make. Any Jedi would rather accept risk than endanger others."

All very true. But Qui-Gon had never forgotten the look of pure terror and abandonment on Pianna's face as she fell. Yes, her mind had been sliced, but she had still known her Master. She was unable to control her actions, but her emotions had remained her own. Her Master—the person she was supposed to be able to trust above all others in the galaxy—had killed her. That was the last thing she'd known before she died.

She would never have been exposed to a slicer dart attack if Rael had obeyed protocols.

Perhaps a Jedi Knight with a more conventional background wouldn't have been excused so easily. But Rael was an extreme latecomer to the Temple, fully five years old before he was identified on Ringo Vinda—the oldest youngling ever brought in, so far as Qui-Gon knew. Those years made a profound difference. Rael had never fully mastered the subconscious controls that were trained into most Jedi from infancy. The members of the Averross family were people he missed terribly. The large majority of Jedi didn't know their birth families at all; the exceptions went no further than speaking—on rare occasions—to relatives who were little more than strangers. Rael's manners were rough, those of the orbital-station rat he'd been rather than the Jedi he hoped to become. He never lost his Ringo Vindan accent.

Some children would've been ashamed of this; others would've worked as hard as possible to conform to their companions' ways. Not Rael. He'd gone in the opposite direction—using his station-rat slang, remaining informal in every situation, and wearing clothes that a laborer would've thrown away as rags. In this way he tried to bandage the wound of his lost childhood, but it was a wound that never healed.

No one at the Temple was fooled by Rael's defiance, not even himself.

So he was treated with compassion. Even Dooku, who was in most ways a strict Master, had made allowances for Rael. As a result, Rael had flourished as both a Jedi and an iconoclast. He'd become a brilliant pilot and a lightsaber master and had served the Order nobly for many years. So after the *Advent* incident, the Jedi had made allowances once again—and for the first time, Qui-Gon thought, those allowances had gone too far.

He knew Rael better than most in the Order did, which was why he doubted the official explanation for why the cargo bay had been targeted ahead of the bridge. In Qui-Gon's opinion, Nim Pianna's life had been risked, and lost, mostly because Rael wanted a straight-on fight instead of the tedious work of overriding bridge controls.

That didn't mean Rael had been completely reckless. After four years teaching Obi-Wan, Qui-Gon could understand that losing a Padawan would be one of the most intensely painful experiences a Master could endure. So he hadn't challenged the findings. When he'd learned that the Council had given Rael a long-term, faraway mission, Qui-Gon had liked to think of his old friend in a place where he had time to meditate, and could do some humble good as a means of penance. In this way he might find peace.

But no. These past eight years, Rael Averross had been living in a palace. Ruling a world.

Obi-Wan would only have been a youngling when this happened. Probably he'd never heard anything of the tragedy aboard the *Advent*. In Chancellor Kaj's office, Obi-Wan had betrayed no recognition of the name Rael Averross.

It felt like the worst possible time to talk with Obi-Wan about a Master killing his Padawan. But Qui-Gon would tell him the whole story, as soon as possible.

Maybe he wouldn't be Obi-Wan's Master much longer—but in that time Qui-Gon would give him nothing but honesty. Obi-Wan deserved that much, at least.

He received a message. Putting aside the records, Qui-Gon turned to his comm, then raised his eyebrows in surprise. When he turned it on, a hologram took shape in his quarters. "Master Yoda. Can I help you?"

"Wished to speak to you, I did."

"About the mission to Pijal?"

"Among other things." Yoda studied Qui-Gon carefully. *"Linked strongly to Averross, are you. Yet that connection has not always been best for you both."*

"Rael's always been a friend to me." The defense was almost automatic. "If he's something of an outsider—I don't think that's a bad thing."

Yoda's ears flattened, a sure sign of irritation. *"Think you we judge on such trivial things?"*

"Of course not," Qui-Gon admitted. "If you did, you wouldn't have picked me for the Council, would you?"

"Pick you, I did not. Unsuited you are, in many ways. Yet the Council has spoken, and by that decision I shall stand."

It took Qui-Gon a moment to process what he'd heard. Yoda hadn't wanted him for the Council? Maybe it shouldn't have mattered, in light of the fact that Yoda wasn't opposing the invitation any longer—but it felt like a kick to the gut. "Did you call just to flatter me?"

Unsurprisingly, Yoda didn't take the bait. *"Dooku is the link between you and Averross. Of Dooku, you must speak. Ominous, is his absence from the Jedi. More understanding of his reasons for leaving, we need."*

At the moment, it was easy for Qui-Gon to imagine reasons not to deal with Yoda. "I'll ask," he promised. "I'll find out what I can."

Yoda nodded, and the hologram shimmered out of existence, leaving Qui-Gon to wonder why, when the rest of the Council embraced him, Yoda had not.

CHAPTER EIGHT

———— ✦ ————

Obi-Wan had many duties aboard the transport to Pijal. First he volunteered to help the crew double-check cargo manifests—tedious work, but important, as these materials would help build the modern spaceports needed for the new hyperspace corridor. Then he felt he should discuss the finer points of handling a *Consular*-class cruiser with the pilot; after all, Obi-Wan loved flying and wanted to become an even better pilot, so he ought to learn about as many kinds of craft as possible. Once they were en route, he went along with the engineers to check the cruiser's sensor dish, just in case repair assistance was needed.

What with one thing and another, he managed to avoid Qui-Gon until the final hour of their journey to Pijal.

"Padawan," Qui-Gon said as he ducked into the service tunnel where Obi-Wan was triple-checking some readings no one had asked for. "The crew seems to have the ship well in hand."

"I only wanted to help," Obi-Wan protested—then stopped himself.

Maybe Qui-Gon had failed to be honest with him, but that was no reason for Obi-Wan to be dishonest in return. "I haven't known what to say. So I was avoiding you. Not very mature."

"You're extremely mature for a seventeen-year-old. Whereas I'm forty, and I let you get away with it for hours."

Qui-Gon had always been quick to admit his own faults and errors, a kind of humility rarer among the Jedi than it should've been. Obi-Wan had always respected this trait in his Master. "I ought to have said before—congratulations on being invited to join the Council. It's a very great honor. They'll be lucky to have you."

"You really think so?" That made Qui-Gon chuckle. "Thank you, Obi-Wan. I thought probably you pitied them."

"Of course not." As difficult as their partnership had sometimes been, Obi-Wan realized he would miss it. Whatever had gone wrong between them wasn't all Qui-Gon's fault, and there had been more to learn from this man, which now Obi-Wan would never know—

"I wanted to talk with you about Rael Averross," said Qui-Gon, becoming grave. "You probably have some questions."

"Actually, after Chancellor Kaj described him as 'controversial,' I went digging for answers on my own." Obi-Wan's mood darkened as he remembered the footage he'd seen of the long-ago mutiny on the *Advent*. "What did you think, after . . . after Nim Pianna's death?"

Qui-Gon said nothing at first. He simply gestured for Obi-Wan to walk out of the cramped service area into one of the main corridors of the cruiser. They were the only passengers other than the crew, so the corridor was empty save for an astromech busily at work on a distant panel. Was his Master searching for a private place for them to speak? Obi-Wan wondered. Or maybe his questions had pushed too far.

Then Qui-Gon leaned against the wall to gaze at the electric-blue light of hyperspace visible through one long oval viewport. His voice was heavy as he said, "Rael was reckless. Bad enough to be reckless with your own life, but criminal to be reckless with another's. Worst of all to be reckless with your Padawan's."

"What?" Obi-Wan caught himself. "I mean, you didn't accept his reason for going to the cargo hold?"

"I think Rael probably believed in his own rationale. But he believed what he *wanted* to believe. We all do that, sometimes." Qui-Gon's gaze went distant for a moment, as though he was thinking of something else, but he went back to his topic. "Rael Averross never had the patience for complicated tasks like going through levels of computer security to *slice* his way onto a bridge. He violated mutiny protocols in favor of doing something he liked better—whether he ever consciously realized that or not. And his Padawan paid the price."

It *did* put Obi-Wan's issues with Qui-Gon into perspective. "Chancellor Kaj said you were the best person to deal with Rael Averross. That you knew each other before. Were the two of you friends?"

"In a manner of speaking." Qui-Gon began strolling back toward the bridge, and Obi-Wan fell into step beside him. "We shared the same Master. Rael was Dooku's apprentice before me. As fate would have it, we were on several missions together those first few years. So we got to know each other rather well. He helped me see what kind of man Dooku was, and how best to serve him. He helped teach me—even introduced me to the prophecies, as a matter of fact. We weren't intimates, but we . . . forged a bond of trust, which I believe survives."

If only there had been someone to tell Obi-Wan how to handle Qui-Gon. "How can you think of him as a friend when you judge his actions so harshly?"

This earned Obi-Wan a look. "We *were* friends, my Padawan. I believe on some level, we still are—but that changes nothing. Never assume your friends are above wrongdoing. Even good people can make terrible mistakes. But I believe they should be helped to understand and account for those mistakes, a point of view the Council doesn't share. At least, not when it comes to Rael Averross."

Obi-Wan's curiosity sharpened. "Why? Is there some particular reason the Council didn't hold Averross accountable?"

"Rael was . . . an unusual case. The seekers didn't find him in infancy, as they do most Force-sensitive children. He wasn't identified until he was five years old."

"*Five?*" Obi-Wan at first thought he must've misheard. "I was brought in late, and I was only three."

Qui-Gon nodded. "I doubt the Council will ever again accept a Padawan so old. Those years made the difference between Rael thinking of Ringo Vinda as his home, rather than the Temple. It shaped his attitudes, his progress—even the way he speaks, as you'll hear for yourself. As such, Rael Averross was always something of an outsider. Rare allowances were made for him, from childhood all the way to the hearings on Nim Pianna's fate. It's always better to err on the side of mercy, but . . . I suppose I'll always wonder."

"I suppose that's something you'll have to deal with, once you're on the Council," Obi-Wan said. The Council must've come to understand that some of Qui-Gon's criticisms were valid. Maybe Obi-Wan should've been looking harder for that validity a long time ago.

Qui-Gon didn't answer the question directly. "My invitation to the Council isn't relevant at the moment. And what Rael Averross did in the past mustn't overshadow our mission. Our attention has to be on Pijal and the princess. Don't lose sight of the now."

"I won't," Obi-Wan promised. It was one of those promises he couldn't be sure of keeping, but he made it anyway.

Millennia ago, according to local legend, Pijal had been one of the first worlds to adopt planetary shield technology. Qui-Gon suspected the equipment had not been updated since.

He and Obi-Wan stood on the small observation deck of their Corellian cruiser, taking in the vast spacescape before them—both the planet itself (broad blue oceans, smallish continents in green and gold) and its moon (darker green, densely wooded). Neither Pijal nor its moon looked especially noteworthy, but the shield technology was another matter. The ancient, clay-colored shield generators—twelve of them—slowly orbited Pijal, projecting almost invisible, glinting golden beams that swirled outward to form the shield, such as it was.

"This can't be a fully operational shield," Obi-Wan protested. "Generators this old couldn't possibly produce enough energy."

Qui-Gon inclined his head. "That depends upon your definition of *fully operational.* The Pijal shield doesn't prevent ships from flying in or out—but it never did, and was never designed to. It exists to shelter the world from the extreme solar flares that arrive every decade or so."

"I see, Master," Obi-Wan said. "But surely newer and more efficient generators would be safer. These look as though they might fall to pieces at the tap of a micro-asteroid."

"Replacing the technology is expensive, and Pijal's prosperity faded a long time ago." Qui-Gon folded his hands together within the broad sleeves of his robe. "But it looks as though Czerka Corporation plans to step in."

In the distance was an enormous Czerka ship, a *Branch*-class vehicle, which would serve as a manufacturing center, personnel transport, and office complex. The cruiser's bridge info screen identified this as the *Leverage,* under the command of Sector Supervisor Meritt Col.

Obi-Wan said, "Czerka's everywhere, it seems."

"And has been for thousands of years." The corporation was so ancient some believed it might even predate the Republic; the facts had long since been lost to time. "If the hyperspace corridor is opened soon, maybe Pijal won't be so dependent on Czerka. They could make their own repairs."

"In the nick of time, it seems." Obi-Wan shook his head in disbelief. "Hard to believe anyone on the planet could sleep at night, with a solar shield this weak."

How sheltered he still is, Qui-Gon thought. Some of their missions had taken them to less developed worlds, but Obi-Wan persisted in thinking of them as the exceptions, rather than the rule. To him, "normal" meant Coruscant.

Why should the Jedi raise so many of their younglings on the richest, busiest planet in the galaxy? It made sense for the Jedi Council to be located there, at the center of government. But Council members didn't need to be in constant contact with the younglings.

Perhaps we might move more of the schools, or at least the crèches, Qui-Gon thought. *There are numerous worlds safe enough for us to shelter the younglings where life is lived more simply, in ways more familiar throughout the galaxy. Where the children might be surrounded by farmland, or fisherbeings. Where we interact more with the communities around us, and train new Jedi to be as much a part of the worlds as separate from them—*

He caught himself. He was focusing on the future rather than the present. The lecture he'd given Obi-Wan would have been better delivered to himself.

"What in the worlds is that?" Obi-Wan pointed to a small spherical vessel rising slowly from the planet in the direction of the closest shield generator. Probably its tiling had been pure white, long ago, but countless reentries into atmosphere had left gray charring around seams and edges.

"Didn't you review the planetary report?" That was unlike Obi-Wan, Qui-Gon thought. "Those are the soulcraft. Ships that go back to the first settlers of this planet thousands of years ago. At some point, apparently, the local form of Force worship began urging pilgrims to travel into space periodically to experience the darkness and zero-gravity for themselves—so as to make them truly grateful for the beautiful planet they had. For some reason, circles and spheres tend to be sacred shapes on Pijal."

"*That's* a soulcraft?" Obi-Wan was practically sputtering. "But—of course I read the report, Master, I just—I can't believe they're still using ships that old."

"I believe over time the soulcraft have gained a certain talismanic quality of their own. They're valued because they're ancient, not in spite of it." Though Qui-Gon wondered how long such belief would last when—not if—one of these ships failed.

As though his thought had summoned it, a blue flare of plasma energy erupted from the soulcraft's side.

"Blast!" Qui-Gon wheeled around to the data terminal. Radiation levels were terrifyingly high—plasma venting into space but not into the ship itself, not yet—

"It's exploding." Obi-Wan hurried to the navigator's chair. "The ship finally failed?"

"The explosion is external," the cruiser's navigator said, gesturing toward the ice-blue haze of energy rippling into the space around the soulcraft. "That's an incendiary device."

A plasma bomb? Qui-Gon took a deep breath. Those were crude weapons, but powerful—used by attackers with few resources and no limits on cruelty. If the plasma fully penetrated the soulcraft, the deaths suffered by those within—

"The plasma explosion's still external?" Qui-Gon asked. When the answer was a nod, he pointed toward the soulcraft. "Get us within ten klicks, immediately."

"You can't get any closer to that thing," the navigator protested, meaning, *I can't*. "You'll fry yourself and everyone else on this ship!"

"Not if we act quickly." Qui-Gon shucked his robe, preparing for what lay ahead. As his garment fell to the floor, Obi-Wan's fell beside it. Some Padawans might've hesitated, but not his.

"You heard my Master," Obi-Wan said to the navigator. "Take us in."

I *am a Padawan of the Jedi,* Qui-Gon told himself as their shuttle drew closer to the forbidding black surface of Shurrupak. *I'm good with my lightsaber. I've been apprenticed to Dooku for four months. I'm ready for battle.*

Surely the Council agreed, or they wouldn't have sent him here with his Master.

But he gripped his lightsaber hilt more firmly when the ship shuddered again. They'd come under heavy weapons fire four point three minutes ago, according to the ship's chrono. Qui-Gon suspected the chrono was broken, though, because it felt much, much longer.

"Coming in for landing!" shouted Master Elio as the shuttle began the telltale shimmy that meant they'd hit atmosphere. "We'll be at Primus Base within five minutes!"

From the pre-mission briefing, Qui-Gon knew that Primus Base wasn't on the front line of battle. It was a whole three hundred kilometers away. But three hundred kilometers had seemed like a much bigger distance during the briefing than it did now.

Next to him, Master Dooku remained as tall and stoic as a tree. He was truly fearless in a way most Jedi could only appear to be. Instead of offering explicit support to Qui-Gon, he was providing an example to aspire to. Qui-Gon resolved to live up to that example if he could.

Assuming they didn't get blown up.

The shuttle took one more burst of fire as it neared the ground, rocking it back and forth so that even the most experienced Jedi stumbled. Qui-Gon managed not to fall down, barely, but felt as if he'd only just gotten his balance when the shuttle trembled again. That was the feel of landfall.

When the door swung open, everyone hurried forward, splashing onto a beach at low tide, still puddled with water. The wet sand dragged at Qui-Gon's boots, but he hurried to keep up with his Master's long stride. Every few seconds, the echoing boom of battle sounded, and the horizon lit up, but he tried very hard not to hear or see.

He reached the border gate of Primus Base just as Dooku did. His Master was a veteran of many military campaigns, so Qui-Gon expected him to look calm. To his astonishment, when he looked up, Dooku was . . . smiling?

"Rael!" Dooku called in his sonorous voice. He marched forward, his dark-green cape rippling in the harsh Shurrupak wind, to greet the young man who stood before them: short for an adult, his black hair rumpled in a dozen directions, wearing a ragged cloak and boots that looked older than Dooku himself. Of course Qui-Gon knew the name Rael Averross—a famous lightsaber duelist, and Dooku's first Padawan—but it couldn't be the same Rael. This person had to be a refugee.

But Rael cheerfully called, "Master! About time you got here. You were on the verge of missin' all the fun!"

"You always did enjoy combat more than you should." Dooku's amusement eclipsed his disapproval.

When they reached him, Rael quickly embraced Dooku—a gesture that startled Qui-Gon nearly as much as the fact that Dooku allowed it. "Seems like longer than five months since we've seen each other," Rael said.

"You spent ten years seeing me nearly every day. I should've thought that would be enough." This was what passed for humor with Dooku. "Meanwhile, I've taken a new apprentice—Qui-Gon Jinn."

Qui-Gon nodded in greeting. Rael's grin widened as he bent down to inspect his successor. "I'm finally taller than someone! About time." Before Qui-Gon could feel embarrassed, though, Rael put his foot next to Qui-Gon's own. "Okay, I see it now. You're gonna outgrow me in no time. When the rest of you catches up to your feet, you'll be as tall as our Master. Maybe taller. Dooku, someday you're going to have to get used to not being the biggest guy in the room."

Dooku shook his head, tolerant of teasing from Rael to a degree Qui-Gon would've believed impossible. Or maybe Dooku was only focusing on the battle to come, because he strode away across the dark-green Shurrupak sands to confer with the nearby generals. In the distance, through the fog, Qui-Gon could make out stun cannon tanks and troop transports. The horizon lit up again with weapons fire, and Qui-Gon shivered.

Rael put one hand on his shoulder. If he comforted Qui-Gon, the embarrassment might be worse than the fear.

Instead, Rael said, "Master Dooku can seem stiff sometimes. Know why that is?" Qui-Gon shook his head no, and slowly Rael's grin widened. "That's because he *is* stiff. Like a plank. Even in his sleep. How does he do that?"

Qui-Gon couldn't help laughing. "I don't know."

"Never figured it out, either." Rael straightened, now addressing Qui-Gon as an equal. "Dooku's a hard guy to get to know. Eventually you're gonna feel like you can tell him anything . . . but it's gonna be a while, right? Well, listen. Sometimes, a Master's previous Padawans help out the newer ones, if they get the chance. It looks like we do. So any questions you have that you might not feel comfortable asking Dooku yet—you bring 'em to me. We can spar, too, if you want."

The prospect of fighting a dueling expert like Rael Averross would've seemed intimidating at any other time. With his first battle looming, however, Qui-Gon couldn't worry about much else. "I'd like that."

"Good. C'mon, then, let's talk to the generals." Rael made it sound like a natural thing for a twelve-year-old to do.

Qui-Gon felt as though Rael Averross were the bridge—the link between the Padawan he was and the Jedi Knight he so desperately wished to be. The journey would be easier, now that he had a friend to show him the path.

CHAPTER NINE

———————— ✦ ————————

Princess Fanry felt frozen to her throne. She could not bear to watch the horror playing out on the screen in front of her—but she couldn't look away, either. She didn't deserve to look away while her people suffered.

While they died.

"This is turning into a nightmare," she said, her throat tight with tears. "I never thought it would come to this."

"Why not?" snapped Minister Orth, a tall, rangy woman whose salt-and-pepper curls were pinned haphazardly atop her head. It was the only haphazard thing about Orth, whose dark brocade dress was stitched tightly from ankles to throat. "Why wouldn't Halin Azucca follow things through to their natural conclusion? This was inevitable. There's nothing the Opposition won't stoop to."

Fanry braced herself. *You will be queen,* she thought. *You must not be weak. Pijal doesn't need a weak queen.*

Instead she looked up at tall, grave Captain Deren, who hadn't left her side since the latest report. His expression remained calm; only his eyes betrayed his sadness. To her he said, "The *Leverage* reports they'll be on the scene soon. Supervisor Col has taken charge personally. We may yet avoid any loss of life."

Will Czerka be the savior of the day? Fanry wondered. *I should've ordered more patrols, so my forces could rescue these people themselves . . .*

"Look, Your Serene Highness." One of the technicians shyly pointed to a blur at the edge of the screen. "It looks as if one or two other ships are already coming to help. There's a transport—a big one, a *Consular*-class cruiser—"

Instantly Fanry knew what that meant. Her pulse leapt as she turned to Deren and whispered, "The Jedi!"

"Don't be afraid." Dooku's voice rang out over even the howling winds of Shurrupak. Qui-Gon clung to the carbon-fiber-rope riggings of the Shurrupakan ship, salt spray stinging his face and hands, as they rounded the cape to approach the battle from an angle the enemy wouldn't expect. "They're shielded against skycraft and energy weapons. Not against seafaring vessels!"

He made this sound majestic, courageous, brilliant—nothing like the last-minute, last-ditch attempt it actually was. Qui-Gon took a deep breath and stared up at the stars. Big mistake. The stars weren't moving, and his stomach was, and the queasiness that swept through him made him feel weak. It was as though the fear of hanging on to the rigging was doing the work for him, more than his will.

"C'mon, hang in there," called Rael, who clung to the rigging just behind him. "You'll be all right, kid. The first battle's always the worst."

"It's not the battle I'm afraid of!" Qui-Gon protested. "It's the water."

"—the water?"

Despite the chill of the seawater drenching his clothes and hair, Qui-Gon's face flushed warm with embarrassment. "I can't swim!" Now Rael Averross—the Padawan before him, the stronger one, the better one—

would laugh at him, and no bravery in combat would ever eclipse Qui-Gon's shame.

Rael didn't laugh. "Don't worry," he called over the roar of the waves. "You fall in, I'll levitate you out. And after we've won this thing, tomorrow, I'll teach you to swim."

He made the victory sound inevitable. Tonight, battle—and then came tomorrow. It erased Qui-Gon's fear faster than anything else could've done—

"I've never taught you to swim, have I, Obi-Wan?"

Obi-Wan looked up from his space-suit fittings, confused. "No, Master. But I know how—well, a little bit."

"We'll practice," Qui-Gon insisted as he fastened his own space suit. "Every Jedi should be able to swim like a Mon Calamari."

Obi-Wan paused, and Qui-Gon could almost hear his Padawan's thoughts: *So why didn't you teach me before, and when exactly are we going to practice? After you join the Council?* These were excellent questions, but Obi-Wan was too good to ask them aloud. "We're approaching the soulcraft, Master."

He's making the transition to no longer thinking of me as Master, Qui-Gon told himself. *Before you join the Council, you'd better adjust as well.* "All right. Seal up."

Once they were encased in their space suits, Qui-Gon hit the panel that cycled the air lock. As the room depressurized, he double-checked the energy shield and personal thrusters at his belt: fully charged. He and Obi-Wan exchanged glances—*this is it*—before the external shield dropped, exposing them both to deep space. Qui-Gon pushed off into the void and, as soon as he was clear of their transport, hit the accelerator.

The energy shield shimmered greenish around him as he was propelled forward through space—more like a ship, or a missile, than a man. Most sentients couldn't master the muscle control to remain functional within a thruster-accelerator shield; even many Jedi found it difficult. But over many years, Qui-Gon had gotten the knack.

(Obi-Wan had mastered it in only a few weeks. There were skills no one could easily teach; a person possessed them, or didn't, and Obi-Wan possessed this.)

An accelerator shield essentially sheathed its wearer within an energy blast. The toughest part, usually, was to deactivate the acceleration in time to steer away from a collision that would be as destructive to the wearer as to its target. However, plasma fire interacted with accelerator shields in unusual ways—ways that at this moment were very useful to Qui-Gon Jinn.

The interaction would also be very painful, but not for long. That didn't matter. He simply needed to mentally prepare for it.

As the soulcraft grew closer, it seemed to expand in Qui-Gon's vision until it had almost erased space around it. The instant the surrounding blackness had disappeared, he braced himself for impact, calling on the Force for strength.

It hit him. It *owned* him. Every bone, every cell, every atom of his being seemed to resonate on a different frequency from every other, painful and strange. But it lasted only a moment. Then he was able to steady himself against the hull of the soulcraft. Qui-Gon looked up to see that Obi-Wan, too, was in position. Plasma fire rippled around them, a sickly green haze of light that seemed to be writhing. Horrifying as it looked, the writhing was a good sign. The accelerator shields had set into motion a chain reaction that would eventually dull the plasma to nothingness.

Meanwhile, he and Obi-Wan could help the process along. Already Obi-Wan had his field laser in his hand, a thin white beam carving up the plasma as though it were a gelatin, sending small blobs scattering into space where they would soon harmlessly dissipate. Qui-Gon got to work as well, hacking through the stuff as quickly as possible. The soulcraft had begun an emergency descent toward Pijal, but at this rate they'd finish their work long before the ship hit the scorching resistance of the atmosphere.

If we're so far from the atmosphere, why is the soulcraft already outlined in light?

The faint glow around the spherical soulcraft's horizon sent horror jolting through him. *Another plasma fire,* Qui-Gon thought, his skin prickling as his hair stood on end. *A second incendiary device. Separate from the first. Still fully active.*

How much good could his field laser be against that? It didn't matter. Qui-Gon had to handle this himself if he could; the risk was too great for Obi-Wan to be exposed to it. First he attempted to reach out with the Force, but plasma responded poorly to such commands. Next he reached for the magnetic tethers that would allow him to move across the hull, toward the second plasma fire.

But as he did so, a small, distant shape darted into range and fired a single antiplasma charge at the soulcraft. The charge hit the second plasma fire, dousing it to darkness. Vibrations rippled through the ship again at the impact, but the magnetic tethers kept him in place. Qui-Gon's relief shifted into curiosity as the unknown vessel—a light freighter, he thought—darted away.

Who could their savior have been? Why didn't they want credit for what they'd done?

Maybe the mystery rescuers wanted only what Qui-Gon and Obi-Wan wanted: the safety of those inside.

Pax Maripher's voice was sharp enough to cut through a Mandalorian shield. "What in the blazing fires of Lola Sayu was *that*?"

"That was an antiplasma charge." From her place in the pilot's seat, Rahara Wick pushed the engines to the max, making sure they'd be safely hidden behind the moon long before any other ships took notice. "I would've thought you'd know an antiplasma charge when you saw one."

"I am not *addled.* Of course I'm capable of recognizing an antiplasma charge. What I don't recognize is why you would insist on our anonymity, for protection from Czerka Corporation, and then do something almost guaranteed to attract attention? Something risky? Something *utterly* unnecessary?"

Rahara inhaled deeply. She reminded herself that the *Meryx* was

Pax's ship, not hers, so as long as she was aboard, she had to try to get along.

But that didn't mean never doing the right thing.

"Look." She stabbed at the screen with one finger. "Their manifest wasn't locked. So this was here for everyone to see."

The screen read: *15 passengers, 37 items of sentient property.*

"That means Czerka property." Rahara felt her throat beginning to tighten. No, she couldn't tell Pax all of this again and hope that this time he got it. She'd just tear up, and displays of emotion weren't the way to get through to Pax. "Let's get this straight. If I see people like that, in that kind of trouble, and there's something I can do to help them, I'm going to do it. If you can't accept that, then find yourself another pilot."

"By Elath. Such *drama.*" Pax held up his hands in sarcastic alarm. "It's not as though I were about to toss you out the nearest air lock. I merely wanted to know why you did it. You have told me. Therefore our conversation has come to a satisfactory conclusion."

Rahara knew that Pax was capable of feeling deep kindness and compassion, even if that better side was difficult for him to express. Sometimes, however, he simply lacked the emotional savvy to look past the practical aspects of any situation. So was he genuinely sympathetic to what she'd done, or did he simply not care, as long as they were both fine?

It didn't matter to her either way. Or it *shouldn't,* at least. She'd saved the lives of fifteen free people and thirty-seven "items of sentient property." That was good enough for one day.

Obi-Wan had thought it would be a relief to pass through the air lock into the soulcraft. At this point, it seemed, the Czerka Corporation ship would arrive to rescue them before the soulcraft had to test its damaged hull on reentry. Still, he didn't like being isolated in deep space without a ship around him.

But then he got inside the soulcraft and realized, for the first time, what it was like to be with dozens of people and *without* gravity.

"Sorry!" called one woman as she collided with Obi-Wan's legs. "I'll try to push off over here—" But as soon as she was gone, a man even larger than Qui-Gon bumped into him and knocked his helmet against the wall.

He and Qui-Gon were tethered to the interior hull with short cables, but the pilgrims inside floated freely. They wore simple white unitards or gray coveralls seemingly designed for this purpose, and those with longer hair had taken the precautions of braiding or tying it back, or wearing tight-fitting caps. But apparently part of the religious element of the pilgrimage kept them from strapping into their seats at any time other than ascent and descent. The rest of the time—regardless of any crisis, or of unexpected rescuers coming in through the air lock—they were spiritually commanded to fly free.

Obi-Wan had never felt queasy in zero-g before, but that had always been in the darkness of space, when he was more or less looking only at distant ships, or stationary planets and stars. Now, with bodies in every orientation bobbing and twisting around him, his stomach churned.

A shudder went through the ship, followed by the dull, heavy metallic thud of the engines shutting down. He relaxed as he recognized the pull of a tractor beam, no doubt pulling them toward the Czerka vessel *Leverage*. Which would have gravity. Wonderful, soothing, underappreciated gravity . . .

"Breathe easy," Qui-Gon said. He sounded faintly amused, and didn't appear to be queasy at all. Maybe once you were a Jedi Master, little things like "lack of gravity" could no longer concern you. Obi-Wan hoped to reach that stage soon.

Slowly, gravity began to take hold within the ship. As people began settling lower in the sphere, both Jedi unclipped their cables and descended to the floor along with them. Some of the Pijali seemed as relieved as Obi-Wan did, though most of them seemed oddly . . . let down. Sad, even. Maybe they hadn't gotten the full religious experience they'd hoped for.

Then he noticed that the quieter people all wore the gray coveralls, rather than white unitards. They also had odd bulges atop their left hands. It looked as though something flat and rectangular had been inserted between skin and muscle. Obi-Wan turned to Qui-Gon and murmured, "Their hands—"

"For scanning as part of cargo manifests," Qui-Gon said quietly.

Oh. These people were enslaved.

Obi-Wan had of course seen enslaved people before—the practice, though abolished by the Republic, was still widespread throughout the galaxy. But most he'd seen were part of smaller groups: a household staff, a farm's crew, extra dockworkers. He'd never seen any of them fitted with tags as part of an enormous corporate organization . . . or he simply hadn't noticed.

Maybe Qui-Gon hadn't, either. His Master studied the downcast faces around them, his gaze almost as sorrowful as theirs.

With a thud, the soulcraft settled onto a hard surface—the floor of the Czerka ship's docking bay. The air lock spun open, and a column of harsh bright light streamed through the shadowy space. "All right, then," barked a Czerka staffer. "Everybody out. We'll sort through the lot of you." Since Qui-Gon and Obi-Wan were closest to the air lock, the staffer turned to them first. "Don't recognize *that* getup. Slave or free?"

"Free," Qui-Gon said in his deep rumble. "Free Jedi, as a matter of fact. Summoned to Pijal by the lord regent."

The Czerka staffer straightened up so quickly he whacked his head on the air lock rim. Obi-Wan saw a few of the enslaved people stifling laughter. "Sir! Yes, of course. The lord regent is on board. We'll take you to him immediately."

"See that everyone here is checked out by a medical droid," Qui-Gon said. "The plasma fire could've caused unseen lung damage."

"Sir! Absolutely, sir. Right away."

After Qui-Gon and Obi-Wan had shed their space suits and stood in simple gray lining suits, a silvery protocol droid led them through the corridors of the Czerka vessel. Every control panel signaled that this ship had the finest equipment; every surface gleamed. The feel of the place was both very efficient and very cold. It was not the sort of place where Obi-Wan could feel comfortable wearing a thin, skintight lining suit.

To distract himself, he said to Qui-Gon, "What lung damage could the passengers have suffered from the plasma fire? None of the fumes got inside, surely."

"There's no damage they could've suffered." Qui-Gon gave him a sly look. "But a medical checkup ensures the enslaved get some time to pull themselves together afterward before being put back to work."

"Of course."

That was another thing Obi-Wan had always respected about Qui-Gon: his compassion. Obi-Wan wasn't uncaring, at least he hoped not, but sometimes it took him longer to see when someone was hurting, or what they might truly need. Qui-Gon seemed to instinctively understand such things.

So I don't suppose he could've taught me that anyway, Obi-Wan told himself. That was a quality he'd have to cultivate on his own.

The protocol droid led them through a gilded arch, more ornamented than anything else Obi-Wan had yet seen on board. When the doors slid open, they revealed a luxurious space—an observation deck furnished with long couches in rich fabrics. The most beautiful flowering plants of a dozen worlds bloomed from exquisite ceramic pots. A faint whiff of incense softened the air as a Cerean band played a lilting ballad. Seated in the plushest chair, in the center of the room, was a man drinking Toniray wine from a fine crystal goblet, and wearing . . . rags, basically. Clothing so threadbare it hardly deserved the name. His dirty boots were propped on another chair and had already marred the velvet. The man's unshaven face widened in a grin as he spotted his visitors.

A Czerka official, I guess, Obi-Wan thought. *But I wouldn't have thought a corporate officer would be so casual—so extravagant—*

"Rael Averross," Qui-Gon said to this man who couldn't possibly be a Jedi but . . . was. "Good to see you again."

CHAPTER TEN

Qui-Gon smiled before he could stop himself. Whatever else had happened, however much they might have changed, this was still *Rael.*

He hadn't realized how much their reunion would move him, not until now, when he finally stood face-to-face with Rael again.

"Qui-Gon Jinn!" Rael called, holding his hands out wide as he strode forward. His old brown robe had been lined with pale-blue shimmersilk, in the Pijali fashion—though, over time, it had of course been worn as threadbare as most of Rael's garments. "It's been too long, kid."

"Agreed." Qui-Gon allowed a welcoming embrace before stepping back to take a better look. "I think palace life agrees with you."

Rael laughed. "It tends to agree with most people. I mean, what's not to like? Now, let me guess—this is your Padawan, right? Can't believe they trusted you with one. The Order's really going downhill."

His grin turned wolfish. "Their decline started around the time they accepted me. Not a coincidence."

"Obi-Wan Kenobi, Rael Averross," Qui-Gon said, gesturing between them. Obi-Wan made a polite short bow. His student could be difficult to read at times, but overall he looked as bewildered by Rael as . . . as virtually everyone else was, at first.

Rael Averross wasn't a tall man; he barely came up to Qui-Gon's shoulder. Time had swirled Rael's thick black hair with a few touches of gray, but that only set off the deep tan of his skin and the strong features of his face. Rael's frame remained muscled and strong despite his increasing years. None of that was as striking as the warmth—the charisma—that still shone from Rael like a light. And obviously he cared no more for conformity now than he ever had.

"I'd tease you about your version of royal robes," Qui-Gon said, "but in my current state I can hardly comment on anyone else's clothes."

"At least I've *got* clothes." Rael's dark eyes sparkled with humor as he took a pointed look at their lining suits. "As much fun as it would be to have you show up on Pijal in your underwear, I wouldn't do that to Fanry. You there—Cady, isn't it?"

A young girl cleaning in the corner hurried forward and ducked a quick bow. "Yes, Lord Regent."

"Head to ship's stores, will you? Basic tunics and trousers will do for now—we'll have their stuff sent from the Corellian cruiser to the palace." Rael dismissed the girl with a quick wave.

Qui-Gon studied Cady as she hurried out. Probably a year or two younger than Obi-Wan, but already doing adult work. Dark hair tied back with plain cloth. A royal emblem on her gray coveralls. The telltale rectangular shape on the back of her hand.

"That stunt out there with the soulcraft?" Rael said as he led them both to the nearest of the sofas. "That was worth watching. I mean, it doesn't measure up to what we managed on Riosa that time! But still, not bad."

"We'd need an entire squadron to be in danger to equal our adventure on Riosa." Qui-Gon saw Obi-Wan's interest had been piqued. Maybe he should share a few more of his old war stories. Adult Jedi might know how little war was worth, but the young were always fascinated, despite themselves.

"Dooku would be proud." Rael's smile faded slightly. Qui-Gon always remembered Rael smiling—but somehow, he seemed more himself now, with that touch of melancholy. "Heard he left the Order. Can you believe it? I tried to reach him on Serenno, but no luck."

Qui-Gon was taken aback. "He didn't answer you?"

With a shrug, Rael said, "Ah, he's a ruler now. Probably surrounded by courtiers and bureaucracy and all the other bantha poodoo I've had to deal with here for the past eight years. Bet you one of his new flunkies tossed my message out with the rest of the trash people send a count of Serenno. Sounds like he talked to you, though . . ."

"No. I haven't reached out to him at all." Qui-Gon sighed heavily. "I think he left partly for Serenno's sake, after inheriting the title of count, but partly because he no longer agrees with the work of the Jedi. It's an argument I'm not ready to have."

Rael gave him a knowing look. "An argument you don't want to lose, you mean. You've always been a rebel, Qui-Gon. If Dooku talked to you long enough, you'd probably walk out the door right after him."

"Not anymore," Obi-Wan ventured. "I mean, Master Jinn isn't a rebel, not really. He can't be, now that he's joining the Jedi Council."

Qui-Gon wanted to wince, though it was hard to say why. Rael's eyes widened as he sank back on the cushions in astonishment that didn't seem to be exaggerated. "Is he joking? Or did the Jedi Council get more interesting all of a sudden?"

"Obi-Wan isn't joking. As for the Council—well, they finally seem open to hearing other points of view." Qui-Gon shook his head in disbelief. "My surprise is even greater than yours."

"We've *gotta* reach out to Dooku again," Rael said with a laugh. "If he hears the news on his own, unprepared, he's gonna drop dead on the spot. A planet will lose its ruler. So galactic politics hangs in the balance, right?"

Obi-Wan laughed, too. Rael's charm had settled around the room like velvet, soft and warm, muffling any discomfort, any sound.

But a vague sense of uneasiness remained within Qui-Gon—and would, until he had a chance to talk with Rael alone.

Once the Padawan had left to watch the pilots bring them in for a landing, Averross could speak freely. Maybe now he could get Qui-Gon to loosen up.

"You grew at least seven centimeters taller than me. More, I think. How *dare* you." Averross shook his head in mock dismay. "I spent ten years with Dooku towerin' over me. Then you came along, and I finally had someone to tower over. Now I'm out of luck."

"I didn't do it on purpose," Qui-Gon said. He seemed amused, but didn't laugh. Even as a little kid, he'd never been the type to joke around freely. Averross had at first wondered if the boy was troubled in some way Dooku hadn't caught on to. Yeah, Dooku was a good man, but he was tall and dark and imposing and strict. Averross would bet the last time his old Master laughed, the stars hadn't even cooled yet. That made him an imposing figure, especially to a kid. That wasn't the sort of person a boy would relax around, or tell all his secrets to.

But Averross had come to understand that Qui-Gon had a kind of natural bedrock steadiness, that it was as much a part of him as his flesh and bones. You weren't going to find *him* in the extremes.

Which was where Averross preferred to spend most of his time.

Still, he and Qui-Gon understood each other. Averross felt sure their bond endured.

"We should discuss the Opposition, and their leader, Halin Azucca," Qui-Gon said. "Performance artist terrorists—now I've finally seen everything."

Averross held up a hand. "Don't say that until you've been to a bachelorette party on Kashyyyk."

"Wait. You weren't really—"

"Maybe someday you'll find out. Not now." Averross grinned. "And let's hold off on the debrief until Fanry can be a part of it, too. She's gotta start handling this stuff on her own soon."

Qui-Gon nodded. "Very wise."

Okay, he wasn't being unfriendly, but he was distant. What the hell was wrong with Qui-Gon?

It's about Nim.

It's not about Nim. Qui-Gon would understand, more than anyone. He doesn't blame me.

For an instant Averross could see Nim's face as he'd seen it last—her wide eyes shadowed by the haze of the slicer dart, tears welling—

Move on.

"Like I said, you'll be able to get through to Dooku now," Averross said as he strolled by the long viewport of the observation deck, with Pijal bright and blue against the darkness of space.

"I wish I could be as certain." Qui-Gon shook his head. "Yoda's concerned about Dooku's departure from the Order. He thinks there may be more to it than anyone knows."

Averross shrugged. "That guy's concerned about all kinds of ridiculous stuff." He shifted his voice into an imitation of Yoda's. *"Up the hell, he should shut."* Qui-Gon tried not to laugh, but failed, which only made Averross grin wider. "Seriously, *this*? It's the bait of the century. When you tell Dooku you've been invited onto the Jedi Council, he'll want to spill on what it's *really* like."

"Do you think I should be cautious?" Qui-Gon held his glass of Toniray but had yet to take a sip. "That I ought to hear Dooku out before I make a decision?"

"What decision? C'mon, are you seriously considering *not* joining the Council?"

Qui-Gon shrugged. "I intend to accept. But I know that accepting means . . . change. For me, for the Council, even for Obi-Wan. It's not something to undertake lightly."

"Responsibility can be heavy," Averross admitted. "My work here on

Pijal isn't nearly as big a deal as serving on the Council, and still, sometimes, it feels—let's say, daunting."

This earned him a sharp look. "It doesn't seem that daunting from here."

Averross turned around, as if only just noticing his old robes. "What, you think I ought to be swanning around in shimmersilk and satin? Wearing shiny medals, something like that?"

"As though you would ever. I was referring to your comfort with Czerka Corporation," Qui-Gon said, gesturing toward the luxurious interior of the observation deck. "Certainly they seem comfortable with you."

Averross shook his head ruefully. "Listen, there's a time for straight-forward negotiations, and then there's a time to play the game. I'm playing the game with Czerka, because they can help Fanry. They can help the whole planet, if I handle it right."

Finally, Qui-Gon relaxed. "I too often use—less direct methods, shall we say."

"Yeah, I know. Or were you hopin' I'd forgotten Riosa?"

"I wish *I* could forget Riosa." Finally Qui-Gon drank some wine, relaxing into the moment.

Averross was relieved. Now they could enjoy themselves—at least, until the time came to handle the Opposition.

"Man, that makes me think—you remember the old prophecies?" he asked as he poured himself more wine.

Qui-Gon stared at him in surprise. "I—of course. Actually, I've begun studying them again, the past couple of years."

"Why?" They'd both studied them under Dooku, who considered them an important element of Jedi history. Averross had found them an entertaining curiosity, but he remembered Qui-Gon being en-chanted by them, and worried about them, to a degree he'd never un-derstood.

"It occurred to me that I'd have a greater understanding of the prophecies when I had a greater understanding of myself," Qui-Gon said. "But why do you ask?"

"Because, wasn't there one . . ." Averross snapped his fingers. "It went, 'One will ascend to the highest of the Jedi despite the foreboding of those who would serve with him.' That was it, right?"

"Roughly." Qui-Gon shook his head. "You think that prophecy refers to me? That the Council's wary of me?"

"Hey, they were, right?" Averross said. "But obviously they got over it."

"The prophecies aren't to be taken literally."

"That's what I *always* said. Don't you remember, it was me who had to talk you out of it, back in the day? You were halfway to becoming a spaceport soothsayer offering to see futures for a credit or two. Still, it's weird, right? You being obsessed with this stuff as a teenager, and then nearly livin' out one of the prophecies yourself."

"I suppose it *is* strange," Qui-Gon said.

"And then some," Averross agreed. His friend seemed distracted again, but this time he could tell Qui-Gon's thoughts had nothing to do with Averross, and so could be safely ignored.

CHAPTER ELEVEN

From the *Leverage*, both the soulcraft and the Jedi were loaded onto a smaller cargo vessel that could land more easily on the planet's surface. As they approached the capital city, the cargo ship skimmed above lanes of tall, thin conifers that striped the rugged hills below. Sunset light shone on a broad ocean as the ship rounded toward its coast. Giant cliffs jutted out into the water, their white stone imposing itself on the seascape.

Qui-Gon stepped to Obi-Wan's side as the ship began its final approach. "Have you learned to pilot yet another type of ship? You'll be able to fly anything in the galaxy before long."

However, Obi-Wan's attention was elsewhere. "Master, the capital city's nearby, but we're still in a wilderness. The readouts say we're practically on top of the royal palace when there's nothing around for kilometers."

Qui-Gon chuckled. "Look closer."

He watched Obi-Wan's eyes widen as he realized that the cliffs had been hollowed out. Windows in various geometrical shapes had been hewn from the rock, and the sunset already revealed that the transparencies there were in various colors. What lay before them was not only the palace, but an entire royal complex. The only hints above the surface were the round temple known as the Celestial Chalice, and grounds so thickly forested with trees that it was easy to miss the manicured lawns and antique iron fences.

"By night, the palace complex shines like a lantern," Qui-Gon said.

"It's remarkable. Why did they do it? Protection from the solar flares?"

Qui-Gon shook his head. "No. Pijali culture believes in focusing on the internal, rather than the external."

"Admirable," Obi-Wan said. "Not to mention, unusual in a royal court."

"Very true." Qui-Gon couldn't suppress a smile as he thought of some of the regal pomp they'd been forced to endure in the past.

As they walked down the gangway, the hiss of steam around them, an honor guard of troops marched in their direction. Their cloaks were plain brown, the cloth visibly rough—but as the guards walked, the flutter of the robes revealed brilliant-green shimmersilk linings.

The guards stopped and pivoted to face one another across a path of smooth stone that led toward a high arched door. As they did so, Rael emerged from within the ship, ready to escort them the rest of the way. "So here we are," he said, stepping in front of them on the path and gesturing ahead. A strange kind of happiness shone from him, one it took Qui-Gon a moment to recognize as pride. "Ahem. Allow me to present Her Serene Highness, Crown Princess Fanry of Pijal."

Emerging from the arched palace door was a young girl with pale skin. Her dress and turban scarf were plain white, but with slashes in the sleeves and skirt that revealed the rich gold shimmersilk of her undergown.

"We are most honored to welcome more Jedi Knights to our realm," Fanry said, coolly and properly—then made a face. "I'm supposed to refer to myself in the plural when I'm speaking officially. No idea why. Makes me want to turn around and look for my clone."

That made Qui-Gon chuckle, and Obi-Wan grinned, too. Obi-Wan said, "When you're crowned queen, can you change that?"

"I won't be absolute ruler, so no." Fanry gave an exaggerated sigh, clearly meant to amuse. "But maybe the new Assembly will have mercy and enact the changes on my behalf. I mean—*our* behalf."

Clever, Qui-Gon thought. *Quick. Very independent. Exactly the sort of student Rael should have.*

Not like Nim.

Nim had died at very nearly the same age Fanry was now.

During his time as a Padawan, Obi-Wan had visited dozens of royal palaces—from a chief's simple fortress on Lah'mu to the expansive, spectacular queen's complex on Alderaan. He thought of himself as too worldly to be awed by such places, or even surprised.

However, the inside-out aesthetic on Pijal impressed him. Every table was gilded below, rather than above; every chair was plain, save for the richly embroidered cushions that would be hidden when someone sat. Even the lanterns that hung from the high ceilings were fashioned from plain black metal, but lined with glittery tile that reflected sparkles of light all around.

There was something fascinating, Obi-Wan decided, about the idea of having such grandeur and concealing it—making it known only to those who would be willing to discover what lay within.

"You're getting to like the place," Averross said, striding past Obi-Wan on his long legs. "Knew you would. Best palace in the galaxy, if you ask me."

"Of course you like it best," Qui-Gon interjected. He remained a few steps behind them, not bothering to keep up with Averross. "This has been your home for nearly a decade. Only natural that you should become fond of it."

That wasn't the same thing as Qui-Gon saying he didn't like the palace. He'd even praised it, before. But Obi-Wan sensed his Master was . . . blunting Averross's pride. Refusing to get caught up in his point of view.

I suppose I should be glad Qui-Gon's not overly impressed with a Master who was responsible for killing his Padawan, Obi-Wan thought. The bleak joke cut too close for him to smile.

They reached the central chamber, where Fanry hurried ahead and took her place on her throne. Obi-Wan noted with amusement that her slippered feet didn't quite touch the floor. She gestured to the courtiers and guards who stood around her. "Our Jedi guests have arrived," she proclaimed, lifting her chin. "This is Jedi Master Qui-Gon Jinn and his Padawan, Obi-Wan Kenobi. Present yourselves to them for introductions."

A tall, skinny woman with wiry graying curls piled atop her head tottered forward in her narrow-cut brown dress, pale lips set in a thin line. "I am Minister Orth." Her imperious tone suggested she expected them to have heard of her. "I advise Her Serene Highness—and of course our lord regent—on internal planetary matters."

There was no *of course* about it. Obi-Wan felt sure most political figures wouldn't trip over the title of an important official they'd been reporting to for nearly a decade. *She resents Averross,* he noted. Maybe it didn't matter for their mission, but he was going to mention it to Qui-Gon—if only so his Master would know Obi-Wan had been sharp enough to pick it up.

Another introduction also struck him—that of the captain of Fanry's guard, a slender man with dark skin, strikingly high cheekbones, and a gleaming bald head. "I am Captain Deren," he said in a voice so low and resonant that he made Qui-Gon sound like a youngling. "My loyalty is sworn to the princess, now and forever." It was a formal phrase any guard might have uttered, but Obi-Wan could sense how deeply Deren meant it.

"With these guys' help, we're finally gonna put the Opposition where they belong. In jail." Averross took his place on the dais beside Fanry, standing to her right, slightly behind her shoulder. Undoubtedly this was meant to suggest his deference to her—but his ragged appearance and unshaven face suggested Rael Averross deferred to no one.

Has he become too accustomed to power? Obi-Wan wondered. *No Jedi should ever fall into that trap. He doesn't seem as though he cares for authority that much—but he definitely likes the fact that no one can boss him around.* The glint in Minister Orth's narrowed eyes suggested she'd like to give Averross an order or two.

Qui-Gon asked, "How much can you tell us about the Opposition?"

"They were actors, of a sort, before they turned to terrorism." Fanry held out her hands, as if helpless. "Performance artists, whatever those are."

Orth interjected, "Halin Azucca had this one show where she wore this enormous white fluffy . . . thing, about four meters across, and invited audience members to cut off bits of it to be clouds in the sky she was painting. Apparently this counts as art."

"It was about the paradox of findin' serenity through destruction," huffed Averross. "*Think* about it."

Minister Orth looked like she'd sooner lick a river toad. Probably Averross's enthusiasm for performance art was mostly about irritating Orth. Then again, Obi-Wan had once heard of a Hutt who collected fine porcelains. You never could tell what people held inside.

Fanry continued as though neither her regent nor her minister had spoken. "Our royal audiences are available to everyone. We've repeatedly asked to meet with this Halin Azucca or other Opposition leaders, under a promise of absolute immunity. But no one appears. No one speaks. Instead we got pranks and stunts, and then vicious attacks." The holoscreen nearby showed a statue breaking apart to reveal tiny shimmering flight droids, which spelled out various words in the air—and then an explosion ripping through a Czerka warehouse. The contrast was even more jarring than Obi-Wan had expected.

"Terrorists are always lookin' for reasons to hurt other people," Averross said. "They don't like the treaty. Yeah, they give all these different reasons why, none of which justifies the things they've done.

Even though the moon is finally gettin' some representation in the Assembly! They never had that before."

"It sounds mystifying," Qui-Gon said. Obi-Wan wondered if anyone else noticed that wasn't the same as agreeing with anything that had been said.

"Well, that's why we've brought you in, Qui-Gon," Averross said. "You're better at sizing up a situation than just about anybody, and we needed someone I knew I could trust. Not some play-it-safe type. Too many of those in the Order. You, though—you can get to the bottom of this."

Mildly, Qui-Gon replied, "I've been fooled a time or two."

"But not often, and not for long." Averross's pride in Qui-Gon seemed almost as great—and as paternal—as his pride in Princess Fanry.

"If I may—" Captain Deren waited for the Jedi to nod before he continued. "—in my opinion, 'getting to the bottom of this' is irrelevant compared with the importance of safeguarding the treaty ceremony. After that ceremony, we'll have all the time we need for investigations."

"*You* might think we can protect the treaty and the princess without getting these answers," Minister Orth spat, "but I do *not*. I only hope the new Jedi on our planet are able to come up with information faster than the one already here."

"Protect the princess?" Qui-Gon said. "Is there any particular reason you think she would be in danger? Have there been attempts on her life?"

Fanry bit her lower lip and stared at the floor. Averross cut in, "Nothin's happened to Fanry. Not on my watch—and not on Deren's, either. The man knows what he's about. But in the end, if the Opposition's hell-bent on preventing the treaty from being signed, they could go after the one person with the power to sign it."

Although agreeing with Averross was clearly difficult for Orth, she nodded. "And the upcoming events will expose her to greater danger. Public appearances, the Grand Hunt—"

"Perhaps the hunt might be postponed," Obi-Wan ventured.

Every Pijali citizen in the room stared at him as though he'd just stripped off his trousers. He was blushing by the time Captain Deren responded, "The Grand Hunt is a traditional rite on Pijal. Every future monarch must prove themselves on the hunting grounds."

Averross nodded. "It's like the ruler has to demonstrate they can provide for the planet."

"Were Her Serene Highness not to hunt," Deren said, "many Pijali would consider her coronation null and void. Her signing the treaty would then provoke a crisis far more serious than the Opposition attacks."

"There's no talking 'em out of it, guys," Averross said. "Believe me, I tried."

Orth's eyes narrowed. "Perhaps you should've spent less time trying to destroy our traditions and more time finding the Opposition."

"Rael Averross is as intelligent and dedicated a servant as Her Serene Highness could wish," Qui-Gon said. He stood with his hands clasped together within the sleeves of his robe. "But whatever I can add through a new perspective is at the court's disposal."

As was often the case, Obi-Wan noted, Qui-Gon managed to sound very reassuring while actually saying very little.

Later that night, after a sumptuous dinner and some courtly music, the Jedi had been taken to their guest suite. It was an ample space, with bedrooms for them each, and a central room with tall windows that looked out onto the sea. Pijal's troublesome moon illuminated the water, revealing each wave, each curl of foam. Staring out at the tide, Obi-Wan ventured, "Deren's the only one I feel entirely certain of."

"That's usually the one who causes trouble." Qui-Gon's smile was rueful. "So you *don't* feel entirely certain of Rael Averross?"

One thing Obi-Wan had learned from his Master: When in doubt, answer a question with another question. "Do you?"

Qui-Gon shrugged, using the gesture to free himself of his heavy robe. "I feel certain that he cares about Princess Fanry, and is committed to the treaty. That's enough for now."

His Master was being cryptic again. By now, Obi-Wan ought to have been used to it. He *had* been used to it. But the abrupt, unannounced end to his apprenticeship had scoured his feelings raw. He wanted to snap, *Just* tell me *what you're thinking, can't you for once just—*

"How shall we begin?" Obi-Wan said as coolly as he could manage. "By visiting the moon?"

"Yes." Qui-Gon kicked off his boots. Normally he left them in the center of the floor; it would be Obi-Wan's job to look after his things. Tonight, however, he collected them under one arm. Apparently the duties of a Padawan were slowly being taken away. "We'll fly to the moon tomorrow morning in a small, short-run vessel—preferably without any military escort. Less formal, and much better for snooping around."

Despite his dark mood, Obi-Wan smiled slightly at the word *snooping;* Qui-Gon's tone made it clear how much he was looking forward to that. Still, he had to ask: "Do you seriously expect we'll be able to turn up the Opposition just by flying around the moon? When we've never been there before, and hardly know what we're looking for?"

"Of course not." Qui-Gon freed his hair from its leather tie, so that it fell loose to his shoulders. "That would be absurd."

"Then why are we doing it?"

"It's not the Opposition we'll be searching for," Qui-Gon said. With that he walked into his own bedroom.

Cryptic. On purpose. Again. Obi-Wan had sometimes found this habit of his Master's endearing. Tonight he didn't.

But he couldn't help feeling curious about whatever Qui-Gon had planned.

CHAPTER TWELVE

———————— ✦ ————————

Ships of enormous size and grandeur were put at the Jedi Knights' disposal, as well as the finest pilots of the royal star fleet. Qui-Gon refused them all except for a small cruiser for Obi-Wan to pilot himself. Nothing larger was necessary. Obi-Wan would enjoy the experience, and besides, it was bad form to ask for too many favors at the beginning of a mission. Better to keep them in reserve. It was too early to test Rael's hospitality.

Not Rael, Qui-Gon told himself as Obi-Wan brought the cruiser out of Pijal's atmosphere. *The "lord regent." That's who Rael Averross is here.*

No wonder the Jedi Council had chosen Rael for this mission. Of all the people Qui-Gon had ever known, Rael Averross was the least likely to be bowled over by riches, finery, and grandeur. Eight years in a palace, and the man still dressed like a Drexelian shell-digger.

But the temptations of power were subtly different, and far more dangerous. Had Rael fallen prey to those? Time would tell.

"Lunar gravity taking effect," Obi-Wan said. Even as he spoke, Qui-Gon felt the faint pull on the cruiser drawing them in. "If you'd care to enlighten me as to our specific destination, this might be a good time to mention it."

"Settle us into low orbit while I run some scans. When I find what I'm looking for, that's when we'll land."

"When?" Obi-Wan gave him a curious look. "Not *if*?"

"They're here," Qui-Gon murmured. "We just have to find them, wherever they are."

Obi-Wan opened his mouth, obviously to ask who "they" were, then closed it again. He was learning patience, Qui-Gon thought—discovering when to wait and let a mystery unfold for itself.

(That, or he was completely sick of dealing with a deliberately obtuse Master. If that was the case, Qui-Gon couldn't blame him.)

Qui-Gon input a datacard he'd requested from the Czerka ship the day before. A holo began to play, showing yesterday's plasma attack on the soulcraft. He ignored the images, looking only at the scan findings at the bottom.

"Are we reliving our past triumphs?" Obi-Wan said. He was joking now, trying to leaven the mood between them. "If so, I'd like to ask that the Hutt palace on Teth be stricken from the record."

Qui-Gon simply pointed at the findings as they scrolled along. "It's not our triumphs we're reliving. Ah—*there*."

The shadowy mystery ship appeared at the edge of the holo, barely visible, firing to stop the plasma fire. Qui-Gon paused the holo there to study the information beneath. "We made some new friends yesterday. I suggest we look them up."

Obi-Wan frowned. "Those are literally the only people on this moon we can safely assume *aren't* in the Opposition."

"Agreed. That's one reason why they might be useful to us." Qui-Gon pointed to one particular set of findings hovering at the lower edge of the holo. "This is another."

"That's . . . a scanner-blocking field. A rather powerful one, but small." Obi-Wan spoke faster as he became more intrigued. "The field's limited to only one section of the ship, which isn't that big to begin with. Maybe it could stretch to cover the whole ship, though, as powerful as it is. Master, I didn't think small ships could project scanner-blocking fields, much less ones this strong."

"We're dealing with someone rather ingenious." Qui-Gon stripped out most frequencies from the cruiser's scanners, setting them to search for only the energy by-products of this unusual blocking field.

"And rather secretive," Obi-Wan pointed out. "Are you sure you can get them to help us?"

Qui-Gon smiled as the first faint hit came up on scans. "Let's find out."

Obi-Wan brought them in low, the cruiser skimming over thick forests of trees with distinctively knobby, gnarled trunks and branches. The terrain was uneven, rich with both cliffs and caverns. From their scans, it appeared the blocking field was at work within one of these caves.

A hiding place within a hiding place, Obi-Wan thought as he and Qui-Gon strode out onto the moon. *I'm not sure these people will be eager to work with us.*

But he followed Qui-Gon as they made their way toward the cave. It was important to stay attentive, because the beauty of their surroundings could so easily lull him off his guard. Soft light filtered through the leaves far overhead. Sinuous vines twined around low shrubs and tree trunks, fruit gleaming in various shades of deep purple and a green so pale it was almost gold. Temperate breezes caressed his skin, tousled Qui-Gon's hair. Calling upon the Force here would be easy— only a few moments of serenity would surely connect any Jedi to the abundant life of this moon.

Pijal carves its beauty out of stone, Obi-Wan thought. *No such effort is required here.*

The rambling terrain dipped lower, revealing rocky hillsides—and the mouth of a cave, nearly hidden by vines. Obi-Wan's sharp eyes picked out the torn leaves here, the odd winding there, which revealed that these vines had been broken recently, then tugged back into place from within.

Qui-Gon gave him a look. Obi-Wan nodded, and they both took their lightsabers into their hands without activating them. Silently they slipped through the vines and began walking into the cave.

Sunlight became weaker as they went. Just when Obi-Wan thought they would soon be in complete darkness, he became aware of a dim glow ahead, which outlined a small ship of unknown make. They continued on, taking care to step as quietly on the gravelly surface as possible, as new sounds became audible.

"I *cannot* believe this," said a reedy human voice in a Coruscanti accent more precise than most. "Every single one of them? This is outrageous."

The feminine voice that replied was more amused than angry. "You're going to be *outraged* that some rocks aren't doing what you want them to do?"

"More that they have the gall to be something other than what they pretended to be." Obi-Wan made out a man's silhouette against the pale, pinkish glow of hovering candledroids. "Never in the history of mineralogy has anyone been so betrayed."

The unknown woman laughed. "We'll lay a curse on them later, okay? For now we should—wait. Do you hear that?"

She had sharp ears; Obi-Wan wouldn't have detected anything yet at this point. For once his reaction and Qui-Gon's were in perfect sync; instantly they both leapt forward and ignited their lightsabers. The two people inside the cave jumped back behind their ship, maybe going for weapons—

—and yet what was that sparkling along the cave walls?—

"We mean you no harm," Qui-Gon said, in his gentlest tone. "We only want to ask a few questions."

"Your questions be damned." The man half showed himself from the edge of his ship, holding something long and black in one hand.

The woman murmured, "Pax, they're *Jedi*. They're not going to—"

"They're not going to stop us," said the man evidently named Pax. "They're going to turn around and back out of here if they know what's good for them. And if not, well, I stand ready to fight."

Qui-Gon sighed. "Stand down."

"Surrender?" Pax said. "Give up before the battle's even begun? Why would I do that?"

"Because you're not holding a blaster in your hand, only a shovel," Qui-Gon said patiently. "Also, we have lightsabers."

A short pause followed before Pax said, "Your point is well taken. Allow me to congratulate you on your persuasive rhetoric."

"I can't believe you tried to bluff two Jedi Knights with a *shovel*." The woman appeared, hands raised. "We surrender."

"Surrender isn't necessary," Qui-Gon said. "But we need to talk."

"Just want to talk." A likely story.

Pax Maripher stood in his hold, arms crossed against his chest, glaring at the Jedi Knight and his student who dared interrupt his work. Granted, the work had turned out to be utterly fruitless, a waste of time. But that didn't give the Jedi the right to barge in waving their lightsabers about.

Rahara, meanwhile, had introduced herself and was now chatting with these two like they were old friends. "Can you believe it?" she said, gesturing toward the brilliant orange crystal the tall fellow called Qui-Gon held in his hand.

"It looks almost exactly like kyber," Qui-Gon said, turning the crystal back and forth. "The same heft. It even possesses some vibration with the Force. The differences are incredibly subtle. I see why you were fooled."

The young one with the stupid haircut, whatever his name was, shook his head in disbelief. "Are you positive it's not kyber? Not some—new form, a different kind of crystallization?"

This was too much to be borne. "*Yes,* I'm positive," Pax said, in a tone of voice he hoped would be described as "withering." He held out his scanner as evidence. "On the macro level, this stuff is identical to kyber, but if you get down into the microscopic, they've got about as much in common as Coruscant and Ceiran."

"Apparently they're called kohlen crystals," Rahara explained. "We just looked 'em up. Turns out they're not unknown, just rare—even rarer than real kyber. But they're no good in lightsabers, and so unusual there's not even a jewelry market for them. Which means this whole trip is nothing but a wild-mynock chase for us." She shrugged in a way that made her silky hair fall past one shoulder. Pax wondered if she was doing that on purpose, not remembering that the Jedi were supposedly celibate.

Then he wondered if he was simply noticing Rahara's hair far too often.

"Not *only* that," Qui-Gon said, smiling at Rahara while continuing to pretend Pax was the least important individual in the room. "It also gave you an opportunity to save many lives."

Pax's eyes met Rahara's. It seemed to him that he ought to be indignant that her stunt had drawn exactly the attention they'd hoped to avoid. Instead, he saw the pain she tried so hard to hide, so well, most of the time. Quietly she said, "There was no reason not to help."

"There was also no reason to run away afterward," said the little one with bad hair, Obbie whatever. "Why did you?"

Pax was ready to leap in with one of many possible explanations, each in his opinion more deceptive than the last, but Rahara—after years of never speaking about it—instead simply held out her left hand. "Here," she said. "That's why."

Visible on the back of her hand was the faint scar from the long-removed Czerka tag.

"The scars won't heal," she said quietly. "They treat the tags with a chemical that burns in ways bacta can't fix. So you have to wear it forever—the proof that you're enslaved, or were before you were freed."

"Your last owner freed you?" Qui-Gon said.

Rahara's expression grew steely. "I freed myself."

This was more than Pax could bear. "If you think for one instant that you can repatriate her to Czerka, let me make it very clear that those lightsabers won't stop me from stopping *you*."

Qui-Gon held up one hand. "I've no intention of returning Ms. Wick to Czerka." Something in his voice made Pax want to trust him, which was highly unusual, as he trusted nearly no one. "I only need your help."

"I knew it. Pax was right." Rahara hugged herself, a gesture of fear that had nothing to do with the pure rage in her voice. "You're going to make me do—do something, or else you'll turn me over to Czerka for—"

"Ms. Wick," Qui-Gon said again. "I repeat, I have no intention of returning you to Czerka whether you cooperate or not. However, I'm more sympathetic to those who've escaped from slavery than I am to jewel thieves."

"Who said we're jewel thieves?" Pax demanded. "You can't possibly prove such a thing."

Obi-bad-hair held up a datapad with their past inventory and sales records, which obviously hadn't been securely locked. "I think we can."

Rahara raised her eyes to the ceiling. "Pax, it's obvious what we're doing. So let's not waste time denying it." Her gaze focused on Qui-Gon next. "What favor is it you want from us, anyway?"

Pax thought he was braced for any answer, until Qui-Gon smiled easily and said, "I need you to help me find some terrorists."

CHAPTER THIRTEEN

———— ✦ ————

"The *Meryx,* you say?" Qui-Gon took a seat in the ship, studying its inner workings, which were a unique patchwork of state-of-the-art tech and materials so old they might've predated the Republic. "An interesting namesake. Have you ever found any?"

"No, more's the pity," said the wiry, wild-haired man called Pax Maripher. His resentment of the Jedi was clear—but not as powerful as his pride in his vessel. He ran a hand along one gleaming wall as he added, "Should we ever get our hands on some meryx, oh, the upgrades I'll give her."

From his place near the scanner-blocking field, Obi-Wan turned with a frown. "What's meryx?"

"Probably the single rarest gemstone in the galaxy," answered Rahara Wick, who was placing orange kohlen crystals in an analysis cylinder. "It's a kind of amber—specifically, the fossilized amber of the white wroshyr trees of Kashyyyk, which have been extinct for millennia."

"Meryx appears cloudy and white until the light hits it *just so.*" Pax's face could actually look quite handsome when he was smiling. Qui-Gon suspected few people ever learned that. "Then it shines the most brilliant gold you can imagine."

Obi-Wan was as interested in jewels as the average seventeen-year-old Padawan, which was to say not at all. "Why did you name your ship after a jewel you've never found?"

"It's about hope," Rahara said. Pax gave her a look—that wasn't the answer he would've given, Qui-Gon saw. But he didn't contradict her, either.

The man has a soul, Qui-Gon thought. *But he makes her carry it.* "Their ship is named after their ultimate goal," he said to Obi-Wan. "It's an aspiration. A reminder to strive for great things. Something any Padawan should relate to, surely."

Obi-Wan looked at the floor as he nodded. "Perhaps you should explain to our new friends—"

Pax snorted. "Hostages, more like." This earned him an elbow in the ribs from Rahara.

"—exactly what it is we need from the *Meryx,*" Obi-Wan concluded. Which meant that his Padawan hadn't yet put it together himself. He'd been distracted these past several days, still wounded by Qui-Gon's failure to tell him about the Council. Even the innocent remark about having goals to aim for seemed to have stung. Qui-Gon wondered how things could've gotten so bad, so quickly.

The probable answer: They'd been that bad for a while, but he'd failed to see it. He'd been so busy judging Obi-Wan that he hadn't thoroughly judged himself.

Without missing a beat, Qui-Gon replied, "We need to search this moon rather thoroughly, without signaling to anyone that the search is under way. Using Pijali ships would attract attention and cause alarm. The *Meryx,* however, has been expertly fitted to avoid detection."

The word *expertly* soothed Pax, as it had been intended to do. His tone was marginally less acidic as he asked, "In other words, you mean for us to chaperone you about this entire moon while you look for—what, precisely?"

Qui-Gon gestured upward, toward the space between Pijal and the moon where they'd first encountered each other. "For whomever sabotaged that soulcraft, nearly killing everyone inside."

"The Opposition, right? I read that on the feeds." Rahara leaned against the wall. The static of the scanner-blocking field tugged strands of her hair out, almost as though she were standing in the wind. "Look at it this way, Pax. We're going to be flying around this moon as well protected as the princess herself, with two Jedi by our side. And we're not going to go to jail. I'm not seeing a downside here."

"The downside is, I don't like it. But I must admit—we're stuck." Pax turned to Qui-Gon, as though making a very great concession. "Very well. Give us your desired search pattern, and we can begin."

Qui-Gon held up a finger. "We'll begin tomorrow. Scouts might've seen our ship today, and be on alert. If they have sources within the palace, they'll definitely know. Tomorrow morning, when you pick us up on Pijal, no one will be the wiser."

Pax rolled his eyes at the thought of having to get them from Pijal, but he raised no further objections. When he took himself off to the refresher, Qui-Gon mildly said, "Interesting fellow, your partner."

"You don't have to be tactful. Pax is a lot to take. But you have to understand where he comes from." Rahara looked from Qui-Gon to Obi-Wan and back again. "When Pax was just a kid, four or five years old, he was on a ship on the border of Wild Space that got attacked by Delphidian pirates. He hid in an equipment hatch, because he was still little enough to fit. Nobody else was. Which means every other sentient on board was killed, including his parents. Pax was left behind."

"How terrible," Obi-Wan said.

Rahara nodded. "Yeah, but I don't think that's the main reason why he is the way he is. That has more to do with the fact that the ship went derelict—it wasn't found for a long time, and while it had tons of emergency rations in storage, it didn't have the fuel to get anywhere on its own. See, the only equipment the pirates left behind was a shipment of protocol droids. Threepio units, mostly. Those protocol droids raised Pax for the next fifteen years, until the ship was finally rediscovered. And they taught him to behave exactly like they did."

Qui-Gon considered the 3PO units he'd known. "That must be . . . challenging."

"That's one word for it," she said, with a laugh. "But once you figure out how to deal with him, honestly, Pax is pretty great."

Obi-Wan gave Qui-Gon a look that clearly meant, *We'll have to take her word for it.*

But they had more than Rahara Wick's word. Qui-Gon could feel the subtle flow of the Force around these two—the sense that they were people drawn to greater things. Despite Rahara's past traumas and Pax's bad attitude, there was very little darkness here.

Some people, he thought, *are drawn to the light as surely as flowers that bend toward a sun.*

Pax returned just as Qui-Gon began inputting an initial search grid. Rahara beckoned Pax to their equipment table and whispered, very low, "It looks like there are some whirlpool opals on this moon."

"Semiprecious at best," sniffed Pax.

"Okay, maybe people don't pay that much for them, but they'll pay *something.* We might as well harvest what we can. Then this trip could still be profitable for us—or we'll at least break even."

"Assuming," Pax said, "we're not blown to atoms."

"Yeah, that would help."

Stifling a smile, Qui-Gon settled down to work.

Although there were no specific references in the ancient royal charters, most of the Pijali courtiers believed that, for at least the last hundred coronations, Czerka Corporation had thrown a preliminary celebration for the heir to the throne. Not any of the rallies Czerka promoted, nor the orchestral events they sponsored—a small, private party. Something personal for the heir, and the current sector supervisor.

Which was why Fanry was spending her afternoon on a yacht with Meritt Col.

"Your Serene Highness," Col said, settling into the cushioned repulsor chair next to Fanry's, near the prow of the ship. "When you take office, we'll have so many important matters to discuss. But today is only for pure—"

"What matters?" Fanry asked innocently.

Meritt Col paused. Although she wore a free-flowing silvery robe—the sort of thing one might wear on a yacht—it looked as uncomfortable on her as her stiff Czerka uniform would've looked on anyone else. Her pale hair ruffled in the sea breeze. "Well. Of course, we'll want to negotiate various terms and permissions. For instance, we'll need greater authority on the moon, because of course we need both the Pijal and lunar anchors for the hyperspace corridor to remain intact. And the docks reserved for the soulcraft—some of them could be put to greater commercial use. But as I say, there's time for all that later."

Rael Averross had tutored Princess Fanry in the corporate structure of Czerka. (This was no small feat, since that structure was as labyrinthine as the government of any planet she'd ever studied.) She could envision some of the requests Col would have. The specific requests, however, were beside the point.

"You won't really need me, though." Fanry took a sip of fruit punch from her pink glass. "Since I won't be an absolute ruler. Just a constitutional one."

"That doesn't mean you won't have power!" Col laughed brightly. "The people still look to you. Care for you. Haven't they asked you to bless the soulcraft next week? Your symbolic authority is greater than any real authority could ever be."

Symbolic authority, Fanry thought. That had a nice ring. The sound of it—well, it was friendlier than *absolute monarch*, wasn't it? Kinder. More in touch with the greater galaxy. Not cemented into the traditions of the past. It was something entirely new.

She smiled up at Col and said, "Then I guess we'll have *lots* to talk about after the ceremony."

"So very much!" Col held her glass out for them to clink them together, as though toasting the brighter future to come.

Throughout their work with the crew of the *Meryx,* Qui-Gon noticed that Obi-Wan largely remained silent. Not peculiar behavior, for a Padawan ... but unusual for Obi-Wan, who generally weighed in whether it was appropriate or not. Qui-Gon didn't acknowledge this until much later, after they'd bid farewell to Pax and Rahara for the evening and were taking the cruiser back to Pijal.

"What troubles you?" Qui-Gon said.

Sometimes Obi-Wan tried to pretend he wasn't troubled, but today he didn't bother. "We made a deal with thieves."

"Jewel thieves," Qui-Gon added. "When you put it that way, it has a bit more panache to it, don't you think?"

"*Panache?*" Oh, how red Obi-Wan's cheeks could get when he was on the verge of high moral outrage. "These people steal for a living. And we agreed to let them get away with it! And—and you're laughing at me."

"I'm laughing at moral absolutism. You just happen to be displaying it at the moment."

Obi-Wan remained unamused. "We made a deal with the Hutts because we had to, if we were going to get off Teth alive. But this? We can't find a better way of disguising our movements? Surely there's something more clandestine than a flashy thieves'—excuse me, *jewel* thieves' ship."

"No doubt there is," Qui-Gon said, settling back in his chair as the gravitational pull of the moon released them with a faint shudder. The tug of Pijal would take them in soon enough. "But I was curious about them. They took a great risk, exposing themselves to help save the people aboard the soulcraft."

It was like watching Obi-Wan wilt, as the realization washed over him. "They're more than just thieves. I ought to have remembered that."

"I think at the moment you're a bit weary of me," Qui-Gon said gently. "Under the circumstances, no one could blame you. Pax and Rahara were never the ones you were truly upset about."

Obi-Wan didn't acknowledge this out loud, but already his temper had improved. "So we investigated them. That didn't mean we had to partner with them. Is that also about your curiosity?"

"Partly. Partly because it actually is excellent cover for us to move around the moon without being exposed. And partly because I wanted to give them a chance to be . . . better. Bigger of spirit. That rescue suggests they have it in them."

"People are more than their worst act," Obi-Wan recited. It was something Qui-Gon had said to him many times, which at last seemed to be sinking in. "At least, most people. And they are also more than the worst thing ever done to them."

The dark scar on Rahara Wick's left hand flashed through Qui-Gon's mind. "We could both bear to keep that in mind while dealing with Rael Averross, as well."

Obi-Wan didn't look up from the cruiser's controls, despite the fact that there was virtually nothing for him to do until they got much closer to Pijal. "You still have doubts about him?"

I do, Qui-Gon wanted to say—but couldn't. "Despite everything that's happened, Rael remains a Jedi Knight. A man committed to his duty. You can't have missed his devotion to the princess."

"I didn't," Obi-Wan said quietly. "But perhaps we should evaluate Jedi by criteria other than their dedication to the younger people they protect."

The jab pierced Qui-Gon, all the more painful for the element of surprise. It wasn't that Obi-Wan had never tried to say anything hurtful before; he'd just never hit the target so squarely. Worst of all— Qui-Gon wasn't sure Obi-Wan had even meant to hurt him. He simply meant what he said. *That* was what really stung.

"You're too dedicated to ideals rather than reality, Obi-Wan," Qui-Gon said, hating the answering sharpness in his voice, but unable to resist it. "To the point of sacrificing your principles."

Evenly, Obi-Wan replied, "I thought members of the Jedi Council were meant to represent the ideal."

"The Council deals with the messier aspects of reality all the time." This conversation had gone far enough. "Obi-Wan, why don't you check the alluvial dampers? The readings on those are a bit strange." They were mere fractions of a point off optimal range, but it was the first distraction he could think of.

Rarely was he so transparent. Obi-Wan did him the courtesy of not gloating, and instead went to check the obviously fully operational alluvial dampers. He paused at the cockpit archway, though, and said, "I guess this is another point in favor of the old prophecies."

"What do you mean?"

"I just remember—wasn't there one that talked about the kyber that isn't kyber?" Obi-Wan frowned. "It was something like that, anyway."

"You're right." Qui-Gon's curiosity got the better of any awkward feelings. "I'll look it up."

As Obi-Wan got to work, Qui-Gon did so as well, using his datapad to search the translated texts he'd been studying. There it was: *When the kyber that is not kyber shines forth, the time of prophecy will be at hand.*

It's only a metaphor, he thought, as he always did. *Even the ancient mystics probably never meant for it to be taken literally. It's not as though some "time of prophecy" was meant to come around and make all their symbolic predictions become real.*

So Qui-Gon had believed, at least since he was thirteen years old. So he would have said to anyone who asked him, and would say to Obi-Wan if his Padawan brought up the subject again.

Yet he couldn't deny the uncanny thrill that swept through him.

The orange glow of the kohlen crystals. The kyber that is not kyber.

The time of prophecy will be at hand.

CHAPTER FOURTEEN

Qui-Gon stands in the cave. The orange crystals glitter around him, reflecting a source of light he cannot see.

Then the crystals darken, turning red—as though with Sith fire.

He hears a scream. No, several screams. He can no longer see the crystals, because the cave has turned white. Has turned glorious, with gilded walls and a glass ceiling that looks up at the sky. Beneath his feet are midnight-blue tiles.

And ahead of him, he glimpses the colorless image of a blazing lightsaber superimposed over Princess Fanry's face.

"The Skykeeper!" someone shouts. Qui-Gon looks for whoever spoke—looks for anything he will recognize or understand—but he looks in vain.

Another voice shrieks in terror as the lightsaber slashes downward. In the very far distance he hears somebody say, very calmly, "Even the Jedi can fall"—

Qui-Gon woke with a start. Using the traditional exercises, he slowed his heartbeats and breath, reasserting calm over his physical form. Most dreams faded quickly upon awakening, but this one only grew more vivid.

There was no reason for him to have a dream about the Sith. No reason to fear that anyone with a lightsaber would interfere with the treaty ceremony, and surely Rael's blade would always protect Fanry. No reason to think the Jedi Order would ever fall.

And yet the dream shook him to a level few others ever had. It felt . . . more than real.

It felt *certain*.

The ancient mystics had sought visions of the future. In return, they'd been visited with dreams like this one, dreams they spun into cryptic "predictions" that really were nothing of the sort. That was what Rael had always believed. What Dooku had determined. What Qui-Gon had told himself for a quarter of a century.

But now, sitting in this broad bed, he could not believe that convenient, rational interpretation. Instead he sensed he'd glimpsed something that could truly come to pass.

But what?

Averross lay in his bed, staring up at the richly ornamented ceiling. Everything else in his chamber had gotten more comfortable over time—regular old chairs, his stuff in reasonable piles, that kind of thing—but the ceiling he couldn't do anything about. It always reminded him that he was in a palace.

He should have asked for a bottle of something good to be put in his room, Corellian ale or Port in a Storm, maybe. But he couldn't ask for it now, no matter how much he'd like to put away a glass or two. Well, it wasn't like he hadn't had a good night anyway—

"Rael?" Qui-Gon Jinn's voice came from the doorway. "May I speak with you?"

"Qui-Gon?" Averross scrambled out of bed, grabbing for his dressing gown. "Be right with ya!"

But for those who lived in the Jedi Temple—a communal space—privacy was more a concept than a reality. Averross remembered when it had been that way for him, too. So he couldn't be angry when Qui-Gon walked straight in.

Just embarrassed.

"Ah," Qui-Gon said, staring at the woman in Averross's bed. "Forgive my intrusion."

"Selbie was just leavin'," Averross promised. It happened to be true—she'd already tugged her underdress on, despite his wheedling. But this still won him a glare from Selbie, who might've preferred a warmer introduction.

She knows why this is so awkward, he reminded himself as he draped her cloak about her and saw her to the door. *She'll get over it soon enough.*

If Selbie didn't get over it—well, this was no more than a matter of convenience for either of them. There would be others for her, others for him.

Once Selbie had stalked out with her head held high, Averross had no further excuse to avoid eye contact with Qui-Gon. The man's face was as inscrutable as ever, but the moment the door swung shut behind Selbie, Qui-Gon said, "Have you forgotten yourself entirely?"

Averross laughed. "Oh, please. Like you didn't—"

"This isn't about what happened in my past," Qui-Gon said.

"Oh, no? Guess it's about hypocrisy, then."

"There is a difference," Qui-Gon insisted, righteous as ever, "between falling in love and simply giving oneself license to do as one pleases."

"Yeah, there is." Damn, but Averross wished he had that ale around now. "Falling in love—that's what the Jedi Code forbids. Getting laid? Not so much, not if it's casual, like me and Selbie. That doesn't compromise my emotions, doesn't divide my loyalties, anything like that. I might've broken the letter of the law, but not the spirit. On Felucia, you broke the spirit of that law into a dozen pieces."

Qui-Gon tensed. These words cut deep—or the memories did. The latter, Averross figured. He wasn't sorry he'd pushed back against Qui-Gon's empty moralizing, but it wasn't like he'd wanted to cause his friend pain. So instead of bringing up old stories, or naming long-unspoken names, Averross moved on. "I take it you didn't storm in here to try to catch the local innkeeper in my bed."

"The local innkeeper," Qui-Gon muttered. But already he was moving on. "I came to talk about—about a dream I had."

Averross scoffed as he lit a cigarra. "Seriously? You came runnin' in here because you had a bad dream?"

Qui-Gon gave him a dark look. "This wasn't a mere nightmare, Rael. It was troubling, but more than that, it was vivid. Startlingly so. And it seemed to be during Princess Fanry's coronation."

"All right, go on." Averross hoped this story was worth hearing. No chance it was worth losing out on another few minutes with Selbie, but he had to take his fun where he found it.

"The sequence of events isn't clear. But it was so strong—so urgent—"

"Wait, wait, wait. Are you about to tell me you've turned into a *prophet*?"

Qui-Gon groaned. "It sounds ludicrous when you put it that way."

"Sounds ludicrous because it is," Averross said, before taking another long drag on his cigarra.

"But you studied the prophecies. You know that the mystics truly saw things, that the Force did work through them."

"Yeah, but that's not the same as actually learning the whole future. A vision's way short of an actual *prophecy.* And those guys spent their entire lifetimes searchin' just for visions. You seriously think you would've learned more about the future than they did?" Averross sighed.

Qui-Gon remained restless, disturbed. *Must've been one hell of a dream,* Averross figured.

More gently, he added, "Get yourself together, man. You're probably just worried about the mission."

Averross believed fully that bottling up worries and concerns muddied the spirit. That was why he acted on his urges—immediately, harmlessly, before they could sink in deep to rot. Too bad Qui-Gon wasn't doing the same.

"The mission's a concern, of course, but I'm more troubled about Obi-Wan, actually."

"Yeah?" Averross shoved some dirty clothes aside to take a seat in the chair near the fire. "What's the matter?"

"He disapproves of my methods. He always has, but it's worse now." Qui-Gon ran one hand through his long hair as he admitted, "He found out about my invitation to the Council from someone else. Understandably, he was hurt. But now he's becoming more rigid. Less understanding."

"The Force plays jokes with us, doesn't it?" Averross shook his head. "History repeats itself. You were a kid who wanted to do everything by the book, until you wound up with a Master who thought for himself. Looks like Obi-Wan's on the same road."

"I was never as upright as Obi-Wan. At least, I don't think so." Qui-Gon leaned forward, resting his forearms on his knees. The firelight illuminated his long hair, revealing the first glints of gray. It gave Averross a turn, thinking of little Qui-Gon becoming gray-haired. How old did that make him?

"What's going on, exactly?" Rael asked. "I'm guessin' *you* don't have an arrangement with the local innkeeper, unless Selbie's better at time management than I thought."

Qui-Gon's dark glance meant, *That wasn't funny.* Averross didn't agree, but whatever.

"The details don't actually matter that much," Qui-Gon said. "I was wondering how to get him to relax. To think for himself more."

"While givin' me hell for not toeing the line?" Averross shook his head. "Listen. This"—he gestured toward his unmade bed—"this doesn't matter. Not really. Being lord regent doesn't leave me much time to relax. Neither does taking care of Fanry—trying to help her become a leader, like Nim would've been—"

Averross stopped. He'd sworn to himself he wouldn't talk about

Nim with Qui-Gon. With anyone, really. He'd spoken to Fanry about her plenty of times, but at this point Averross had spent more time with Fanry than any other living being except his old Master, Dooku.

Yet there had always been something about Qui-Gon, even when he was barely more than a child, that made people want to tell the truth.

Qui-Gon murmured, "You think that if you succeed with Fanry, it will make up for what happened to Nim."

"Nothing makes up for it." Averross's voice had already grown hoarse. "Nothing ever can, nothing ever could. But at least it won't make me feel like I'm poison to anybody I get close to."

That made Qui-Gon grimace. "I've been feeling as though I were— not poison to Obi-Wan, but completely incapable of helping him."

"I don't see it. You two wouldn't be together after this long if you weren't."

"I'd considered ending our partnership before now," Qui-Gon confessed. "Only the invitation to the Council kept me from having to take such a step directly."

"So what? Now you both have a safe way out. No hurt feelings."

"A bit late for that." Qui-Gon didn't elaborate, which was a relief to Averross. It was tough, listening to the man pretending to be so worried about a Padawan who was clearly smart and capable, bound for a bright future no matter what Qui-Gon had gotten wrong or right.

He kept having to bite back the words, *At least Obi-Wan will get out alive. Nim wasn't so lucky.*

Because she had me for a Master.

"Look," Averross said, casting aside his darker thoughts. "What your Padawan's doing is totally normal. Adolescents go one of two ways—they're either rebels to the core, or even stricter than their elders. So Obi-Wan's the latter. He'll relax after a while. Know what? If his new Master is stricter than you, I bet he'll loosen up immediately, just to be contrary."

Qui-Gon looked thoughtful. "Interesting."

"Okay, I've provided midnight advice, and now I'm going back to bed." Averross rose to his feet, which prompted Qui-Gon to do the same. "Though going back to bed is gonna be a whole lot less fun than I'd planned, since Selbie left early."

This joke didn't earn a laugh from Qui-Gon, only a bent smile. Maybe he'd become a bit of a prig after all. How disappointed Dooku would be, if and when they ever talked it over.

It had been a long time since Rael Averross felt the need to justify himself to anyone on Pijal, but as he walked Qui-Gon to the door, he found himself saying, "You know, there've always been a few Jedi—let's be honest, more than a few—who see celibacy as an ideal, not a rule."

"I'm coming to believe that we must all interpret the Code for ourselves," Qui-Gon said, "or it ceases to be a living pact and becomes nothing but a prison cell." Which sounded nice and all, but was a long way from letting Averross off the hook.

"Get some sleep," Averross grumbled, "and if you have any more bad dreams, don't—"

A scream shattered the midnight silence, and he recognized the voice.

Fanry.

When Qui-Gon first heard the screams, he thought, *It's coming true already. It's coming true right now.*

Then duty took over, propelling him through the door of the chamber. Rael had taken off at the first shriek, not even looking back for Qui-Gon.

He was equally proud and chagrined to see that Obi-Wan was also ahead of him in the corridor; by the time they'd reached the threshold of the royal chamber, Qui-Gon had caught up. So together they saw Princess Fanry appear at the door, breathing hard, her tiny body trembling so pitifully that it seemed she might fall. Her nightcap had been knocked askew, revealing a few bright-red curls of hair.

"Fanry?" Rael put his hands on the princess's shoulders. All the nonchalance from earlier in the night had been forgotten, Qui-Gon could see. The man's terror for his charge was very real. "Fanry, what's happened?"

"The alarm went off—I turned to my window, and I saw someone there—" Fanry whipped around to face Cady, the young servant girl who seemed to be the key royal attendant despite being Czerka property. "Did you see anything?"

"No, Your Serene Highness." Cady ducked her head so that her long, dark-brown hair fell past her shoulders. It concealed her expression, yet not her wide, wary eyes. "But I found this lodged in the windowsill."

Cady held up a small device, silvery and pointed. Qui-Gon didn't recognize it at first, not until Rael sucked in a breath so sharply that he seemed to be in pain.

"A slicer dart," Qui-Gon murmured. Obi-Wan instantly looked at Rael—a tactless gesture, however understandable—but Rael was past noticing it. The man had gone so pale that he seemed to be in danger of falling over.

Slicer darts were rarely used. The law-abiding had no chance to deploy them, because the darts were outlawed on nearly all civilized worlds; criminals seldom bothered, because the results were so unpredictable. When slicer darts were used, it was usually an act of deliberate cruelty. Qui-Gon had no doubt that was the case here.

"What did they want to do?" Fanry cried, shrinking back from the bladed thing, even as Rael took it from the girl. "Make me go mad, just before the ceremony?"

"They could've been aiming at me, Your Serene Highness," Cady said quietly. "Hoping I'd assassinate you." Fanry covered her mouth with one hand at the mere thought.

But Qui-Gon knew what the unknown assailant had intended: to hurt Rael Averross. To scare him. To give him notice that Princess Fanry was in danger, and that he could no more protect her than he'd protected Nim all those years ago.

And surely Rael knew it, too.

CHAPTER FIFTEEN

Some Jedi Knights' sensitivity to the Force allowed them to expertly plumb the emotions of everyone around them, sifting through and assessing feelings in a way that allowed them to perfectly gauge their responses to all. This was a talent Qui-Gon didn't share. He generally had to assess mood and tempers like any non-Force-user—through tone of voice, expression, things said and unsaid.

But Captain Deren's shame and misery were so great that Qui-Gon not only felt them, but shared them as though the pain were his own.

"I personally checked the perimeter of the palace compound," Deren said. Though he spoke quietly, his deep voice still commanded the room—specifically, the regent's audience chamber, the richly decorated suite. It was a sumptuous, pristinely clean place, which led Qui-Gon to suspect Rael rarely came here. No one had gone to sleep since the incident with the slicer dart a few hours ago, and even the moon had set. Despite this, Rael and Qui-Gon agreed that the interviews should take place immediately; potential witnesses' memories would fade after time and sleep. They needed all the information they could get. But few were able to share anything of use, including Deren. "I myself made a full sweep of Princess Fanry's rooms. My astromech cycled through all sentry data, and I double-checked those findings. Yet the responsibility must be mine."

"We're dealing with dangerous people here," Rael said. "Some of you kept telling me that this Halin person wasn't so bad. That the serious attacks maybe got out of hand. But now they've shown their hand. They're assassins. They're murderers. And they're after Fanry. So I don't ever want to see security slip up again. Got it?"

Deren bowed his head, as though he'd been condemned. "Yes, Lord Regent."

Another official Qui-Gon and Rael interviewed closer to dawn was less subdued. "This is an *outrage,*" Minister Orth snapped. "That anyone would blame a fourteen-year-old girl for political change—however unasked-for that change may be—and how little the girl herself has to do with *any* of it—"

"What?" Rael raised one arched eyebrow.

Orth lifted her pointed chin, defiant and proud. "*You're* the architect of change around here. Not Princess Fanry, not the people, and certainly not me. You're the one who wants to make Czerka even more at home than they already are. And everyone on both planet and moon knows it."

"You'd want Pijal to stay a backwater?" As hotly as Rael spoke, Qui-Gon could tell this discussion had occurred before; both participants seemed very sure of their lines. A sideways glance at Obi-Wan suggested his apprentice had seen it as well. "This planet's not going to catch up to the rest of the galaxy the way things are going now. This whole planet has no future without change."

"There can be no future for Pijal without its leader," Orth insisted. "Its *true* leader. And that is Fanry, not some . . . some . . . *constitutional assembly.*"

"You've never lived in a democracy, minister," Qui-Gon ventured. "Yes, larger governing bodies have their own problems, but they can get things done."

Orth laughed. "Tell that to the Galactic Senate! Unless they're too busy posing for their reelection holos."

Qui-Gon said no more. He didn't want to argue with Orth—particularly when so many senators answered to her description.

After the meetings were over and Rael had dismissed them from his chamber, Qui-Gon walked a good distance down the palace corridor before saying to Obi-Wan, "Your thoughts?"

"They're angrier with each other than they are with the Opposition. Perhaps they blame each other for the Opposition rising up in the first place." Obi-Wan shook his head. "Such displays of temper seem counterproductive at best."

"Very true. Yet last night, that anger took a turn—as did our mission."

Obi-Wan frowned. "Why do you say so?"

"The fate of Nim Pianna isn't widely known beyond the Order," Qui-Gon said. "Slicer darts are unreliable weapons, thank the Force, or else we'd see them more often. Last night's attacker got close enough to have, say, tossed in a thermal detonator. Or fired a blaster. Or gone after Fanry in any number of ways that would've been far more likely to kill her."

Understanding lit up Obi-Wan's eyes. "You mean, the weapon was deliberately chosen. It was meant to send a message to Averross."

With a nod, Qui-Gon said, "And whoever did it knows Rael well enough to know exactly how to hurt him. This isn't just an assassination attempt. It was also an attack on Rael Averross."

The sun had not yet risen when Qui-Gon finally went to bed, but the horizon had become faintly grayish, warning that dawn would be on them soon. A meditative trance would allow him to reset his mind, greatly reducing the amount of sleep he'd need, but he was not yet calm enough to attempt one. No single element of the current situation disturbed him so deeply that rest was impossible—but they jarred and jostled with one another in his brain.

Someone wishes to hurt both the princess and, through her, Rael Averross.

Rael wants to protect the princess so much that it may color his judgment.

Rael is desperate to make up for failing Nim.

I have failed Obi-Wan.

The Opposition's efforts to disrupt the treaty signing have accelerated rapidly in the past weeks, even since our arrival on Pijal.

Both lives and the treaty are in imminent danger.

All true. All troubling. Yet—to Qui-Gon's chagrin—none of these critical problems captured as much of his mind as the constant soft whisper in his memory: *the kyber that is not kyber.*

And his dream, presaging trouble for the crown princess of Pijal, trouble that was already coming to pass—

That, surely, was only his subconscious working faster than his conscious mind, scarcely an unfamiliar phenomenon. He must've picked up on discrepancies in the behavior of those around him, intuiting imminent trouble.

Yes, that would explain the dream. Rael had been correct, last night, not to overreact to what Qui-Gon had seen.

But while subconscious warnings explained the dream, they *didn't* explain the kohlen crystals. The kyber that wasn't kyber.

Qui-Gon groaned. How calm he'd been, discussing this with Obi-Wan, explaining that the lure of the ancient prophecies was no more than intellectual curiosity. He hadn't shared how different it had been for him as a boy—about the days when he'd believed it all, when he and Dooku had shared their fascination with these visions of what would be—

He hadn't been honest with Obi-Wan primarily because he hadn't been honest with himself.

Maybe Yoda had glimpsed this hint of zealotry in him all along. If so, no wonder he'd disapproved of inviting Qui-Gon onto the Council.

Qui-Gon slept as much as he could, which wasn't enough rest for the kind of search he and Obi-Wan needed to conduct that day. He could meditate enough to make up for the lost sleep, though, and so he headed to one of the balconies that looked out onto the sea. The soft thunder of the waves would be ideal for lulling him into a deep meditative state.

But as soon as he stepped outside, he heard a different, even lovelier sound: hundreds of voices raised in song.

He went to the railing and looked down at the waters. There, arranged on floating platforms, stood choruses of singers—most human, like the majority of Pijali citizens, but including some Twi'leks and Pantorans, and even one little Ugnaught in the front row. They wore plain gray robes that hung open at the front to reveal golden garments beneath, and directed their attention to another balcony, farther up in the cliffside palace. Qui-Gon followed their gazes to see Princess Fanry standing there, listening with apparent delight.

Who in the blazes allowed her to step outside hours after an assassination attempt? Qui-Gon thought. Before he could call Deren, however, he detected the faint shimmer of a shield around Fanry's brown dress and headscarf. Relaxing, he recalled that Rael had mentioned this event before—some sort of tradition associated with the coronation. Probably the royal security team had planned adequate protections for Fanry even before the incident with the slicer dart.

But they hadn't plumbed the sea. Bubbling water disrupted the waves, and the singers, whose voices faltered as they struggled to remain upright on their platforms. Qui-Gon prepared himself to leap down and help anyone who fell in the water—it would be a long dive, but one he could survive—but the bubbles popped as an enormous black sphere emerged from the waves and rose into the air.

Qui-Gon's alarm shifted to bewilderment. The intruding force was . . . a *balloon*?

The balloon's upward journey stopped short when its cable tether reached its limit. That tug of resistance made the black surface shimmer, then shatter into dust swiftly blown away by the ocean breeze. Now the balloon was revealed as white, with a message painted in red letters at least two meters high:

END TYRANNY! END CZERKA!

After that, nothing. The balloon bobbed at the end of its cable, casting shadows on the confused, but stabilized, singers beneath. Fanry, who had been pulled back by her guards at the first sign of trouble, tentatively stepped forward again. It had been no more than a harmless protest prank—the sort of thing the Opposition had been known for in the beginning.

Why, Qui-Gon wondered, would terrorists shift from an assassination attempt to a mere political stunt?

Yet one more answer he'd search for on the moon.

After Qui-Gon had been Dooku's Padawan for almost a year, they'd achieved a kind of rapport. Not friendship, not even informality, but Qui-Gon now understood what his Master's expectations were, what support would be given, and what he would need to handle for himself.

For instance, Dooku would never, in a thousand years, help Qui-Gon with his homework. He would, however, let Qui-Gon do that homework in the main room of his Jedi Knight's quarters, where he could munch on leftovers.

As he labored over his latest research report, Qui-Gon was startled to hear the door slide open. Dooku never came home early—

"And here's the kid." Rael Averross came striding in, a wide grin on his face.

"Rael!" Qui-Gon got up to greet him; he didn't hug Rael, but wished he could. "What are you doing here?"

"Finished up on Shurrupak, so it's back to base until I get my next mission." Rael flopped down on Dooku's couch, looking absurdly out of place. Dooku kept his quarters pristine—everything sleek and shining, glass and metal, as though it had never been touched. How had Rael Averross ever kept company with Dooku, much less for years? On Shurrupak, Qui-Gon had assumed Rael dressed like that because of the difficulties of war. Yet here he was on Coruscant looking even sloppier than before. "Come to think of it, what are *you* doing here? The schedule said Dooku's tied up in conference with some muckety-muck from Badtibira for another few hours."

"He lets me do my homework in here, if I won't be disturbing him."

"Homework." Rael made a face. "What've they got you stuck doing?"

"A report on the different schools of theosophy a century ago."

Rael's grimace went from mock to real. "Theosophy? The worst. Did you get on your teacher's bad side or something?"

Qui-Gon admitted, "I picked the topic. I knew it wouldn't be interesting, but . . . it seemed easy. It isn't."

"Say—is it too late for you to change your topic?"

"No, why?"

With a grin, Rael rose from the sofa and motioned for Qui-Gon to follow. "Let me show you some history worth studying."

Several minutes later, Qui-Gon sat next to Rael in the Jedi Archives, looking at the one and only holocron that had ever interested him— the one that held the ancient prophecies. Some were majestic. Some were mysterious. A few seemed laughable. But they were all fascinating. Qui-Gon kept reading, unable to stop.

Only through sacrifice of many Jedi will the Order cleanse the sin done to the nameless.

The danger of the past is not past, but sleeps in an egg. When the egg cracks, it will threaten the galaxy entire.

When the Force itself sickens, past and future must split and combine.

A Chosen One shall come, born of no father, and through him will ultimate balance in the Force be restored.

"The ancient mystics had these visions in trances?" Qui-Gon asked.

Rael nodded. He sat on the opposite side of the long table, going through holocron archives as raptly as Qui-Gon himself. "I don't even want to know what kind of spice they were smokin'."

Qui-Gon wondered whether, or how, he might be able to learn more about that. That was something to worry about later. Right now, his head buzzed with all the prophecy he'd read, all the possibilities of the future they hinted at. The entire universe seemed to have grown larger in an instant—full of incredible possibilities.

But should he trust it?

"Dooku said I shouldn't pay attention to this holocron," Qui-Gon said. "He doesn't believe in the prophecies."

"Since when?" Rael's confusion was totally sincere. "He's the one who turned me on to it. Used to be, you could hardly pry this holocron out of his quarters."

"I don't know when, or why. He didn't explain."

"I'm going to have to ask him about that," Rael said. "If that changed—wow. Then a lot's changed about Dooku."

"Don't ask him yet!" Qui-Gon protested. When Rael looked at him in surprise, he shrugged. "Not until I've finished my report, anyway."

Rael laughed so loud that Jocasta Nu gave him a stern look.

CHAPTER SIXTEEN

S *omeday,* Rahara Wick told her younger self, *you'll be guiding two Jedi Knights around the most backwater moon in the galaxy.*

Her younger self couldn't believe it. She wouldn't have been able to believe just about anything that had happened in her life in the past fifteen years, beginning with her escape from slavery. Yet Rahara repeated the mental exercise often, because trying to convince her past self was one of the few ways she could get her present self to believe anything about her life.

The older Jedi, called Qui-Gon, was a tall man with long brown hair and wise eyes. Qui-Gon sat at her shoulder, nodding as she input his suggested flight path. Meanwhile Obi-Wan, the "Padawan" or whatever you called it, had gotten stuck arguing with Pax.

"But if you can extend your scan-blocking field to cover your whole ship," asked Obi-Wan, "why don't you?"

"Let me enumerate our reasons." Pax began counting them off on his fingers. "First, it taxes our power unnecessarily. We usually have enough power for it, but possessing enough of a thing is no excuse for wasting it. One never knows when an emergency will occur. Second, we do not seek to completely disguise our voyages, only their true purpose. If we are found attempting to conceal our travel entirely, then we have created a presumption of wrongdoing. If, however, we travel openly while only acting clandestinely, no one has any particular reason to suspect us of anything. Furthermore—"

"Pax." Rahara shot him a look over her shoulder. "The point's been made."

Although Pax would've liked to continue putting the younger Jedi in his place, he folded his arms and went silent, his expression suggesting great forbearance with Rahara's whims. She resisted the urge to sigh and simply hit the ignition.

The *Meryx* rose through the swaying trees into the cloudy morning. Winds buffeted the ship, which made Rahara itch to take them higher—but the Jedi needed them lower. Rahara needed not to be arrested. So, motion sickness it was.

"Such a joyful way to spend a morning," Pax said. He'd begun making some Chandrilan tea for her, pointedly not asking the Jedi if they wanted any. "Looking for terrorists. This afternoon, for fun, why don't we set ourselves aflame?"

Wisely, Qui-Gon didn't reply to this—but he didn't ignore it, either. To her he said, "We don't want to put either of you in danger. But the situation is growing more threatening for the crown princess, among others."

Pax scoffed. "Oh, has it become slightly inconvenient, being a monarch and living in a castle?"

That irritated the younger Jedi, Obi-Wan. "Someone tried to *assassinate* her in her own bedroom."

Time to speak up before Pax went from acting like a jerk to acting like an irredeemable jerk. "She's a kid," Rahara said, giving him a sharp look. "Yeah, she's an absurdly overprivileged kid, but that doesn't give anyone the right to kill her."

"I'm not sure," Qui-Gon said, "how much of a privilege it is to have one's entire future predetermined—in this case, by an accident of birth."

Okay, she needed to be more diplomatic with the Jedi—but Rahara couldn't help it. She snorted.

Pax gave her an appreciative look, probably pleased she'd helped him meet today's sarcasm quotient. That much she expected. What she didn't expect was Obi-Wan frowning at his Master. "It matters what that future is, doesn't it? Fanry was born a princess. That's a privilege."

"It's still something chosen for her," Qui-Gon insisted. "Not what she herself chose."

"*Nobody* chooses how they're born." Rahara input a few more lines of the search parameters, mostly to give herself something to do with her hands, so they wouldn't shake. "We all get what we get. And most of us don't get thrones and crowns and—and—forget it."

A few moments of silence followed, during which she pointedly stared down at the screen. This would be a great time to find some terrorists. No such luck.

The Jedi seemed to have all kinds of Force powers, but "tact" wasn't one of them. "So you were born into enslavement," Qui-Gon said.

Pax stiffened. The only thing meaner than Pax in a cranky mood was Pax in a protective mood. She'd have to keep him quiet, even if the only way to do so was by speaking up. "Yeah," she said. "I was. On Hosnian Prime."

"But"—Obi-Wan looked confused—"there's no slavery on Hosnian Prime."

"Of course not. The Republic doesn't allow slavery." Pax held up one finger. "They *do* allow Czerka Corporation to do business, though, and naturally Czerka can bring in whatever workers it wants. If those workers are owned instead of paid—well, that's an internal corporate matter, isn't it? Nothing to do with the governments of the planets their 'sentient property' is sent to work on."

"It could've been worse," Rahara said. She always reminded herself of this. The alternative was forgetting so many of the people she'd grown up with. "As a little kid I had pretty low-level work to do—sorting minerals brought to Hosnian facilities for processing. Then they taught me more about mineralogy, more than I bet most students learn at universities. But that just meant I had to go into worse and worse mines. Deeper and deeper underground. And the lower you go, the more dangerous it gets."

Cave-ins. Lava spurts. Poisonous gases. There were a lot of ways to die underground, and Rahara had witnessed them all. When she was thirteen, the Czerka mining vessel she was assigned to caught fire on Ord Mantell. Chaos had erupted throughout the spaceport. Rahara had taken advantage of that to slip away, and to steal a small knife from a fried-nuna vendor.

Cutting the tag out had hurt *so much,* but she hadn't flinched once. The minute it fell to the ground, stained with her blood, Rahara had started running. She didn't look back.

"You weren't talking about the princess at all, were you?" Pax said, jolting her out of her reverie. The silence had lasted longer than she'd realized. Pax's stare was fixed on Qui-Gon. "You were talking about *yourself.* Because it's not a choice for Jedi, either, is it? I mean, supposedly they allow you to leave, make your own decisions, blah blah blah, but they steal you when you're babies and train your minds thereafter. What kind of freedom is that?"

Obi-Wan looked like he'd swallowed a gundark. "Being a Jedi is an *honor.* A responsibility. A—a noble calling—"

"Yes, Padawan," Qui-Gon said quietly. "It's all those things. But it's very hard for most of us to determine whether we chose it freely, being raised as we were. That said, I *did* have a choice. Dooku helped me to see that. And I chose the Order."

"Just as Dooku chose otherwise," Obi-Wan said stiffly. By this time, Rahara knew, the level of tension in the *Meryx* had risen sharply, but Obi-Wan Kenobi looked more uncomfortable than anyone else as he asked, "When did you decide knowing the future was a bad thing, Master?"

Qui-Gon didn't respond.

Pax, meanwhile, was starting to have fun. "This unfortunately named 'Dooku' actually quit being a Jedi? He sounds worth knowing. I don't suppose we'll be enjoying the pleasure of this person's company anytime—"

"We've got something." Rahara pointed to a glimmer at the edge of their sensors, then began zooming in on it. "Energy levels that suggest sentient presence, even though there's no Czerka presence around for kilometers. Let's see what else we can figure out when we get closer."

"Getting closer?" Pax said. "It sounds dangerous. I don't like it."

Rahara wanted to roll her eyes but resisted the urge. "What part of this have you ever liked? We know you're upset, Pax. So stop being redundant."

The droids who'd raised Pax didn't know anything about the finer points of human behavior—but they all knew, down deep in their programming, that "redundant" was a terrible thing to be. Sure enough, that shut Pax up.

In a conciliatory tone, Qui-Gon added, "We're not landing today. Just mapping areas worth investigation, for Obi-Wan and I to pursue on foot later."

"Check this out," Rahara said as their sensor readings gained detail. "The energy readings look like—well, like weapons signatures."

Obi-Wan peered over her shoulder. "I agree, Master. We should take a very close look."

"*Carefully*," Pax insisted.

Qui-Gon took the controls, guiding the *Meryx* so skillfully that even Pax couldn't protest. He stayed on sensors as they came in low over the trees. The *Meryx* remained distant enough not to tip anyone off to their presence, but close enough to gather intel.

"No buildings," Rahara said, squinting down at the scans. "Some life signs, but they're . . . blurry, somehow. Maybe in the caves, or underground."

"Underground?" asked Obi-Wan.

Pleased to know more than the Jedi, Pax interjected, "Czerka drills all over this moon, and with very little interest in maintaining geological stability. At least they've had the relative decency to steer clear of populated areas, thus far. But out here? You'll find all sorts of tunnels and chambers you wouldn't expect." In a lower voice, he added, "But not a single kyber crystal. Oh, no indeed."

Wisely, Qui-Gon ignored this last. He checked her readings for himself. "To me this looks like—twenty, maybe thirty individuals. Do you agree?"

Rahara nodded. "But weren't you looking for a larger group?"

"Yes," Qui-Gon said distantly. "And there are no remnants of space or even air traffic in this area for days."

"Does that mean they couldn't have been behind the—behind what happened in the palace last night?" Obi-Wan said.

That sounds interesting, Rahara thought.

Qui-Gon shook his head. "No. The Opposition could have operatives permanently stationed on Pijal." He then sat upright to face Rahara and Pax. "It would help if you both understood the dangers we're dealing with. I sense that I can trust you both, but I must emphasize—this is in the strictest confidence."

"Of course," Rahara said.

"Palace intrigues," Pax said with relish. "This is more fun than I thought."

That afternoon, Obi-Wan would've liked to prepare for the Grand Hunt. He'd be riding, not flying, which he'd rarely done before; he trusted he could manage, but it might've been nice to at least see the animals more than a few minutes before he was expected to get atop one. As an alternative, he'd have liked to nap. (Already he'd shrugged off the late interruption the night before, but he understood that the Grand Hunt often lasted until well after sunrise, and wanted to be at his best throughout.) Third choice—sit down and talk with Qui-Gon about what he meant when he'd said the Jedi had no choices, or whether Rael Averross was worth trusting, or any of the myriad subjects about which his Master was behaving strangely. Obi-Wan had ceased to believe he'd ever understand Qui-Gon, much less in the short time remaining to them as Master and apprentice, but he couldn't dull the urge to at least *try*.

Instead, Averross had whisked Qui-Gon away to discuss the Opposition's bizarre prank and what it might mean. Meanwhile, Obi-Wan was assigned to help Captain Deren protect Princess Fanry.

Which sounded very exciting, but in practice actually meant *entertain* Princess Fanry. Mostly, she just wanted to talk.

"I can't believe they kept singing after that," she said, grinning like a child even younger than her age. "I thought they'd jump in the ocean and swim for shore, but they stayed."

Minister Orth practically gleamed with pride, as though she'd personally kept the singers in place. "The ceremonies and traditions of the monarchy still hold tremendous meaning for our people. None of this constitutional nonsense can stop them from paying their future queen due tribute. And none of the Opposition's nonsense will prevent her coronation."

Obi-Wan wasn't sure he was in a position to speak up, but he decided to err on the side of curiosity. "It struck me as strange that the slogan wasn't about Her Serene Highness or the treaty. Only Czerka Corporation."

"A cheap ploy for sympathy," sniffed Minister Orth. "The crown princess is a popular figure, and this 'representative government' fad hasn't faded yet. Czerka, however, is not so well liked." Her tone of voice made it clear she didn't like Czerka, either.

"I've heard that Czerka has drilled extensively on the moon," Obi-Wan said, "to the point of causing geological damage. Is that one of the reasons people are angry with Czerka?"

Captain Deren, who'd been standing by the door in solemn vigilance, spoke for the first time in many minutes. "Where did you hear that?"

"It's commonly known, up there." Obi-Wan shrugged, as though he weren't covering for two jewel thieves. His casual demeanor apparently proved reassuring, because Deren resumed his former position.

Orth, however, seemed alarmed. "Why are you conducting interviews with lunar citizens? It would be just like the Opposition to plant someone who could convince you how evil everyone is down here. At least a few of them are actors."

Best, Obi-Wan thought, to sidestep this. "We're not conducting in-depth interviews, just learning more about the terrain we must search. Master Jinn and I would need to be prepared for any confrontation that might lie ahead."

The diversion worked. "But you're Jedi," Fanry said. "How could you not be victorious? You have your lightsabers, don't you?"

"We do," Obi-Wan said, pointing at his blade where it hung at his belt, "but lightsabers aren't that useful against bombs."

"Aren't they?" Fanry wrinkled her nose. "After all these years, the lord regent has still never shown me the exact workings of his light-saber. So I thought maybe there was some big secret about how they operate."

"Not at all, Your Serene Highness." Should he have said that? Maybe Averross had lied about it, to keep her from treating his weapon like a toy. Fanry was old enough now to hear the truth. "The construction of lightsabers isn't mysterious, though there are elements that ensure the weapons will always remain singular to the Jedi."

"What do you mean?" Fanry asked.

"Well—" Obi-Wan considered for a second, then set his lightsaber on a small table near the princess and began to disassemble it. "I'll show you the inner workings and explain from there."

Fanry bit her lower lip. "You won't break it?"

He stifled a laugh. "No, Your Serene Highness. We're required to know how to disassemble and reassemble our lightsabers in the dark. A Jedi's lightsaber is his life."

With Fanry and her ministers leaning in intently—and Deren sud-denly at his side—Obi-Wan carefully unscrewed the pommel cap and hand grip, then revealed the lightsaber's core. "Here you see the con-trols, and the main hilt—"

"What's that?" She pointed straight to the gleaming heart of his lightsaber. "Is it a jewel?"

"In effect. It's a kyber crystal, which focuses the power of the light-saber's beam." Amid the metal workings surrounding it, the kyber crystal sparkled tantalizingly—while the rest was a machine, the crystal looked more like magic. He couldn't blame Fanry for her fascination; he'd felt the same way when he first learned how to assemble a lightsaber.

Still felt that way, sometimes.

"It's blue, isn't it?" Fanry said curiously. "Are all lightsaber blades blue?"

"The kyber crystals do determine the color of the blade, but they only take on their colors after their bond with the Jedi who've chosen them."

Fanry's eyes widened. "Kyber crystals *bond* with Jedi? Does that mean you . . . communicate with them?"

With a grin, he said, "No. Just—their particular properties are affected by their proximity to a Force user. Very swiftly, the bond forms, and then the kyber crystals change. Most turn blue or green, which is why most Jedi's lightsabers are those colors. A few crystals even turn purple."

"Purple?" Fanry laughed. "Is that what you wished for? Do any of the colors mean something?"

Legend had it true darkness, such as that wielded by the ancient Sith, turned crystals red. But Obi-Wan had no intention of discussing ancient history with the princess. "I was just happy to have a kyber crystal bond with me at all, Your Serene Highness."

"Lightsabers are the sole weapon of the Jedi," Minister Orth interjected. "Are they not?"

Obi-Wan shook his head "They're far from the only tool we have at our disposal—but in combat, a lightsaber is an unparalleled weapon for both attack and defense. And because using the blade requires immense concentration and keen reflexes, no one but a Force user can wield lightsabers skillfully or efficiently."

Fanry said, "Is a stronger Force user's lightsaber stronger, too? What happens when two Jedi fight each other?"

"The blade isn't stronger. Only the Force user's ability to wield it," Obi-Wan said. "In ceremonial combat, of course, we're displaying forms more than actually testing strength—"

"But what about non-ceremonial combat?" Fanry persisted. "When two Jedi are on opposite sides of a conflict. What happens?"

"It . . . it *doesn't* happen." The idea made so little sense that Obi-Wan could hardly parse it. "We are members of one Order. We serve the Jedi Council and, through the Council, the Republic. The Jedi are united in this way."

"Well, *that's* boring." Scowling, Fanry kicked her little feet beneath her throne. "And nobody but the Jedi ever uses lightsabers? You'd never fight anyone else who had one? For real, I mean. Not 'ceremonially.' "

"The ancient Sith used lightsabers," Obi-Wan said. "But they've been extinct for a millennium. So, no. A Jedi just wouldn't be involved in a lightsaber duel to the death. It couldn't happen."

Fanry seemed to realize she was being a bit bloodthirsty, because she smiled impishly and made the next question a joke. "Never?"

He smiled back as he shook his head. "Not ever."

CHAPTER SEVENTEEN

—— ⚜ ——

A royal ship found itself unable to take off when a dozen green-clad people perched on its hull, then tethered themselves in place with magnetic bonds. One of them was Halin Azucca herself, her hair braided into tight knots she wore like a crown. Security droids arrived quickly, but at their first appearance, the protesters activated personal flight packs and managed to escape.

Pijal had been building a magnificent Hall of Assembly to house its new representative government, an entirely spherical structure with a mirrored surface, which would appear almost invisible until sundown, when the last rays of light would make it burn like another star. Security cams captured the moment late at night when the mirrors turned cloudy, then totally gray, then crumbled to dust. Only later did investigators determine that nanotech had been planted inside, and had devoured the building's framework from within.

Panic had broken out one night when the moon of Pijal rose in the sky—no longer golden-green but a stark, ominous red. The Opposition turned out to have extensively seeded the moon's atmosphere with a harmless chemical that would disperse within a few days, but ensured the moon would remain crimson the whole time. On the next morning, an ominous message was discovered painted on one of the larger temples in the capital: CAN YOU FORGET US NOW?

A droid rolled into a Czerka facility, seen on various security cams, until it suddenly exploded. The resulting flames burned so hot they were blue in the night. Had any living being been within the facility at that late hour, they would surely have been killed.

"And they couldn't have known the facility would be completely empty," Qui-Gon pointed out as he shut off the holos of known Opposition actions. Deren had been reluctant to share them—his paranoia about protecting Fanry had grown. Qui-Gon had insisted on having them, but had waited until late in the evening to review them with Obi-Wan, when they could be alone.

Obi-Wan looked thoughtful. "No, they couldn't. Anyone might have decided to return to work—or a servant might've been forced to stay behind for some reason. Whoever did this was willing to risk taking lives."

"So it would seem," Qui-Gon replied. He stroked his beard, considering the possibilities.

"Chancellor Kaj told us the Opposition's violence was escalating," Obi-Wan said, "but the behavior seems more erratic to me. Not something that could be plotted on a line."

"The various incidents are—wildly discordant. Nor do they follow a straight chronology. Some of the more harmless incidents occur after the bombings began."

"Maybe some of the 'pranks' were programmed before the violence escalated," Obi-Wan said. Then his eyes widened. "Or maybe there's not one single head of the Opposition, but many. Halin Azucca could just be the one leader we know about. There could be other cells, both more and less violent. All of them working toward one cause, but in very different ways."

"A valid theory, my Padawan." Qui-Gon still sensed there was more to the puzzle—but he felt certain the shift in pattern was important. "Rael considers all of this to be mindless violence. Pure terrorism. I suspect that's why he didn't recognize this pattern himself."

Obi-Wan said nothing. Qui-Gon was relieved. Whenever Obi-Wan doubted Rael, the impulse to defend his old friend strengthened. That impulse interfered with Qui-Gon's judgment.

Rahara objected to Pax's plan. Sometimes Pax felt as though she objected to any and all fun, purely on principle. This time, however, he understood her concern.

But he still intended to ignore it.

"You want to deal with *Czerka*," she said, arms folded, as he dressed for the big meeting to come. "They're scum. No, worse. They'd have to work their way up to scum."

Pax examined his best coat—blue, oversized, velvet lapels—then regretfully laid it aside. Pijali citizens were so *boring* in their attire. "Sadly for the galaxy, the scum often winds up with a great deal of money."

"Blood money," Rahara insisted. "They've made untold trillions, over untold centuries, largely through slave labor. Czerka's money is tainted, forever."

"I quite understand your point of view."

"Then why—how can you be willing to do business with the company who—"

Her words trailed away. It didn't matter. Pax knew what she meant.

"Czerka treated you abominably," he said, settling on a black cape that looked rather dashing, if he did say so himself. "Their slavery practices are worthy of the deepest contempt. The company deserves not one chit of its gargantuan wealth. Which is why I consider it my moral duty to deprive them of as much of that wealth as I can."

Rahara tilted her head. "You mean . . . you're going to scam them."

"It will appear to be an honest mistake." Pax gestured toward the pile of kohlen crystals he'd gathered together. "So few people can tell the difference between these and true kyber. It could take them quite a while to figure it out—long enough for us to have left Pijal, even. So I foresee no negative repercussions for us, only for the vipers of Czerka Corporation."

". . . I guess I can see the good in that." One corner of her mouth lifted, not quite a smile. Still, it brightened Pax's mood considerably. "But be careful."

"Of course." Pax gathered the crystals into a small antigrav crate. He'd be able to fit this aboard his single-pilot craft. "I know perfectly well what Czerka is capable of."

So he said, and so he believed, the entire way to the nearest Czerka office. Naturally he couldn't bring the *Meryx* on this errand, but he had a single-pilot craft, which he'd dubbed the *Facet,* stashed in the hold for just such occasions. Really, he thought, he ought to take it out more. He ought to improve his flying, if only to keep up with Rahara.

After he'd landed the *Facet,* gone to the guard station, and gained admittance, however, he was walked through the work yard. There he saw a group of enslaved people in their gray coveralls, at hard labor.

The labor was far from the worst that could be assigned, nor was it the worst Pax had ever personally witnessed. They were merely polishing and cleaning an elegant personal craft, probably the supervisor's. So it wasn't the nature of the work that struck him.

It was that all the workers were children.

The oldest human couldn't have been nine years old yet. Pax wasn't as good at estimating the ages of Ithorians, but the one scrubbing hard with a cloth was the tiniest he'd ever seen. The Wookiee looked older, though it was hard to determine his height; he hung his head so sadly. One of his hands had been shaved to insert the Czerka tag, and the fur hadn't grown back yet. This child had been enslaved for only a few days.

Rahara was even younger than this, Pax thought as he followed the security guard, guiding his crate. Suddenly he wasn't sure he'd be able to put on a smile for any Czerka officials—even if it was in the noble cause of ripping them off.

He suspected he didn't put on a very convincing performance for the sector supervisor, but it hardly mattered. As soon as Meritt Col opened the crate to see the crystals—what, as far as she knew, was a treasure trove of kyber—her attention was purely focused there.

"You say these are found extensively throughout this region of the moon?" Col held one crystal up to the light. It shone as bright an orange as the skies of Abafar.

"Indeed, Supervisor Col." *Keep it cool. Keep it steady. Pretend you're G-3PO.* "I was so excited at first, but an independent trader like me—how am I supposed to do business with the Jedi Order?"

"It's very insightful of you," Col said, smiling not at Pax but at the crystals. "Few independent traders would be as ready to face their own inadequacies."

Inadequacies? Pax held on to his temper, barely. Half of him wanted to explain all the ingenious ways he'd already planned to work with the Jedi Order, had this stuff proved to be true kyber. Fortunately, the other half won out.

Ultimately he made a deal for a large sum—not enough for him and Rahara to retire, but more than enough to upgrade the ship and take a long vacation. Pax had considered negotiating for more, but the bigger Czerka's payout was, the more suspicious they would be of the person who'd sold them a useless box of kohlen.

You see? he thought as he flew away in the *Facet. It was worth sticking around for a while, Jedi or no Jedi. You've pulled more of a profit on this than you will from the Alderaan haul.*

All very true. But he couldn't look at the credits without hearing Rahara's voice whispering in his head.

Blood money.

"No comms, Master?" Obi-Wan felt naked without the comm device he'd worn at his belt as long as he could remember. "What if someone needs to reach us?"

"The only individuals who could need to urgently talk to us will be on the Grand Hunt, too," Qui-Gon said. "Besides, it's custom to leave behind all advanced technological devices. Apparently, centuries ago, people used them to cheat."

To Obi-Wan it sounded primitive to the point of barbarity, but following local traditions and habits was encouraged, so he resisted the urge to go back for the comm device. Instead he and Qui-Gon marched across the rolling ground toward the stables. High grasses swayed and parted for them as they went. In the distance, he could see torches blazing—actual torches—against the deep purple of late sunset. Musicians had begun to play, and more and more people were headed toward the starting ground.

Qui-Gon gave him an appraising glance. "You haven't ridden much up until now, have you, Padawan?"

"No, Master. But it doesn't look so difficult."

"Depends on your mount." Qui-Gon looked amused. "Just remember, riding a living thing is different from riding a ship or speeder. The Force binds you together. You can use that."

Although Obi-Wan had looked the creatures up beforehand, he was still taken aback by his first glimpse of a varactyl. Its scarlet feathers glimmered iridescently in the torchlight, and it pawed at the ground, eager to begin. They were huge—and when he thought about trying to get atop one, they seemed even huger—

"Here you go," Qui-Gon said, a roguish smile on his face. He patted the side of one varactyl, which chirruped at him. "It's all ready for you, yes?" When the attendant nodded, Qui-Gon motioned toward the saddle. "Why don't you see if you can get up there?"

His Master was enjoying his confusion—not meanly, because that wasn't Qui-Gon's way, but that didn't make it less irritating. Obi-Wan tried to ignore Qui-Gon and any other person who was watching, to think only about the varactyl . . .

And then he felt it. The beast's soul, simpler and purer than that of a sentient, yet still intelligent in its way. When it cocked its head to study him, Obi-Wan realized this could not be a matter of his mastering the varactyl; instead, they would have to meet as equals.

He put one hand on the varactyl's neck, stroking the feathers. It chirruped again, and the end of its tail flicked once . . . from excitement, Obi-Wan thought. Perhaps it was looking forward to the hunt as much as any of the humans were. Through the Force he sent back his own dawning enthusiasm for the event.

The varactyl ruffled its feathers, then crouched low on the ground, until its belly lay in the grass. That let Obi-Wan easily swing up into the saddle and take the reins. Rising to its feet, the varactyl chirruped happily. They were friends now, Obi-Wan realized—friends who were about to have a lot of fun together.

"Well done," Qui-Gon said. His expression was a mixture of amusement and wonder. "Very well done indeed."

Obi-Wan leaned down to whisper in the varactyl's ear. "He says you've done well." It thumped the ground with its tail, which he instinctively knew was a good sign.

Was it possible riding might be even more fun than flying?

Applause, muffled through gloves of shimmersilk and velvet, made him look up. Two handlers were leading out an unusual droid—a modified crab droid, from the looks of it. Was it of Czerka manufacture? Its dark surface made it all but invisible in the encroaching dusk; soon only the blue and white lights on its many-jointed legs would betray its place.

"The prey," Obi-Wan said.

Qui-Gon—who'd managed to get on his own varactyl, if not quite so gracefully—nodded. "Thousands of years ago, of course, they hunted live game. That practice was abandoned long ago."

"That's a relief," Obi-Wan said. "I don't know if I could've killed a living creature merely for sport, or helped anyone else do it, either."

"Don't be too relieved." Qui-Gon sounded amused. "The main motivation for hunting a droid rather than an animal was increasing the level of challenge. A droid has defenses and resources no living creature could ever claim."

More applause heralded the arrival of Princess Fanry. Her varactyl's feathers were all tipped with white, which made it the most striking of all the beasts. Obi-Wan wondered if it had been chosen for its appearance alone, or whether it was fast, too. Already he wanted his varactyl to win.

Fanry's riding habit was plain in Pijali style, a sandy color of no particular note, but with wide sleeves and a shorter hem that revealed the brilliant-green underdress beneath. The servant girl Cady walked alongside her, carrying a basket that seemed to be piled high with whatever luxuries the princess might desire during the course of the night. Fanry's expression was more serious than he'd ever seen it, even when discussing the Opposition attacks.

Is that a sign that she's frivolous, and cares for nothing but her amusements? Obi-Wan wondered. *Or is it a sign of how important this hunt is on Pijal?*

More applause—and cheers—as Rael Averross rode up on his varactyl. He held up one hand, simultaneously acknowledging the crowd and hushing them. The man's rugged riding gear contrasted less with his shaggy hair and unshaven face than the regent's robes did; this was the first time Obi-Wan thought he'd seen Rael fully in his element. Rael's lopsided grin suggested he enjoyed this even more than he let on, and he let on a fair bit.

Obi-Wan's varactyl ruffled its feathers. "The others are larger than you, I know," he murmured. "But that means you're faster. We'll capture the prey. Wait and see."

But there was more happening here than the Grand Hunt. Princess Fanry was in danger—from someone on the inside, someone who might be on this hunt. If anyone tried to hurt her, that person became his new prey.

"Assemble!" called the herald, and the riders and varactyls all took their positions. Wordlessly, Obi-Wan steered away from Qui-Gon, to the other edge of the crowd; the farther apart they were, the more ground they could cover. By now the sky was almost purely dark, and the torchlight seemed to blaze brighter. The smell of fresh-cut grass and damp ground filled the air. Obi-Wan felt his varactyl tense under him, and the energy was catching. He could see it in everyone around him—Captain Deren, flanking the princess, was smiling broadly, the only time Obi-Wan had ever glimpsed that. Even Minister Orth's hair was down, and she'd tied a scarf around her neck, maybe so it could ripple behind her in the wind.

The horns blew once. Obi-Wan seized the reins tighter as his mount stamped its feet.

Twice. Everyone leaned forward in their saddles. Beneath the murmur of activity, Obi-Wan could hear Averross chuckling softly with anticipation.

Three times. *Go!*

The varactyl leapt forward at the moment Obi-Wan wished him to; he didn't think he'd made a move. Already the Force had tied them together, and now he knew that for the varactyl, running was the greatest joy imaginable. So he leaned in, letting his ride choose their speed, but keeping them close to Princess Fanry.

"There it is!" the princess cried. A flickering of light had betrayed the droid's location, in a thicket farther up the nearby hill. Fanry's varactyl broke from the others, galloping over a trench. Some of the other varactyls balked, but Obi-Wan's took the jump effortlessly. He didn't see Qui-Gon or Averross make it over, but in only minutes he sighted them atop their varactyls at the far side of the hunting party.

As darkness had deepened, the automatic sensors on the varactyl harnesses had begun to turn a pale shade of purple, outlining the beasts' forms, painting their feathers more brightly, and casting eerie lights on the riders. It felt almost like being in a primitive simulator, Obi-Wan thought, except that no simulator could possibly match this.

The cool air that smelled of conifers, the workings of the varactyl's muscles that could be felt even through the saddle, and most of all the thrill that couldn't be experienced in mere fantasy. Only reality.

Another trench, this one deeper and muddier than the last. Once again, Fanry soared effortlessly over it. More of the varactyls shied from this trench, growing skittish long before they even reached it, but Obi-Wan reached through the Force to reassure his beast. *If you can't make the jump, I won't make you try. If you can, though, don't hold back.*

His varactyl's answer came when he bounded across the trench without so much as a pause.

Obi-Wan laughed out loud. Finally, he'd be the one sharing adventures with his friends.

It must have been tremendous, back in more primitive times. To know that their survival depended upon this, to race ahead on creatures far less tame than the one he rode now, to see monarchs genuinely desperate to protect their right to the throne.

If Fanry had been crown princess in those days, Obi-Wan thought, she would've fared just fine. Only a handful of riders had made it this far yet, and Fanry was the first among them. She urged her beast forward, toward the faint lights of the crab droid flickering among the high grasses. Finding the prey was only the first part of the hunt—outwitting the droid was the next, more difficult step, but he felt sure the "kill" would be hers, not because of a ceremony, but by right. Obi-Wan was impressed. Nothing stood between Fanry and victory—

—until the dark underbrush lit up with blaster bolts, firing at the princess.

CHAPTER EIGHTEEN

Qui-Gon's varactyl faltered at the second trench, rearing back. Only by clinging tightly to the saddle did Qui-Gon prevent being thrown off. *I was a good rider, once,* he thought as he straightened himself, remembering a race he'd had with Dooku long ago.

The memories shattered with the sound of Fanry's scream.

"The princess!" Deren shouted, and he turned his own beast into the trench, forcing it to run down and through. Qui-Gon followed along with the pack, or tried to; he was blocked by Minister Orth, who had lost control of her varactyl entirely. Its feathers had fanned out into a ruff around its head as it hissed angrily. Orth, white-faced, simply clung to the saddle, apparently unable to manage anything else.

Blast it! Qui-Gon stood in the stirrups to get a better view of the fray. In the meadow, he saw blaster bolts being fired from the underbrush that grew more thickly upon the hills of the hunting grounds. In the murk of nighttime he couldn't make out who or what was firing. Each bolt illuminated another split second of the scene:

Rael streaking toward the princess at top speed.

Fanry ducking low over her ride, protecting herself.

Obi-Wan charging toward the underbrush, his lightsaber shining in the night.

Despite his fear, Qui-Gon felt a flush of pride. *That* was the apprentice he knew Obi-Wan could be—and the shadow of the great Jedi Knight he would yet become.

Assuming you don't both die here first. Now move!

When his mount balked again, Qui-Gon stopped fighting it, dropped the reins, and called on the Force to execute a jump that far exceeded anything a human could've done under his own strength. His boots thudded on the ground, but he sprang up instantly. His leap had brought him well over the trench, halfway to Fanry.

As he landed, a flash of blasterfire from within the underbrush illuminated the attacker—and it was the prey. The crab droid had turned the ritual of the hunt upside down.

The princess huddled behind her varactyl, but she had taken up her energy bow and fired over the beast's shoulder. The princess's spirit was stronger than her aim, though; the crab droid remained untouched. She was still in danger. Qui-Gon ran at top speed toward the fray that had ignited in the underbrush.

Two lightsabers now shone in the night, both Obi-Wan's and Rael's. Rael's blade spun around like a windmill, blocking nearly every bolt fired. He was fighting defensively, protecting Fanry rather than going on the offensive. A wise move, given that Obi-Wan was already two meters ahead, slicing underbrush out of the way with every swing of his blade, clearing the way to the attacker. Qui-Gon reached out, sensing the patterns of Force and fire, so he could run as quickly as possible to his Padawan's side.

"About time you got here, Master!" Obi-Wan called, never looking away from the assault.

"Thought I might lend a hand." With that, Qui-Gon ducked low, igniting his own lightsaber to slash through the brush almost at ground level. At least the droid couldn't fly. Destroy the legs, and the fight was over.

Together they pushed deeper into the brush. By now Qui-Gon could peer through the brambles and see the prey droid with his own eyes. It didn't register him at all. This droid had been programmed with a ruthless single-mindedness; even as he and Obi-Wan got closer, it fired directly at them no more than a handful of times.

Whoever did this wanted the droid to complete one task, Qui-Gon thought. *Kill the princess.*

Finally, Qui-Gon got close enough to stab his lightsaber blade beyond the final layer of brambles, through two of the crab droid's legs, straight into its base. It made a screeching sound, harsh with electronic interference, before sending out a spray of sparks and then going dead. Toppling sideways, it fell to the ground with a heavy thud.

Some people cheered, but most of them were still screaming and weeping. Fanry had already stumbled out from behind her varactyl, alive and well, to be comforted by Rael. In the distance, Minister Orth was still struggling to get her varactyl under control.

Obi-Wan wasn't even winded. "So, Master," he said, putting away his lightsaber. "Are any more of the upcoming coronation events this exciting?"

"I doubt it." Qui-Gon didn't approve of his Padawan's cockiness, but let him enjoy the moment while he could.

It hardly mattered. Had any of those blasts hit the princess, she would now be dead.

Animals. Monsters.

Averross made himself think in those terms, because he'd worked hard to break his habit of swearing when he'd come to help six-year-old Fanry. But the profanities of a dozen worlds threatened to burst through at any moment.

What about the treaty, the coronation, *anything* about Fanry could make the Opposition want to murder a young girl?

Averross put his hands on Fanry's shoulders and gentled his voice as much as he could. "Hey. Kid. Are you sure you're all right?"

Bravely, she nodded. "I only scraped my knee when I slid off my varactyl."

"Wasn't talking about your skin." He meant her soul, though he was grateful not to have to say it out loud. Fanry probably knew more about Averross's soft side than anyone else living, but he didn't like to broadcast it even to her.

Sure enough, she understood. "I'm fine. I think we all ought to have expected this."

"You shouldn't have to expect people comin' at you in the middle of a sacred ritual," Averross said, but he knew she was right. They couldn't afford to take anything for granted now. There was nothing the Opposition wouldn't stoop to. No moment he could ever relax and assume Fanry was safe.

Qui-Gon joined them, his expression grave. "I take it you're well, Your Serene Highness." When Fanry nodded, he continued, "This is far worse than we knew."

"Yeah, because these lowlifes will stop at nothing—" Averross stopped himself before he swore words that would fry Fanry's innocent ears.

"Yes, they're ruthless," Qui-Gon agreed, "but that's not what I meant. I reviewed the security measures alongside you, Rael. The stables and hunting ground had been extensively secured by droids, autosentries, and human guards."

"We even hired a few Rodian mercenaries, put 'em out in the far woodlands," Rael said. "But somebody got to the prey droid anyway."

Qui-Gon lowered his voice. "Therefore, the droid could only have been sabotaged by someone within the palace."

The truth struck Rael with the force of a blow. He couldn't catch his breath. Couldn't move. Because the greatest danger to Fanry came from one of her own courtiers or guards.

From a traitor.

"You think it's one of my people?" Fanry said to Qui-Gon, shaking her head in disbelief. "They've all been with me my entire life. None of them would try to kill me, not ever."

"They sent a slicer dart after you," Rael said. "Whoever did that knew what that weapon meant to me. I don't like it any better than you do, Princess, but we've gotta face facts. There's a traitor among us."

A traitor who was going to be very, very sorry for the brief remainder of his or her life.

Fanry looked as though she didn't know whether to laugh or cry. Cady slipped a thick shawl over the princess's shoulders and led her away, no doubt for some water, quiet, and rest.

Which left Averross to stare at the group around him, wondering which individual could be cold enough to betray a little girl who'd put her trust in them all.

The scene was almost pathetically comic. Orth was still flopping around atop her varactyl like the terrible rider she was. A nobleman was whining about his torn doublet, which revealed the entire gold satin lining and was now too gaudy to be worn *anyplace,* how *gauche.* Captain Deren, at least, was proving himself useful by swiftly disassembling the droid down to its component gears, wiring, and panels. But the rest of the Pijal court was distinguishing itself mostly through its utter silliness.

At least there are two people here I know didn't betray her, Averross thought as he followed Qui-Gon to Obi-Wan's side.

"Perhaps we should examine the droid's workings," Obi-Wan was saying to Qui-Gon, when he broke off at Averross's approach. "How is the princess?"

Averross breathed out heavily, wiping sweat from his forehead with the back of his grimy hand. "She acts brave, but that shook her up."

"And no wonder," Qui-Gon said. "We'll have to go through security footage immediately."

"Anybody smart enough to reprogram the prey droid's smart enough to reprogram the security terminals," Averross muttered. "But we're going through them anyway. We see one shadow, I swear by the Temple I'll follow that shadow straight to the scumbag that tried to hurt her."

Qui-Gon remained almost damnably calm. Easy to be calm when you didn't really care about anyone involved. "Were you able to see anyone whose presence you can't explain? Maybe someone you thought was a sentry but wasn't in a preapproved location?"

"You think I wouldn't have mentioned that by now if I had? I was too busy saving Fanry to count heads."

Averross saw Qui-Gon and Obi-Wan exchange a look. Most Jedi Knights would see it as their duty to remember every possible detail of an important battle or skirmish, so as to analyze it and extract maximum information.

But when Rael Averross was in a fight, he was *fighting*. He wasn't going to let any Padawan sneer at him for it, either. To Obi-Wan he said, "That okay with you?"

Obi-Wan's blue eyes widened. "I—well, I only meant—you obviously protected the princess very ably."

It used to be fun to shake the Padawans up like that, he remembered. There'd been a time when he could joke with Nim that way.

Maybe that wasn't a kind of fun he needed to revisit.

He called out to the entire gathering, "The Grand Hunt is over! Now get yourselves back to your rooms and remain available for questioning. *Nobody* leaves the palace compound without my express permission. Got it?"

The various nobles all nodded, murmuring among themselves as they began shuffling back to their varactyls, obviously shaken and disappointed in equal measure. Qui-Gon and Obi-Wan were walking back already, talking to each other. And in the distance, Captain Deren was trying valiantly to get Minister Orth down from the saddle.

"Are you sure you're uninjured, Your Serene Highness?" Cady asked.

Fanry nodded, though one of her ankles twinged every time she stepped on it. Whatever was wrong there, it wasn't bad enough to require a medical droid's help, and besides—she wanted to be alone with her thoughts.

The look on Rael Averross's face—that would stay with her for a while. She'd seen hints of that kind of guilt and sorrow before, but only when he talked about Nim Pianna, the Padawan who had died. Fanry had never expected to see him that scared for *her*.

But there was nothing to be afraid of. Fanry refused to give in to distractions or doubts now. The ceremony would take place so very soon. Deren would be there to protect her; Orth and Col would be there to watch her; and even Cady would be there to help her. Everything would proceed according to plan.

A small quiver of uncertainty shivered through her, but Fanry squelched it. Timidity might be all right for little princesses who still covered their hair.

Not for a queen.

Qui-Gon helped settle the various riders after the hunt, losing track of Obi-Wan during the process. At the end, he found Obi-Wan in the stables, standing in his varactyl's stall and absently scratching the beast on its neck.

"I think you're turning into a rider," Qui-Gon said.

"Master?" Obi-Wan looked up hurriedly. "I don't think—I mean, yes, I like riding a lot more than I expected to, but—you need to see this."

He let Rael rattle him, Qui-Gon thought as he stepped into the varactyl's stall. *Obi-Wan needs to stand up better than that.*

Then he saw that his apprentice was holding a datapad. On its screen were images of the sabotaged crab droid, or what remained of it; *this* was what had shaken Obi-Wan. "You've learned something?"

"Not much, I'm afraid. But I wanted you to see this." Obi-Wan expanded one area to reveal a sort of shield device—one totally unfamiliar to Qui-Gon. "Do you know of any shields like this?"

"No, I've never seen anything like it. I'm no weapons expert, but this is definitely unusual." Qui-Gon took the datapad into his own hands. "The shield doesn't connect to the main power supply. What was in its cell?"

"Destroyed, according to Deren. His team dug out nothing but ash." Obi-Wan looked sheepish. "I, uh, may have swung my lightsaber directly into it as it fell."

Qui-Gon briefly touched Obi-Wan's shoulder. "It's all right. You couldn't have known." The shielding must've been centered on the body of the droid, not the legs, where Qui-Gon had struck. Once systems failure began, the shield would have lost power—and of course a lightsaber could pierce any shield, in time.

"There's something else, too. Deren's still going over the security footage, but they've found just one image of interest so far." Obi-Wan brought it up on the screen.

There, amid a thicket in a narrow ravine, was the outline of a human, crouched low, holding something that might've been a remote tether to the droid. The image revealed little. But Qui-Gon thought one element of the image wasn't a trick of the night.

All they knew about their attacker was that this person had been completely clothed in black.

CHAPTER NINETEEN

———————————— ✦ ————————————

"I don't see why we don't just leave," Pax complained as he stretched out on the long cushioned bench in the mess hold of the *Meryx*. "As of yesterday, thanks to my exemplary skill at negotiation, we've made a profit on our trip to Pijal. And if we've left the system, do you really think the Jedi are going to take time out from searching for terrorists to track down two jewel thieves?" From where she stood, pouring herself a cup of Chandrilan tea, Rahara gave him a withering look. He sighed. "Two 'independent marketers of unregistered gemstones,' then?"

He was hoping to stoke a conversation of some length and fervor, which would fill the dull time they had to pass waiting for the Jedi. It might also bring a flush to Rahara's cheeks, if she got wound up enough. (He knew this wasn't a good enough reason to wind her up, but he seemed to do that whether he meant to or not, so he saw no reason not to enjoy the aesthetic effects.) Pax considered arguing a hobby.

Rahara only shrugged. "We made a promise to the Jedi. I like to keep my promises. Besides, if Czerka's on high alert, I'd rather stay put for now. Better to leave when they won't be on their guard." With this she took her steaming mug of tea and wandered back toward her corridors.

Disappointing. His invitation for a vigorous row had been declined. Apparently "sulking" was a bad habit, one he was supposed to be breaking, so he resisted the urge. But he couldn't help thinking fondly of the ship where he'd grown up, where everything had made so much more sense.

"Oh, heavens," Z-3PO had said when she found five-year-old Pax hiding in the equipment locker. "A child! A human one, quite alive! Whatever are we to do?"

Copper-plated G-3PO bent down to study Pax, who was too terrified to speak yet. "Are you sure it's human? It's rather pale."

Z-3PO swiveled on her jointed torso, revealing more of the coiled wires within. "Am I sure? I'm programmed to recognize more than thirty thousand sentient species, you know. Of course I can identify a human!"

That made G-3PO totter back a few steps. "How rude! Is this the thanks I get for trying to help you identify a stowaway?"

"Whatever are the two of you bickering about?" said blue-and-silver B-3PO, shuffling into the hold. "Oh, my. A human!"

"I told you so," Z-3PO said. . . .

. . . and that was more or less the way every day of Pax's life had unfolded from the age of five until the age of twenty, when the ship had at last been found by a Republic cruiser. He'd been the center of the droids' universe—the one human on board, amid eighty-three droids who had all been programmed to serve humans and other sentients—and was thrown off by the fact that now he didn't seem to be the center of anyone else's universe. (Except, of course, his own.) The droids had all been cheerful about their recovery, because they were ready to get back to work; this had convinced Pax he shouldn't be sad, either. Really, in his opinion, all beings ought to behave more like protocol droids. What exactly was wrong with that?

A great deal, it seemed, but Pax didn't intend to change himself to fit the universe. If the universe wanted him to blend more, well, then it could change to fit him.

Rapping against the *Meryx* hatch startled Pax, then irritated him. He went to open the door, muttering, "If only someone had invented comlinks. Then nobody would have to knock, like some primitive—"

The hatch slid open, to reveal Qui-Gon Jinn (solid and genial) and Obi-Wan Kenobi (small, wiry, curious). "Oh, bliss," Pax said. "Just what I needed this morning."

"We made arrangements yesterday to return to the source of those strange life signs," Qui-Gon pointed out, obnoxiously in Pax's opinion, even though the Jedi was correct. "Are you and Ms. Wick ready for the trip?"

"Ready? No. Stuck, yes." Pax sighed. "All right, then, let's go."

The slicer dart. The crab droid.

Someone wanted to kill Fanry. Someone wanted to ruin the future of the entire planet of Pijal. And this someone also wanted to make damn good and sure to hurt Averross at the same time.

Halin Azucca must figure I don't care about Pijal or Fanry, Averross brooded as he stalked along the castle grounds at dawn, his old boots already crusted with mud. *Or if she does give me enough credit to care, she's so angry it doesn't matter. She wants to make this* personal, *Force knows why.*

Well, if Azucca wanted a grudge match, she could have one. He grabbed his communicator and called, "Deren!" The man was undoubtedly already up. "We need to review procedures."

"At your service, Lord Regent," Deren said—not via comm, but only a few meters away, and now walking straight toward Averross. The man's timing was uncanny—exactly as it should be, for a captain of the guard. But then why wasn't he applying some of that foresight to Fanry's attackers?

Averross bit back his irritation. "You could've told me you were coming out here to search."

"Forgive me, Lord Regent. I believed you would expect me to do so." Deren bowed his head. "I *did* inform Master Jinn, so that he and his apprentice could return to their investigations on the moon. But I should've let you know regardless, if only so you wouldn't feel the need to search the grounds yourself."

"Both of us doing the same job isn't necessarily helping Fanry," Averross said, "unless one of us is doing his job wrong."

Deren drew himself upright, as firmly stiff and correct as ever, but Averross could see the pain in his eyes. "If you feel that I should not be in Her Serene Highness's service any longer—"

"C'mon, that's not what I meant." With a sigh, Averross put away his comm unit. "You're the one person on this whole planet that I can be sure doesn't want Fanry dead, and I only trust *you* because, by now, if you wanted to kill Fanry, you could've done it twenty times over."

"Her life is more sacred to me than my own," Deren said solemnly, the way someone might swear an oath. His expression and bearing remained as rigid as though he were carved from a blackbark tree. Did the guy ever wear casual robes, swimming suits, even pajamas? Averross had lived in the same castle as Deren for eight years now and never once seen the guy out of uniform. Never seen that uniform be anything less than pristinely correct. Never heard Deren call him anything but Lord Regent.

Most people who'd lived and worked together in such close quarters would've become friends by this point . . . that, or bitter enemies. Deren remained at a remove.

No, not Deren, Averross thought. *Me. I'm the one at a remove. Every single human in the palace besides Fanry has made sure of that.*

Just like it was back at the Temple. Just like always.

(Dooku had told Rael, many times, that his isolation was a self-fulfilling prophecy. "*Do you not keep your own customs rather than adopt those of the Jedi around you? Do you refuse to explain yourself more often than not? Why then does it surprise you that you stand apart from the rest?"* Master Dooku had liked that about his Padawan, had always encouraged it. So Rael had cultivated that quality within himself—his isolation was at least half his own doing. Yet the solitude kept its sharp edge, always.)

"I wasn't sure, sir," Deren said, lifting the scanner he held, "what kinds of searches you were running. I've been looking for repulsorlift signatures that would reveal speeder activity, in case that's how they're slipping in and out. But if you're doing the same, I could—"

"I've done that. I've reviewed the safety droids. Even sent probes down to check the coastline, in case they were coming in via submersibles. Nothing. Not even a picture, except that one blurry guy in the brush." Averross felt wired. Every muscle was tense. Nothing was right, and nothing could be right until the treaty was signed, and nothing was safe.

Deren bowed his head once more. "I swear to you, Lord Regent, I've run all such searches before and will do so again, personally."

"What do you feel is goin' on here?" Averross met Deren's eyes, searching for the man inside the uniform. "What does your gut tell you? Forget the evidence, or politics, or anything else. I want *instinct.*"

After a long pause, Deren said, "I obey procedures, sir. Not instincts."

Like a blackbark-wood door being slammed in my face, Averross thought. "All right, all right. Just . . . go back to what you were doin'."

Captain Deren immediately returned to his tasks. Maybe he was grateful not to have to talk to Averross any longer; maybe he just didn't give a damn. More likely the latter.

Seabirds shrieked as they began their morning flights, circling high overhead. Averross remembered what he'd sworn to himself when he first arrived on Pijal and saw Fanry, only six years old and newly orphaned, clinging to her slave girl in her loneliness. He'd looked down at her and inwardly promised, *Nobody else matters. Nothing else matters. Not the Jedi Council, not politics, not glory, not me. Just you.*

But it was becoming clear to him that he should've made more friends in the palace. If he had, maybe he'd have a better idea who their enemies were.

He stared at the horizon, where the setting moon showed as a pale sliver against the brightening sky. Qui-Gon was up there, trying to find Halin Azucca. Maybe his fresh perspective would let him do it. Averross wished he was with him.

Because Halin Azucca's Opposition needed to be hit hard. Harder than Qui-Gon Jinn would ever allow.

That was Averross's job.

"I'd like your opinion," Qui-Gon said.

Obi-Wan looked up from the *Meryx*'s scanners. "Well, that's a first."

The look Qui-Gon gave him made Obi-Wan realize, *I don't think I should've said that out loud, even if it's true.* But maybe Qui-Gon saw truth in it, too, because he said only, "I had a curious dream about the treaty ceremony."

"Not prophecy, I hope," Obi-Wan joked. Then his heart sank as he took in Qui-Gon's expression. It hadn't been a joke at all.

"Obviously—obviously not literal prophecy," Qui-Gon said, unusually tentative. "But I wondered whether my dream might not be worth analyzing. Perhaps my subconscious has picked up on some clues that we haven't noticed consciously."

Obi-Wan figured that if Qui-Gon was finally asking for his opinion, he could have it. "Surely we have more pressing concerns. Better ways of searching for an answer. Dream analysis would be guesswork at best."

Qui-Gon frowned. Maybe this was the beginning of an argument. Obi-Wan braced himself—then startled as the sensors began chiming. "Looks like we're here."

"Same place as yesterday." Rahara Wick slid into the seat next to him, double-checking the readings. "And I'm picking up even higher levels of concentrated protons."

Protons? Obi-Wan and Qui-Gon shared a look, their disagreement forgotten. That indicated weaponry: torpedoes or missiles, probably. Anybody who had missiles had other weapons, too.

Had the Opposition finally been found?

"All right, put it down," Qui-Gon commanded.

As Rahara obeyed, Pax Maripher rolled his eyes, something he did often. (Obi-Wan wondered whether maybe it was a medical condition.) Pax proclaimed, "The only thing worse than being made to search for a guerrilla army is being made to face one."

"You're not facing anyone, Pax," Qui-Gon said. "You're staying on the ship, as is Rahara. This is for me and my apprentice."

Despite everything, Obi-Wan felt a small surge of pride. *Qui-Gon does trust me, at least in some things. I've earned that much from him, anyway.*

Rahara brought the *Meryx* down low, until its bottom hull brushed along some treetops. Obi-Wan followed his Master to the hatch, which Rahara had already released for them. Silently Qui-Gon pried the door open. Strong winds whipped into the bay, and Obi-Wan squinted against them.

"Ready, Padawan?" Qui-Gon said. How many more times would Obi-Wan hear that?

He looked down into the thick green cloud of treetops moving beneath them. Somewhere beneath those leaves a terrorist army was hiding.

Maybe waiting.

"I'm ready, Master." With that, Obi-Wan jumped from the ship, into the unknown.

CHAPTER TWENTY

———— ⟨⟩ ————

Qui-Gon leapt with Obi-Wan, reaching out with the Force to sense the trees, the life in each branch and leaf. He sensed the winds and the ground, and anchored himself to them to slow his fall. Obi-Wan was doing the same, his own efforts a second note in the great chorus of the Force around them—

—and the others. So many others.

We're jumping directly into the center of the military unit, Qui-Gon realized.

Good.

The sound of rushing leaves marked the final moments of the fall, and Qui-Gon positioned himself to land on his feet, legs slightly bent. He didn't need the Force to tell him Obi-Wan was doing the same.

Impact. The jolt was minor, and Qui-Gon scarcely noticed. At that instant he activated his lightsaber and reached out with his senses to detect their foes.

(And they were foes. At this range, their hostile intent surrounded them all, cold as Cadomai.)

Fourteen adversaries—four to our right, three to our left, one behind, and six straight ahead. Qui-Gon plunged forward, into the heart of the fray. Behind him, Obi-Wan turned backward to the one enemy standing alone.

Not what I'd have done, Qui-Gon thought as he swung his lightsaber up to parry incoming fire. *But smart. Once Obi-Wan is done, we'll only have three directions to worry about instead of four.*

As blaster bolts sizzled around him, Qui-Gon carved his way through the underbrush, silently resolving to do a healing meditation in the forest afterward. He reached his first black-clad attacker, felt no chance of a surrender, and so struck out—

—and his lightsaber bounced off the man.

What the . . .

Qui-Gon compensated for the bounce almost instantly and brought his lightsaber up at a different angle. It bounced off again.

His attacker laughed.

Shields, he realized. Now that he was looking for them, Qui-Gon could detect a faint reddish glimmer along the outlines of the black-clad soldiers. Few fighters used individual shields, cumbersome and energy intensive as they were, and most energy shields were of limited use against lightsabers—a blow from a lightsaber would still shock and stun anyone wearing one. After that, disarming them and removing the shield generally took no time at all. Never had Qui-Gon come across a shield so powerful that a lightsaber's blade had no effect, and instead pushed the Jedi Knight backward.

An opponent untouchable by lightsabers could fight on and on, waiting for one of the Jedi to make a mistake, leave an opening. Even the best Jedi would tire eventually. A mistake would inevitably be made.

"Master?" Obi-Wan called over the *hiss-crackle* of blasters. "Something's wrong with my lightsaber!"

"It's not your lightsaber," Qui-Gon shouted back. "Retreat immediately. Head to the south." That was the clearest direction possible.

"Qui-Gon, no! I can fight—"

"That's an order, Padawan!"

The wave of chagrin and fear that swept past Qui-Gon told him Obi-Wan was obeying him. Now to ensure that heading south would do his apprentice any good. He swung around so his back was against the thickest nearby tree. That way he could use one arm to wield his lightsaber as a defensive weapon, the other to grab his comlink and call the *Meryx*. "We need you back here."

"*I beg your pardon?*" Somehow Pax Maripher even *sounded* like a protocol droid. "*You're summoning us back toward the firefight? The one that apparently is too fierce to be handled by two Jedi Knights?*"

"*We're not leaving anyone, Pax,*" Rahara Wick insisted. "*Where do you need us?*"

"South of our drop point. As close as you can get without putting yourselves in jeopardy. Obi-Wan will rendezvous with you shortly."

Qui-Gon dropped his comm unit back in his robes, though it didn't shut off before he overheard Pax: "*I wasn't saying we* would *leave them, only that we shouldn't be expected to—*"

He refocused on this attack. One against fourteen, no offensive weapon. Therefore Qui-Gon's best tactic was to use these fighters against one another.

A tree nearby was very old and dry, already dying. Qui-Gon dived into a roll that took him to its trunk; with a thought of apology, he slashed his lightsaber through the trunk. With a heavy creak, the tree toppled down—earning shouts of fear and surprise from the attackers. It only hit one, and that glancingly, but Qui-Gon could sense him leaving the fight, with another guard's help.

Two down, twelve to go.

Qui-Gon crouched for cover behind the trunk of the fallen tree, placing one hand on the stump to ease it gently into death. The trunk had landed in the middle of the attackers, dividing them into two groups. *Now to get them firing at someone in the middle . . .*

He crawled forward, using his lightsaber to deflect the lowest bolts and suggest the center as a target—then heard a scream as a higher-aimed bolt hit another guard. Eleven remaining, and if they didn't adjust formations, others would soon fall. Friendly fire could be more deadly than any enemy attack. Would they have the sense to stop now?

"This way!" someone shouted. Someone to the south.

Qui-Gon tucked himself into the V of a large branch, buying himself a few moments to look around. The *Meryx* was descending through the trees, finding a narrow clearing, to which Obi-Wan seemed to be running. But now all the guards were after him, and after the ship, ignoring Qui-Gon in favor of easier targets. Normally Obi-Wan would've been more than able to handle such a situation, but against foes shielded from lightsabers?

"Blast it," Qui-Gon muttered, throwing himself forward, following Obi-Wan.

What's wrong with my lightsaber? Obi-Wan thought as he tried to run serpentine through the underbrush of the forest. Qui-Gon had claimed that wasn't the problem, but Qui-Gon hadn't seen how ludicrously his lightsaber bounced off a fighter wearing an ordinary energy shield.

If the energy shield is ordinary—

He had no time to pursue that thought. The *Meryx* was descending to pick him up, a dangerous maneuver for all involved. So Obi-Wan's job was to get on that ship immediately, then figure out how to rescue his Master.

From his pocket, his comm unit spoke in Rahara's voice: *"We're drawing fire—hang on, we'll find a way to—"* Static broke off the transmission as a blaster bolt struck the hull of the *Meryx*. It wasn't a dangerous hit, but they were exposed to open fire now, and the attack would only worsen.

Obi-Wan fumbled for the comlink, then called, "You're too exposed. Forget me—I'll find refuge. See if you can provide any cover for Qui-Gon."

"Cover for Qui-Gon?" Pax protested. *"What about us?"* But either he

was only complaining or Rahara ignored him, because the *Meryx* immediately rose above the treetops, heading north.

His Master would soon be safe. Now to find some safety for himself. Obi-Wan hurried deeper into the brush, hoping to find a patch so thick it provided real barriers to blasterfire. The crunch of leaves and twigs underfoot seemed so loud, like he was signaling his location for the attackers' convenience—*no, no, it's louder for you than it is for anyone else, just keep going*—

The grove ahead of him was darker, almost blocking out light entirely. Obi-Wan dashed for it. This might give him the safety he needed.

He felt the slight instability underfoot only an instant before the ground gave way under his feet.

Obi-Wan grabbed for purchase, and wrapped one hand around a thick branch jutting from a heavy log. That alone kept him from tumbling down with the soil beneath his feet, the loose ground and small stones and roots, all of which were swirling down into—

A sinkhole, he thought. *A bad one. One of the ones Rahara warned us about.*

The log shuddered on the lip of the widening sinkhole. Already the soil underneath was shaking, loosening, threatening to give way. When it did, the log would fall—taking Obi-Wan with it.

CHAPTER TWENTY-ONE

---⚔---

Qui-Gon saw the *Meryx* rising above the firefight. He saw a strange trembling among the leaves and trees in a distant dark patch of the wood.

But he *felt* Obi-Wan fall, through the Force, through the sheer jolt of alarm that passed straight from his Padawan's heart to his.

"Sinkhole!" shouted one of the soldiers attacking them. They were frightened and, at least for the moment, disorganized. That gave Qui-Gon a chance to reach Obi-Wan.

He braced himself, called once again upon the Force, and leapt upward to the higher limbs of a nearby tree. It swayed under his weight, then bent in the opposite direction—closer to Obi-Wan. Qui-Gon silently thanked it and jumped again, using all his power to clear five meters to another of the trees.

"Get back in there!" shouted another of the soldiers, perhaps their commander. "The sinkhole's only going to open so far! We've got the Jedi where we want them!"

Irrelevant. Qui-Gon would get to Obi-Wan and help him. He'd worry about the attack after that, not before.

He attempted to send a wave of reassurance to his Padawan through the Force, encouragement to hold on, but he felt no answering sense of relief. Either Obi-Wan hadn't perceived it, or the situation was too dire for his fear to be so easily allayed.

Through the branches, from his perch several meters above ground, Qui-Gon caught a glimpse of his Padawan's predicament—a sinkhole opening wide like the maw of some terrible beast, a felled tree shuddering from the upheaval at the sinkhole's edge, and, hanging on to one of the tree's broken branches, Obi-Wan. The loose churn of dirt and stone beneath Obi-Wan's feet, at the bottom of the sinkhole, chilled Qui-Gon to the marrow. If his apprentice slid down into that stuff, he would be pulled beneath it within seconds, dragged inexorably down deeper underground, farther and farther from air. From the sheer weight and velocity of the groundslide beneath him, Qui-Gon wasn't even sure Yoda could've gotten himself free.

Blast and damn! He leapt down from the trees, propelling himself closer to Obi-Wan. Loose leaves underfoot meant he had to slide to a stop, but at least now he was within sight of the sinkhole. Qui-Gon ran toward the sinkhole, deactivating his lightsaber. When blasters fired at him, he reached out with his feelings to dodge them, not bothering to parry. He didn't need to worry about the attackers right now, save for keeping himself alive long enough to reach Obi-Wan's side.

At last he plunged into the clearing—what was now a clearing, thanks to the trees sliding deeper into the sinkhole. About two meters away, Obi-Wan had managed to climb halfway up the log—which only did so much good, as the log was now itself toppling down.

When Obi-Wan saw him, his blue eyes widened. "Master!" he called. "No! Save yourself!"

This is the boy who believed I found him unworthy as an apprentice. The one I failed to tell about the most significant change in my life, and maybe his.

I don't deserve him. I never have.

Qui-Gon ignored the protests and got down on his belly, the better to stabilize himself on the trembling ground. "I'm going to pull the log back. Just hang on."

"But, Master—"

Qui-Gon tuned this out and slid forward far enough to reach the exposed, long-dead roots of the log. One of them had taken on a withered, almost ropy texture, but remained strong. He wrapped this around his left arm, shoulder-to-wrist, then dug his feet into the loose soil as best he could. Then he began creeping backward, scuttling like a desert lizard in sand, making tracks with his elbows, knees, and belly. The log creaked in protest, but began sliding up the lip of the sinkhole.

Would the sinkhole widen yet farther? If it did, all Qui-Gon's efforts would be useless. But he sensed it deepening instead, suggesting that the older, taller trees nearby had such deep root systems that they stabilized the ground beneath them. If he could make it to the tree line, they'd be out of danger.

Well, he thought as he heard the enemy troops approaching. *Out of one danger, anyway.*

"It's working!" Obi-Wan called. Qui-Gon felt the angle of the tree shifting, less and less vertical until it was finally horizontal again. He kept going, crawling backward ceaselessly until he reached the edge of the clearing. The ground beneath them now was steady and strong.

He propped himself up on his elbows to peer over the tree. Peering back at him, dirt smudged all over his face, was Obi-Wan. When their eyes met, Obi-Wan grinned, and Qui-Gon couldn't help smiling back.

Then a blaster bolt slammed into a nearby shrub, setting it smoldering.

"Out of the saucepan," Qui-Gon muttered, "and into the stove."

Obi-Wan scrambled to his feet, ignoring the bloody scratches on his hands and arms, and ignited his lightsaber. That could do them no good when fighting enemies shielded against lightsabers.

Yet what portable shields had ever been impervious to lightsabers? Droids could sometimes power such shields, but he'd never witnessed any individual shields with that kind of ability. Qui-Gon half doubted what he'd seen before. Maybe the haze of battle had confused him. No amount of experience could prevent that from happening sometimes.

"The *Meryx* isn't—they can't—" Breathless, Obi-Wan simply gestured at the *Meryx*. To Rahara and Pax's credit, they were still attempting to approach for a pickup. But the guards kept up their fire on the ship, enough to keep it at a distance. Their vessel was small enough to be at serious risk from hand-weapons fire.

"I see it," Qui-Gon said. He made his way to stand by Obi-Wan, back-to-back, the better to defend themselves. It was a delaying maneuver, no more. Even the greatest Jedi Knights could only block enemy fire for a finite amount of time. If the attackers were shielded as well as Qui-Gon feared they were, they could simply keep firing upon the two Jedi for hours, even days, until finally one of them failed to parry and took a fatal shot. The other wouldn't be able to hold out much longer after that.

Obi-Wan saw it as well as he did. "Master?" he said, keeping his tone light. "I don't suppose you'd tell me why you kept me at the beginning forms in lightsaber dueling, would you? This is probably my last chance to find out."

Qui-Gon took a deep breath. "You see, Padawan—"

A blaster bolt flew through the air—from the opposite direction of their attackers. Then another. Shouts of alarm went up from the soldiers, echoed by shouts from the unknown others, fast approaching. Qui-Gon and Obi-Wan exchanged glances, then simultaneously dived to the ground to take cover.

"We have either new friends," Qui-Gon called over the din, "or double the enemies."

Obi-Wan managed to smile. "Look on the bright side. It's not like our situation could've gotten any *worse.*"

Through the Force, Qui-Gon felt their attackers' resolve weaken, then give way. They broke ranks and ran, the fury in their minds growing distant like storm clouds being blown away by a strong spring wind.

The others approaching them weren't as angry. No, Qui-Gon realized, not angry at all. Surprised, and scared, and even confused.

"Our cam droids showed us Jedi Knights in this area!" called a woman's voice. "Were they killed? Or are they here?"

Qui-Gon looked at Obi-Wan, who shrugged.

He's right. It's not getting any worse. "We're here," he called back. "May I know who it is who's looking for us?"

"First you'll surrender your weapons!" the woman demanded. Something in her tone made him think she hadn't made demands like that very often.

"No, we won't." Qui-Gon kept his tone reasonable, but resolute. "We don't intend to surrender ourselves as your prisoners—but we don't intend to take you as prisoners, either. Either you'll show yourselves and we'll talk like civilized beings, or we'll fight this out. I'd prefer the former. But the decision is yours."

For a few seconds, no one spoke. The only sounds were leaves rustling in the breeze, and the far-off hum of the *Meryx*'s engines, where Rahara and Pax were apparently trying to figure out if it was safe to land. Qui-Gon was trying to figure that out himself.

The woman finally said, more calmly, "All right. We're putting our weapons away. You do the same."

Obi-Wan looked skeptical, but Qui-Gon nodded. He could sense the honesty in this woman.

Qui-Gon slipped his lightsaber back into his belt and got to his feet, Obi-Wan right behind him. Through the brush, he could see several humans approaching, all of whom wore outfits in various shades of green. No practical coveralls or uniforms were to be seen; some of these people had even decorated their garb with bits of lace, patches of velvet. They could've been mistaken for theatrical performers, were it not for the holster belts they wore, heavy with sheathed blasters and other weapons.

But they *were* performers, after all. This was probably the only performance troupe in the galaxy ever to turn to terrorism.

Their leader appeared to be the woman walking toward him. Given her resonant voice, he was surprised to see that she was actually rather small—a few centimeters shorter than Obi-Wan. Her skin was deep reddish brown, and her black hair was pulled up in small knots all over her head. The lines on her face suggested that she smiled broadly, when she smiled . . . and that at least in the past, that had been quite often.

At this moment, the main emotion he sensed in her was bewilderment.

When at last she stepped into the clearing, they were only two meters apart. Shaking loose dust from his hair, Qui-Gon said, "May we know to whom we owe our deliverance?"

She snorted—not quite a laugh, but not a denial, either. If he could get her to take credit for their rescue, that brought this situation one step closer to *being* a rescue.

"My name is Halin Azucca," she said, and gestured at the people around her. "We're the Opposition. And we'd like to know why we're being framed."

CHAPTER TWENTY-TWO

———————— ☩ ————————

"Follow me," said Halin Azucca, gesturing deeper into the forest.

That meant her group's base was probably in the exact opposite direction. Qui-Gon made note of this for later.

Navigating a nebulous situation like this one was always tricky. Qui-Gon understood that he and Obi-Wan were not truly prisoners, but that they needed to behave as if they were.

He and Obi-Wan walked just behind Halin, as casually as if this were just a stroll, but always mindful of the other Opposition members beside and behind them. Qui-Gon noted that several people in the Opposition held their weapons awkwardly—as though they'd never been trained in their use, or simply felt profoundly uncomfortable being armed. *Odd, for a guerrilla army, even one that began as a group of performers. Perhaps Halin Azucca is telling the truth about their being framed.*

It would take more than a few badly held blasters to convince Qui-

Gon of the Opposition's innocence. But the contrast between these unlikely soldiers and the black-clad figures who had attacked him and Obi-Wan was clear.

Qui-Gon's comlink buzzed with Rahara Wick's voice. *"Are you guys all right?"*

Several Opposition members froze in apparent alarm. Halin Azucca met Qui-Gon's eyes evenly. "Is that a palace ship? Official troops?"

"No," he answered. "As a matter of fact, those are jewel thieves."

A moment's disbelief in her eyes gave way to amusement. "You must be telling the truth, because that's much too weird to be a lie." She nodded, signaling permission for him to answer.

He took the comlink in hand. "We're fine."

"Oh, good," Rahara said. *"We were worried about you."*

Pax chimed in, *"You see, if the two of you were killed up here, we'd be the prime suspects."*

"Undoubtedly," Qui-Gon said. "For now, hold your position. We'll be in touch if and when we need a pickup."

"Got it." With that, Rahara signed off.

Obi-Wan muttered, "Remind me again why we didn't just get a palace ship for this?"

Halin answered before Qui-Gon could. "If you guys had arrived in a palace ship, we couldn't know whether or not you were Deren's troops or even Czerka operatives coming to haul us in. We'd have to shoot a palace ship, or try. Jewel thieves, though . . . they're not going to report our location, are they? They couldn't turn us in without turning themselves in."

Obi-Wan blinked. Qui-Gon smiled slightly. Perhaps his Padawan was at last beginning to see that there were advantages to not doing everything strictly by the book.

After several more minutes, their group reached a rockier, more uneven area bordered by a hillside. The mouth of one of the moon's many caves was half shrouded in vines. Halin gestured toward it. "The blackguards haven't found this one yet. Only a matter of time."

With a frown, Obi-Wan said, "Blackguards?"

"That's what we're calling them—the black-uniformed troops that attacked you," Halin replied.

Qui-Gon and Obi-Wan shared a glance. They were both remembering the dark figure that had been sighted on the night of the Grand Hunt.

"They've attacked us, too. At first we thought they might be Czerka operatives, but the blackguards have hit a couple of Czerka ships as well. Nobody knows who they are, or where they came from. But I'd bet a million credits that they're the ones behind all this. Well, the recent stuff, anyway."

Qui-Gon caught the filtered admission. "The recent stuff," he repeated. "But not all of it?"

The Opposition members exchanged glances, and Halin sighed. "Come on. Let me show you what we've got."

The cave had no lights, no equipment stores, nothing to contradict Qui-Gon's reasoning that this wasn't one of their bases. However, a couple of canteens sat in a small cranny, and a few mats had been pulled into a semicircle near enough to the cave's mouth to get a little light. A hideout, then. An emergency meeting place. A few Gatalentan meditation candles sat in an alcove; someone had tried to find peace here.

He and Obi-Wan sat on a couple of the mats while Halin fiddled with an ancient astromech droid. Eventually it began playing holograms of a dance performance outside a temple, one with Halin Azucca twirling in the middle of it all. Several of the other members danced alongside her as the crowds watched.

"This is the kind of thing we came together for," Halin said. Her expression was wistful. "Political art. Acts that might uplift the spirit while they informed the public. We staged shows in public places, played pranks, did whatever we could do to get attention. But we never, ever hurt anyone. That's the last thing any of us wanted."

"And yet the violence has escalated to bombings," Obi-Wan pointed out.

"That's not us!" scoffed a younger Opposition member. "Reckly over there? He's a drummer. Bajjo focuses her eye-lenses to create abstract holos. I trained as a *puppeteer*. Do you seriously think I'd know how to build a bomb? That any of us would? We're artists."

"Artists with weapons," Qui-Gon said.

"We got some blasters together, after we were on the run, *only* to protect ourselves," Halin insisted. "The first violent attacks scared us as badly as anyone. When the security forces said we were responsible? It was so absurd. Some people wanted to turn themselves in, just to prove their own innocence. I didn't allow it; I thought Czerka might pressure the government to find us guilty even without evidence. But the longer we stayed hidden, the more atrocities piled up. Proving we were innocent went from difficult to impossible. And whoever it is that's doing this—they're not even under suspicion, because the government is so sure we're the terrorists."

Qui-Gon could sense her honesty. Even without the Force, he would've known that her account tracked better with the pattern of attacks than any other theory they'd come up with so far. The early, targeted, bloodless operations contrasted sharply with the deadlier attacks that came after. It made sense that these might be the work of two separate groups instead of one.

Yet some points remained unclear. "You continued your pranks after the terrorist attacks began, even after the Opposition was blamed. That could only encourage the idea of a link between you and the so-called blackguards."

"You pulled a stunt just two days ago," Obi-Wan interjected. "Did you think that balloon outside the palace would do your cause any good?"

Every Opposition member in the cave grinned, or laughed, or both. The puppeteer shook Halin's hand as she said, "That went off? Oh, fantastic."

By now Qui-Gon understood. "You arranged many of these pranks weeks or even months in advance."

Halin nodded. "Easier to put stuff in place when security's not watching. They'd check the areas for weapons, but not for the kinds of things we planted, like holos and signs."

"And balloons." Qui-Gon sighed. He now had to prove the innocence of a group of performance artists. He remembered Chancellor Kaj saying, *The galaxy is big and strange.*

Obi-Wan seemed warier. "For a political group, you haven't done a very good job of getting your message across. It's rather muddled."

"It isn't!" Halin insisted. "If you look at our work—just our true work, in isolation—it's perfectly clear that we're protesting the Governance Treaty. It doesn't give lunar citizens fair representation, and it cedes over even more of the government's power to Czerka Corporation. But they've lumped in our work with the blackguards', which means nobody understands what we're saying."

It occurred to Qui-Gon that Halin Azucca might have analyzed the blackguard attacks more precisely than even the palace had, because she alone knew what acts the Opposition had and hadn't committed. "Have you picked up on any pattern to the blackguards' attacks?" he asked. "This is your world, your system. You might see significance where we cannot."

"Sorry to disappoint you." Halin sighed heavily as she sat on another of the mats. "We can't make any sense of it. Their targets sometimes seem deliberately chosen, but others seem random. The only thing we've noticed is that they don't seem to be going after palace ships. That's odd, seeing as how the palace is the ultimate authority on this planet, at least until the damn treaty ceremony. Then again, that's only here on the moon, where the royal guards have a smaller presence. For all we know, the blackguards may be going after them constantly on Pijal. The palace would keep it quiet, if they were."

"They've attacked the palace," Obi-Wan said. "In fact, they've twice attempted to assassinate Princess Fanry."

Murmurs of dismay went through the Opposition, heightening Qui-Gon's curiosity.

"You seem concerned for Her Serene Highness's welfare," he said. "And you've indicated your displeasure with the coming Governance Treaty, but I suspect you're not monarchists."

Halin sat up straighter, a glimmer of something like hope in her eyes. Qui-Gon wondered how long she'd been waiting for someone to ask her for her side of the story—or for someone who might be willing to believe it.

She began, "No, we're not monarchists. Most of us aren't opposed to the idea of a constitutional monarchy, but we'd like democratic representation."

"So why do you oppose the idea of an Assembly?" Obi-Wan asked.

"We don't oppose the idea," Halin said. "We oppose the reality, as it's set up in the Governance Treaty. Have you read through the entire thing?"

"Of course," Qui-Gon said. "As did my apprentice, and the chancellor's team on Coruscant. All appears to be in order."

Halin's expression darkened. "All is not what it *appears* to be."

The legalese was difficult to recall exactly, and in such matters precision was important. "Please explain."

"The Assembly sounds like a great idea, but when you dig into the details, you realize how shoddy this Governance Treaty really is. There's only token representation for the citizens of Pijal's moon, even though we're a solid quarter of the system population."

The moon had been described as "sparsely populated," and the census records had seemed to back this up. Yet Pijal, with its sparse island continents, undoubtedly had fewer inhabitants than the average planet of its size. "Why would anyone obscure the real population of the moon? And who would have the power to do so?"

"Czerka," Halin said. She offered no further explanation, but she didn't need to. Qui-Gon had seen for himself the influence Czerka held on this planet. Czerka's mining efforts took a far higher toll on the moon than on Pijal itself. The corporation had made sure that the planet's leadership—most recently, Rael—would never be face-to-face with the worst damage. By now, the lunar citizens knew better . . .

which was precisely why Czerka would work to keep them disenfran-
chised.

"So you want proper representation," Obi-Wan said. "Did you not
try normal political channels for your protests? Before turning to, um,
dancing?"

"We tried," Halin said, "but a fat lot of good it did us. The lord regent
wouldn't even listen. He sees any opposition to the treaty as a personal
attack on the princess. That, or he's too arrogant to admit he might've
made a mistake. Typical high-handed—"

Her voice trailed off in a way that made Qui-Gon suspect the next
word out of her mouth would've been *Jedi.*

"Rael Averross is devoted to the princess," he said. "It's possible that
has affected his judgment." Qui-Gon had no doubt that Rael's ego
could also have played a role in his obstinacy, but that was not a matter
to be discussed with outsiders.

Halin nodded, grateful to be given a tactful out. "Sure. That would
make sense. But what doesn't make sense is the fact that this treaty
doesn't benefit the moon *or* the planet as much as it benefits Czerka
Corporation."

Obi-Wan looked confused. "The corporation's not named in the
treaty."

"Of course not," she said. "But there are clauses giving the Assembly
the authority to 'renew all contracts applying to privatized industries
and such industries' land use.' That might not look so ominous until
you realize *all* of those contracts go to Czerka. They have for centuries,
though Czerka's tightened its grip during the Regency. Then it says,
'This shall be preserved as the sun preserves the moon.' "

"I thought that was merely ritual language," Qui-Gon admitted.

"It is ritual language," Halin said, "but there's no 'merely' about it.
Only a Pijali native would understand; in our law, that phrase means
'forever, and ever, and ever.' As in, absolutely irrevocable, no matter
what laws are passed afterward. In other words, while the Assembly
can renew the contracts, it lacks the power to *cancel* the contracts."

Obi-Wan had a finer mind for such legal details than Qui-Gon ever had. Already he'd come to a conclusion. "You mean that if the treaty is signed, Czerka's presence on the Pijal system will be codified into law, permanently."

"Exactly." Halin exhaled heavily, apparently relieved that someone close to authority had seen her point. "That would be abhorrent to us even if Czerka weren't massively abusing their power."

"How so?" asked Qui-Gon. "The more details we have, the better."

"One of the 'privatized industries' Averross put Czerka in charge of is the penal system," she said. "A generation ago, the Pijal system rarely resorted to lengthy jail sentences. Now they're mandatory for a long list of crimes, including minor ones. And a larger number of crimes are now punishable by life sentences at labor."

"Slaves," Qui-Gon said as understanding dawned. "You mean Czerka takes these people and enslaves them."

One of the Opposition members standing watch at the mouth of the cave added, "And if they have children while enslaved, those kids are legally Czerka property, too."

"Rael Averross helped to write this?" Qui-Gon's feelings toward Rael had been mixed for so long—but never had he imagined an ethical failure as great as this. "He approved it?"

"Less that he did it personally, more that he lets Czerka do what they want and doesn't ask any inconvenient questions," Halin answered. "Czerka's powerful. They use that power to support the princess. Even after the Governance Treaty, Fanry will have enough authority to make sure Czerka doesn't run into any difficulties. And she's *grown up* with Czerka. Had their supervisors to dinner in the palace at least once a week. Yes, Fanry's our crown princess, but she's also still a child, one who doesn't have the perspective to comprehend exactly how screwed up this all is."

Obi-Wan had taken on a thoughtful look. "Even if she does figure it out when she gets older, it won't matter. By then Czerka's contracts will be made permanent by the treaty."

It was possible that Halin Azucca was exaggerating some of this, or misunderstanding certain elements. Yet Qui-Gon was now convinced that the largest part of what she was saying was true. He'd observed Czerka's omnipresence in the system for himself, as well as the palace's reliance on forced labor. A closer inspection of the Governance Treaty would no doubt confirm the greatest dangers.

Rael was fighting so hard to protect Fanry—to make up for failing Nim—that he was instead failing an entire system.

"I'm going to address this directly with Averross," Qui-Gon promised Halin. "And with the Jedi Council, and possibly Chancellor Kaj herself. Surely we can change this."

Her expression was difficult to read by the flickering hololight—hopeful, yes, but uncertain, too. "If anyone can, the Jedi can."

"The chancellor and the Council will want to hear about the blackguards, too," Obi-Wan pointed out. "And we're no closer to figuring out who they are."

"If the blackguards are trying to interfere with the treaty process, we may learn a great deal about them if the treaty is delayed or canceled." Qui-Gon recalled something Halin had said earlier. "You mentioned, when we first reached this cave, that they 'hadn't found this one yet,' or something similar. What did you mean by that?"

Halin shrugged. "The blackguards seem to love raiding the various caves. At first we thought the caves must be their hideouts, but that doesn't check out. Maybe they're trying to trace Czerka activity underground, but why? That's all we know about these people. They raid caves, and they're willing to take lives in service to an agenda nobody knows." Smiling crookedly, she added, "A mystery worthy of a Jedi?"

Qui-Gon said, "Absolutely."

CHAPTER TWENTY-THREE

R ahara tapped her fingers on her seat as she stared at the chrono. The Jedi had been gone too long for her liking.

"If they're dead," Pax said, "we'll be the ones blamed. Mark my words."

"That's only the thousandth time you've said that." It would've been easier to dismiss Pax's worries if she didn't share them. Two missing or dead Jedi Knights would, at minimum, attract considerable attention from the authorities. At least one of those authorities was sure to notice the scar on her hand, which would lead to—

The comlink crackled with static before resolving into Qui-Gon Jinn's deep voice. "Meryx? *Do you read?*"

"Loud and clear," Rahara said. The relief sweeping through her was so deep that it came close to joy. "Ready for your ride?"

"Very much so. We'll be waiting at these coordinates."

The data lit up on-screen, and instantly Pax went to work laying them in. "So they were fine the entire time? We spent all this time worrying for nothing. Worrying, and remaining inactive, when we could be harvesting opals—"

"At least we're not on the hook for losing two Jedi, Pax. So drop it." Rahara sank into the pilot's chair, ready to roll.

A low fly-by between some of the nearby hills revealed Qui-Gon and Obi-Wan standing in a small clearing. They were incredibly dusty, and when Qui-Gon boarded the *Meryx*, Rahara spotted a twig tangled in his hair—but otherwise, they seemed none the worse for wear. "How did you guys get out of that one?"

"Often I have to ask myself that question," Qui-Gon said. "This time, we were saved from one secret paramilitary organization by another secret organization."

"Uncanny luck, that." Pax raised an eyebrow. "I suppose diplomacy or Jedi protocol precludes any chance you'll explain it all to us?"

To Rahara's surprise, Qui-Gon turned thoughtful. He and his apprentice shared a look, and Obi-Wan shrugged. Qui-Gon said, "There's no rule against it, and the two of you have been searching this moon for a while. It's possible you might've picked up on clues that could shed some light."

Pax sighed. "Oh, so now we're forced to be advisers to the mission?"

Apparently protocol droids complained every other sentence, which she figured was the reason Pax did the same, but that didn't mean Rahara had to like it. "Pax, you literally *just asked* the man for information."

"I didn't ask to *opine* upon it," Pax said haughtily as he steered the *Meryx* back toward their landing grounds.

"Forgive me," Qui-Gon said, "but I suspect you'd share your opinion on this or any other topic, whether we asked for it or not."

Slowly Pax began to smile. When people punctured his vanity, he began to respect them. "Rather perceptive of you."

Qui-Gon studied Rahara's and Pax's faces as he finished speaking. He'd wondered, at first, whether they would keep back anything they knew; it was possible they were up to illegal acts beyond the ones they'd already admitted to, in which case they would have motivation to conceal some facts. Yet he sensed no deception, no reticence, from either of them. Pax merely looked curious.

Rahara, however, had withdrawn within herself—as people did when they were in pain.

"Whatever are these blackguards spelunking about in the caves for?" Pax said. "There's nothing in there but whirlpool opals, which aren't valuable enough to motivate a paramilitary operation. They're not even valuable enough to motivate *me,* and I do this for a living. Then there are the kohlen crystals, but those are absolutely useless. Unless maybe they've mistaken them for kyber?"

"The shields," Obi-Wan said. "Their shields seemed impervious to our lightsabers. Could kohlen crystals power such a thing?"

"Not that I've ever heard of, though it's an interesting concept." Pax looked thoughtful. "Hmm. Must consider."

Qui-Gon weighed the information they had. "That seems the likeliest scenario—that these kohlen crystals are used in these shields, which is why the blackguards raid various caves."

However, Obi-Wan wasn't satisfied. "But why bother with an operation on such a scale? There are, at present, exactly three people in this system who have lightsabers. Designing a shield just to defend against three people—isn't that overkill?"

"Obviously they plan to distribute," Pax said.

Qui-Gon had just reached the same conclusion, though he couldn't speak of it as calmly as Pax Maripher did. "A means of complete protection against a lightsaber . . . that could be a powerful defense. A dangerous one, if it falls into the wrong hands."

"Not *that* dangerous." Obi-Wan took up a cleanser towel and began scrubbing his dirty face. "We have other weapons, even if they're not exclusive to us in the way lightsabers are. And the shields do nothing to affect our connection to the Force. With the Force as our ally, we're always strong."

"True, Padawan. Unfortunately, it's also true that you and I wound up cornered today, with no way out. We survived only because the Opposition intervened. Some Jedi become complacent—even arrogant—about the power the Force gives us. That power is great and profound, but it is not absolute. Never forget that."

Chastened, Obi-Wan nodded. "I won't. Still . . . I can't see the point of attempting to distribute a weapon that only works against the Jedi, but doesn't provide that much of an advantage against the Jedi, either. If we hadn't been so significantly outnumbered, the blackguards wouldn't have had much chance."

"A fair point," Qui-Gon conceded.

Obi-Wan, now deep in thought, went back to cleaning himself. Probably Qui-Gon should do the same; if his face was as begrimed as his hands, he was utterly filthy. Yet he couldn't ignore the waves of emotion rising within Rahara Wick. He sensed her pain, and her anger.

Although Pax Maripher was more deeply Force-blind than almost any other human Qui-Gon had encountered, he was capable of telling when something was wrong with Rahara. "What is it?" he said, his voice startlingly gentle. "Rahara?"

"Slaves," she said flatly. When she lifted her face from her knees, tears were welling in her dark eyes. "They want even more. It's not enough for Czerka that they already own millions upon millions of sentient beings, and the children they'll have, and the children *those* children will have. Czerka still wants more. Sometimes I think they want to own everyone in the galaxy."

"Allowing slavery as a sentence for crime is . . . abased, in the extreme." Qui-Gon shook his head. "That will be the first subject I take up with Rael Averross."

This placated Rahara not at all. "Yeah. Abased. In the extreme. But owning people who were born into forced labor—what, that's okay?"

Qui-Gon answered her gently. "Of course not. The Republic has abolished slavery."

"But the Republic doesn't force Czerka to stop using them, even in Republic space. They don't aggressively police trafficking on their borders. Why not?"

He sat for a few long moments, considering this, to be sure he was answering honestly. "The Jedi don't *make* the Republic do anything. We serve the Republic, not the other way around. But as to why the Republic doesn't act . . . I have no good answer for you."

Rahara wiped her cheek roughly, with the back of one hand. "If the Republic can't do something as decent and basic as attack slavery, why do we have a Republic to begin with?"

Qui-Gon repeated, "I have no good answer."

Enslavement was one of the evils that existed outside the Republic— a dirty fact of life there, one the Republic had never sought to eradicate. Some planets had never operated under any other system of labor. And different species interpreted slavery in different ways. The concept meant something rather different to humans than it did to, say, the T'zaki, insectoid beings who shared a hive mind. In the T'zaki language, the word *freedom* translated roughly as "purposelessness."

But for the overwhelming majority of sentients, slavery was deeply painful, and its operation extremely corrupt. Qui-Gon understood that the Republic's powers ended at its borders . . . but its influence did not. Surely that influence could be brought to bear more often, to help enslaved persons. Why had this never come to pass?

This rot has been festering within us from the beginning, he thought. *Little wonder Czerka has abused it.*

Was that something Qui-Gon had the power to change?

Rahara had pulled herself together somewhat. "So, am I right that you guys are going after Czerka?"

"In terms of ending their undue influence on this planet," Qui-Gon said, "yes."

"Then I want in." Her smile was as sharp as any blade. "Because there is nothing in this world I'd enjoy more than making Czerka run scared."

Qui-Gon expected Pax to protest about his safety, or the difficulty of taking on a corporation of such size, or simply for protest's sake. Instead, he grinned at Rahara. "Sounds like splendid fun to me."

Once the *Meryx* had dropped them off on Pijal, Obi-Wan and Qui-Gon hurried across the grassy plain where their personal ship waited. Pax and Rahara were decent pilots, but Obi-Wan looked forward to flying again, even if it was a simple in-atmosphere hop.

Though really, a flight like this one wasn't as much fun as riding the varactyl had been—

"All right," Qui-Gon said as they entered the vessel. "Let's get out of here."

Obi-Wan kept the ship low, skimming tree lines, dipping into any large clearing. Scanners stayed on auto-function, with Obi-Wan taking over only to ensure in-depth coverage of any hills that seemed likely to contain caves—which, on this moon, meant most of them. Qui-Gon remained silent for a long time, which Obi-Wan took as a sign of affirmation that he was doing the right thing.

Yet he proved to have misinterpreted Qui-Gon yet again.

After a long while, almost at the point of returning to Pijal, Qui-Gon said, "Padawan, do you remember what I said to you about my dream?"

Oh, no. He's been over there obsessing about prophecies? But Obi-Wan was determined to hear him out. "Yes, I recall, though you hadn't shared many details."

"I saw the treaty ceremony." Qui-Gon's voice was low, contemplative. "As vividly as though I were there, or more so. Yet there were surreal elements—screaming, blood. A vision of my lightsaber, brought up as though to block an attack. But maybe it was the treaty itself I was meant to be blocking."

Obi-Wan worded his response carefully. "That does sound rather . . . symbolic." Surely that was safe to say. Many dreams were symbolic.

To judge by his heavy sigh, Qui-Gon must've sensed Obi-Wan's uncertainty. He didn't seem to blame him. "Perhaps this is madness, or at least hubris. To believe that the Force is at work in all this. That it would be at work in me."

"The Force is in all things, Master." That much, Obi-Wan felt sure of. "I can't tell whether it has anything to do with your dream—yet it *is* present, guiding us, if we listen."

"Very true. But whom, or what, do I listen to? Can it possibly be that I should listen to my dream?"

Obi-Wan summoned his courage. "Right now, your dream agrees with your conscious mind. So I don't really see the conflict."

Qui-Gon shook his head, not at what Obi-Wan had said, but perhaps at some unheard dialogue within his own mind. "Visions from the Force always have a meaning deeper than what first appears. If this is a vision . . . then I must find what is hidden within it."

Qui-Gon sat in Dooku's quarters, alone in the dark, except for the light of the holocron.

Many months had passed since that fateful history assignment. Receiving top marks on his essay had only spurred his fascination. The prophecies had become nearly an obsession with him.

But it was an obsession not unlike those of other Padawans his age—who would review lightsaber holos for hours on end, or follow their favorite racer pilots and boast in any victories. Qui-Gon never spoke of it, not out of any sense of shame or wrongdoing, only because Rael had suggested Master Dooku's opinions about the prophecies and mystics were complicated.

Had he been afraid of being caught, he would've been more cautious. He wouldn't have taken the holocron to Dooku's quarters to study it in private. And certainly he would never have become so enraptured with the prophecies that he lost all track of time and was still at it when Dooku returned home. When the door slid open, Qui-Gon turned to say hello to his Master as usual. Only the expression on Dooku's face told him he'd made a mistake.

"What," Dooku said, pronouncing every word distinctly, "is the meaning of this?"

By now Qui-Gon knew it was better to admit any mistake or doubt to Master Dooku immediately; he respected forthrightness, and besides, he'd always figure it out in the end. "It's the holocron of prophecy, Master. I studied it for a class project, and since then I've been—" What was the right word? "—interested."

Dooku came into the room then, shrugging off his dark robe. He stared at the holocron, not with anger, but with a fascination Qui-Gon recognized. "Padawan, such knowledge is . . . tempting, but it is also dangerous."

"Why? I know you said wanting to see the future could lead to the dark side, but I don't think it's doing that to me." Like any other adolescent with an obsession, Qui-Gon dug in. "It's even made me a better student! You can ask my history teachers, both Jedi history and galactic—"

"Your teachers' opinions are irrelevant in this matter. They don't know the prophecies as I do. They haven't studied them as I have. They cannot know the risks."

Even as Dooku pronounced such dire judgment, he kept walking toward the holocron. Its glow fell on him as he stared at it. Qui-Gon couldn't read that stare. Was his Master in pain? Was he in awe? With Master Dooku, those reactions weren't so different.

"I'll take the holocron back," Qui-Gon promised. That was the only thing he could think of to do. "I won't ever bring it here again, I promise."

"My worry is not that you're studying the holocron here, it's that you're studying it at all," Dooku said. He didn't sound as angry anymore, though. Maybe he was calming down. Qui-Gon hoped so. "You'll keep looking at it, won't you? Regardless of what I tell you."

Disappointment made Qui-Gon slump in his chair. "I won't disobey you, Master. If you tell me not to study the holocron, I'll leave it alone for as long as I'm your Padawan."

Dooku drew himself upright, folding his arms. "Which means you'll study it thereafter?"

Qui-Gon hadn't thought that far ahead, but now that he did— "Maybe," he admitted. "If I'm still interested."

"You will be." Dooku walked away from him, staring out the window at the bustle of Coruscant.

After a long pause, Qui-Gon realized his Master would say nothing more. He closed the holocron and left Dooku's quarters, determined to go straight to the Archives with it, and never to disappoint his Master again.

That night, however, Qui-Gon couldn't rest.

The holocron contains the prophecies. And the prophecies tell us the future. How could anyone not want to know the future, if they could? He flopped over in his bed, groaning. *That isn't the dark side. That's just being* awake, *isn't it?*

Qui-Gon had already made so many connections that he thought might be borne out. It was a mistake, he thought, assuming that the prophecies still referred to his future; they'd been made nearly ten thousand years ago, and surely some had since come to pass. The prophecy about the woman who was born to and would give birth to darkness—that might refer to an ancient duchess of Malastare whose father had waged wars that were vicious even by Malastarian standards, and whose daughter had become a Dark Jedi. Another prophecy said the Sith would disappear yet appear again. Most of the notes on this prophecy interpreted it as the potential reincarnation of the Sith Order, but Qui-Gon wondered whether it might not be referring to a specific Sith, a legendary Darth Wrend, who had been believed dead but returned to wage war against the Jedi once more . . .

But he shouldn't even be thinking about that. Not if he wanted to be a good apprentice to Dooku.

Qui-Gon pulled his blankets over his head and tried to go to sleep.

The next morning, sleepy and grumpy, Qui-Gon made himself presentable and headed to Dooku's quarters. He expected another lecture, and maybe even some extra duties as penance. *As my Master wills it,* he thought to himself.

But when he walked through the door, he saw Dooku sitting at the same table Qui-Gon had been sitting at the day before—with the holocron of prophecy open in front of him. In its golden light, Dooku's face looked younger than Qui-Gon had ever seen it.

"Padawan," Dooku said. "It occurs to me that if you'll be studying this anyway—it only makes sense for you to do so with the proper guidance. Someone to make sure you don't go too far."

Qui-Gon grinned. "You mean, you'll teach me yourself?"

"It's my responsibility," Dooku replied. "As your Master." He never looked away from the holocron.

CHAPTER TWENTY-FOUR

———————— ✦ ————————

"All hail Her Serene Highness!" called the tribune.

Cheers rose from the crowd within the central metropolitan dome of the capital city—a gathering as large and cheerful as any Rael Averross had seen in his eight years on Pijal.

He'd personally seen to it.

Averross stood on the hover platform with Fanry, watching her wave to her subjects. She had been kept sequestered in the palace complex for most of her youth, meaning she was still somewhat awkward at such huge public gatherings. It was perhaps Averross's final duty as regent to help Fanry get accustomed to the role of queen. Even a constitutional monarch had to be able to own the spotlight.

Certainly Fanry looked the part. Her dress and headscarf were a pale enough green to meet Pijali standards of outer plainness, but the rich gold embroidery glinted subtly in the dome lights. She held herself proud and tall . . . well, as tall as the little thing could manage.

Cady helped her up on a step, where the princess could be better seen by the crowd.

The rally had been extensively promoted—Averross had seen to that—and Czerka Corporation had even been sharp enough to offer free transportation for those from outer provinces. Many of these cheering, flag-waving citizens had bustled off Czerka ships just a few hours ago, eager for their first trip to the capital dome. And every single one of them had been searched and scanned. No slicer darts would get inside today.

Cam droids hovered around the platform, getting good footage of the striking young princess who would soon be Pijal's queen. Averross had made good and sure none of them focused on him for long. It had been a long time since public attention had been welcome.

In his mind, a memory flickered: *The Council chambers. Yoda shaking his head sorrowfully. "Mourn we, Nim Pianna's death. Too soon, and unnecessary it was." Walking along the Temple corridors afterward, stares burning into him like lasers, hearing echoes of Nim in the voice of every Padawan, his already depthless anguish somehow made worse by the knowledge that every single person around him blamed him as much as he blamed himself—they'd never wanted him here, never thought he belonged, and his failure had proved them right—*

Averross snapped out of it. This wasn't about Nim, not any longer. It was about Fanry.

Guard platforms hovered around the edge of the crowd as the royal orchestras began warming up for the celebration concert. Captain Deren rode atop the largest one, his vigilant eyes forever examining the perimeters. As Averross watched, Deren suddenly straightened, as though in alarm—then relaxed. Averross followed the captain's gaze to another platform that had just entered the arena. *Good. It's just Qui-Gon and Obi-Wan. Maybe they've had some luck up there on the moon, dragging Opposition scum out in the open.*

Once Fanry had been guided to the royal box, Cady carrying her train, Averross gestured that he'd return later. Listening to fancy music never was one of his favorite pastimes, and he wanted to hear what Qui-Gon had learned.

So he thought.

"And you *believed* that?" Rael said, pacing in front of Qui-Gon. "A bunch of blaster-carrying thugs surround you in the forest, and then they tell you they're not actually dangerous, and you bought every word of it?"

"I'm not naïve," Qui-Gon replied. "Obviously Halin Azucca's story has to be thoroughly questioned. But a group of performance artists isn't what I'd call 'thugs.' And everything she said fits the fact patterns we'd observed before."

Rael shot back, "You mean, the lady knows how to tell a really good lie."

Qui-Gon had known this would surprise Rael; he hadn't understood that it would enrage him. He took a moment to be grateful that he'd sent Obi-Wan back to the palace; apparently he'd need to draw on their old friendship to get through to Rael at all, and that was more easily done with his apprentice absent.

However, Obi-Wan had accompanied Qui-Gon as far as the dome perimeter, so he, too, had seen the jarring artificiality of this ceremony. Protesters were relatively few, but they'd been cordoned off into an area that allowed them no access to the interior of the dome. The final attendees had been filtering in as he and Obi-Wan arrived, collecting flags, banners, and other previously prepared items to show their support for the princess and the Governance Treaty. To judge by their smiles, Qui-Gon suspected the attendees genuinely were happy about the coming changes—but this group had nonetheless been carefully curated to present a uniformity of opinion that didn't actually exist.

How many of the Pijali understand Czerka's role in all this? he wondered. *How many of them have lost friends or relatives to slavery?* Probably a great many, none of whom were inside the dome.

Rael had brought them to an antechamber at the rim of the dome for their conversation. It was a small space, cramped and claustrophobic. Or maybe it just felt that way, with Rael's fury so great that it drew the air out of the room.

"They admitted they were behind some of it," Rael said, still pacing. "Admitted it. And you're still trying to give them a free pass."

"They admitted to political stunts. Not any acts of violence. And as I see it, the fact that they admitted to some crimes makes their denial of the others more persuasive, not less," Qui-Gon said.

Rael's first response was a sneer. "As you see it. You always had a weakness for seeing what you wanted to see, Qui-Gon. Always were a soft touch for a sad story. Halin Azucca sized you up pretty good."

This wasn't entirely untrue. Qui-Gon refused to be ashamed of it. "I attempt to understand the viewpoints of everyone I deal with. That's not a weakness. It's how I operate. And I've learned more that way than I ever would by being too quick to cast blame."

"Best-case scenario, they're still criminals," Rael retorted, "and I don't believe in her best-case scenario. So why are you in here arguing their case?"

"Because I've undertaken a preliminary review of the treaty, and it appears to me that many of the Opposition's criticisms are well founded. If the phrase 'preserved as the sun preserves the moon' means what she claims it means—that it means forever, beyond amendment—then the treaty is deeply flawed." Qui-Gon currently had Obi-Wan doing a much more thorough review, so tomorrow he'd be able to raise specific objections. For today, he just wanted to get Rael to listen. "There *isn't* much representation of lunar citizens in the proposed Assembly—"

"The moon is ruled by Pijal! Always has been!" Rael's voice had taken on a thick veneer of contempt. "Since when does our mandate as Jedi allow us to change the way things have always been done on a planet?"

"You're lord regent, Rael. The Council wouldn't have named you to the position and expected you to do nothing. Your mandate is to help govern a world! And if you're willing to shift from an absolute monarchy to a constitutional one, why shouldn't the status of lunar citizens be reexamined as well?"

"Because that's not how things work here. Fanry's still going to be queen, of both Pijal *and* its moon."

Rael was smarter than this; his zeal to preserve Fanry's power and status had gotten the better of him. Qui-Gon had to find a way to get past his anger. Then, perhaps, Rael would listen. He needed to turn the discussion to something further from the princess.

"The treaty tacitly gives Czerka Corporation immense power," Qui-Gon began. "Their contracts will effectively be enshrined in law."

"So what? Czerka might be even older than the Republic. They've got contracts all over the galaxy. That's probably never going to change, not on Pijal or anywhere else," Rael said.

"Czerka's not in charge of the penal system all over the galaxy. They're not claiming every planet's citizens as forced labor."

Rael scoffed. "Pijal's hardly the only planet that punishes crime with long terms of labor."

"That doesn't make it right," Qui-Gon said. "And this isn't just 'long term.' It's *permanent.*"

This made no impression. "Is this your first time on the fringes of the Republic? Is this seriously the first time you've seen proof that this exists? Because, if not, I don't know where this attitude is comin' from."

Qui-Gon paused. "Punishing crime with forced labor isn't traditional on Pijal. You yourself just said, you're not here to change the way things have always been done—"

"And you yourself just tried to make me change things!" Rael's face had flushed as deep a red as it did in battle. "Listen, Qui-Gon, you're not here to help draft the treaty. That's already been done, and done well, with no assistance from you. You're here to make sure the treaty gets signed. Because until that treaty is signed, Fanry doesn't have the authority to make permanent agreements with other worlds. Once the new Assembly has that authority, they can establish the hyperspace corridor. And once that's done, Pijal has a new future. Fanry can rule on a world that's safe, and stable, and prosperous. I've done everything in my power to create that for her, and I don't understand why you want to interfere with that."

Qui-Gon waited several seconds before responding. "As you said, the treaty's already been drafted. Who drafted it, Rael?"

That finally made Rael pause. "Okay, so, we had some help from the local Czerka supervisor. But Meritt Col's solid. She's done a lot of good on Pijal—"

"Perhaps, incidentally," Qui-Gon said. "But I assure you, she's only ever been working for the benefit of Czerka Corporation. Not for the good of this planet."

"In this case, they're one and the same," Rael insisted.

Qui-Gon held on to his temper only with the greatest difficulty. "That's not possible."

Music began filtering into the room from the dome; apparently the orchestra had begun playing the triumphal symphony composed for Fanry's coronation. The gentle strains of the overture almost seemed to be mocking their anger.

Rael finally said, "Czerka's authority helps the treaty. The treaty helps Fanry hold on to the most important parts of her royal power while allowing her to finally have a halfway normal life. So I'm not backing down."

"Your role as lord regent is about more than protecting the princess." Sorrowfully, Qui-Gon shook his head. "You have a responsibility to all the citizens of Pijal, including those who live on its moon."

"You know who I don't have a responsibility to? Terrorists that have already bombed multiple municipal buildings and are going to try to interfere with the treaty—the same treaty that's going to guarantee a good future for Fanry and for Pijal." Rael lifted his chin. "And I don't have a responsibility to anybody who tries to get in the treaty's way."

A rap on the door startled them both. Qui-Gon turned to see Meritt Col walking in, wearing her best suit and an obsequious smile. "Lord Regent. The music has already begun. We're expecting you in the

Czerka box—since, after all, you wanted Fanry to have the spotlight to herself during the concert—"

"Yeah," Rael said. "She deserves it. Let's go."

Qui-Gon could only watch as Rael offered his arm to the Czerka supervisor and walked away.

CHAPTER TWENTY-FIVE

⸺ ⟁ ⸺

After the capital dome event, the palace turned chilly—in a way that had nothing to do with drafts or the sharp winds from the sea. Princess Fanry herself seemed oblivious to any strife, but Rael Averross's rage had shifted from hot to cold. From his long experience with Rael, Qui-Gon knew this was a dangerous shift.

If he didn't need me to ratify the Governance Treaty in two days, Qui-Gon thought, *Rael would throw us out of the palace tonight.*

And surely Rael suspected that Qui-Gon now hoped *not* to ratify that treaty.

Meeting with Obi-Wan in the palace library afterward only confirmed his worst fears. "These are the 'official' census results," his Padawan said, bringing up the charts on a datapad screen. "But by going into local census records, I was able to pull other sets of numbers—which I suspect are more accurate. It turns out Halin Azucca was wrong about twenty-five percent of Pijali citizens living on the moon—it's closer to thirty percent."

Although Obi-Wan spoke in a low voice, every word echoed slightly in the cavernous, marble-tiled library. The room showed signs of infrequent use—dusty windowpanes, out-of-date data solids, no resident droids to speak of—but it was hard not to feel paranoid that someone might be spying on them. Rael Averross, Halin Azucca, the mysterious blackguards: All of them would have their reasons for wanting to eavesdrop on the Jedi, and for planning to intervene if they didn't like what they heard.

Besides, there was still a traitor in their midst.

Qui-Gon scratched his beard, as he often did when deep in thought. "In other words, this treaty gives the vote to seventy percent of the people of the Pijal system, while nearly disenfranchising the other thirty percent."

"Exactly. And that doesn't even count those they've enslaved." Obi-Wan pressed the datapad to bring up holographic data. "As for the role Czerka Corporation plays in Pijal, everything we've been told is true. Averross didn't start the process of allowing Czerka to take over so many parts of the government—they've been here for generations—but he definitely accelerated it. And yes, the phrase about the sun preserving the moon turns out to be legally binding in a very permanent sense. The Governance Treaty would set Czerka's monopoly here in stone."

"I can understand why Averross wouldn't know the traditional power of that phrase. What I can't understand is why he let anyone else draft the constitution, much less anyone from Czerka. And yet he did it out of loyalty to the princess." Qui-Gon still felt guilt about the many failures he'd had as Obi-Wan's Master . . . but at least he hadn't smothered him in falsehoods, as Rael had Fanry. The very acts Rael thought were for her benefit were the ones that would mire her rule and her planet in corruption.

Obi-Wan's voice broke his reverie. "How do we proceed, Master?"

"We begin by contacting the Jedi Council," Qui-Gon said. How odd, to think that someday soon he would be the one other Jedi contacted for advice. That his judgment would supersede that of the individuals who were on the scene, actually dealing with the problems at hand. "I'll handle that myself. You get some rest. It was a hard day for you."

"I'm still shaking dust out of my clothes," Obi-Wan confessed. "A bath has never sounded so good."

He could joke about nearly dying in a sinkhole, not even six hours after the event. Qui-Gon once again realized what a fine Padawan he'd had, and what a shame it was they'd failed to get on.

Just before Obi-Wan reached the door, Qui-Gon called, "Padawan?" Obi-Wan half turned to listen as Qui-Gon continued, "Sorry to stick you with yet more library duty."

He was answered with a broad smile. "Compared with clinging to a log for dear life, research isn't half bad."

What was evening for the palace of Pijal turned out to be the middle of the night for the Jedi Temple. Only one member was available to speak immediately, but it was the one member whose judgment was most likely to be final.

"*Troubling, this is,*" Yoda said. "*To Chancellor Kaj, I must speak.*"

Of course—Kaj would've reviewed the treaty. But she wouldn't have understood the full meaning of that ritual phrase, and so hadn't seen the trouble it would cause. "Do you think she'll withdraw the treaty? Or at least ensure amendments?"

Yoda's ears drooped. "*Difficult to say. Ready to retire, the chancellor is. Surrounded by planetary ministers, corporate interests, and others who desire her influence in the final days of her rule. Complications in this matter will not be easily brought to her attention.*"

"Something must be done," Qui-Gon said. "I cannot in good conscience represent the Republic at the ceremony, not unless the treaty is changed."

"*Careful, Qui-Gon.*" Yoda's holographic image blurred momentarily as the tiny Jedi Master adjusted himself in his bowl chair. "*Jeopardize the hyperspace corridor, you must not.*"

"The hyperspace . . . ? Master Yoda, forgive me, but are you putting the profit of corporations ahead of the people of Pijal?" Qui-Gon had long thought the Council was in danger of losing its way, but this was colder than he would've imagined possible.

Yoda pulled himself upright, ears rising. *"Serve planets long cut off, this corridor will. Planets struggling with poverty and famine. Will you save Pijal at the cost of their lives? Is this how you will serve the Force?"*

"Forgive me. I spoke in haste." And, Qui-Gon knew, in repressed anger at Yoda's *no* vote against him. That was unworthy of them both, and he strove to set the feeling aside. "However, the essential problem remains. We cannot neglect others to save Pijal, but in turn, we cannot neglect Pijal to save others."

"Reason with Averross, you cannot," Yoda said in a tone that suggested long experience. *"This assignment—we thought to help him. Always he has felt himself to be alone. To be judged and found wanting. Thought we that as regent, he would struggle no more for status. His pride would be fed. Instead, it has only fueled his weaknesses."*

Qui-Gon thought again of the laughing young man who had stood by him before he went into his first battle. At the time, Rael Averross had seemed like the bravest, best Jedi Knight the Order could produce. Qui-Gon had been too young to see the cracks in the bravado—the pain that all Dooku's guidance and all Rael's accomplishments had never been able to erase. "That he would effectively sell citizens into slavery—"

"Grievous, this is," Yoda agreed.

Into Qui-Gon's mind came the echo of Rahara Wick: *What's the point of having a Republic in the first place?*

"We should put an end to it," he said.

Yoda shook his head. *"Not ours to decide, the fate of the treaty is—"*

"Not the treaty. Slavery." Qui-Gon folded his hands in front of him, allowing the robes to obscure them—the most formal way in which a Jedi could address another. "Why do we allow this barbarism to flourish? The Republic could use its influence to promote abolition in countless systems where the practice flourishes. How can we fail to do this?"

Yoda remained silent for a few moments before saying, *"Know of the planet Uro, do you? Devour their weakest children, they do."*

"... they're arachnids, whose instincts are unstoppable."

"*What of Byss?*" When Qui-Gon shook his head no, Yoda said, "*When their elderly grow too old to regenerate, beat them to death, the Abyssin do, to conserve their resources.*"

Qui-Gon's patience began to wear thin. "This isn't about imposing human ethics on nonhuman species. This is something humans do to one another, an atrocity we should put an end to."

"*We? Not the chancellor, not the Galactic Senate, not even the people of the Republic, but the Jedi?*" Yoda thumped his gimer stick on the floor. "*Want to rule, do you? Dangerous this is, in one who would join the Council. Dangerous it is in any Jedi.*"

Qui-Gon knew all of this. On one level, he accepted the truth of it. On the other—"If we don't stand for the right, what *do* we do? Why do we exist?"

"*Many ways there are of serving the right,*" Yoda replied. "*We work within our mandates, and there do as much good as we can. To do otherwise, to substitute our judgment for that of the Republic, is to repeat the mistakes of the past.*"

So instead we make different mistakes in the present? Qui-Gon kept this to himself. A galactic crusade against slavery beyond the reaches of the Republic would need to be larger than one angry Jedi Knight. But enslavement here on Pijal . . . *that* was within his mandate. And it would not stand.

He said only, "You'll talk to the chancellor as soon as possible?"

Yoda nodded. "*Well you have done, to reveal the shortcomings of the treaty.*"

Praise from Yoda was rare, and Qui-Gon tried to take satisfaction in it.

Yet it was difficult for him to go to sleep that night.

He stood in the Celestial Chalice, the curved amphitheater to the ancient gods within the Pijali palace. This was the place for the treaty ceremony, and everything was about to begin.

Fanry walked toward him, her dress shining white, her brilliant red hair hanging free, her clothing all the more vivid against the dark-blue-tiled floor of the Chalice—

—and everything went mad, turned into a jumble Qui-Gon couldn't comprehend. People screamed. Minister Orth pushed roughly through the crowd, toward the altar. Rael shouted, "Fanry, no!" Qui-Gon brought up his lightsaber, ready to strike—but at what? At whom? Something had to be done—

Qui-Gon opened his eyes. He lay in his bed, far from the Celestial Chalice. It felt as though he had traveled through time and back again. The events yet to come were more real to him than the sheets, the mattress, the sound of his own breath.

Another vision granted by the Force, he thought. *No. More of the same vision. Another angle. A deeper look.*

Maybe. Or maybe he was only dreaming. There was no way to tell—or was there?

He put on his robe and hurried out into the palace corridors. This late at night, they were utterly deserted, save for one astromech burbling along the floor on its errands. Qui-Gon's feet, still bare, were chilled by the marble floors, and when he went by the windows, he heard the soft rushing of the tides.

During their first day on Pijal, Rael had talked Qui-Gon and Obi-Wan through the details of the ceremony, gesturing toward two large, plain wooden doors at the end of the royal reception hall. Those doors opened onto a tunnel, which led directly to the Celestial Chalice. They were opened only when the monarch went to the Chalice for one of the momentous ceremonies that took place only two or three times in a reign.

Luckily, the hinges were kept oiled.

As he walked into the tunnel, two sentry droids with Czerka logos scanned him. They weren't programmed to ask questions, only to recognize previously approved individuals and attack all others. Qui-Gon felt relieved he'd already been entered into the system . . . and that Rael Averross's temper hadn't led to his deletion. Yet.

The tunnel was dark, illuminated only by a few candledroids spaced far apart. But everything the tunnel lacked in visibility, it provided in audibility. Qui-Gon heard other footsteps ahead of him—coming his way. He readied himself, one hand on his lightsaber's hilt—

Someone yelped in fright, then swore, "Sacred *bats,* what are you doing here?"

"Minister Orth?" Qui-Gon stepped forward to see her, still wearing her bronze-colored court dress from earlier in the evening. "I might ask you the same question."

"I'm double-checking security procedures," she snapped. "It's too important a job to be left to Czerka droids."

"I quite agree."

"You haven't answered my question." Orth folded her arms in front of her chest. "What are you doing here?"

". . . I wanted to have a look at the Celestial Chalice for myself, before the ceremony."

"You could've had anyone give you a tour during the day," Orth said, "which would make sense and provide a better view. But as you will."

She hustled back toward the palace, apparently satisfied with his explanation. Qui-Gon wondered if he should be satisfied with hers.

He continued on until he reached the other set of doors, which were carved of the same smooth white stone found on the cliffs by the sea. These swung open easily at his touch, revealing the Celestial Chalice in all its glory.

And Qui-Gon had seen it before.

The gilding around the lower edges of the domed ceiling, the octagonal altar, the arrangement of the seats around it—every single detail matched. When he looked down at his own bare feet, he saw the bright-blue tile beneath them.

It was exactly like this in my dream, he thought, then caught himself. What Qui-Gon had experienced was no dream. It was a vision.

CHAPTER TWENTY-SIX

"I will not take part in the treaty ceremony," Qui-Gon said. "The Republic will have no representative, and therefore the treaty cannot go forward."

Were the stakes any less important, he might have been amused by the reactions around the banquet table. Obi-Wan's eyes widened. Minister Orth dropped her knife. Captain Deren squinted at Qui-Gon as though his vision had suddenly gone blurry. Little Fanry bit her lip, maybe not to smile at the astonished adults around her.

Rael, as expected, was furious. Rising to his feet, he said, "You raised your objections yesterday, Qui-Gon. I told you then, it's not your decision to make—"

"This isn't about my personal opinion. It's about a vision of the future—a warning—given to me by the Force." Remembering the images from his dream, and the sheer feeling of horror that bound them together, steeled him against any objections. Qui-Gon knew what he knew.

"Why did I ever show you those prophecies?" Rael shook his head as he paced the length of the table. "Dooku had the sense to keep them from you, but I didn't know any better. I figured you were smart enough to tell legend from fact. I assumed you weren't a fool who'd lose your head over other Jedi's visions, much less your own. Well, Qui-Gon, you proved me wrong."

Minister Orth put her head in one hand. "*Prophecies?* This just keeps getting worse."

Was it still possible to reach Rael on any level at all? If so, Qui-Gon knew, it would be in their shared past. "You showed me the work of the ancient Jedi mystics—the work you collected with our Master—because it expanded your understanding of the Force, and helped to expand mine. Dooku believed in them. Will you call him a fool, too?"

Orth said, "Who is this . . . Dooky?"

From her place at her gilded chair, mouth full of breakfast, Fanry said, "*Dooku.* I've heard lots of stories about him. He taught Rael and Qui-Gon both. But I don't think he's a Jedi anymore."

Rael gestured at the child. "That's right. Dooku *left* the Order, because he got sick and tired of the hypocrisy—the judgment—all of it."

"I don't know why Dooku left the Order," Qui-Gon said, "and neither do you. What I do know is that I've had two separate visions that predict disaster at the treaty ceremony."

Captain Deren finally spoke. "What kind of disaster?"

Qui-Gon admitted, "It's unclear."

"Unclear." With one fist, Rael pounded the table. "You want to sabotage the coronation and the hyperspace corridor for something that's 'unclear.' "

"What's not unclear is the screaming I hear in the visions." Qui-Gon looked around the banqueting table, piled high with more breakfast than a dozen courts could ever eat, making eye contact with each person in turn. "Nor fighting with a lightsaber. Nor blood on the floor of the Celestial Chalice. And if any of you could feel the fear and despair that came with that vision—that is as much a part of it as any image or sound—you wouldn't doubt this any more than I do."

Minister Orth put her hands on her hips. "I ran into you last night headed to the Celestial Chalice. Are you sure you weren't sleepwalking?"

"No, Minister. I was checking details from my vision against the reality of the Chalice. Even though I had never been inside it before, I had seen it all, precisely as it is, down to the tiles on the floor."

"*Cool*," Fanry breathed. "Does that mean we can't have a treaty ceremony?"

"We're signing the treaty!" Rael insisted. "On schedule, as planned. The Jedi Council will soon set Qui-Gon right."

Qui-Gon had not yet shared his vision with the Council, nor did he intend to. They would spend all their time bickering about the viability of the hyperspace corridor. They were too bound to Coruscant. Too bound to the chancellor. Too far from the living Force.

They were no longer the sort of Jedi who could trust in a pure vision.

It shocked him that he *was* that Jedi. That he could still find it in him to believe so profoundly, so unshakably, in pure mysticism. Qui-Gon had often felt out of step with the Order as a whole, but never to this degree.

He had also never felt this close to the Force.

Rahara Wick had received instructions from Qui-Gon Jinn the day before, requesting that the *Meryx* check out the Czerka landing pads throughout this section of the moon. She would've done it anyway. How could she mess up Czerka's plans on this moon if she didn't know more about what those plans were?

As she'd expected, Pax was less excited about their task. "I don't like this."

"Have you ever liked anything, ever, since our journeys began? Besides finding jewels, I mean."

"You say that as though finding jewels were incidental to our travels, rather than the *entire point*. But I digress." Despite his complaints, Pax had already laid in a course to the nearest Czerka facility and was already steering them in that direction. "We agreed to help the Jedi, not do their dirty work for them."

"That's before any of us knew we'd be going up against Czerka Corporation," Rahara said, rubbing absently at the back of her left hand. "If we're taking Czerka on, we can't be scared of a little dirty work."

Soon the Czerka facility came up on the scanners, then became visible to the naked eye. Rahara began working with instruments to zero in on as many details as possible.

"Looks like they've rerouted almost all energy from this hemisphere's solar generators straight to their own places," she muttered. "And check out those shipment cases. What's in those?"

Pax examined the readings before she could. "Ores, mostly. Not stuff found near the surface, either. These mines delve deep—perhaps halfway to the moon's core. Rather drastic."

Rahara nodded slowly as she recognized some of the mining droids rolling about, models she'd been familiar with since childhood. "Czerka's willing to dig the heart out of a world, as long as it makes them a credit or two. The shafts get colder and colder the farther they drill down. Then it starts getting warm again, and you know they're going too deep—and if they ever weaken the layer beneath you too much, the magma could boil up through it, and—" She stopped herself. "That never happened to me, obviously. But I always knew it could."

Once, after her escape, Rahara allowed herself to research exactly what happened to human workers in a shaft exposed to magma. She'd thought knowing the details would exorcise the nightmares she'd always had about it. That had been a mistake. The details only made the dreams more real, and more horrifying.

"Oh, dear." Pax leaned closer, getting between her and the dashboard. Before she could review for him the concept of "personal space" and why people shouldn't invade it, he said, "We appear to have, ah, new workers coming in."

It felt as though she were back in one of the cold mineshafts again, numb all over, surrounded by darkness. "You mean new slaves."

He nodded. "Don't look," he said, in the gentle tone of voice he used so seldom. "If it will hurt you—"

"It will," Rahara said. "But I'm gonna look."

Pax grimaced. "Willingly inflicting pain on oneself is irrational—outside certain fetishistic pursuits, I mean."

"These people deserve a witness. They deserve to have someone who cares see exactly what's happening."

Slowly, Pax nodded and leaned away from her, allowing her a view of the facility's perimeter, where a large tram had been parked. Sentry droids were herding dozens of people into the warehouse; that was probably where they'd be implanted with the Czerka tag. Some of the people were crying, but most of them looked dazed and exhausted, unable to process what was happening to them. They had on the telltale gray coveralls, still crisp and new. Rahara had worn most of hers until they were threadbare.

These people are criminals, part of her mind said. It seemed easier to blame these people in some way than to relive her own past. *They actually did something to get in this mess. They weren't born into it, like you were.*

Didn't matter. Nobody deserved to live like that. No one.

"That tram must've come in from the nearest town," Rahara said. Her voice didn't tremble; she was proud of that. "We ought to go there and check it out. Land, walk around, talk to some people. We might learn a lot."

Pax replied, "I bought you a gift."

She leaned back in her seat and closed her eyes. Awkward conversational segues were one of Pax's specialties, but this one was spectacularly weird. "Since when do we buy each other gifts?" Was he rethinking the whole rational-co-workers-do-not-get-romantically-involved thing? That wasn't something she could deal with right now.

"I propose that we buy each other gifts," he said, "when we see the other has a need that has not been met." After some fishing around in the cluttered cockpit storage compartment, he withdrew a slim rectangular box and presented it to her.

Rahara opened it, less curious than resigned, and saw—a pair of gloves.

Beautiful gloves. Gundark leather, she thought, tinted a blue so dark it looked almost black. When Rahara slipped her left hand into one, she realized the lining was some kind of shimmersilk; it was soft against the ever-tender scar. These were probably the nicest things she'd ever owned.

But it wouldn't have mattered if they'd been a pair of Gamorrean underwear. The gloves were a way to protect her from Czerka, and a way to help her feel less afraid. That was what made her choke up.

"I got them yesterday evening, when I took the *Facet* to pick up more supplies." Pax looked from her face to the gloves and back again, unsure what to make of her silence. "You, ah—you like them?"

"They're wonderful," Rahara said hoarsely. She gave him a watery smile. "You have your moments, Pax."

"Bosh," he said. "I'm marvelous all the time. This is simply one of those occasions when you've noticed."

There were undoubtedly many, many factors Qui-Gon had taken into account when he decided to make his announcement over breakfast. Obi-Wan knew that.

He also knew that a factor Qui-Gon had *not* taken into account was how thoroughly he would ruin his Padawan's day.

"You work for a highly unstable individual," Minister Orth said, more than an hour after Qui-Gon had made his announcement and left. "Do you know this, Mister Kenobi?"

Of all the complaints Obi-Wan had ever had about Qui-Gon, *unstable* wasn't one of them. "This is very unusual for him," he said, as tactfully as he could manage.

Rael Averross had spent most of this time trying to convince Princess Fanry that this was, in fact, a very serious problem. (Fanry seemed amused by the whole thing . . . which, given that her elders were all losing their tempers and looking foolish, maybe wasn't so surprising.) However, now Averross turned on Obi-Wan, dark eyes blazing. "When did he revert to his childhood, huh? When did he decide all that prophecy nonsense was real?"

"As far as I can tell," Obi-Wan said, "this morning."

Though Qui-Gon had, in fact, been talking about the possibility of a future vision for a couple of days now. His general interest in the prophecies had been growing for some months. Was it possible his Master had lost his objectivity? Even lost his way?

Obi-Wan felt queasy. Padawans weren't supposed to be more objective than their Masters. Their Masters were meant to guide them, to always be the stronger, surer ones. This dynamic had been reversed, and it discomfited him as much as zero-gravity had, when he'd hardly known which way was up.

"We need to know whether the coronation and treaty ceremony are taking place as scheduled," Captain Deren said in his deep gravelly voice. He, alone of all the people in the banquet hall, remained calm. "And we need that information as soon as possible. Otherwise, I can't take proper security measures."

"It's happening," Averross growled. "Trust me on that. Qui-Gon Jinn is going to get his head on straight, or—"

"Let me talk to him," Obi-Wan said. Qui-Gon and Averross would only clash more stridently in future versions of this argument, and would make little progress. "He might share more of his thoughts with me, as his Padawan."

Slowly, Averross nodded. Minister Orth said, "I'm glad you understand him, because nobody else does."

Obi-Wan's heart sank. He never had figured Qui-Gon out—but today, maybe for the last time, he had to try.

"I'm in pursuit!" Qui-Gon shouted into his comlink, hoping his voice would carry over the rush of air around his speeder bike as he swerved through jungle foliage. "Track me!"

His voice cracked on the last word. *Great,* he thought, but there was no time to dwell on anything except the chase.

He and Dooku were part of a Numidian Prime strike team, organized to find the notorious bounty hunter Shenda Mol. She collected her bounties not by murdering individuals—which would've been bad enough—but by sabotaging passenger ships, detonating devices in crowded public areas, or once even releasing a deadly virus. Tens of thousands of deaths on fifty different planets were, for Mol, no more than collateral damage.

The Jedi had tracked her to Numidian Prime, where she had a small stronghold and a handful of followers. But the followers had all been apprehended now, and it was up to Qui-Gon and his Master to bring in Mol herself.

He gunned his speeder bike, trying to fly over the thick jungle underbrush but under the heavy palm leaves. Qui-Gon's Padawan braid streamed behind him, and he wished he'd worn goggles to protect his stinging eyes.

No time for that. He crested the hill, which revealed the stony valley where they'd detected Mol's hideout. Qui-Gon pulled back on speed, bringing his speeder bike to as quiet a stop as possible. From now on he'd travel on foot.

Numidian Prime could be a swampy, treacherous world, but Shenda Mol had hidden herself on high ground. Qui-Gon could walk silently on leaves and vines that were still soft and green. Other than a few birds circling overhead, no fauna seemed to be in the area. Keeping one hand on his lightsaber, he pulled out his scanner to make sure he was heading toward the right coordinates.

A few large, stony hills provided the likeliest place for Mol's hideout. Qui-Gon paused at the foot of one of them to put away his scanner and prepare for an altercation. Dooku would be along any moment now, but there was no guaranteeing his target wouldn't be—

"Don't move," said Shenda Mol. She leaned against a rock formation a few meters up the hill, and pointed her blaster at his head.

Qui-Gon went still. His hand remained on his lightsaber; against an ordinary opponent, he would've trusted himself to pull his weapon in time to block blasterfire. But this was Shenda Mol. She was a Falleen, with ultra-fast reptilian reflexes—and even among the Falleen, her reputation as a sharpshooter was unparalleled.

"Tell me something," he said, remaining motionless. "I've always heard you had perfect aim—"

"You heard right." She tossed her head; her long black ponytail fell across her green shoulder. "If you doubt it, make a move and find out."

Qui-Gon had no intention of making a move . . . yet. "If you can target any individual from a tremendous distance, why do you resort to bombs or viruses? Why do you kill thousands when you could kill only one?"

Mol smiled. "I have a little game I play. I need more kills to win—though, of course, I'm only competing with myself. That's the only competition that really matters, you know. More people ought to understand that."

Dooku would be along at any moment, he reminded himself. Master Dooku would've been tracking his speeder bike. All Qui-Gon needed to do was stall Mol for a brief time.

"You're one of the trainees, aren't you?" She cocked her head, studying him. "Not much of a catch. The kind I'd usually throw back."

Qui-Gon didn't like being called a "trainee," but that was the least of his problems. "I'm not yet a full Jedi, no."

"I knew *that*," Mol said. "I've eaten cheese older than you."

"I'm fourteen."

"Fourteen." She hissed, as the Falleen sometimes did when they were amused. He thought it best not to respond to that.

Mol slid over a few rocks—practically slithered—while keeping the blaster at the ready. Qui-Gon felt sure her aim hadn't wavered for a moment. Now she was a full meter closer to him.

She said, "What am I to do with you?"

"The smartest thing to do would be to turn around and leave," Qui-Gon said. "Of course, that's what I want you to do, but it happens to be true. Others are coming. The sooner you leave, the more chances you'll have to lose them."

"When you'll just hunt me down again."

This, too, was true.

Mol narrowed her eyes. "Shall I tell you of my little game, trainee?"

"It sounds like you're going to," Qui-Gon replied evenly. His palm was becoming sweaty against the hilt of his lightsaber.

"It goes like this. I'm trying to kill one target of every age. At least up to two hundred—I can't go chasing ancients all the time. But I want all two hundred years represented. So far my oldest was a Whiphid who was one hundred and sixty-two. My youngest was four days. I count her as zero."

Mol said it all proudly. It turned Qui-Gon's stomach.

"Here's the thing." Her grin widened. "I've killed a thirteen-year-old and a fifteen-year-old. But that leaves me with a little gap. A gap you'd fill perfectly."

She's going to kill me. Qui-Gon's hand tightened on his lightsaber—he'd just have to try to block her, even if it was futile—

A flash of light exploded from the jungle, striking Shenda Mol. She screamed in agony, dropping her blaster and tumbling down the hillside to fall to the ground. Qui-Gon could no longer see her—thick undergrowth blocked his view—but he could hear a strangled gurgling coming from her throat. Scratching against the dirt, as though she were clawing or kicking at the ground. Before Qui-Gon could ask what that light had been, the foliage rustled to reveal Master Dooku.

"You kill the helpless and brag of it," Dooku said, walking past Qui-Gon into the underbrush, focused only on Mol. Although Qui-Gon wanted to see his Master, to show himself, he knew better than to interject himself into an encounter Dooku had well in hand. "You think to murder my Padawan merely to fulfill your pitiful ambitions. You find yourself impressive, do you? You know *nothing* of true power!"

Brilliant light flashed again, and again. Qui-Gon still couldn't see it directly, though he could feel his skin prickling and his hair standing on end. The air tasted of ozone.

None of that seemed to matter, not when he could hear Mol's wretched shrieks of pain.

Then Shenda Mol's cries choked off. For one instant Qui-Gon thought she was dead—but then he heard her moaning brokenly. The sound wrenched him into action.

"Master, *stop.*" He pushed his way through the underbrush to stand between Dooku and Mol. The assassin lay at his Master's feet, curled in on herself, trembling. "Please. I'm all right. We're taking her into custody. It's over."

Dooku's expression was unreadable at first, but slowly he lowered his hand. "It's over," his Master repeated. Suddenly he seemed almost normal again. "You're all right, my Padawan?"

"Yes, Master." Every other time Dooku had saved his life, Qui-Gon had thanked him. He couldn't now.

What had his Master done?

"Let me summon the others." Dooku stepped away to speak into his communicator, while Qui-Gon remained there, "guarding" Shenda Mol as she shivered on the ground.

CHAPTER TWENTY-SEVEN

NO REPLY RECEIVED

Qui-Gon sighed at the words on the screen. Count Dooku had proved an enigma ever since his sudden departure from the Order, and Qui-Gon had refrained from contacting him since, mostly to allow his former Master some time and privacy. But now he needed his old Master's advice more than ever. Dooku had had his own difficult relationship with the prophecies, believing in them, then casting them aside, then taking them up once more during Qui-Gon's time as his Padawan. Surely he would understand why Qui-Gon believed in this vision so firmly. Maybe he could even help find the words that would convince the others to listen.

But from Serenno, he received only silence.

The door to the bedroom chimed, signaling a visitor. He braced himself. "Enter."

When Obi-Wan walked in, Qui-Gon exhaled in relief. Although he was a strong-willed man who had faced down warlords and crime bosses without flinching, he preferred to delay another round with Rael Averross. The history that had led to Qui-Gon receiving this mission was now making the mission even more fraught.

He asked, "Has the royal retinue calmed down yet?"

"Not even close." Obi-Wan walked past Qui-Gon, farther into the bedroom than he'd ever come before. He picked up the smooth, opalescent pebble Qui-Gon had collected from the cave yesterday. "You're always gathering bits and pieces, of everywhere we've been."

"I like to remember."

"You like remembering nearly dying in a sinkhole and getting caught between two sets of blaster-wielding outlaws?"

"Memory is, in the end, all we truly possess." Qui-Gon took a seat in one of the tall-backed, carved chairs in the room; he suspected this would take a while. "You're not here to discuss my habit of taking souvenirs."

"You're right," Obi-Wan said. "I'm here to ask you what in the worlds you think you're doing."

"Listening to the Force. Heeding the vision it has sent me."

Obi-Wan's expression darkened. "Forgive me, Qui-Gon, but it seems . . . terribly convenient that this vision aligns perfectly with your opinion about the Governance Treaty. Are you sure that you're not just seeing what you *want* to see?"

He didn't understand. Maybe nobody who hadn't had a vision of the future could comprehend how powerful it was, how persuasive, how true. "My vision may agree with my opinion, but neither one influenced the other. My objections are real. So is this vision sent through the Force."

"But—we talked about this on Coruscant." Obi-Wan paced along the wall of windows, which looked out onto the cliffs at the shore. "You said yourself, the mystics' visions of the future shouldn't be taken literally. That they were merely interpretations of their current circumstances, projected upon the future. Isn't that precisely what you're doing here?"

Qui-Gon felt as though he'd said those words half a lifetime ago. "Obi-Wan, I was wrong. A true vision of the future is more than a simple dream, or a figment of the imagination. It's the simultaneous perception of two points in time—beyond anything my mind, or yours, had previously encountered. So it's no surprise that I didn't understand it before, and that you don't now."

"So now you believe that 'she who was born to darkness will give birth to darkness'?" Obi-Wan asked. "That a Chosen One will come and restore balance to the Force? Are you going to take every single one of these hazy mystical prophecies literally from now on?"

It took Qui-Gon a moment to admit it, not to Obi-Wan but to himself. "Yes. I think I have to. Now that I stand where the prophets have stood, I must listen to them in humility, not in judgment. When I was younger, I was capable of that. I only hope I can find the strength to believe again."

Some Jedi would've begun to listen at this point, but not Obi-Wan Kenobi. His apprentice's thinking remained as rule-bound as ever. "Wanting to see the future, to predict it and change our behaviors accordingly—that's a kind of control we're not meant to have, Qui-Gon. You're reaching for a power that others cannot have. That path can lead to darkness."

"I'm not turning to the dark side," Qui-Gon snapped. "Not every disagreement with Jedi orthodoxy turns you into a Sith Lord overnight."

"I didn't mean *that*." Obi-Wan sighed. "If you won't listen to me about the visions, will you at least listen to me about our mission? Our mandate on Pijal comes straight from Chancellor Kaj herself, and she was very clear. We're here to protect Princess Fanry and witness the treaty, so the hyperspace corridor can be opened. If we have to push for the treaty to be amended and made fair, then that's what we will do. But you *can't* refuse to sign on behalf of the Republic. You don't have the authority to make that choice."

His apprentice wasn't wrong. But when facts collided with ideals, Qui-Gon preferred to change the facts.

"I may have the authority to sign a treaty that condemns people to servitude and slavery," he said. "But that doesn't mean I have the *right* to do so."

"So you're turning your back on Averross and Fanry, instead of working to convince them?" Obi-Wan said. "We can still succeed on this mission, and do what's fair for the people of Pijal. If you persist in quoting mysticism and refusing to compromise, however—"

"I will persist," Qui-Gon replied. "Rael Averross is beyond listening to reason. His dedication to protecting Fanry has turned into a mania. We'll get nowhere with him. Fanry is a child, who must look up to Rael as something like a father. If he won't budge, I doubt she will, either. This is not a matter for negotiation, Obi-Wan. It is a matter of principle, and we must stand firm."

Obi-Wan lifted his chin. "Yes. It's a matter of principle. The principle being that we as Jedi must not go beyond our mandate, that we must work within that mandate to do what is right."

That was the second time in the past half day that Qui-Gon had been lectured about the limits of the Jedi mandate. His conscience twinged him slightly; it *was* important for Jedi not to become arrogant, not to impose their wishes and values on all others around them.

But this situation was different. It had to be, because the only thing Qui-Gon knew to be absolutely true was that his vision was real. He said, "In this case, my Padawan, we cannot both work within our mandate and do what is right. I've chosen the latter."

Obi-Wan walked toward the door, obviously outdone. "At the beginning of my apprenticeship, I couldn't understand you," he said. "Unfortunately, that's just as true here at the end."

Only yesterday they had worked together as never before. How did Qui-Gon manage to get closer to Obi-Wan at the same time he was moving further away?

Just before Obi-Wan would leave the room, Qui-Gon said, "Once, you asked me about the basic lightsaber cadences. Why I'd kept you there, instead of training you in more advanced forms of combat."

Obi-Wan turned reluctantly to face him again. "I suppose you thought I wasn't ready for more. The same way I'm not ready to believe in all this mystical—"

"That's not why."

After a long pause, Obi-Wan calmed to the point where he would listen. "Then why, Qui-Gon?"

"Because many Padawans—and full Jedi Knights, for that matter—forget that the most basic technique is the most important technique. The purest. The most likely to protect you in battle, and the foundation of all knowledge that is to come," Qui-Gon said. "Most apprentices want to rush ahead to styles of fighting that are flashier or more esoteric. Most Masters let them, because we must all find our preferred form eventually. But I wanted you to be grounded in your technique. I wanted you to understand the basic cadences so well that they would become instinct, so that you would be almost untouchable. Above all, I wanted to give you the training you needed to accomplish anything you set your mind to later on."

Obi-Wan remained quiet for so long that Qui-Gon wondered if he were too angry to really hear any of what he'd said. But finally, his Padawan nodded. "Thank you, Qui-Gon. I appreciate that. But—"

"But what?"

"You could've said so," Obi-Wan replied, and then he left.

The lump in Obi-Wan's throat wouldn't go away for several minutes, no matter how many times he swallowed, or how hard he tried to turn his mind to other things.

He was trying to help me this whole time, he thought. *Qui-Gon cared about me more than I knew. He does even now.*

Knowing this soothed something deep in Obi-Wan's soul, an ache and an uncertainty that had dwelled within him for many years. He wondered how much of his apprenticeship would look different to him when he reexamined his memories through this new perspective.

But none of that came any closer to resolving the problems on Pijal.

Only one solution came to mind. It was a major violation of protocol—beyond the proper boundaries of any Padawan. Obi-Wan rejected it for that reason alone, but when every other idea he had failed, this came to him again. This time he couldn't shake it.

There are rules for what Padawans can do, and what Masters can do, he told himself. *If I do this, I will break almost all of those rules.*

After a few hours of consideration, however, Obi-Wan knew he had no choice.

It was time to go over Qui-Gon's head.

He went back to the palace library, which was still completely empty, and activated one of the comm terminals. When its screen lit up, an artificial voice said, "State location and identity of recipient."

"Coruscant, the Jedi Temple." Obi-Wan took a deep breath. "The message is for the Jedi Council."

CHAPTER TWENTY-EIGHT

I t wasn't as though Obi-Wan had never spoken to the Jedi Council before. But he'd never done so alone, without Qui-Gon beside him—and had never had anything to say that would shock the Council so much.

"*Qui-Gon's gone rogue before*," Saesee Tiin said, "*but he's never deviated from his mandate so greatly, or in such a serious matter.*"

Poli Dapatian shook his head, disbelief apparent even through the hologram. "*Of course the treaty must somehow be changed to protect the people of Pijal. But disrupting the entire diplomatic process is dangerous, especially when multiple armed forces threaten the rule of law on Pijal and its moon.*"

Nearly the entire Council was arrayed, via holo, in a circle around Obi-Wan. Full projection was best for a meeting of this seriousness, he knew—but it felt eerily as though he were in the Council Chamber itself. Only the occasional flicker revealed the palace library around him.

He gathered his courage. "I would argue that Czerka's undue influence on this planet, and on Averross in particular, already threatens the rule of law. But I fear my Master's extreme stance makes change less likely, not more. There's no room for negotiation between them."

The Council members exchanged troubled glances. Eeth Koth said, *"We cannot allow this to stand. Both Jinn and Averross should be recalled, immediately."*

Obi-Wan didn't like saying this, but he had to: "Averross has been the de facto ruler of this planet for nearly a decade. He and the crown princess appear to be inseparable. If he's pulled offplanet just before the ceremony, the public mood could turn ugly—possibly winning converts to both the Opposition and the blackguards, whoever they may be. I also suspect that any power vacuum would quickly be filled by Czerka. They're entrenched here."

"What a mess," said Koth, his irritation evident. *"I fear, Master Yoda, that the rest of us should've listened to you. Inviting Qui-Gon Jinn to the Council—"*

"Has been done," Yoda said. *"Undone, it shall not be."*

Yoda voted against my Master? Obi-Wan felt the rejection as sharply as though he had been the one found wanting, not Qui-Gon. The divide between them had somehow made Obi-Wan treasure his Master more, not less. It was as though he'd had to stand farther back before he could see the man clearly.

But seeing Qui-Gon clearly had not helped Obi-Wan get through to him.

"So sure are all of you that Qui-Gon is wrong to put faith in his vision?" Yoda drew himself upright. *"Certain, you are, that the Force does not speak to him?"*

The silence that followed went on for what seemed like a long time. Doubtfully, Depa Billaba said, *"The future is always in motion. We cannot put our entire faith in such visions."*

"No, we cannot. Qui-Gon errs in this. Yet also an error it is to say that such visions cannot have meaning." Yoda turned to make eye contact

with every Council member present in turn, then finally Obi-Wan. *"What evidence is there that Qui-Gon's dream may see true?"*

Obi-Wan admitted, "In the dream, Qui-Gon envisioned the entire Celestial Chalice—the chamber for the coronation and treaty signing—in great detail. When he saw the Chalice for himself, it was identical to his vision in every sense."

Poli Dapatian cocked his head, apparently impressed; he wasn't the only Council member who reacted that way. But others remained skeptical. *"Jinn may well have seen a holo or picture long ago,"* Koth insisted. *"The place may look the same as his dream, but that has no bearing over whether events will unfold as he says—and it's a rather disjointed version of events, at that."*

"Besides," added Saesee Tiin, *"seeking to know the future is a path to the dark side."*

Obi-Wan had said the same, but it sounded harsher coming from Tiin.

Yoda harrumphed. *"Seeking to know, yes. But seek this vision, Qui-Gon did not. Came to him unbidden, it did. Such visions may be false—but not darkness in themselves."*

"Can anything that leads to such temptation to control the future be said to be free of darkness?" Tiin said.

Dapatian nodded sagely. *"We cannot evaluate the tactical implications of these visions without also considering the ethical implications."*

Are they truly going to waste time debating theoretical ethics instead of dealing with the crisis at hand? The thought shocked Obi-Wan—such criticism of the Council was something he would've expected from his Master, but had never really confronted in himself. Maybe Qui-Gon had a point about the Council's tendency to bicker rather than lead . . .

Don't be childish, Obi-Wan told himself. *They're the Council. Of course they consider all aspects of every situation.* And at any other time, he might've found this discussion interesting. Now, however, it was a distraction from the critical questions he needed the Council to answer. "Masters, please—I'm to return to the moon with Qui-Gon later today to monitor Czerka activity and hopefully find and identify the blackguards." The summons from his Master had come up on Obi-Wan's datapad as he briefed the Council; guilt had weighed heavily on him ever since. "What are you going to do?"

"The question, this is not," Yoda said. *"Determine we will what* you *will do, young Padawan."*

After a long, mostly silent trip with Obi-Wan to the rendezvous point, Qui-Gon was grateful to see the *Meryx* landing nearby. Even Pax Maripher's attitude would be a welcome break from the awkwardness between him and his apprentice.

"So," Pax called from the ship's hatch, "ready to endanger our lives again today?"

"Looking forward to it," Qui-Gon replied.

Pax raised an eyebrow but simply gestured for them to get in for takeoff.

"Okay," Rahara Wick said, once they were in space again, "we got the coordinates you sent, but we haven't done recon yet. After that blowup yesterday, we wanted some Jedi along for the ride before we got anywhere near people who are potentially armed."

"Understandable." Qui-Gon leaned farther into the *Meryx* cockpit to study her readouts. "We're headed to a Czerka mine—not one of their larger operations, but it's close to areas the blackguards have attacked before. So whatever Czerka's doing there seems to be of interest to the people we're trying to find."

Pax folded his arms as he leaned against a wall. "Why are you only turning your attention to this now?"

Obi-Wan spoke up. "Because before, it was difficult to detect meaningful patterns. But we've learned which acts were the work of the Opposition, and which were the work of the blackguards. Once we went through the record with that knowledge, the patterns became clearer. This place is important to the blackguards. That makes it important to us."

"Well put, Padawan." Qui-Gon meant the praise sincerely. Why did it make Obi-Wan flinch?

Soon they were descending into the moon's atmosphere. Sooty haze on the horizon signaled the Czerka facility. At Qui-Gon's signal, Rahara brought the *Meryx* down. Finding a landing spot proved tricky on this rockier, more uneven terrain, but she managed to settle the ship at the very border of scanner range. At this distance, only specifically targeted scans would pick up much. Pax and Rahara would be able to monitor the Jedi as they scouted out the Czerka facility, but Czerka was unlikely to detect the *Meryx*.

Qui-Gon and Obi-Wan set out on foot, lightsabers in hand and blasters at their side. Anyone who wore one of those unusual shields today would be much less protected than before. They moved as quietly as possible, bending branches aside and slowly releasing them, placing their feet on grass or soft leaves instead of dead ones. The silence between them was not awkward but necessary, and they were united again by a shared purpose.

We'll get through this mission well enough, Qui-Gon noted. It had occurred to him that his invitation to the Council might not survive his defiance of the mission mandate on Pijal; if so, would Obi-Wan continue as his Padawan? The rest of their time on Pijal would provide the answer.

The smell of smoke signaled that they were coming close. Both Obi-Wan and Qui-Gon drew their cloaks around them and pulled up their hoods as a sort of camouflage. Obi-Wan, who held the scanner, motioned for Qui-Gon to take a closer look. "The ores they're mining don't appear to be particularly rare or precious."

"No," Qui-Gon agreed, double-checking the mineralogy readouts. "Czerka's not mining here because it's necessary. Just because it's possible. This is interesting, though—" He pointed to unusual spikes in the graphs from an area near one edge of the Czerka facility compound.

"Kyber . . . no, of course, it's kohlen crystals." Thoughtfully, Obi-Wan tapped one finger on the edge of the scanner. "If Czerka's actually looking for kohlen crystals—"

Qui-Gon completed the thought. "They may be behind the black-guards after all. This may be how they gather the crystals to power those mysterious shields."

"We don't even know the shields use kohlen," Obi-Wan said, contradicting not Qui-Gon but his own train of thought.

Nodding, Qui-Gon answered, "Nor are we entirely certain our lightsabers are ineffective against these things. One battle can't be absolute proof."

"We ought to make sure of that—though I don't think it would be fun finding out." A grin lit up Obi-Wan's face, just for a moment.

"Let's see if we can find out what they're doing with the kohlen crystals." Qui-Gon motioned for Obi-Wan to follow him.

Together they kept moving until they were almost at the perimeter of the compound. Only brief bluish sparks of light revealed the electronic fence that marked the boundary. *Good,* Qui-Gon thought. *This way we can see everything.*

At first glimpse nothing about this facility looked any different from countless other mining operations Qui-Gon had seen over the years. Sifter droids mindlessly went through raw material, separating ore from dross, which was picked up by loader droids lumbering along the ground, taking the ore for initial processing. Enslaved humans were present, too, in their gray coveralls, doing maintenance on droids. More were probably inside, performing the more complex tasks that simple worker droids weren't programmed to handle. It was dull, grueling labor—another example of the arduous work they were forced to perform throughout the galaxy.

There has to be some end to this, Qui-Gon thought. *Yoda's correct—the Jedi cannot assume the authority for putting a stop to slavery throughout the galaxy, not without taking on more power than we should ever have. But somehow, this must change.*

Their scanner blinked faster as they moved quietly through the trees, approaching the area with the kohlen crystals. "Here, Master," Obi-Wan whispered. "It should be coming into view now."

A new area of the compound became visible. The Jedi stopped and stared at it for the several moments it took to believe it, until an ASP-7 clunked toward the uneven area, an enormous metal container balanced on its arms. The ASP-7 emptied the container, shook it once for good measure, then began carrying it back to be filled again.

"The trash," Obi-Wan said in disbelief. "Czerka's throwing the kohlen crystals into the trash?"

Qui-Gon might not have believed it, either, if he hadn't glimpsed a few telltale orange glints amid the rubble. "Apparently they're mining for the other minerals we've detected, and the kohlen crystals are merely . . . debris. Well, that tells us one of two things."

"We know Czerka isn't behind the blackguards," Obi-Wan said. "If they were, they'd need the kohlen crystals."

"That, or the kohlen crystals aren't used in the blackguards' shielding after all." Qui-Gon straightened. "Either way, I doubt we have much more to learn by searching this facility. There's nothing special about Czerka's operation, and we're not getting anywhere near the blackguards."

The electric sizzle of a blaster bolt startled them. The Jedi both looked up just in time to see one of the mining droids explode.

Alarms began to wail. Red lights blinked on the corner of each facility. Worker droids dropped their tasks, wheeling around to provide what meager defense they could. Qui-Gon scanned the horizon and saw three small troop movers hovering just over the tree line, approaching the compound. The troop movers were descending— coming in to land just within the fence.

He knew who it would be before the first soldier appeared, and surely Obi-Wan knew, too. But when that figure jumped out, blaster in hand, Qui-Gon still had to say it: "The blackguards. They're here."

CHAPTER TWENTY-NINE

———— ☖ ————

The boredom of sitting around waiting for the Jedi ended abruptly, with telltale signals blinking their way into sensor range. Pax took a look at them, sized up the situation, and thought, *Oh, bloody hell.*

"Scanner-blocking field up," he said. "At our first convenience, we're getting out of here."

Rahara came in, a haroun bun in her hand. "Wait. What about the Jedi?"

"Qui-Gon had the decency to say we shouldn't put ourselves in mortal danger on their account. We are not *currently* in mortal danger, but it's rather too close for comfort." Would he have to do a full readings analysis to convince her? Then a simpler solution came to mind, and he pointed through the cockpit viewport toward the flying shapes near the horizon. "*There.*"

She gasped. "Whose ships are those?"

"I've no idea, and it doesn't matter anyway. The ships' weapons are powered up and they're flying in attack formation. That's all I need to know to assess the likelihood of the aforementioned 'mortal danger,' which is extremely high."

Distant blasterfire showed as little more than greenish streaks of light above the trees. Pax preferred the fire to come no closer. Rahara murmured, "Whoever they are, they're attacking the Czerka facility."

"People after your own heart," he said. "Let's leave them to it, shall we?"

He hoped she'd return to the cockpit beside him and take the helm; Pax was a perfectly adequate pilot, but he lacked Rahara's magic touch. They stood a far better chance of getting away from here without being noticed if she was in the pilot's seat. Besides, she'd been back in the mess, snacking, for some time now, and he was in the mood for more companionship and entertainment. (He had previously been in-structed that it was not acceptable to interrupt her eating, sleeping, refresher time, or holovids for this reason alone. The crisis gave him the perfect excuse.)

But she was already shaking her head no. "It's not just Czerka scum in the facility," she said. "The people they've enslaved are there, too. They'll get cut down before anyone's able to touch the inner rooms where their owners are." Rahara straightened. "I can't let that happen."

"Although I shudder to ask," Pax said, "how do you propose to stop it?"

"By taking the *Facet* in to provide some cover." Rahara grabbed a helmet from the rack and headed toward the hold.

This was unacceptable on many levels. Pax hurried after her, calling, "You won't be able to do much good in the *Facet*—each one of those ships is five times larger, and has ten times the firepower. Roughly. Exact figures can be calculated if you need convincing."

"I don't need exact figures. I need to get down there."

With that, Rahara pushed a panel on the wall. The plating on part of the floor retracted, providing access to the launch bay below. There, gleaming like a silver dart, lay the *Facet*.

Pax had felt so clever when he'd purchased a single-pilot fighter. If the *Meryx* were ever attacked, then he had the ability to strike back—while keeping his valuable cargo out of harm's way. But he'd always pictured himself going into the fight. Not Rahara.

"Get us off the ground," she said. "I'll take it from there."

It was tempting to refuse. Even a pilot as skilled as Rahara Wick couldn't manage to launch a fighter within half a meter of the ground.

Refusing to take off, however, would only start an argument. Pax already knew how that argument would end. He might as well help her do as much good as she could.

"Rahara?" he called, as she took her seat. "Wear your gloves."

She grinned up at him for the split second before the *Facet*'s mirrored cockpit slid shut.

Obi-Wan's brief hopes that they could stay out of the fight vanished when several blackguards pivoted and began running directly toward them. "They've spotted us."

"So it would seem." Qui-Gon ignited his lightsaber, and Obi-Wan did the same. The electric hum of it was almost soothing, a reminder that whoever his opponents were, *he* was a Jedi.

One of the blackguards fired in their direction—but not at them, Obi-Wan realized. Instead the bolt hit one of the fence control posts. For a moment, the electronic fence glowed so brightly it was as opaque as any stone wall. Then it vanished, and there was nothing between the Jedi and the blackguards but some mining droids and twenty meters of mud.

Qui-Gon ran forward, taking point. With his free hand, he grabbed a blaster dropped by a blackguard and fired at another, but the shot impacted on his opponent's shield, causing no damage. Obi-Wan swore to himself. Why did the shields have to guard against conventional weapons, too? Qui-Gon's defensive moves were perfectly executed—but their enemies remained untouchable. That meant all the blackguards had to do was bide their time and wait for one small mistake by the Jedi.

Obi-Wan ducked behind an ASP-7, taking cover. He expected Qui-

Gon to do the same, but instead his Master kept fighting. His robe and hair spun with every move he made, and when Obi-Wan glimpsed his face, he saw only serenity. Complete calm.

I am one with the Force, Obi-Wan thought, recalling an old saying of the Guardians of the Whills. *The Force is with me.*

He relaxed and let the Force flow through him. Usually, in battle, the Force seemed to fall silent—not to desert him, but to become no more than instinct. This time, however, Obi-Wan found himself connecting to everything around him—as though he were in a meditative trance. He wasn't waiting for his Master to guide him. At last, he was guided purely by the Force.

The next few minutes seemed to take place in slow motion. Obi-Wan felt no fear as he emerged from behind the loader droid and re-engaged the blackguards. Life and death were all the same, within the Force; there was nothing to hide from, nothing to distract him. Instead he could perceive the path of every blaster bolt before it was fired. His body required no help from his conscious mind to angle his lightsaber to deflect each shot.

Qui-Gon had always encouraged him to enter a meditative trance during combat. Obi-Wan had always thought that absurd, if not impossible.

But now, at last, he fought as his Master had taught him.

Rahara kept the *Facet* so low that it skimmed some of the treetops. She'd feel the thud, dip to one side or the other, momentarily lose some speed—but it was nothing her ship couldn't handle.

I'm not sorry we never had to use the Facet *as an actual fighter before,* she thought, *but I'm glad we've got it now.*

All the attacking ships had landed by this time, so there was nothing to worry about in the air. Once Rahara had cleared the facility perimeter, she could see what was happening on the ground. On this side of the main building, the two Jedi Knights were up against at least a dozen fighters, and from the looks of it were holding their own. They moved so fluidly, their lightsabers so brilliant, that she could almost have believed they were dancers. Rahara felt a shiver of awe. She'd always heard about the Jedi using their powers, but she'd never witnessed it before.

The *Facet* flew over the nearest building, revealing another slice of the compound and the battle. It showed her what she'd come here for.

Alongside this building—a processing unit—a dozen or so Czerka workers had huddled beneath an overhang, attempting to shield themselves from blasterfire. The attackers, whom Rahara figured had to be blackguards, weren't firing at these poor people directly, only at the building itself. But if the building blew, all the enslaved would be killed as surely as if they were inside.

There was a door only a meter away from them. Rahara remembered the old protocols, knew that the Czerka personnel had already taken shelter and locked all the entrances, because everyone who mattered was safe. Slaves didn't matter.

Someday she'd get her shot at Czerka proper. For now she could only help those Czerka had abandoned.

Rahara took the *Facet* in low, almost ground-level, flying between the enslaved people and the blackguards. Blasterfire pummeled the hull, but these were personal firearms, not the more powerful cannons ships used; the bolts barely scarred the surface, and didn't even slow her down. As soon as she was done, she swooped back again, closer to the blackguards. Her reward was seeing them skitter backward to escape being physically run down.

She banked around for a third sweep of the area. By now the enslaved workers had dashed away from the Czerka building and were hurrying into a mineral silo—more than strong enough to hold up to blasterfire. Should she keep buzzing the blackguards? Probably not; then she'd be helping Czerka, not the people Czerka had enslaved. So Rahara took the *Facet* higher to get another look around. Dots on the distant horizon drew her attention.

Wait. Those are approaching ships. Out loud, Rahara muttered, "Who the hell is *that*?"

Green-white light exploded all around her, surrounding the *Facet,* which dipped dangerously to one side. She fought for control, but the ship was no longer responding well. Apparently at least one of the blackguards had a surface-to-air weapon, which had just been used to take her out. Rahara could do nothing besides pull up hard to try to break the force of the crash that was coming.

"Don't look now," Obi-Wan called over the din of battle, "but I think we have reinforcements!"

Qui-Gon looked toward the horizon and saw approaching ships—troopships, not unlike those of the blackguards, but each of them proudly showing the royal colors of green and white. Despite Rael's protests, Fanry's guard had come to back them up.

The blackguards didn't seem to have planned for this contingency. Several of them lowered their weapons and looked around in apparent confusion. But some others had already broken and run for their ships. A full retreat seemed likely.

Then the sound of crashing metal echoed through the camp. Qui-Gon wheeled around to see a small ship, a single-pilot fighter, sending up plumes of mud as it skidded to a stop along the ground. That must be the fighter from the *Meryx,* he thought. Although Qui-Gon hadn't seen the fighter before, Pax had already taken the opportunity to brag about it.

Whoever was in the cockpit of that ship was in serious danger of capture or death. Whether it was Pax or Rahara, they were only there because Qui-Gon had insisted.

Which meant it was his responsibility to get them out alive, if he could.

CHAPTER THIRTY

Obi-Wan saw his Master running toward the downed fighter, and understood instinctively that he was to hold his ground against the blackguards until they retreated. The pilot's rescue would be up to Qui-Gon.

Or so he thought, until weathered droidekas began rolling up from chutes within the ground. Czerka's defense had finally kicked in. Several of the droidekas headed for the blackguards, but two aimed themselves directly at Qui-Gon.

The wave of surprise and fear that went through the blackguards told Obi-Wan they were about to run. That let him ignore them completely and run toward Qui-Gon.

Calling upon the Force allowed him to jump farther and higher than he ever had before—at least five meters—somersaulting in midair to land in defensive position, slightly in front of his Master. Qui-Gon shouted, "What do you think you're doing?"

Obi-Wan's only answer was deflecting droideka fire. These blasts could be blocked by their lightsabers, but the droidekas could shoot five times faster than any human, and were at least ten times harder to stop.

The entire compound had sprung into action at the same time as the battle droids. Some Czerka higher-up huddling in one of the buildings must've belatedly signaled for an evacuation. Although Obi-Wan remained focused on the battle droids, he could perceive more of the scene around them: blockish automated craft emerging from concrete shafts, doors opening to Czerka workers hustling in all their property, droids and equipment—

—and people.

"Owww." Rahara popped the pilot's harness in the *Facet* so she could brace herself. Her ship had skidded to a halt on the edge of a ditch, tilting it sharply to one side. With one arm under her, she could prop up to see what was going on.

The cockpit was half covered with mud. Through the smears she glimpsed droids moving in set patterns, toward autopiloted hauler craft. Rahara recognized the evacuation protocol immediately. She'd gone through a handful of these, when a mineshaft threatened to blow and damage equipment.

Okay, Czerka's leaving. Rahara felt relieved, then guilty for feeling that way when just a few meters from her ship, enslaved people were being loaded onto haulers. But she knew the evacuation procedure well enough to understand that there was nothing she could do, unarmed, with a ship that would need some repair before it could fly again.

I wonder, she thought, *if some of them are people I know.*

Tears filled her eyes as Rahara envisioned some of their faces—the fellow slaves who'd been kind to a small child sold away from her parents, comforted her as best they could—

A security droid rolled up to the *Facet,* blocking Rahara's view of anything else but mud. Through the cockpit she could hear its tinny voice: *"Scanning."*

Rahara froze. It felt as though the back of her left hand were burning, like the tag she'd cut out long ago were trying to signal Czerka on its own. She looked down at her midnight-blue gloves and repeated to herself, *You're safe. You're safe.*

The security droid projected a beam of green light into the cockpit, momentarily blinding her. She was still blinking when it pried off the cockpit, exposing her.

"Initial scan inconclusive," it said as the beam swept over Rahara one more time. Its long, multijointed arms unfolded with its next words: *"Confirmed via facial recognition. Czerka property."*

"No!" Rahara clambered from the cockpit, ignoring the ache in her crash-bruised chest, scrambling to get away. The Jedi were around here somewhere—if she could only reach them, they'd help her—

But the security droid's clamp seized her, knocking the breath from Rahara's lungs as it snatched her into its grip. Her feet dangled several centimeters above the ground, so she couldn't get any traction to push away. A miniature pincer clicked out from a panel to snatch off the left-hand glove. A needle jabbed the back of her hand, piercing the skin, and she cried out in pain.

"Temporary tag in place," the droid said.

Rahara had been prepared to die in deep space. To go to jail as a jewel thief. To run afoul of the Hutts. To get shot down by blackguards. She'd accepted all the dangers her life contained, except one. The only one she had begged the Force to spare her was a return to slavery.

So much for the Force, she thought numbly as the security droid dropped her in a hauler with the rest of Czerka's stuff.

The palace troopships were coming closer as the Jedi Knights fought against two droidekas at the perimeter of the compound. Ozone from blasters filled the air, a strange counterpoint to the organic smells of conifers and mud. A haze covered the ground—smoke, puddles evaporating from the heat of blaster bolts, ore dust—hampering visibility, as though they were fighting their way through a swirling fog that came up to their knees.

Qui-Gon wasn't fazed. All he and Obi-Wan had to do was stall for a little more time. Then they'd have extra firepower on their side, and defeating the droidekas would be easy.

But as he observed Obi-Wan in action, fighting as brilliantly as any full Jedi Knight, Qui-Gon decided extra firepower might not be necessary.

"Obi-Wan!" he called. "Triangulate!"

His apprentice lit up, for once understanding Qui-Gon completely. The two of them moved closer together, almost back-to-back. Under his breath, still furiously defending them with his lightsaber, Obi-Wan murmured, "Say when."

Qui-Gon had a near miss of a bolt that jolted his lightsaber in his hands, but he recovered immediately. He watched the two droids pivot, each toward the Jedi it had locked onto as its main target. *"Now."*

Together they jumped more than two meters sideways, to the exact midpoint between the droidekas, and then ducked to the ground.

Blaster bolts flashed over their heads, fired by each droid—straight at each other. Crackling blue electricity raced along their plating as each vibrated, then collapsed.

Obi-Wan half turned to smile at him. "That's more like it."

"Come on." Qui-Gon hadn't forgotten that the *Facet* had gone down a few minutes before. The heavy, swirling fog around their feet became more opaque by the second, and he wanted to search before the murk became impenetrable.

Airspace above the Czerka facility had turned into a three-dimensional traffic jam worthy of Coruscant. Blackguard ships were attempting to escape in one direction, pursued by palace vessels; Czerka cargo haulers were taking off in another; and a few remaining royal ships had begun descending through the middle of it all. Qui-Gon hoped the palace troops were getting detailed scans of the blackguard vessels. Then, perhaps, they could be traced, and the mystery of their origins could be solved.

His boots trudged through mud as they walked farther back into the compound, into the area where Qui-Gon had seen the *Facet* go down. Neither Pax nor Rahara showed themselves. He quickened his steps; the pilot might be injured.

"The other droids have all headed to Czerka haulers," Obi-Wan said. "We're safe."

"For the moment, at least." Qui-Gon looked sideways at his apprentice. Obi-Wan had a few tiny flecks of mud on his face mixed in with his freckles, and he'd torn the hood of his robe. Never had Qui-Gon seen him so elated. "You fought splendidly."

"I know! Oh—I mean, thank you, Master."

Qui-Gon chuckled. "Go ahead, Padawan. Claim it. You've earned the right."

Obi-Wan ducked his head, trying to be modest, though the broad grin across his face told another story. "Always, before, when you talked about achieving trance state during battle—I thought it impossible. But today, I reached it. I felt the presence of the Force as never before."

"Meditate upon that tonight," Qui-Gon said. "Remember the feelings that guided you. The more you accomplish that state during battle, the easier it will be in the future, until it becomes second nature and—oh, no."

A strong breeze had stirred the soupy fog, revealing a patch of bare ground, including the *Facet,* slightly damaged, lying alongside a shallow ditch. The cockpit had been popped open. No one was inside.

Obi-Wan's smiled faded. "What's this?"

"The fighter from the *Meryx,*" Qui-Gon said. "Either Pax or Rahara came here to help, but neither is in the ship."

"Which means they're injured or—" Obi-Wan half turned and called, "Rahara? Can you hear me? It's Obi-Wan Kenobi! You're safe, just let us know where you are!"

Nobody answered.

At first Qui-Gon thought to chide Obi-Wan for assuming that Rahara had piloted the ship, but then his intuition agreed. Rahara Wick was the one with a personal grudge against Czerka Corporation, and deeper empathy for the people under its control. Pax would never have flown into the thick of this; no one could've stopped Rahara from doing so.

"Master Jinn," said the deep voice of Captain Deren. Qui-Gon looked back to see the captain approaching them in his flight uniform, guards flanking him on either side. "Thank goodness you're all right."

"Captain Deren," Qui-Gon said. "Tell me, did you have to fight Rael Averross to come here? Or were you able to sneak out?"

A shadow of a smile briefly flickered on Deren's face, but had vanished in an instant. "Princess Fanry herself ordered me here, so you two wouldn't be traveling through such dangerous territory alone. When we realized you were in danger, protecting you became our first priority."

So Her Serene Highness was capable of defying her regent when the stakes were important enough. Qui-Gon wondered if that was a sign of maturing wisdom, evidence that Fanry was indeed growing into the queen Pijal needed—or simple adolescent rebellion. Either way, the palace troops' arrival was fortuitous. "We've been working with—" Qui-Gon paused momentarily to find the most prudent way of referring to Pax and Rahara. "—independent pilots, who brought us to this location. One of them flew into the fight to try to help us. We're searching for her now."

Deren nodded. "I'll task two of my officers to help you."

"That would be much appreciated. But we also badly need any scans you have of the blackguards' ships. We've been able to determine that they're not sponsored by Czerka—obviously." Qui-Gon gestured around at the mayhem, then paused as he saw the refuse area he and Obi-Wan had observed before. Enormous gouges had been scooped out of it by some sort of droid. There was only one thing Czerka was throwing away that the blackguards could want. "This entire raid may've been no more than an attempt to steal kohlen crystals."

"Who knows why the Opposition does anything?" Deren said, contempt in every syllable.

Qui-Gon frowned, ready to object, but then another figure emerged from the forest—Pax Maripher, in an absurdly oversized blue coat.

"Where is she?" Pax called. "Rahara's not back by now, which suggests she set down here, and as I couldn't fly through this melee—" He waved his arms about in the general direction of the air traffic, even though by now it had largely died down. "—I was forced to walk here to fetch her."

"Independent pilots," Qui-Gon said to Deren in a low voice, before turning back to Pax. "I'm afraid the *Facet* was downed during the fight. Rahara's no longer in the cockpit. We're searching for her."

Pax's face turned pale as he hurried toward the *Facet*—even paler than it usually was. "Were there security droids here? Scanning equipment and people?" When Qui-Gon nodded, Pax stopped in his tracks, fisting his hands in his wild hair as he muttered, "She wasn't tagged any longer. She had her gloves. They didn't get her. They couldn't have."

Captain Deren removed his hat, as he might when approaching the loved ones of one who had fallen in combat. "Forgive me, but—are you speaking of a Czerka slave tag?" When Pax turned toward him in alarm, the captain hastily added, "No word of this will ever be shared with a Czerka representative. This I swear."

"Then yes, that's what I'm speaking of," Pax said.

"I regret to inform you that in recent years, Czerka has upgraded most of their scanner droids with facial recognition technology. They have holos on file of every sentient they've ever owned, going back generations." Deren shook his head sorrowfully. "If this missing person was once owned by Czerka, the security droid probably identified her."

Qui-Gon expected Pax to erupt in fury, to turn on one or both of them, or stalk into the woods without another word. Instead, he simply stood there in the mud, his eyes blank and fearful. Pax resembled nothing so much as a lost child. He didn't move until he spotted something in the mud. Then he knelt and picked up a blue glove, which he folded almost tenderly between both hands.

It was a private moment, one Qui-Gon should witness no more of. He turned to Deren. "You're still assuming the blackguards are affiliated with the Opposition. There's no proof of that, not here or any-where else."

"I know that people who would attack one building would attack another," Deren said. "I know that people who resort to violence will continue to be violent. That tells me all I ever need to know about the Opposition." With that he marched away.

Qui-Gon didn't bother calling after him. There was no point in calling someone who would never listen.

CHAPTER THIRTY-ONE

———————— ✦ ————————

Two days to the coronation, and Fanry had finally gotten nervous. "How about this one?" said the court jeweler, opening yet another antique, plain, wooden box to reveal a jeweled crown—ornate and ostentatious in the extreme, but less so than the first one she'd tried on. Fanry took the crown in her hands and laid it on her own head.

"Now, that's lovely," said Czerka Sector Supervisor Meritt Col, who sat with the other ladies of the court to witness the occasion. "Don't you think so, Minister Orth?"

Minister Orth looked as thrilled as usual, which was to say not at all. "The first crown is the traditional one for coronation ceremonies."

"This coronation is going to be different from the others," Fanry said. Every other Pijali monarch had been assuming absolute power, without a constitution in sight. As she put the second crown aside, she told the court jeweler, "Something less showy would be better."

"Hmm." The jeweler frowned. "Usually 'showy' is the whole point of a crown, even here. Let me go through the treasury records."

As the jeweler began sorting through the treasury via datapad, someone knocked on the door. To Fanry's surprise, it was Rael Averross who said, "Princess, we need to talk."

"It has to wait," she called back. "I'm not done choosing a crown."

"We need to talk *now*," he insisted. He was furious. She'd heard him furious many times, but never at her. It shook her more than she would've thought.

"For shame, Lord Regent!" Minister Orth bustled to the door, the better to shout through it to Averross on the other side. "She isn't fit to be seen. How dare you outrage her modesty this way?"

Fanry put one hand to her hair—which, unlike every other day of her life until now, fell free instead of being wrapped in a headcloth. Only at maturity did a Pijali woman put aside the cloths. The coronation would be the first time Fanry had ever shown her red hair to the world.

"All right, all right, whatever. If we've gotta talk it out like this, we will." Averross paused, maybe to catch his breath; it sounded like he might've run all the way from the palace to the treasury. "Fanry, what the hell were you thinking? Sendin' royal troops to the moon?"

From the corner of her eye, Fanry saw Meritt Col stiffen as though she'd been slapped. Apparently the supervisor was well aware that the Jedi didn't care for Czerka's presence on Pijal. In an even tone, Fanry said only, "Master Jinn needed assistance."

"Master Jinn's the one trying to screw up the treaty, the hyperspace corridor, your coronation—everything we've worked for since I got here!"

Fanry sighed. "Master Jinn is a Jedi, sent to help us by the Jedi Council. So, while he's on Pijal, he's under our protection. It's our duty to make sure that he remains safe. We must do our duty, even when he fails to do his."

"*Very* well said, Your Serene Highness." Minister Orth drew herself upright, as though Averross were somehow able to see her through the door. "Are we done here, Lord Regent? May the princess return to her task?"

"Yeah, whatever." Averross said no more.

Probably he'd go work off some of his anger on a long ride. Fanry wondered what it would be like when they spoke again. For now all that mattered was that Minister Orth was calm, Meritt Col had relaxed again, and her hair had not been revealed too soon.

The crown jeweler held out the smallest box yet. "Try this, Your Serene Highness."

Opening the lid, Fanry saw a delicate circlet, beaded with tiny gemstones that would catch the light and sparkle in a dozen different shades. She laid it on her head and looked at herself in the mirror—as the queen she would soon be. "Oh, it's perfect," she said. "This is the one."

Qui-Gon returned from Pijal with Captain Deren on one of the royal ships. Obi-Wan would fly back later, after helping Pax Maripher repair the *Facet*; given what had happened to Rahara Wick, they owed the man all the assistance they could manage. The trip back might've provided an opportunity to hear whether all the royal troops shared Deren's thought about the blackguards and the Opposition. Instead, Qui-Gon was treated to several rounds of marching songs, in varying degrees of cheerful obscenity. He returned to the palace none the wiser.

Rahara Wick's fate troubled him deeply. She'd taken a risk he hadn't asked her to take, one she'd faced with a full understanding of the dangers involved. He knew he wasn't directly responsible for her fate. Yet she would never have been anywhere near the Czerka facility if he hadn't strong-armed the *Meryx* crew into assisting with his mission.

Qui-Gon paused in the hall leading to his chamber in the palace. His spirit was in turmoil. He needed to still it, through a deeper level of meditation. For this he needed solitude.

He wound his way through the palace until he found a lesser-used area, and within it the stairway to a tower. The steps had been carved out of rock long ago, their edges worn soft and rounded by centuries of feet. Qui-Gon had to duck most of the way. Certainly it seemed as if very few people came to this part of the palace; maybe this would offer him an hour of silence and peace.

Instead, when he reached the top terrace and stepped into the open air, he found Rael Averross standing there.

Rael's arms were crossed against his chest, and he was looking across the pathway that led to the palace, lined by heavy, ancient trees. When he glanced over, he made a sound that might've been a scoff, or a laugh. "Figures. I try to get away from it all, and you follow me anyhow."

Qui-Gon felt much the same. Saying so would get them nowhere.

Instead he walked out onto the terrace, taking a good look around at the splendor of their surroundings. "You must've enjoyed spending eight years in a place as beautiful as this."

Rael shrugged. "Never gave a damn about this kind of stuff."

Which was true. "That's why you were able to handle this assignment when many other Jedi couldn't have."

"The Jedi live in the fanciest building on the fanciest planet in the galaxy. I imagine most of 'em could deal with Pijal just fine." Rael rested his elbows on the stone wall that ringed the top of the tower. "The Council sent me here because they knew how I felt about Nim. They knew I'd never get over it unless I got to do right by some other kid, but I told 'em not to give me another Padawan—not then, not ever. So they sent me here to bring up Fanry."

Qui-Gon asked, "Has it helped?"

"Some. But it doesn't fix it. Nothing's ever gonna fix it." Pulling back from the wall, Rael shook himself out of his contemplative mood. "What're *you* doing up here?"

"Searching for solitude and quiet."

"We've gotten pretty good at sabotaging each other. At least, you've gotten good at sabotaging me. Don't know that I'll get any chances for payback."

"Do you *want* payback?" Qui-Gon wondered just how far Rael had deviated from Jedi teachings.

"Don't know. What I do know is that I'm in a bad mood, and if I can't meditate it away, I'm gonna have to work it out." Rael took the hilt of his lightsaber in his hand. "Wanna spar?"

Since it looked like Qui-Gon wasn't going to get a chance to meditate, either . . . "Let's."

They ignited their lightsabers at the same moment—Rael's blue, Qui-Gon's green. The two Jedi circled each other, taking stock. They'd sparred against each other many times, but not since Rael was a young man and Qui-Gon no more than a boy. Past experience might not apply.

Rael swung first, going low; Qui-Gon parried and followed through on the movement, turning so that he was now closer to the wall.

"So these days, you make sure to cover your ass," Rael said, shifting his weight from foot to foot. "Used to be, you threw yourself into a fight like you meant it."

"Dooku taught us caution," Qui-Gon said. "Well. He tried to."

That made Rael laugh. "First he taught us to trust our instincts. So that's what I do."

He moved forward at such speed Qui-Gon scarcely had time to bring his lightsaber up to block. The electric hum of their weapons turned to the crash of static as their blades collided. One push backward and Qui-Gon had driven Rael out again.

"Dooku also taught us about the ancient mystics." How much Qui-Gon would give to know his old Master's thoughts about this situation. "But only after *you* introduced me to the prophecies."

"Because they were a hell of a lot more interesting than anything else you could learn outta books," Rael said. "Still, I never took that stuff literally."

Qui-Gon raised an eyebrow. "Dooku believed in them once, and eventually did again."

At the last word, he went on the attack. Qui-Gon swung his blade, sharp short moves that forced Rael back several steps, until they stood together at the center of the terrace.

But Rael remained undaunted. "Dooku left the Jedi. You've gotta admit, it doesn't sound like he's putting his full faith in the Jedi teachings anymore."

"Do *you* still have faith?" Qui-Gon asked, taking a step forward. Their lightsabers weren't touching, but were so close sparks crackled between them. "That's all that matters here."

"Let's say I do," Rael answered. "Let's say I believe that someday there's going to be perfect balance in the Force, thanks to some kinda 'Chosen One.' Did you ever really think about what that would mean, Qui-Gon? It would mean the darkness would be just as strong as the light. So it doesn't matter what we do, because in the end, hey, it's a tie! It doesn't matter which side we choose."

Qui-Gon straightened and deactivated his blade. Rael took a step back, lowering his lightsaber but keeping it on.

"It matters," Qui-Gon said quietly. "It matters which side we choose. Even if there will never be more light than darkness. Even if there can be no more joy in the galaxy than there is pain. For every action we undertake, for every word we speak, for every life we touch—it matters. I don't turn toward the light because it means someday I'll 'win' some sort of cosmic game. I turn toward it *because it is the light.*"

Rael turned off his lightsaber then, but the contest wasn't completely over. "You've made mistakes, Qui-Gon. You've touched darkness."

"Yes, I have. No doubt I will again. This isn't a choice we make once and walk away from. It's the work of a lifetime." Qui-Gon headed for the door. Strangely, despite everything, he had found a greater sense of peace. "Take up that work again, Rael. Let yourself be guided by the Force."

"I'm not your Padawan," Rael replied. "So save it."

Qui-Gon saved it. He went downstairs wondering when—or if—his old friend would again be guided by his principles rather than his shame.

———

In the early evening on Pijal's moon, the sky took on a vivid shade of pink. Pijal hung enormous and golden in the sky, giving the scene a kind of beauty it didn't deserve.

Obi-Wan knelt in the muck that had been a Czerka compound and then a battleground. Next to him was the *Facet,* and in its cockpit sat Pax Maripher, who wanted to test their repairs.

"All right. What do you see when I do this?" Pax asked, to the sound of a flipped switch.

"The wing curvature increases the degree of its arc," Obi-Wan said, reaching toward a panel by the wing.

"Splendid. And what about this?"

"Ow!" Obi-Wan pulled back his hand. After sucking on his singed finger for a second, he answered, "The antigrav units warm up—literally."

"Well. That's good then. That's good." Pax said the words absently, as though he didn't wholly remember where he was. "I suppose there's no reason for me to stick around, then."

They'd double-, triple-, and quadruple-checked the minor repairs the *Facet* had needed. Obi-Wan strongly suspected Pax was putting off his departure out of the irrational hope that Rahara Wick would suddenly appear and explain where she'd been. But night was falling, and more than one armed group was running amok on this moon. They both needed to leave.

"Pax?" he asked. "If it would help, you could head back to the *Meryx* and bring it up. That way I could pilot the *Facet* into its hold."

"Oh. Yes. Of course. Very logical."

Slowly, as though his muscles were sore, Pax climbed from the *Facet* cockpit and wandered into the woods. How long would it be before he could bring himself to take off? A while, Obi-Wan thought. So he didn't climb into the *Facet* himself right away.

His comlink buzzed. He took it up and said, "Kenobi here."

"*Padawan Kenobi.*" It was Mace Windu's voice. "*Is this an opportune time to speak?*"

The Jedi Council had made its decision.

CHAPTER THIRTY-TWO

W hat action could not do, diplomacy might accomplish.
Or, failing that, money.

"Supervisor Col," Qui-Gon said, taking a seat in her luxurious office. "Thank you for agreeing to see me on such short notice, and at such a late hour."

"I'd been hoping to speak with you, too." Meritt Col folded her hands together on her desk. Through the enormous window behind her, he could see the palace silhouetted by the last fading light of sundown. "Besides, we're all putting in long hours preparing for the coronation. Czerka's sponsoring numerous fairs and activities in honor of the future queen."

"A sector supervisor helps organize public events?" Qui-Gon asked mildly, accepting a small cup of tea from a little LEP servant droid. "That seems—well, beneath your station."

Corporate types were always protective of their status, and Meritt Col was no exception. She was quick to explain. "I prefer to think of it as an investment in Czerka's future, both here on Pijal and in regard to the new hyperspace corridor. Everything we can do to ensure a smooth transfer of power is, in the end, as much of a benefit to this company as it is to Her Serene Highness."

Qui-Gon nodded as though this were any other pleasant conversation over tea. "Of course, it doesn't look like there's going to be a ceremony."

Col's smile stiffened but didn't fade. "I feel sure the Republic will find someone or other to play the part. Please know, Master Jinn, that I don't mean to cast any aspersion on your religious beliefs. But dreams foretelling the future—well, that's not how Czerka Corporation makes decisions. I'd been hoping to talk to you to see if anything might persuade you to . . . reconsider the basis for your actions."

In other words, she hoped he might take a bribe. Probably Meritt Col had more sense than to offer him money, but other forms of bait might be dangled. Qui-Gon wondered whether any Jedi had ever bitten.

Not many of them, certainly—but one or two? Perhaps, especially since Col was smiling at him brightly in a way that suggested she felt optimistic.

"My decision is final. And I doubt the Republic will be sending anyone else to sign the Governance Treaty, not without significant changes." Although Qui-Gon wasn't sure how quickly the Jedi Council would react, he knew Yoda had listened to his concerns and taken them seriously. For all Yoda's lectures about how the Jedi should not rule, he had a funny way of convincing Chancellor Kaj to listen; action would be taken. No more people would be enslaved on Pijal.

But that wasn't what Qui-Gon had come here to negotiate.

"Let's put political matters behind us," he said, setting down his cup. "Yesterday, on Pijal's moon, a person Czerka formerly held as 'sentient property' was retaken into custody—"

"Not 'formerly.' "

Qui-Gon frowned. "I beg your pardon?"

"Those who escaped, rather than legally purchasing their freedom or having it purchased for them, are not 'formerly' owned by Czerka," said Col. "They're *still* owned by Czerka. Our corporate charters specify this in great detail, and of course, any planet that does business with us must agree to operate in accordance with the charter. That includes Pijal."

Every word of this was odious to Qui-Gon, but he remained calm. He was here to accomplish one task and one task only. "Then, as you would have it, a woman owned by Czerka was taken back into custody after several years at large. I wish to negotiate for, or purchase, her freedom."

Col blinked. Whatever she'd been expecting him to say, it wasn't that. "A Jedi wishes to buy a slave. My. How *novel*."

"In order to free her," Qui-Gon emphasized.

Meritt Col pursed her lips. "Would you be willing to consider a price other than money? Say, your cooperation in the treaty ceremony? Agreeing to represent the Republic?"

The automatic answer stilled in his throat. Could he use this position to bargain for meaningful changes—the amendment of the treaty, or even banning slavery on Pijal? Could he not only recover Rahara Wick, but also benefit the entire planet?

Probably not. Qui-Gon's heart sank as he realized how unlikely the Jedi Council was to back him up on this. It was an overreach of his power as a representative, and he knew it.

Besides that, his vision remained vivid. Qui-Gon had seen bloodshed and mayhem at the treaty ceremony. He knew—as absolutely as though he'd already lived through it—that he could not allow the ceremony to occur. Not even to save his own life.

"That's not possible," he said. "However, I'm prepared to offer a considerable amount of money—or perhaps offer advice on how certain political situations might change when Chancellor Kaj leaves office."

Meritt Col's eyes lit up, and for a moment Qui-Gon thought it might be that easy. His opinions weren't based on any confidential information; many people assumed that the Jedi must have inside knowledge of government workings, which was only partially true. Qui-Gon had no more idea than anyone else in the galaxy about what the other candidates like Elissiar or Valorum might do in office. He would opine at length, though, if it freed Rahara Wick.

Then Col's expression hardened. "I'm afraid I can't do that. Honestly, I'm not sure there's any bargain we could've struck. When a slave escapes, it's important to show the others the futility of that action. Allowing such a person to be purchased and freed immediately— well, it could create unrest. Raise false hopes. I'm sure you understand what I mean."

"You mean," Qui-Gon said, "that there's nothing I can do to change your mind."

With a broad smile, Col said, "Absolutely nothing."

"Wick, Rahara." The cam droid took images of her from every angle as she stood shivering in the processing chamber. Meanwhile the RQ protocol droid shuffled around her, reciting the facts out loud. *"Born to Czerka twenty-nine years prior in the Hosnian Prime factory complex. Reported missing fifteen years, two months, and two days prior. Recovered today at approximately—"*

"I wasn't born to Czerka," Rahara said. Her voice was almost drowned out by the hissing of steam vents and the constant clanking of droids and prisoner footsteps on the metal grid floors. "I was born to parents. Human parents. Don't guess you could tell me who they were?"

Sometimes she believed she remembered them. Most of the time, she knew better.

The RQ unit paused. *"The requested records are irrelevant."*

"You know, I have a friend who was raised by protocol droids." Could Rahara connect with this thing? She'd actually learned how to get through to Pax, from time to time. Maybe she could put that experience to good use. "By threepio units—not arcues—but all protocol droids must have a lot in common, right?"

"We have protocol in common," the RQ said.

"Right! Exactly. Well, my friend, Pax—he said that protocol droids have a well-developed moral sense. Better than most humans, even." Her voice shook as she spoke Pax's name. Half the time, he'd driven her so crazy she'd wanted to toss him out of the nearest air lock. But the other half—Rahara swallowed hard. If she thought about Pax right now, she'd break down, and she was close enough to that already. "He—he said that if protocol droids made the rules, the galaxy would make a lot more sense."

The RQ model pivoted at its waist to study her more closely. *"This is fact."*

Mostly, she was just stalling. Rahara could see the intake doors three meters away, and knew she'd be marched through them, cuffed, and penned, then put to work here while awaiting reassignment. If she could trust her memories of others who had been recaptured, her next assignment wasn't going to be anything cushy. Czerka would pack her off to the spice mines of Kessel, or bitterly cold construction work on Stygeon Prime. There would be no mercy for her.

"So, as a protocol droid, maybe you can tell me something." Rahara wiped steam-damp hair away from her face. The scratchy Czerka coverall clung to her skin as if trying to asphyxiate her. "Why does Czerka keep people, when droids can do the work better, and last longer, and are cheaper? *Why?* What's the point?"

The RQ unit cocked its head. *"Czerka Corporation enslaves sentient beings because it can."* Then it sent her through to finish processing.

Qui-Gon walked from Czerka headquarters back toward the palace. Hovering candledroids illuminated his path, as well as some other areas around the grounds. At first, he took little note of them; the palace was always surrounded by illumination, and he was preoccupied with the idea of freeing Rahara Wick. If Meritt Col refused to either sell or barter for her, maybe he should adopt a . . . less legal approach. An individual starfighter or two might be able to slip through the *Leverage*'s defenses, if a distraction could be created.

But as he considered possible distractions (set a derelict craft to self-destruct?), his attention was gradually drawn back to the present. In the rapidly darkening night, it was becoming apparent that the area around the palace was brighter than usual. Significantly brighter. Stepping from the tree-lined path onto the broad lawn gave him a view of sentry guards and worker droids, hard at work around an entertainment pavilion, the broad balcony over the sea, and especially the Celestial Chalice.

When Qui-Gon walked through the palace door, he was greeted with a similar scene. Fresh flowers in brilliant colors had been heaped into pottery jugs set upon every flat surface. Two droids worked together to wax the floor of the great hallway—one rolling about to spread the wax, the other following behind to buff. One of the cooks was hurrying toward the kitchen, speaking into his comlink: "No, sixty fruit displays won't be enough! We need at least eighty . . . yes, I know about the short notice, but there's nothing to be done . . ."

"Jedi Jinn." Minister Orth appeared, straightening her tan cloak. "Well. You don't lack courage, I'll grant you that."

Qui-Gon elected not to take that conversational bait. "Where are you going?"

"To review the seating charts. Don't worry. I don't hold grudges. You'll have a front-row view." She gave him a thin smile before continuing on her way.

The coronation, he thought. *The treaty. They can't be going ahead with it, can they?*

He hurried toward their quarters. Surely there was some message from the Jedi Council about this. Had Rael contacted them to request another representative? Had they been weak-willed enough to do it? Or had a new version of the constitution and treaty been drafted, setting everything to rights?

"Obi-Wan?" Qui-Gon called as he walked through the entrance into their shared living area. "Are you here?"

"Yes, Master." Obi-Wan appeared in the doorway to his bedroom. He both looked and sounded subdued. "I am."

"What the blazes is going on around here?" Qui-Gon shrugged off his robe.

"They're preparing for the treaty ceremony," Obi-Wan said. "The coronation, the constitution—all of it."

"How, precisely, do they intend to go ahead with this?" Darker suspicions entered his mind. "Has Czerka convinced them they don't need the Republic at all?"

Obi-Wan shook his head. "No, Master. Nothing like that." He swallowed hard. "The Jedi Council—the Council has named me the rightful representative of the Republic, for the purposes of the ceremony."

A Padawan representing the entire Republic? Even a Padawan as strong as Obi-Wan? It made no sense. "Rael contacted them, and this was their answer?"

"I contacted them." Obi-Wan straightened up. "You and Master Averross had reached an impasse. Neither of you was willing to seek the Council's advice. So I had to do it. I never thought this is what they'd decide, but it's what they've asked me to do."

The sense of abandonment—of betrayal—closed around Qui-Gon like a fist. Obi-Wan had done this?

It took him several silent moments to come up with any words. "You're willing to sign a treaty and ratify a constitution that will seal both slavery and Czerka Corporation in place on this planet forever?"

"No, Master." Obi-Wan shook his head so quickly that, in less dire circumstances, it would've been comical. "The Senate committee drafted a clause saying that essentially the treaty's terms are only temporary—really, it's just a way to open the hyperspace corridor and get the democratic assembly into office. Then Pijal has to offer a new constitution and a new treaty to the Republic within one local year. Of course the Senate has strongly indicated the changes they expect to see."

"Which they won't," Qui-Gon said. "Are they naïve enough to think that Czerka won't bribe every newly elected official? Are *you*? The lone advantage of leaving authority in the hands of a monarchy is that you only have to convince one person to create positive change. Now there will be hundreds with scraps of authority, many of whom will already be financially tied to Czerka."

Obi-Wan's expression shifted from shamefaced to stubborn. "You've always claimed to have faith in democratic institutions. You praised them only a few days ago! Is it so different here on Pijal?"

"Maybe not. But maybe it is." Qui-Gon sank down heavily on the nearest chair. The images from his dream flooded into his mind, and he had to envision Obi-Wan amid the conflict and the bloodshed, fighting for his life. "None of this changes the vision I've seen of the future. But of course, you don't believe in the vision. You don't believe in prophecy."

"I believe in *you*, Master," Obi-Wan insisted, crestfallen again. "More than I think you realize. But I also believe that the future is always in motion."

"Thanks to your interference," Qui-Gon said, "Pijal's future is written in blood."

He walked out, leaving his apprentice behind.

CHAPTER THIRTY-THREE

"Useless," said Pax Maripher.

He sat in the cargo hold of the *Meryx*, which was illuminated only by the glow of the scanner-blocking field. Proper procedure at the conclusion of a trip called for taking stock of all items sold and obtained. For this voyage, the profit came solely from his bargain with Czerka, which felt even more stained than it had before. Besides that, he had nothing to show for the trip other than an empty pilot's chair next to him, and piles of kohlen crystals.

Kohlen. The whole reason they'd come to Pijal. *Fool's kyber* would be a better name for it. If he'd been able to tell the difference, then the *Meryx* would've gone on to Gamorr as planned. Instead, he had a mediocre haul of a gem that was semiprecious at best, a bunch of orange crystals that were completely useless, and . . . no copilot/minerals analyst.

Remain calm, he told himself. *Of course it's terribly inconvenient, but someone else can be hired, and quickly, too. There are always a large number of pilots looking for work.*

That's what the droids who raised him would've said. Every bit of it was factual, and therefore it was a reasonable, rational way to react to the loss of his copilot. As he had repeatedly stated, their relationship was strictly one of business, without any time-wasting deviations into friendship or . . .

"Just business," Pax muttered.

Saying it aloud made no difference. No matter how many logical reasons he had for behaving otherwise, Pax's mind refused to quit thinking about Rahara.

What was happening to her at this moment? She'd been a mine worker as a child, and had hated it. Would Czerka Corporation shove her back underground? But there were worse jobs—the worst in the galaxy—and Pax knew enough of Czerka to believe they might be punitive toward a recovered escapee. Or maybe she would be sold off as a "troublemaker." In that case, she could wind up anywhere, doing anything.

None of which was relevant to his situation or his plans.

Pax wondered if maybe he was overlooking certain elements of the situation. His brain could be attempting to alert him to his faulty logic.

Yes, there were always pilots seeking work. But pilots who were willing to perform illegal tasks weren't always the sort of pilots who could be trusted. Rahara was one of the exceptions. Her combination of flying skill and mineralogical knowledge was both incredibly unusual and highly valuable to him.

Rahara's rarest talent of all—she'd *liked* him. She'd understood him in a way few others even tried to. Most sentients found him abrasive, which meant the average time of employment for all the pilots Pax had hired before Rahara was approximately twenty days. He had no desire to return to such high levels of turnover, but it seemed that he missed her as a person, and the warmth she had brought to his life, even more than he'd needed her as a pilot.

In his head, he could just hear B-3PO saying, *Why, that's the silliest thing I ever heard.*

When the derelict station had finally been boarded, more than fifteen years since Pax had been stranded there as a child, the droids that raised him had been pleased.

"Just think," said G-3PO, *"I'll finally be translating again! It's been ever so long."*

"We will miss you." B-3PO had tilted her blue head to study Pax for the last time. *"But now all of us can return to our proper functionality, including you. How wonderful that we've all been rescued!"*

The droids shuffled off, clanking down the corridor. Pax had been left there, clutching his few possessions in a bag, wondering why he wanted to cry.

He felt like that again now. Rahara's presence haunted the *Meryx.* Her black scarf was still wrapped around the copilot's chair. When Pax opened the mess stores, he saw her Chandrilan tea there, waiting for her. The cargo hold still smelled faintly of that complicated floral scent Rahara had bought on Coruscant and insisted on wearing, over his repeated objections.

I believe, Pax said to himself, *that this is known as grief.*

B-3PO answered in his mind: *Well, it's not as though there's anything you can do about it. That's our lot in life.*

The *Meryx* versus the *Leverage*—no, that wasn't a contest likely to end well for him. Nor did he expect Jedi Knights to help him break at least a dozen laws. So he was helpless. But Pax remained paralyzed, unable to leave the system while there was any chance Rahara might still be in it.

His comm chimed. Pax's heart leapt—for absolutely no rational reason—then plunged when he recognized the frequency. He grabbed the comm. "Sorry, we don't do business with the Jedi any longer. So you can take your comlink and—"

"I think we can get Rahara out," said Qui-Gon Jinn. *"Unofficially, that is."*

Pax reviewed what he thought he'd just heard. "Let me make sure I've understood you. Are you, a so-called guardian of peace and justice in the galaxy, suggesting an illegal raid?"

"Precisely."

He knew without being told that any such raid would be dangerous, even with the Jedi on his side; the odds would be against them. He also knew that the rational thing to do was to get out of this system immediately, head to Gamorr, sell off his cargo, and start over with a new pilot.

But Pax also knew—as surely as though he'd decided it long ago—that even if there was only a one in two million, twenty thousand, four hundred and seven chance of getting Rahara back, he wasn't leaving this system without her.

Everyone in Pijal seemed to be referring to the day as "Coronation Eve." By now the entire palace was in an uproar of activity and celebration.

Qui-Gon would have nothing to do with it.

Instead, he stayed inside the palace dock. Tomorrow the area would be crowded with private spaceships and landspeeders, but today his only companions were sentry droids. Qui-Gon lay on a levitator to get under the small craft Fanry had put at his and Obi-Wan's disposal—the one they'd flown to and from their rendezvous with Pax and Rahara. He wanted to know the thing inside and out before he finalized any plans. The ship was in sterling condition, but it wouldn't be very good at jamming signals on its own. However, with the help of the *Meryx*'s field, it might be possible for them to approach the *Leverage* without being detected . . .

"Wait until tomorrow night."

Qui-Gon slid out from under the ship to see Obi-Wan standing there. ". . . I beg your pardon?"

"You shouldn't try to rescue Rahara Wick until tomorrow night," Obi-Wan said. He looked neither ashamed nor defiant, only calm. "Czerka will be on high alert until the treaty ceremony is over. Afterward, though, it sounds like every Czerka higher-up will be attending one of the many parties. Private citizens will take their ships into orbit as part of the celebration. That makes it easier to go unnoticed, and when you get to the *Leverage*, it ought to be all but deserted."

"An excellent plan," Qui-Gon said. "I'm chagrined I didn't think of it myself."

Obi-Wan ducked his head. "You've had other things on your mind."

The nightmarish scenario Qui-Gon knew would unfold at the ceremony had been replaying constantly in his head. He felt sickened every time he thought about Obi-Wan in the middle of that. Yet he knew there was nothing more he could do. The Council had made a terrible decision, and Obi-Wan would always obey the Council. "Yes, I have. And how did you know I was planning a rescue?"

"Because you pulled up full diagrams and schematics of the *Leverage* this morning," Obi-Wan said—then added, anticipating the next question, "I know that because I requested them right after you did. Your name was still listed as the last user of the terminal."

Qui-Gon couldn't help smiling. "So I'm not the only one planning a rescue."

By now Obi-Wan had begun to relax. Some of his old humor came through as he said, "Another advantage of waiting until tomorrow night is that after the ceremony, my schedule is entirely free."

If he's alive. But Qui-Gon couldn't dwell on that any longer. The only way he could help Obi-Wan, at this point, was by attending the coronation. His foreknowledge would help him when disaster struck, and that might give him the chance to save his Padawan, Fanry, and others. It was his one hope.

"Tomorrow night, then." Qui-Gon got to his feet, wiping his greasy hands with a rag. "Thank you, Obi-Wan. I needed that clarity."

"I'm glad you—" Obi-Wan stopped. "Of course you're angry with me. But you'd always put the mission first."

"Always," Qui-Gon affirmed.

It was easier to face tomorrow, now that he and his apprentice had again found some common ground. If the worst should happen, at least they had been able to speak to each other with respect and kindness, one more time.

Maybe Obi-Wan's decision already changed the flow of events, Qui-

Gon thought as he listened to Obi-Wan's laughter. *Maybe that will be enough to change the future.*

Yet he still felt the weight of foreboding—the absolute sureness that deadly trouble was coming—

Obi-Wan went silent, which was when Qui-Gon heard it, too: an enormous commotion outside the palace. As they turned to each other, Obi-Wan said, "What is *that*?"

As Rael Averross saw it, things were finally going right.

Qui-Gon's Padawan had turned out to be more useful than his Master. Fanry was now alight with excitement about the ceremony to-morrow, and if she'd gone rogue sending Deren up to the moon—well, okay, she'd had a point. It was just more proof that he'd done a good job teaching her. Averross had sensed the growing determination within her. Fanry was ready to be a monarch, at least in the constitu-tional sense, and in less than a day Averross would see that crown on her head at last.

"Ready for the party, Orth?" he called as he walked the perimeter of the Celestial Chalice, curving in one giant circle. "Gonna save me that first dance?"

Minister Orth stood on the central dais, checking the lighting or something. He expected her to snap back. Instead, she said, "I've promised every single dance to others, Lord Regent. You'll have to ask earlier next time. However, I *will* allow you to bring me a drink." With the air of someone who had made a great concession, she turned back to her work.

Averross managed not to laugh. So apparently Orth wasn't always as sour with others as she was with him—

"What's going on? What's that sound?" Orth said, straightening her pince-nez, like that would help her hear.

At first Averross thought it was no more than another roar from the crowd that had been mobbed outside since the ceremony's hour had finally been announced. But the noise kept building. Kept coming closer. It didn't sound happy.

His hand went to the hilt of his lightsaber. "What the hell?" he growled as he headed for the door that led not back into the palace, but outside.

The royal grounds remained green and peaceful. Whatever was going on was happening outside the wrought-iron fence surrounding the palace. Averross ran across the grounds toward the main gate, where he could see Captain Deren and his guards beginning to gather.

"Deren!" he shouted. "Any idea what the ruckus is about?"

"We've received reports—" Deren began, but the shouting got even louder. He shoved his scanner toward Averross. Above it hovered a grainy hologram of Halin Azucca. Although he couldn't hear what she was saying over the din, her words appeared under her face: AS WE AP-PROACH THIS CHANGE IN GOVERNMENT, IT IS NECESSARY FOR ALL VOICES TO BE HEARD; FOR ALL VOICES TO BE HEARD, WE NEED THE TRUTH TO BE KNOWN; THE TRUTH ABOUT THE OPPOSITION CANNOT BE KNOWN IF THE PALACE REFUSES TO LISTEN. I KNOW OF ONLY ONE WAY TO MAKE THEM LISTEN.

The noise from the crowd became deafening. Averross looked up from the hologram to see people parting in a wave to reveal Halin Azucca herself, riding on a richly decorated mobile stage that hovered a few centimeters above the ground. She wore extravagant green robes as though she'd been invited to the coronation ball, but she kept her hands raised above her head.

Beneath her hologram appeared the words: I SURRENDER.

CHAPTER THIRTY-FOUR

When Qui-Gon and Obi-Wan received the summons to the royal chamber, Qui-Gon decided to take the long way around—which meant cutting across the palace courtyard. This would let them get a look at the crowd gathering outside, to gauge its mood for themselves.

The shouts and cries from the horde had reached a deafening pitch. Obi-Wan grimaced, but Qui-Gon kept his focus on the Pijali citizens, scanning their faces. Some showed anger, but others looked worried or even hopeful. Through the Force he could sense the swirling eddies of many different emotions. No one mood or thought dominated the crowd.

Once they walked back into the palace, as soon as his ears stopped ringing, Qui-Gon said, "Apparently the people of this planet had more faith in the Opposition than its leadership did."

"Agreed, Master. At least, some of them did, and Azucca's actions today may convince others."

"But can they convince Rael Averross?" The man had one day left as lord regent of Pijal. Was that the best time for Halin to throw herself on his mercy, or the worst?

They walked into a space they'd never been invited to before: the lord regent's private office—a cluttered place, as musty and run-down as everything else Rael surrounded himself with. Various data solids, holoprojectors, and scanners were piled so high they blocked half the light from the dusty windows; Qui-Gon wondered absently whether anything that had entered this office had ever been taken out again.

But most of his attention remained focused on Halin, who sat in a chair opposite the broad regent's desk. She sat up straight and wore her green theatrical robes with flair. Rael, meanwhile, was pacing on the other side of the desk like a caged beast. Ironically, the revolutionary appeared more regal than the regent did.

"I don't know what kind of a stunt you're trying to pull here," Rael said, still pacing. "Showing up here, spinning your stories—"

"This isn't a story." Halin glanced back at Qui-Gon and Obi-Wan; she seemed glad they were there, but she directed her words to the lord regent alone. "This is truth. *Verifiable truth,* if you'll follow up on these leads."

She nodded toward a datapad in Captain Deren's hands, which apparently had been confiscated from her when she turned herself in. Deren glared. "This shows us nothing," he says. "It's locked."

Halin took a deep breath. "Master Jinn can unlock it. Only Master Jinn."

"What do you mean?" Qui-Gon reached out to take the datapad; Deren handed it over, with a frown. "And what truth am I to find here?"

"After you were in the cave with us, we took your thumbprint from something you'd touched. Sorry if that's invasive, but already I knew it could come to this." She stared down at her hands in her lap, shackled together by the binders that mocked her supposedly genteel reception in the office. "The regent's never treated us fairly before, and where the regent goes, the palace guard follows—"

"Treated you *fairly,*" Rael practically snarled at her. "What's 'fair' for a bunch of terrorists?"

Halin ignored this. "After we met you, Master Jinn, we saw that you were impartial, and committed to determining the facts of the situation. So we wanted this information to come through you and you alone."

"Taking a print *is* invasive—but I understand your reasoning." Qui-Gon pressed his thumb on the identiscan. After a moment, the datapad hummed, then displayed its data.

Obi-Wan, who was looking over Qui-Gon's shoulder, read more quickly. "You think you've identified a blackguard base here on Pijal?"

Rael scoffed. "That's nonsense. The armed attacks have all been based from the moon, which by no coincidence is where her Opposition is based."

"The armed attacks *have* all originated on the moon." The admission cost Halin—Qui-Gon could see that—but she was more hopeful than afraid. "So we never really searched the planet before. After the last attack on Czerka, though, one of my people was finally able to lock onto a blackguard signal and follow it to the planet's surface. She used to work in holovids, you know, so she's good at that kind of thing. We were surprised, too—"

"Like hell you were." Rael was still pacing. Anyone who didn't know him as well, Qui-Gon thought, wouldn't have been able to spot these first slivers of doubt.

Halin closed her eyes, as though asking for patience. "What we found is a heavily armed installation. Since we're a theater troupe"—Halin ignored Rael's snarl—"obviously we don't have the skills or the firepower to check this out ourselves. Instead, I've brought it to you. All I ask is that you investigate this base thoroughly, on your own terms."

"We will," Qui-Gon said. "With or without the help of royal officials. Though I'd prefer you were with us, Rael."

Deren looked back and forth between the two men. "Lord Regent? Your orders?"

Finally Rael stopped pacing. He took a deep breath. "We've got nothing to lose. Let's go."

Their craft swept along the coastline, with sand on one side and sea on the other.

On a boundary, Averross thought. *Toeing the line. Like I always am.*

During his eight years as lord regent of Pijal, he'd begun to feel as though he'd carved out a place for himself for the first time in his life. This was a place that understood how a rough exterior could conceal a worthy interior. A place where his raw feelings about Nim's death could serve a worthwhile purpose. His place. Averross trusted himself on Pijal, and he'd never thought he would trust himself again, after the *Advent* mutiny.

But if he'd been wrong about the Opposition—if he'd put royal guards in danger, put *Fanry* in danger—

"Coming into range," said Qui-Gon. He stood beside Averross in the craft, both of them holding on to anchor straps as they were buffeted by winds from the open sides. The scanner Qui-Gon held in his other hand blinked rapidly, white-red-white, signaling their prey.

"All right. Deren, take us in," Averross called.

Captain Deren responded only by bringing the craft down.

A few hundred meters from the ocean, dug-out trenches began to appear. Then stonework. Then a familiar, octagonal shape.

"A Celestial Watchtower," Averross muttered. He didn't realize he'd spoken out loud until Qui-Gon and Obi-Wan turned to him, curious. "It's an ancient fort, built to watch over the soulcraft back in the days when spaceflight was a lot more dangerous. Most of 'em are ruins now. Looks like this one was, too . . . until somebody decided to renovate."

Ground craft. Surface-to-air weapons. Laser cannons. Top-of-the-line droidekas. This was a serious military installation. Beyond anything the Opposition had ever possessed, so far as Averross knew.

Yet there were no signs of life. No paramilitary troops returning fire, no guards hurrying to evacuate leaders. The place was both armed to the death and completely deserted.

"Lord Regent!" Deren shouted. "Stealth shield generators!"

The craft banked right so sharply that even the Jedi scrambled to stay on their feet. Although the other staffed ships did the same, a seeker droid took the curve at too rounded an angle and flew over the invisible barrier to the watchtower—

—Which promptly became visible, as in a fiery orange wall of energy, the moment the droid struck it and then exploded.

Soot curled into the air as the droid's shell went into a spiral, then crashed onto the stone wall. Averross cursed. "A trap. The damn Opposition led us into a trap!"

"Someone did," Qui-Gon said. "But not the Opposition. Look. Does this seem within the means of a small political group on your moon?"

Qui-Gon pointed at the things Averross had noted for himself—the pricey droideka, the sophisticated armaments. This wasn't the kind of junk ex-performance artists had on hand.

Deren wasn't convinced. "We have no idea who else might be funding the blackguards. Plenty of forces in the galaxy would have good reason to interfere with the hyperspace corridor. Forces that would have no compunction about funneling money and arms to terrorists."

It would be so easy to agree with Deren. But Averross couldn't. The truth had finally become clear to him, and he wouldn't deny it.

"So this trap," Averross said, "you think it was set for us or for the Opposition?"

Basically, he was admitting he'd been wrong. Some people wouldn't have been able to resist the urge to rub it in. Qui-Gon was better than that. "I'm not sure. Can we destroy the stealth generators and investigate?"

"Let's do it." Averross didn't know what else to think, but he was ready to blow some stuff up.

Although Captain Deren feared more traps and argued strongly against landing, several targeted scans convinced Qui-Gon it was safe to enter the watchtower; no further probes had stirred up additional defensive measures. When their craft touched down, Averross jumped off immediately, stalking across the grounds to what looked like the central structure, at least in antiquity. Light rain began to patter down as everyone else began exploring the site.

"Scans or no scans, we should operate at a high level of caution," Captain Deren ordered as his troops began to fan out. "In other words, when in doubt, blow it up."

And if it's useful evidence? Qui-Gon kept the question to himself. They'd already gleaned the most valuable fact this site had to offer— confirmation that the Opposition wasn't behind the blackguard attacks—and Deren was protecting his men.

"There's almost too much to investigate," said Obi-Wan as he gestured at the various buildings and equipment around them. "Where do we start?"

Qui-Gon considered. "We look for comm devices. Past messages, channels of contact. It looks as though the blackguards abandoned this place in a hurry; otherwise they'd never have left so much behind. If they failed to wipe any communications logs, those may lead us to whoever's behind this."

Unfortunately, it appeared the blackguards had recognized that danger. Every main building, every large craft, had had its comm logs completely wiped. When Obi-Wan managed to pull up some records from a deactivated astromech, they were hopeful—but it turned out to contain very little information.

"This doesn't have anything that leads to Pijal or its moon," Obi-Wan said, shoulders drooping. "Only messages to and from other systems, and very few of those."

Qui-Gon scanned the datapad plugged into the astromech. Corellia— probably a straightforward purchase of vessels or weaponry. Scipio— since the InterGalactic Banking Clan was based there, this meant money laundering. Czerka Corporation funneled a lot of its money through Scipio, but so did every other large company in the galaxy, as well as several monarchies, so the link proved nothing. And also—

"*Teth?*" he said. "Why would the blackguards be in touch with anyone on Teth?"

Obi-Wan's surprise was the equal of Qui-Gon's own. "The blackguards couldn't be working for the Hutts. Could they?"

For a moment it seemed all too plausible. The Hutts would no doubt love to slither into power on the planet that would anchor a major hyperspace corridor. But in that case—"There are records of only two communications between Pijal and Teth," Qui-Gon said. "If the Hutts were behind this, there would be much more, and the data wouldn't be stored in a low-security droid."

"That makes sense," Obi-Wan agreed, though he was frowning. "Still, if the blackguards were in touch with the Hutts at all, that can't be good."

Although Qui-Gon's gut told him the Hutts didn't lead to the answers they sought, he was as curious as his apprentice about what this meant. A few clicks with his finger linked the droid to Teth again. "Let's call and find out."

It took a few minutes for a live connection to be established. Qui-Gon settled himself on the ground within the droid's holorange, so he'd look at whoever answered face-to-face. To his displeasure—but not entirely his surprise—the figure that took shape was familiar.

"Jedi Jinn?" Thurible had to have been astonished, but he displayed no sign of it. "I had hoped we would speak again someday."

"No doubt you didn't expect it to be today," Qui-Gon said, "or on this channel. Perhaps you could tell me why you're in touch with a terrorist organization on the planet Pijal?"

Thurible did look surprised now; the man had to be an accomplished actor. "Terrorist organization? Certainly not. My employer would never condone such actions. We were planning to do business with the legitimate government of Pijal . . . or, I must admit, perhaps only individuals who *claimed* to represent the government of Pijal. There are so many dishonest people in the worlds."

Indeed there were. Qui-Gon came close to saying so, before it occurred to him—what if the person who'd spoken to Thurible *was* part of the government?

Someone close to the princess. Someone who'd had access to the innermost areas of the palace. Someone who could breach the security defenses because he already knew what they were—or was the person who'd put them into place to begin with.

Someone like Captain Deren.

Qui-Gon glanced over to where Deren worked alongside his fellow soldiers. As the captain of the royal guard, he could have represented himself accurately as a government official. He'd repeatedly tried to convince them not to land in the watchtower and search it. The man's commitment to his duty seemed so absolute—Qui-Gon had even sensed it through the Force—but could it all be a ruse?

He betrayed none of his suspicions to Thurible. "May I ask what kind of business you were planning to do? What did they want to buy from you?"

Thurible smiled, the expression a brief shadow on the wavering hologram. "Nothing whatsoever. We were the customers."

"Then what did you want to buy from them?" Obi-Wan asked.

"We had heard rumors—via some cargo-hauler pilots from Corellia, who will go nameless—that the military of Pijal had developed a kind of shield that was impervious to lightsabers," Thurible said. "Fascinating, from a scientific point of view."

The implications of this began to sink in for Qui-Gon. "In theory, spice smugglers and gangsters might be able to use such a shield to protect themselves from any interventions by the Jedi."

"It takes more than blocking a lightsaber to defeat a Jedi," said Thurible. "But blocking a lightsaber *helps,* doesn't it? In theory."

Enough of this, Qui-Gon decided. "I'm afraid the issue is now purely theoretical, as Pijal has no such shields to offer."

"Such dishonesty is truly shocking. If anyone from Pijal contacts us in the future, claiming to represent the government, we'll be very certain to check them out thoroughly." Thurible half bowed. "Wanbo is expecting a delegation from Garel. I trust you'll excuse me."

As soon as Thurible's hologram faded out, Obi-Wan said, "Have the blackguards been selling these shields all around the galaxy?"

Qui-Gon shook his head no. "Not yet. But they may have been negotiating with Thurible as a sort of test. Seeing how much money they could get, how much interest there might be for an anti-Jedi shield device."

"It's not as though we're defenseless without lightsabers."

"No. But if a Jedi didn't know her opponent was shielded—if she were lulled into believing her lightsaber provided protection when it didn't—it could prove deadly." Qui-Gon wondered whether Pax Maripher was about to get much better prices for kohlen crystals.

"Master—" Obi-Wan paused, obviously doubting himself. "When Thurible said that about the 'legitimate government,' it made me wonder—I don't want to be unfair—"

"I caught it, too, Padawan. Captain Deren would've had opportunity to warn the watchtower blackguards about our raid, which might've led to them abandoning the place in a hurry. He tried to keep us out of here, and encouraged blowing up devices that might hold records."

Obi-Wan added, "The blackguards went after Czerka, the Opposition, us—but never the royal guard."

"Another excellent point." Rising to his feet, Qui-Gon looked across the grounds of the watchtower. Deren was hard at work, accounting for the few weapons left behind; there were multiple reasons he might want to do so.

"But—Master, he seems so loyal to the princess," Obi-Wan said.

"Which he may be. We have no proof. Only suspicions. That means we'll have to watch Deren very closely." Qui-Gon turned to his apprentice. "I saw Deren in my vision. Of course he's playing a role in Fanry's coronation as the captain of her guard, but it's possible his appearance has a greater significance."

Obi-Wan didn't argue about the vision, which was surprising. "I suppose we can only keep a close eye on him."

"At this point, yes. That's all we can do."

Captain Deren would be standing next to Obi-Wan during the ceremonies. If Qui-Gon's vision came to pass—and he knew that it would—his Padawan would be at the very center of the danger.

Although Qui-Gon had recovered his faith in prophecies, he understood better than ever before how that belief could lead to darkness. The desire to know the future sprang from a desire to control the future. The desire to control the future sprang from fear—the fear of the depthless pain and loss the future might hold.

The quest for power could be overcome, but never, ever, the fear of losing what mattered most.

It was difficult to speak of something so fraught, so intimate—but there might never be another time. "I've been angry with you since you contacted the Council."

Obi-Wan looked wary, as well he might. "That's . . . not surprising."

"On the way here, though, I realized that all these years, I'd been urging you to be more independent. To trust your instincts, and act on your own initiative. That's what you did. We disagree on the particulars, but I can't fault you in principle."

They both fell briefly silent while one of the security droids rolled by; it might not be programmed to monitor their conversation, but while Deren remained under suspicion, they had to be careful. Once it had traveled farther along, Obi-Wan said, "You know, I never had problems with that as a youngling. Being independent, I mean. I broke rules right and left. They even called me rebellious. Probably the Masters were surprised anyone was willing to take me on as an apprentice."

In fact, Qui-Gon had been warned about this very thing. He'd long since assumed that the crèche masters' concern was overcautious. But now, finally, he saw what had happened. He began to laugh.

Obi-Wan stared at him. "Master?"

"Don't you see, Obi-Wan? They knew you'd rebel against any Master you worked with. So they made sure you wound up with a Jedi who almost never followed the rules. The only way for you to rebel was to become the perfect Jedi."

"Hardly perfect," Obi-Wan said, but by now he was laughing, too. "They really did that, didn't they?"

Qui-Gon shook his head. "*Never* underestimate Yoda."

In some ways, he knew, he and his apprentice were still far apart—on separate sides of a profound philosophical divide. With completely different understandings of the Force.

But in other ways, the bond endured. Qui-Gon would have to take what comfort he could in that.

"Relax, kid." Rael's hologram shimmered in the center of Qui-Gon's meditation room. "It sounds like Dooku lost his temper, did something he shouldn't've, but really, when it comes down to it, sometimes you've gotta get the job done, you know?"

"That doesn't sound right to me," Qui-Gon insisted. He hugged his knees to his chest. "It felt worse than anger. It felt—it felt as though Master Dooku was close to darkness."

"He was scared because he was worried about you." Rael shrugged. "That's another thing the Council's dead wrong about. They keep sayin', *Oh, the Jedi aren't allowed to love,* and that's why we're never supposed to get laid—"

"*Rael!*" Qui-Gon felt as if somebody might walk in any second. He'd strongly hoped the meditation room would remain empty at this hour so he could speak with Rael in private without being overheard by other Padawans, Dooku, or anyone else. Nobody but Rael could understand the line their Master walked, or the dangerous allure of the prophecies.

But instead of taking this seriously, Rael was joking around and sucking a death stick in a lively cantina on some out-of-the-way planet called Takodana.

"Don't be so prim," Rael insisted. "We're not supposed to love, right? Because it makes us less objective. More likely to respond emotionally instead of rationally. But we still love our friends. We still love our Masters, and they love their Padawans—I mean, somebody brings you up for ten years, unless they're a total jerk, you're gonna love 'em. That's just how people are! Human people, Trandoshan people, Aqualish—"

"I get it, Rael." Qui-Gon pushed aside his irritation to weigh Rael Averross's words for what they were really worth. Even if he wasn't taking this seriously enough, that didn't mean he was wrong.

Rael nodded at the person who brought his drink, a small wizened creature who wore goggles and a strand of beads. "It just makes sense," he said more gently. "Dooku saw your life was in danger. He overreacted. But you're safe, Shenda Mol's on ice at Stygeon Prime, and Dooku's back to himself again."

I don't know that he is, Qui-Gon wanted to say. The holocron of prophecies had not gone back to the Archives in weeks. Dooku studied it constantly, both with Qui-Gon and without. Although Qui-Gon still liked coming up with theories about how past historical events might have fulfilled certain Masters' prophetic visions, Dooku's fascination was all for the future. One prophecy in particular occupied him more than any other: *He who learns to conquer death will through his greatest student live again.*

"Hey," Rael said. "You okay?"

"Sure. I should go." Qui-Gon signed off. If he was going to work through this, it wouldn't be with Rael. He'd have to do it on his own.

He returned to Dooku's quarters that evening reluctantly. It had always been nice, before, when he was invited to eat dinner with his

Master. Dooku made a formal occasion of it, which like most teenage boys Qui-Gon found awkward, but the food was always better than anything being served in the Padawans' hall.

Tonight, though, the holocron would be there, too—almost like a third guest, one Qui-Gon didn't want to see. He still believed in the prophecies, but his Master's fixation on them had taken on an uncanny cast that colored everything else between them.

Maybe I should talk to him about it myself, Qui-Gon thought as he walked along the corridors of the Temple toward Dooku's quarters. He and Dooku were still firmly Master and apprentice, not friends; Qui-Gon knew better than to assume they were anywhere near being equals.

But if he didn't speak to Dooku about it, nobody would.

He was still gathering his courage when the door slid open to admit him to Dooku's quarters. As usual, the table was set with good glasses and dishes, and Dooku wore one of his better robes.

The only change: The holocron of prophecy wasn't there.

"You're early," Dooku said, with satisfaction. He approved of Padawans being early. With a small smile, he made one of his rare attempts at a joke: "You must be terribly hungry, to get here so soon."

"I am. But—Master—where's the holocron?"

Dooku stiffened, but he continued to smile. When he spoke, his voice was more pleasant than before, or at least was meant to sound that way. "We've spent too much time with it lately, I think. Gotten too caught up in our wild theories. It was . . . enjoyable, speculating on how the prophecies might be real, wasn't it? But of course, they're only metaphors. Only comments on the mystics' time, not our own."

"Of course," Qui-Gon said. And he willed himself to believe it.

If the price of his Master's soul was refusing to accept that the prophecies might come true, then Qui-Gon intended to do it. So in the days, and months, and years that followed, whenever he walked by the holocron in the Jedi Archives, or remembered one of the quatrains late at night, he would push the thought aside. He didn't want to believe. So he wouldn't.

Very, very deep down, he sometimes wondered whether anyone truly believed out of pure faith, or whether people believed whatever they had to, in order to keep going.

But most of the time, Qui-Gon's thoughts went no further than: *Only a metaphor.*

CHAPTER THIRTY-FIVE

verross had never done this for anyone before. He never intended to do it for anyone again. But just this once—just for
Fanry—it was worth it.

He stood in front of a mirror, wearing a traditional Pijali court tunic
and trousers, complete with cape. Alderaanian shimmersilk, brand-
new. Plain black except for the lining of the cape, which was a vivid
cerulean blue. The WA-2G droid had even shaved his face, cut and
styled his hair.

I look ridiculous, Rael thought as he studied his reflection. At least,
that was what he'd expected to think. Planned to think.

"Am I nuts," he asked the WA-2G, "or do I look great?"

"The terms are not mutually exclusive."

Rael laughed. *I just got burned by a droid. Today's gonna be fun.*

As long as the damn blackguards keep their distance . . .

"Here, Your Serene Highness."

Princess Fanry held out her arm as Cady placed the thick cuff brace-let on her arm. During the ceremony, of course, it would be out of sight, beneath the long sleeve of the white dress she wore. The under-dress, revealed only through a few slashes of the skirt, was such a dark blue it might as well have been black.

"Thank you, Cady," Fanry murmured. She put one hand to her curly red hair, which tumbled freely down her back. "Does this look all right? It just seems so . . . peculiar, without the scarf."

"It's like any other change," Cady said. "It takes time to get used to it."

Fanry nodded, squaring her shoulders more like a soldier than a princess. "Today changes everything."

Obi-Wan was grateful to be spared any kind of ceremonial finery. Being a Jedi was enough.

Even an apprentice Jedi would do.

He had left their quarters early in the hope of examining the Celes-tial Chalice, but the royal guards had sealed the area long before. "I'm sorry, sir," said the one who stood before the inner doors in his crisp formal uniform. "It's off limits, even to you. Captain Deren's orders."

As he walked away, Obi-Wan murmured, "That's just what I'm afraid of."

Qui-Gon sat on the floor of his bedroom, attempting to meditate. Calm eluded him.

Let me be wrong, he thought. *Let my dream have been no more than a dream. Let the prophecies become mere metaphors once again.*

I would rather protect this planet, these people, my Padawan, than be granted any glimpse into any future.

But it wasn't a choice he got to make. Events today would unfold as the Force willed. Qui-Gon could only make himself ready to answer, no matter what he might be called on to do.

———

Two hours later, Qui-Gon prepared to enter the Celestial Chalice as part of the most honored set of guests. Minister Orth tottered up only moments after him; her narrow-skirted brown dress required her to take many tiny, quick steps. She peered at him. "I'd halfway wondered whether I'd saved your seat in vain. Whether you'd boycott the ceremony in the end. Or are you no longer imagining terrible visions?"

"My vision remains with me," he said gravely. "That's why I must be here. To help in whatever way I can."

"Hmmph." Unimpressed, she took her place by his side. In front of him, meanwhile, was a stranger in black—

Qui-Gon stared. *"Rael?"*

"Yeah, yeah, don't make a scene," said the impeccably groomed, beautifully clothed person standing before him, who somehow was Rael Averross. "It's for the coronation, the end."

"My word." Minister Orth took off her pince-nez, blinked hard, then put it back on to look through it again. "Averross, you actually look *handsome.*"

"The servants said that, too. Some of the droids. A couple of guards." Rael scowled. "That's being repeated a little too often, with a little too much surprise."

Qui-Gon managed to smile, but his astonishment had only momentarily lifted the dread. Already its weight was settling on him again.

When the vision begins to unfold, he told himself, *be ready.*

You're exactly where you need to be.

Music began to play, and the royal guests began their procession through the grand radius of the Celestial Chalice. Sunlight filtered through the glass-domed ceiling, making all the gilding sparkle. Even the drab gray and brown robes of the Pijali seemed beautiful—subtle, gentle—and the light caught the few touches of red, gold, and violet revealed in collars or at hems.

Qui-Gon took his seat behind Rael. He was relieved to see that he wasn't the only one who'd brought his lightsaber. Rael might think of it more as a ceremonial weapon today, but when action was called for, surely he would stand by Qui-Gon's side.

The door of the far radius opened, and in from the grounds walked the religious leader called the Skykeeper, the crown jeweler with a wooden box in her hands, and Obi-Wan. Qui-Gon felt a moment of pride in Obi-Wan's calm composure; he carried himself as though he'd always represented the Republic. As though he had no inkling he might be walking into mortal danger.

Let me be wrong, Qui-Gon thought again. *Please let me be wrong.*

Finally the music came to a crescendo, and Princess Fanry began her walk along the far radius, up to the dais. Her white dress wasn't that different from her usual court attire, but it hardly mattered. Qui-Gon suspected most guests were staring at her newly revealed hair, by far the brightest color in the room.

He, however, was far more interested in the fact that the person escorting Fanry to the dais was Captain Deren.

Deren's in position to strike, Qui-Gon thought. *He could kill Fanry or Obi-Wan or both, faster than I could defend them.*

But there was still no proof Deren was the traitor. Qui-Gon looked sideways at Minister Orth, who seemed very proud of herself. Hadn't she been sneaking around the Celestial Chalice late at night, the same evening he'd had his prophetic dream? Orth was older, apparently unarmed, and wearing a dress that hardly allowed her to walk, much less fight. But who could say how many forces she might have behind her?

Somewhat farther away sat Meritt Col, sector supervisor, haughty and elegant in white. Since Fanry's power would only enhance Czerka's power, Col could have no reason to attack the princess. But he couldn't be certain the vision showed an attack on Princess Fanry. It was an attack, and Fanry was there, but perhaps the violence was aimed at someone else, like Deren—or Obi-Wan—

The Skykeeper began. "In days of old, we Pijali traveled to outer space to feel the effortless embrace of the spirits. Now our crown princess is giving us a new way to reach the stars. Through her wisdom, through the changes she brings, she will connect us with the greater galaxy as never before."

Fanry stepped forward to accept a ceremonial sword from the Skykeeper and hold it aloft, then motioned for Deren and Obi-Wan to join her in the center of the dais. She was unafraid.

"Will you," the Skykeeper said, "wield this blade to defend Pijal, to protect it from its enemies, to preserve its independence?"

"Yes," Fanry said. "I will."

Qui-Gon kept his eyes fixed on Deren—

—which was why he almost missed the moment that Princess Fanry stabbed the Skykeeper.

"Now, Deren!" she cried. He pressed something at his belt that sealed the dais in the golden-orange flickering light—shielding it, Qui-Gon realized—as screams and shouts of dismay filled the room. Obi-Wan moved to help the Skykeeper, but froze when Deren pointed a blaster at his head.

The blood, Qui-Gon thought. *The screams. The light filtering from above. It's all happening.*

My vision was true.

Never had it been so bitter to be right.

"Fanry?" Rael got to his feet slowly, as though in shock. "Fanry!"

"Hear me!" Fanry shouted, and the crowd quieted. The Skykeeper had sunk to his knees, badly wounded but alive. "They would have me sign a treaty that gives away my power. My regent and Czerka Corporation wanted nothing but profit. This *treaty*"—she spat the word as though it tasted bad—"would deny me the ability to do what I should, for Pijal. I wouldn't be able to throw Czerka out. But I will *not* sign the treaty. I will *not* give away my power. And I will be avenged on those who would have made change impossible, because they would have destroyed us."

Rael staggered to one side. Qui-Gon grabbed him by the elbow and pushed him forward. "Faint later. First *help me save them.*"

But what could they do? Qui-Gon had realized, by now, that the dais had to be surrounded by one of the blackguard shields, the ones their lightsabers would be useless against. No doubt this was the moment the shields had been designed for in the first place. As he pushed forward through the panicky crowd, he saw Fanry activate a personal shield of her own via a bracelet hidden under her sleeve. Deren's shield was on already. Only the Skykeeper, the jeweler, and Obi-Wan were unprotected.

Focus on what you can do, instead of what you can't. Qui-Gon turned to Rael. "Go find loyal guards, if you can. Get them to close the airspace above the Celestial Chalice!" It took Rael a moment to obey, but he pulled himself together and ran for the far door.

"Czerka Corporation will own Pijal no more!" Fanry shouted, motioning to Deren. Qui-Gon spotted Meritt Col trying to sneak farther back in the crowd only an instant before Deren fired at her. Col went down amid more screams. Obi-Wan tried to take advantage of the moment when Deren's weapon was pointed elsewhere, but almost instantly Deren had him in his sights again.

"Princess Fanry, please, wait!" Orth tottered forward through the ozone scent of blasterfire with a courage that made Qui-Gon reevaluate her. "You don't know what you're doing. You're hardly more than a child—"

"A *child*?" The princess's voice rose almost to a shriek. "There are queens my age on Naboo! Princes my age on Toydaria! Alderaan's queen took Princess Breha to help her negotiate a treaty, and she's younger than I am! And I've seen how Czerka's strangling Pijal when my elders haven't. Don't lecture me about being 'a child.' " Fanry collected herself. "You're honest, Minister Orth. For that reason I spare you. But doubt me no longer."

Qui-Gon breathed in. Breathed out. Drank in what calm he could. Connected himself as fully as possible to the Force. Then he examined the room with fresh eyes. Security alarms ought to have been blinking frantically, but they remained silent. No doubt Captain Deren had deactivated them. No troops had yet entered this room, despite the fact that they were massed outside; that meant the army must be loyal to Fanry, or at least to Deren. And the sunlight overhead no longer streamed through, but had become spotty, as though the sky were filling with clouds or . . .

"You've taken bribes from Czerka for years," Fanry said to the fallen Skykeeper. "Let them use sacred docks that should be reserved for the soulcraft."

The Skykeeper clutched his bloody shoulder. "Your Serene Highness—I—"

"Keep your lies to yourself," Fanry said, turning from him to the shivering court jeweler. "Oh, honestly. Calm down. You're fine."

The jeweler continued trembling as Fanry opened the box, took out a small circlet, and put it on her own head.

Qui-Gon worked his way closer to the dais, pushing through the throngs of people rushing out. Yet a large part of the crowd remained, watching out of either morbid fascination or perhaps even support for Fanry. He tried to catch Obi-Wan's gaze, but his Padawan remained focused on Deren, clearly hoping for one more chance to defend himself.

It didn't look like he would get one.

I must try, Qui-Gon thought. He leapt forward, igniting his lightsaber. The instant his feet hit the ground, he swung his weapon into the glowing perimeter of the shield. Green blade crackled against orange light, reverberating so hard that the bones in his arms and shoulders seemed to shudder. The lightsaber was useless.

"Jedi Jinn." Fanry half turned to look at him. "You alone argued against the treaty. You alone refused to sit tamely at Czerka's feet. Therefore you will be spared."

Karabast. If I'd been the one on the dais instead of Obi-Wan, he'd be safe. Instead—

"But *you.*" The princess—or, now that she wore the crown, the queen—craned her neck back toward Obi-Wan. "You supported this evil treaty. You thought to make me sign it. There will be no mercy for you."

"Fanry, no!" Qui-Gon shouted.

She gestured to Deren. The captain grimaced—in horror, Qui-Gon realized—but he said only, "As my queen wishes it."

The rest happened in what most humans would have seen only as a blur, which only Qui-Gon's focus through the Force allowed him to witness clearly: Deren raised the blaster. Obi-Wan ignited his lightsaber, even if it would do no good—

—his lightsaber was no longer blue, but orange—

—and when he swung it, the blade easily passed through Deren's shield.

Into Deren.

The captain gasped in pain, then crumpled backward to the floor, moaning as he clutched his bleeding abdomen. Fanry shrieked. Obi-Wan wheeled about to again put himself between the sword-wielding queen and the wounded Skykeeper. Qui-Gon tried to understand what had taken place. What happened to Obi-Wan's lightsaber?

Overhead, the glass panes that formed the dome of the Celestial Chalice began to retract. The gathering shadows proved themselves to be troopships of the royal guard, hovering overhead. Someone cried, "Your Majesty, the shield generator!" Qui-Gon realized it had been Cady—who seemed to have known about this all along.

Queen Fanry grabbed a small device from Deren's belt, only a moment before cables dropped from the troopships snaked down into the Chalice. Cady grabbed one; Fanry seized another. Qui-Gon considered taking a third, but the soldiers would sever his line before they'd let him ascend to the top.

"Farewell, Deren." Fanry looped the cable's harness around her body. She and Obi-Wan stared at each other for a long moment, before she was hauled upward. *The shield!* Qui-Gon thought, afraid its border would slice through Obi-Wan—but the generator proved to be compact. The orange shield faded as Fanry took it with her upward, out of range, beyond the roof of the Chalice. Cady rose just beside her, on her own cable.

Everyone in the Chalice stared upward except for Qui-Gon, who hurried to his apprentice's side. Obi-Wan kept staring at his orange lightsaber until he turned to his Master and said, *"What the—?"*

"It's a revolution from the top," Qui-Gon replied. "Rael thought he was defending Fanry. Czerka thought they were manipulating her. But she was more than they counted on."

"But what does Fanry intend to do now?" Obi-Wan shook his head, trying to focus.

"We're about to find out," Qui-Gon said.

CHAPTER THIRTY-SIX

U ntil a few moments earlier, the flagship of the royal fleet had been known as the *Heavenly Sphere.* As of today, by Queen Fanry's order, it was called the *Righteous.*

As she strode through the ship's corridors, strapping on an armor-weave breastplate over her now-stained white gown, she called out, "Who's in command of the *Leverage*? Who's taking over now that Col's dead?"

Cady had already changed into a blackguard uniform. A line across her left hand showed where the 2-1B had freed her permanently of Czerka, just minutes before. She was alight with triumph, even happier about this than Fanry was herself. "I regret to inform Her Majesty that Meritt Col survived the ceremony."

"What?" The one person Fanry most wanted dead, the most corrupt and soulless of them all, had slithered free of the trap. When she realized what had happened, she swore. "Deren. He spared her, didn't he?"

"He was a good man," Cady replied. "He just didn't understand that these Czerka scum have to die."

"But we do." Fanry strode toward the bridge of the *Righteous*. She had studied all her life to be a ruler, had been preparing for this moment for years. Averross had only seen a child when he looked at her, but that was because he only ever really saw Nim Pianna. Fanry could pity that poor wretch, the girl she'd never met, but knew she would not share Nim's fate.

No, she had at last fulfilled her destiny and become the only thing she ever aspired to be: the warrior queen.

Rael Averross had let Obi-Wan Kenobi guide him onto the Corellian corvette. It didn't seem to much matter where he went, or what he did.

Fanry—why? He tried to imagine asking her, but the scene refused to take shape in his head. Averross could no longer see the clever, funny little girl he'd known . . . or thought he'd known. Instead, when he spoke the words in his mind, the person listening was the angry, contemptuous young woman who had today seized absolute power.

"Padawan," Qui-Gon was saying to Obi-Wan as they all walked onto the corvette's bridge, "what happened to your lightsaber?"

"I'm not sure." Obi-Wan unscrewed the components of his lightsaber. To everybody's astonishment, this revealed an orange kohlen crystal where the kyber crystal ought to have been.

"How is this possible?" Qui-Gon asked.

"It has to be—" Obi-Wan's expression became thoughtful. "A few days ago, Fanry asked to know how a lightsaber worked, and I showed her. Deren told me before the run-through last night that no weapons were allowed in the Chalice until the ceremony itself, so I left my lightsaber in the hall outside. Then someone sabotaged it—or meant to."

"The weight," Averross said dully. "They stole your kyber crystal and replaced it with kohlen so it would stay the same weight, and keep you from catchin' on."

Slowly Qui-Gon began to smile. "Fanry and Deren thought the kohlen crystals were useless, except as a way to fool Obi-Wan. But the crystals were able to project a sort of blade, even if it was less powerful—except, that is, against shields also powered by kohlen."

"Thank the Force it's less powerful," Obi-Wan said. "If it weren't, my blow would've killed Deren."

"Hell, you'd have cut him in two," Averross replied.

After a brief pause, Qui-Gon nodded. "And I should imagine the potential black market for these shields will dry up as soon as it becomes known the Jedi have a way to cut through them after all."

Obi-Wan tucked his lightsaber back into his belt, but then hesitated. "I'm assuming we can get my kyber crystal back. It's probably still in the palace somewhere, right?"

"Probably," Averross said. Even to him, his voice sounded dead.

"Are you sure she's queen?" Qui-Gon said as the corvette headed into deep space in pursuit of blackguards, and of Fanry. "The ceremony wasn't completed."

"I'll say." Averross leaned his head back against the shining white back wall, and focused on the array of lights on the bridge, so he wouldn't have to pay attention to what was on the viewscreen. "But yeah. As soon as a consecrated crown of Pijal lay on her head, Fanry became queen. And since she didn't sign the treaty, the old rules are still in place, which means she's got absolute power."

From the sound of it, one of Fanry's first orders would be for his exile. Or execution.

"Good news," Obi-Wan said, looking up from a comm panel. "Apparently Captain Deren's going to live. At least he can explain some of this afterward."

"Assuming the rest of us live," Averross said.

Qui-Gon gave him a look, and Averross wondered if he was about to get a lecture about being defeatist. Better that than what he did get: "Rael, did you never see any sign of this?"

"No. Yes. I mean, now that I think about it—I'd feel this energy in her, through the Force. This determination to rule. Just figured that meant she was mature, but it looks like there was more to it than that." He sighed. "And she never did cozy up to Czerka. Never figured out that I was only cozyin' up to them for her. And she kept that girl Cady close to her, or to me, pretty much all the time. At the time, I figured Cady was just her favorite. But now she's looking like a partner in crime."

"Maybe so," Qui-Gon said. "Though Cady may simply be following her owner's orders—but I sensed hope within her. Not resignation."

So half the palace knew the real Fanry this whole time, Averross thought. *But not me.* "Okay," he said, pulling himself together, or as close to it as he was going to get. "What do we do now?"

"It looks as though the royal ship—the *Righteous*?—is heading for an assault on the *Leverage*," said Obi-Wan. He frowned down at the array of schematics lit up on the consoles around them. "They've pulled in other royal or blackguard vessels to help. Though I guess the blackguards were royal, all along—"

"Here's what we'll do," said Qui-Gon, as calmly as though he'd had this plan for years. "Rael, you and I need to board the *Righteous* and take custody of Fanry."

Rael laughed. The sound was strange in his throat. "Arrest her? For what? She's got absolute power now. Doesn't matter what she does— it's the law."

Qui-Gon shook his head. "The queen has absolute power *in the Pijal system.* However, she has no power that protects her from the crime of attacking a designated representative of the Republic." With that, he nodded at Obi-Wan.

Obi-Wan didn't seem as confident. "Surely killing several thousand Czerka people counts as a pan-galactic offense."

"It does," Qui-Gon said, "but Czerka sometimes 'takes initiative' and pursues those who've committed crimes against the corporation. They claim to handle such matters without help from the courts—but sometimes, they wreak a bloody vengeance. I have no doubt they would here. Czerka must not be the authority to step in. It must be the Republic."

Even though they had to do something, it still hurt Averross to think of arresting Fanry. "Speakin' of Obi-Wan, where's he gonna be?"

"He's going to be boarding the *Leverage,* both to keep Czerka from taking any punitive steps and to liberate an associate of ours," said Qui-Gon.

"The *Leverage*'s security is tight," Averross said. "Like, tighter than the Galactic Senate's. How do you think you're going to get in there without being spotted?"

Qui-Gon smiled. "As it happens, we have a ship with a scanner-blocking field—and an operative ready to help us take it inside the *Leverage* itself."

Pax Maripher had never felt good about the Jedi's plan. Not because he didn't think it would work—it seemed to have a decent chance of success—but because he hadn't come up with it. Obviously his plan would've been far superior, had he ever devised one.

But his objections had become both more numerous and more pointed as Coronation Day wore on. First, according to the comms, the coronation hadn't gone off *at all,* with the young queen revealing herself as some sort of power-hungry zealot. It sounded quite exciting, and Pax looked forward to watching the many dramatic holovids that would undoubtedly be made about it. Then, in the wake of that fiasco, the *Leverage* had gone on high alert. It would've been difficult enough to slip through Czerka security on a normal day, but on high alert? And the cover for their rescue mission was meant to be provided, at least in part, by masses of Pijali people taking their personal ships into space to celebrate the day. Didn't sound like much celebration was in the offing.

Which meant not only that Rahara was still trapped in that Czerka behemoth, but also that he now had no way to get her out again . . .

The comms chimed, startling Pax out of his cockpit reverie. He opened the channel. "Kenobi? Is that you?"

"*It's me,*" Obi-Wan said. He sounded far happier than the situation called for. "*We're changing the plan.*"

"Obviously. Though I've no idea how you expect to breach—"

"*Rendezvous with our corvette.*" That was Qui-Gon Jinn's voice coming through now. *"Obi-Wan can transfer to the* Meryx *then. After that, I'll provide a diversion to distract the* Leverage *while you slip through."*

Pax squinted suspiciously. "What sort of 'diversion'?"

"You'll see." With that, Qui-Gon signed off. How like a Jedi. Cryptic to the last.

But the annoyance was empty. Mere reflex from his mind. Inside, Pax only cared about one thing: Rahara would get another chance.

The rendezvous took only minutes; Obi-Wan practically vaulted on board, and Pax Maripher had blasted back into space the literal second the atmospheric shield dropped. As soon as Qui-Gon got confirmation that the *Meryx* was away, he gestured to the corvette's comm officer. "Signal the *Leverage*. Inform them that the Jedi Qui-Gon Jinn wishes to speak to whoever's in charge."

Moments later a holo flickered into shape on the bridge, revealing the face of Meritt Col. *"Jedi Jinn,"* she said, tucking a lock of hair back into her elaborate hairstyle, or what remained of it. *"Well. That was unexpected, wasn't it?"*

"You have a gift for understatement, Supervisor." Qui-Gon assumed a look of the deepest concern. "We thought Captain Deren had killed you."

"No. Singed me, yes." She gestured with irritation to a black mark on her white jacket. *"Official supervisor formalwear isn't cheap, you know."*

Czerka charged its own people for their uniforms? That was . . . not surprising, actually. Qui-Gon said, "I felt I should inform you that the queen's ship, the *Righteous*, appears to be planning an attack on your vessel."

Col held on to her temper—barely. *"Really. The queen who just proclaimed my employer to be evil and had her captain attempt to murder me at her own coronation? She might attack me? How very shocking. Thank you for this entirely unpredictable news."*

Out of the corner of his eye, Qui-Gon could see Obi-Wan's tracker getting closer and closer to the *Leverage*. The *Meryx* itself, with its scanner-blocking field activated, was as invisible to him as it was to the *Leverage*. "I can't be sure of this," he said, "but it's possible that the *Righteous* carries some sort of advanced weapon—something purchased on the black market, from the Hutts, some time ago. We can definitely confirm that her blackguards were in contact with Wanbo the Hutt's cartel on Teth."

This was all entirely true. Of course, there was absolutely no reason to think Fanry's ship had any such weapon . . . but it was *possible*.

"The Hutts?" Col motioned to someone off-holo. *"Quick, turn all scanners on the* Righteous, *full strength."*

Qui-Gon resisted the urge to smile as Obi-Wan's tracker zoomed up to the *Leverage* and disappeared inside it.

Obi-Wan held his breath as the *Meryx* slipped into an auxiliary cargo bay of the *Leverage*—the kind of place that should be controlled by autosensor, and empty of sentients or droids. If Qui-Gon had succeeded in drawing Meritt Col's full attention—

"We're clear," he said with a grin as the *Meryx* settled into a repulsor berth, where it would rest in midair. "Once the bay doors close, we can set out in search of Rahara. The palace records provided a couple of diagrams—here, on the scanner—so we ought to be able to find her."

"Correction," said Pax Maripher, who was rolling up the sleeves of his overlarge blue shirt. "*I* ought to be able to find her. You, on the other hand, are going to wait here so you can get us clear of the *Leverage* the first moment possible."

"If I'm with you, that wouldn't put off our departure by more than a minute or two—"

"Which, given the situation, is a terrifyingly large margin of error, and therefore unacceptable." Pax straightened up and ran his hands through his wild hair, rendering it messier than ever. "It's also possible another diversion may be needed, one your Master won't be able to provide while he's confronting the queen."

Obi-Wan would much rather have been in the thick of things, but what Pax said made sense. "All right, then. I'll wait here. But take this with you." He handed Pax his scanner, complete with schematics, and a comlink. "Let me know what you can, when you can."

The *Leverage* bay doors shut. Pax immediately went for the exit. "As I said—be ready!"

Qui-Gon reached out with the Force, attempting to scan the *Righteous*. Reading a large area was difficult, particularly when many people were within it, but he wanted only to get a sense of whether the entire crew supported Fanry's quest, or whether they felt trapped by duty. He picked up veins of both sentiments, yet found it impossible to determine which was stronger.

"Are you ready?" he said to the captain of the Corellian corvette.

The captain nodded. "It's going to tax us to the limit—but we can do it."

With that, the corvette locked its tractor beam on the *Righteous*. As soon as the queen's ship realized its predicament, it began attempting to pull away. Although the corvette shuddered from the resistance, it remained stable. The beam didn't break.

"Signal the *Righteous*," Qui-Gon said. "Tell them it's time to talk."

As the comm officer did so, the security chief straightened. "The *Righteous* is powering up weapons!" The Nautolan must have been a civilian worker, not a soldier, because his tentacles trembled at the thought.

"Get closer." It was the first thing Rael had said in hours that was tactical rather than reactive. "Make it obvious that if she blows us up, we'll take her with us."

Qui-Gon frowned—that sounded dangerously vindictive. But it was a valid tactical move.

Rael's maneuver worked. It wasn't long before the comm officer reported, "The *Righteous* wants to talk to us."

"Very well." Qui-Gon straightened his robe and folded his hands together in front so that the sleeves draped over them. *Be in this moment,* he thought, willing his spirit to achieve the same calm strength as his body.

The hologram that shimmered into being on the corvette's bridge was far larger than the one projected by the *Leverage*. This was a royal vessel, and the effect was meant to be one of a royal audience. Queen Fanry appeared, slightly larger than life, flanked by a heavily armed honor guard—and in the back, wearing a soldier's uniform rather than the usual gray coverall, stood Cady.

To his eyes, Fanry looked transformed. She wore the ceremonial sword at her side and a silvery breastplate over her gown, and her freed hair blazed like fire, but none of that altered her as greatly as the confidence and fury that shone from her like a light. This, he understood, was the first time he'd ever truly seen her.

If I'd tried to see her before, Qui-Gon realized, *the Force would've shown me some of the spirit she hid inside. But I didn't try. I took her for the child she presented herself to be.*

There was no Jedi so wise that he could not be undone by his own assumptions.

"*We welcome the chance to speak with you, Jedi Jinn*," said Fanry. "*Our former regent is less welcome—but as we have granted truce to you, we will honor it for him.*"

Rael rasped out the words, "Fanry—*why*?" Despite the finery he wore, the shaven face, Rael Averross had never looked more derelict to Qui-Gon than he did at this moment. "Didn't you ever see, the only reason I ever worked with Czerka was to make things easier for you? That every damn thing I did was only ever for you?"

"*It was* never *for me*." Fanry lifted her chin, spearing Rael with her gaze. "*It was for Nim. Everything you did was for her. You never stopped to ask yourself if the things a wounded child might have needed were the same as the things a future queen would need. You protected me when you should have taught me. You talked at me when you should've listened to me.*"

Qui-Gon didn't even have to look at Rael to know what he felt now; the horror of it was so strong it resonated in the Force. The horror sprang from Rael's knowledge that Fanry was right.

At least, about this. "Your Majesty," Qui-Gon said, "this isn't primarily a chance for you and your former regent to talk over old times. It's a chance to discuss whether you're willing to stand down and come up with a diplomatic solution. The Republic was already attempting to find ways for your people to cast off Czerka's influence."

"*By taking away my absolute authority?*" Fanry scoffed. "*Though really, the more I studied my history, the more I realized no monarch of Pijal had truly ruled in centuries. Czerka's grip has been too strong. I need the full authority of the throne, Jedi. The Republic is compromised by Czerka's wealth and influence. Only I can free my world.*"

Qui-Gon had doubted that Pijal's future Assembly would be able to stand up to Czerka. Could he be certain the Galactic Senate would do any better?

Yet he remained on his path, attempting to appeal to Fanry's reason. "With the future of the hyperspace corridor on the line, your bargaining position has only grown stronger. Will you negotiate? Will you help us find a peaceful solution?"

"*I've seen the cost of peace.*" Fanry's eyes glittered with a febrile, angry light. "*I prefer war.*"

CHAPTER THIRTY-SEVEN

———————— ✦ ————————

*C*zerka ships are as labyrinthine as their bureaucracy, thought Pax Maripher. *How very unsurprising.*

Thus far he'd been able to sneak through a good third of the *Leverage*'s length, and had gone down one level to what he thought would be the slaveholding area. It had taken more time than he would've liked. The Czerka corridors were enormous—three meters high by almost five meters wide—and twisted and turned as though determined to find the least direct route to lead anywhere. In Pax's opinion, the design aesthetic must have been "intestinal."

A mouse droid rolled by, singing to itself. Pax remembered what B-3PO had always taught him: *If a human behaves as though they belong somewhere, less complex droids will assume the human* does *belong.* He strolled past it without any pause on either side.

Once he rounded the next turn, the eerie hush turned into the clatter of work: Droids beeping, machinery moving, the distant tenor of human conversation. Pax sighed in relief; he'd made it as far as the labor area.

He tugged on the maintenance jacket and hat he'd swiped from the auxiliary bay, took a deep breath, and walked into the thick of it. The corridor opened up, becoming a broad walkway that looked down onto the factory area. Rahara had told him this area was called the pit by those who had to work in it, and the name was well earned. It was poorly lit, too hot, and cramped. Enslaved beings wearing dingy coveralls oversaw machines that clanked so loudly they must have caused hearing loss within months. Bursts of steam occasionally came up from some of the machines, very nearly scalding those working nearby.

Just find Rahara, he told himself as he began to descend a service ladder into the pit. *Find her and run.*

"The *Righteous*'s weapons remain fully charged," said the anxious Nautolan security officer to Qui-Gon and Rael. Fanry's hologram had only just faded away. "But they seem to be shifting their targeting."

Only one other target was possible: the *Leverage.* Qui-Gon breathed in sharply. Obi-Wan was far from the only person aboard that ship who wasn't part of Czerka. Was Fanry truly so angry at the company that she would destroy them even if it meant also destroying innocent lives?

He turned to Rael, whose expression had become hard and set. The question was unnecessary. "She'll do it," Rael said. "Now that I'm thinking about it—going over what I knew about her before, and what I know about her now—yeah. She'll take 'em down to hell no matter who has to go along for the ride."

Was it all a dream? Rahara thought dully as she stamped down the compressor lock, pushed the unit forward, and did it again, and again. *Was I just imagining I was free, that I used to be a jewel thief and go all around the galaxy with diamonds and opals and crystals?*

Maybe she had been. Maybe she needed to believe that, to make herself think it was true. Because otherwise she'd have to live the rest of her life down here knowing she'd once been something so much more than one of Czerka's grubby tools. That she'd been able to fly between the stars. Better to convince herself that this—the work, the pit—was all there ever was, all there ever had been, all there ever would be.

How long would it take to convince herself of that? Years, Rahara figured. But it could happen. *Would* happen. She'd forget about her life before—

"Rahara!"

Startled, she nearly missed the compressor lock. As her hands pressed it down automatically, she looked up to see a face peering through a thicket of pipes. "*. . . Pax?*"

"Yes, *of course* it's me." He sighed in exasperation. "Were you perhaps expecting the chancellor instead?"

Rahara began to laugh at the same moment her eyes filled with tears. Maybe she could've imagined a life as a jewel thief, but she could never have dreamed up anyone like Pax Maripher.

A few other people working nearby—a human and two Sullustans—had noticed Pax, too. One of the Sullustans surreptitiously pulled the gear that would stall the compressor line. Usually that was done to take care of minor malfunctions, so the floor supervisor wouldn't pay any attention at first. The Sullustan had bought them a minute. Rahara looked at her in gratitude before turning back to Pax. "How did you get here?"

"The Jedi actually made themselves useful to *us* for a change. Now, come on."

The shock of it hit her. "You're breaking me out?"

"Why else would I ever be here? To take in the scenic view?" Pax gestured at the dark, dank maze of machinery in the pit.

"I know—it's just—" Rahara tried to wrap her head around it. "You said—you don't put your neck out for me, and don't expect me to do it for you. That would be 'irrational.'"

Pax's expression gentled. "So I said. But—it turns out there are things that matter much more than rationality."

He reached out with one hand, and she took it. But when he pulled her toward him, Rahara resisted. "No."

"Yes, yes, I know it's very dangerous, therein lies the heroic nature of my escapade, but there's no other way to leave this place than to, you know, *leave.*"

Rahara looked back at the Sullustan who had helped her. The others working on her section of the line. Farther down the row, more humans, a few Duros, and an Abednedo. A dozen species within sight, maybe thirty or more represented here—adding up to hundreds of enslaved people, all of whom were trapped just as she had been trapped. Who had never even been able to imagine what they might do with a life that was their own.

"If I'm getting out of here," she said, "so are they."

"You mean instead of sneaking out safely, we're going to lead a slave uprising?" Pax considered this, then smiled. "Excellent."

On the *Meryx,* Obi-Wan had very little to do but wait. The ship's sensors weren't sharp enough to pierce through the *Leverage;* while he could've signaled the corvette to talk with Qui-Gon, that stood a very good chance of alerting Czerka to his presence.

He decided to study the *Meryx*—if he was going to have to pilot it soon, he might as well get to know its quirks. The engines, controls, and such were very much what he would've expected. No *Gozanti*-class freighter could ever be highly maneuverable, but Pax's modifications helped. The only real surprise was how well the lower cargo hold had been retrofitted as a berth for the *Facet.*

A Nivex-*class starfighter,* he thought, looking down at its coppery surface. *Cieran make, I think, but Pax will have modified that, too.* Obi-Wan dropped down into the cargo hold to take a better look—

—which was when alarm klaxons began to ring inside the *Leverage.*

Obi-Wan startled. The quickest way to tap into intraship communications was through the *Facet,* so he jumped inside. He turned on the engines and scanned for comms, just in time to hear: "—*disturbances on lower levels, lock down access bays immediately!*"

"Like the access bay I'm in right now?" he muttered. "Splendid."

But Obi-Wan smiled at the very strong probability that these "disturbances" were the work of Rahara and Pax.

He pressed the control for extraship visuals. As he'd feared, Czerka GA-97 and unipod droids were already rolling into the bay to lock all controls, including those for the doors the *Meryx* would need to get out of here. The droids would have to go. Obi-Wan put his hand on his lightsaber, then remembered the kohlen sabotage—there was no telling what his lightsaber was good for right now, which meant he'd be a fool to take it into combat.

Wait, he thought. *Why am I looking for weapons when I'm sitting in one?*

The Czerka droids halted the moment the lower doors of the *Meryx* opened and the *Facet* dropped down and began to fire. Obi-Wan targeted the first unipod, then the second, blowing them to pieces instantly. This would set off a security alarm, but since the *Leverage* was already on high alert due to the revolt, probably Czerka's response would be slowed—

His console lit up with the words AUTOPURSUIT INITIATED.

"No—I don't want—" Obi-Wan's eyes widened as the *Facet* not only targeted weapons without him, but began to move forward. "How do I shut this off?"

He had no time to find out. The *Facet* zoomed ahead, targeting droid after droid; Obi-Wan could steer the ship, but he couldn't stop it, not even as it flew toward the inner doors. His hands clenched the controls as his starfighter zipped into the open corridor. Now he was in a tunnel—one that twisted and turned—with no more than a meter of safety on each side.

You always wanted a real flying challenge, Obi-Wan told himself as he took a sharp left turn, narrowly avoiding destruction. *Here it is.*

Another voice inside him answered, *I take it back!* But it was too late to do anything but plunge on.

Rahara had never enjoyed any moment in a Czerka vessel as much as the one when she swung a metal bar straight into a control panel. The sparks that shot across the room looked like fireworks.

All around her, the newly freed were allowing themselves to cele-brate through sheer pandemonium. Every panel that could be pried off was; the others were smashed. Whatever tools and gear they could scavenge were being distributed among the crowd, which became more and more "armed" by the second.

"As charming and well deserved as this orgy of destruction is," Pax shouted over the din, "it shouldn't take precedence above escaping from the *Leverage!*"

Assuming they *could* escape. Rahara had heard the commands to shut down access bays. Other counterinsurgent moves would follow. Czerka knew how to put down uprisings. As much as Rahara wanted to believe they'd get away, she knew that this was equally likely to end in bloodshed.

But if Pax could hope, she would, too. She grabbed his hand and began leading the way forward, faster and faster, until she broke into a run.

"Master Jedi—" The corvette's comm officer pointed to a screen for Qui-Gon to read. "This is what just came over intraship on the *Leverage.*"

At the moment, the corvette was fighting a losing battle to keep the tethered royal ship from angling itself to fire on the Czerka ship. They could hold the *Righteous* in place, more or less, but could not keep the ship from turning within that place. Already they were within range of the *Leverage,* and the corvette couldn't tow it away fast enough.

So Qui-Gon's mind was preoccupied when he looked down at the comm officer's panel, but not after he'd read what was there. "A slave uprising?"

"Thought the plan was for Obi-Wan and your guy to slip in, slip out, nice and quiet," Rael said. He'd been pacing the floor ever since Queen Fanry's holo.

"The plan appears to have altered." Qui-Gon considered the possi-bilities. He asked the comm officer, "Is the *Righteous* able to intercept those messages as well?"

"Quite possibly, sir, though I don't know if they're doing so."

"Let's find out. Put me in touch with the queen again."

Inwardly, he thought, *I hope Obi-Wan's all right.*

As the *Facet* plunged through the twisting corridors at intense speed, Obi-Wan had given up trying to come up with any coherent thoughts. It made more sense to just yell, "AAAAAAUUUGHHHH!"

"Four minutes to targeting range," said the weapons officer.

"Excellent." Fanry settled into the captain's chair. Her feet still didn't touch the floor. She'd have to have it lowered. "Keep pushing back against our former regent, would you? Let him try his hardest to stop us, and fail."

The comm officer said, "The Jedi's corvette is signaling us again."

"We have nothing to say to Averross!" Fanry snapped.

"It's the other one, Qui-Gon Jinn."

She respected this Jedi, who had stood up to Czerka, but she was fast losing her patience with him. "Let us humor him one last time."

Jinn appeared via holo, seeming to stand on her own bridge. "*Your Majesty, may I call your attention to what's happening within the* Leverage?"

"What's happening to the *Leverage* is that it's going to be destroyed." The *Righteous* wasn't as large as the Czerka ship, but it was far better armed, as she was about to demonstrate.

"*Not to it. Within it. Turn your sensors to their intraship communications—you do have all the Czerka codes, don't you?—and see for yourself.*"

So, they'd done a search and realized how much Czerka intel her team had amassed. No matter, Fanry decided. The comm officer obeyed Jinn's suggestion without waiting for Fanry's order, a breach of protocol she would address later. But her concerns about that faded when she saw the word UPRISING.

"Your Majesty." Cady lit up, happier than Fanry had ever seen her. "The people inside—they're trying to get away! We could help them!"

Fanry laughed. "And let Czerka go? Hardly. We have sworn to show them no mercy, and we shall not." Cady's face fell.

"*Fanry, it's Rael.*" Her old regent appeared in the holo. Just the sight of him angered her almost past the point of reason. But she still heard him when he said, "*You can punish Czerka, or you can save innocent lives. You have one choice. Make it a good one.*"

She hadn't listened to Rael Averross in years, and didn't intend to start now. "Weapons officer?"

"Yes, Your Majesty?" The officer's voice was strangely hoarse.

Fanry opened her mouth to give the order to fire—then stopped when the cold muzzle of a blaster pressed against her temple.

"I helped you do this," Cady said, trembling even as she held the gun on her queen. "No. I made this possible. Planting the slicer dart, helping sabotage the crab droid—you made the plans, but *I* had to do the hard work. And I did it all because I thought that getting rid of Czerka meant getting rid of slavery. But this is just about you, isn't it? About having power for yourself."

It was scary having a weapon pointed at her head. Fanry somehow had never realized that before. Via holo, she could see her fear reflected in Rael Averross's expression. How dare he pretend to truly care about her? And why weren't any of the bridge officers coming to her aid?

But Fanry ruled over Cady. Always had. Always would. Some things could never be changed. "As your queen," she said evenly, "I order you to put your weapon away."

Cady shook her head no. "Looks like we're having our second revolution of the day."

Qui-Gon was relieved to know Fanry had been overthrown, at least long enough to prevent vast bloodshed—but the real battle was still going on inside the *Leverage*. He had to make sure the right side won.

As soon as the holo from the *Righteous* faded out, he connected to the *Leverage* again. When Meritt Col reappeared, she looked more frazzled than before.

"*Yes, yes, the queen's no longer a problem,*" she snapped. "*If you had anything to do with that, thank you, but I have other issues to deal with.*"

"Such as setting free the people currently rebelling within your ship," Qui-Gon said. "The former slaves."

"*How many more times must I tell you?*" Col asked. "*They will always be slaves.*"

"The situation has changed, Supervisor Col, as you would know if you were better versed in Republic jurisprudence. 'During extreme political upheaval, any group found to be imprisoned against their will, without having been convicted or accused of any offense against the law, shall be liberated. Anyone responsible for imprisoning these people is committing a criminal act.' "

Col scoffed. "*This is one day of problems, Jedi. The crown princess is now queen, as planned, even if the particulars are unfortunately very difficult. Who's to say that this counts as 'extreme upheaval'?*"

"Only a designated representative of the Republic can make such a finding," Qui-Gon said. "Such as Obi-Wan Kenobi. Granted, Obi-Wan hasn't yet done so, but he'd be happy to once he gets the chance. And as it happens, Her Majesty has already been overthrown."

"*You're twisting the law to suit your own purposes. You think this momentary disadvantage will make me agree to anything.*" Meritt Col rose to her feet, apparently ready to leave the bridge and take on the uprising herself. As the doors to the wide outer corridor opened, she said, "*I promise you, Jinn, this will not stand longer than—*" Her voice broke off, and turned into a scream.

Qui-Gon's eyes widened as a starfighter inside the Czerka ship barreled through the outer corridor, flying straight onto the bridge. Czerka officers, including Col, fell to the ground. The starfighter then landed, snapping chairs and consoles as its weight settled onto the deck. Was it his imagination, or did that ship look familiar? Qui-Gon's astonishment peaked when the starfighter's hatch opened to reveal—

"Obi-Wan?"

Obi-Wan's face was pale, his stare somewhat dazed. He looked at the holo for a long moment, taking gulping breaths, then ventured a weak smile. *"I don't suppose you believe I meant to do this?"*

"No." Qui-Gon began to smile. "But as it turns out, you're right on time."

CHAPTER THIRTY-EIGHT

———————— ⚜ ————————

"You flew *through the ship's corridors*?" Qui-Gon put one arm around Obi-Wan's shoulders as they walked away from the corvette's docking bay. Behind them, Rahara Wick and Pax Maripher were helping the ship's crew register approximately three hundred former "units of sentient property" as refugees. "Congratulations on being in one piece."

Obi-Wan still appeared to be in shock. "It was terrible," he said, his eyes staring fixedly ahead. "I don't ever want to fly again. *Ever*."

"Oh, come now, Padawan."

"I *hate* flying."

"You're only shaken up," Qui-Gon said. "That feeling will pass."

"No, it won't."

"We'll see. For the time being, we have enough to do on the ground—on Pijal."

————————

Within two days, faced with public outrage over the blackguards and the judicial ruling that a coronation by violence was illegal, Queen Fanry agreed to abdicate in favor of a distant cousin. The new Queen Lamia's reign lasted only a few hours, just long enough to sign new treaties that set up a democratic Assembly with ample representation for lunar citizens, abolished slavery in the system, freed any enslaved persons brought *to* the system, made possible the new Pijal Hyperspace Corridor, and last of all—the item that *had* to go last—ended the Pijali monarchy forever.

There was, however, a nominal head of state, a governor who would help focus the Assembly's efforts.

"As for my first act," said Governor Orth as she sat at her new desk, "I intend to cancel any and all contracts the government has with Czerka Corporation."

"You never did care for them," Qui-Gon recalled.

"Nor did I make any secret of it. Yet the princess never realized we had so much in common. If she would've confided in more of us, she might have realized how much support there was for standing up to the company. But of course, Czerka wasn't the point. Only the excuse that let her feel righteous about seizing absolute power." Orth sighed, and for a moment her expression became wistful. But then she was back to her usual brisk self. "Princess Fanry remains under house arrest—which in a palace is scarcely harsh punishment."

"How is she taking that?"

"Not very well. Honestly, I think it's begun to hit her, the weight of some of what she's done. Deren pulled through, and she's asked to see him to apologize." Orth shook her head. "Poor man. He wanted nothing to do with the blackguards. But he'd sworn to obey the princess in all things, and he held true to his oath. It nearly killed him."

Qui-Gon asked, "How long does Fanry remain under arrest?"

"Four years. Although she was briefly head of state, she's legally a minor for all other purposes. So her punishment ends when she turns eighteen. After that, I'm thinking a university on a faraway planet sounds like the right idea." Orth looked thoughtful. "*Very* far away."

"Fanry doesn't lack courage," Qui-Gon said. "Or will. She may have a great deal to offer, once she's grown. What's become of Cady?"

"A clever girl, that one. She's accepted our offer to send her to the school of her choice; she picked a leadership academy on Alderaan. I hope she'll return someday, but frankly I wouldn't blame her if she never set foot on Pijal again." Orth folded her hands on her desk. "I suppose you and Kenobi will be off, then."

Qui-Gon nodded. "After saying a few goodbyes."

First he went to see Pax and Rahara aboard the *Meryx*. To judge by their joyful moods and newly intimate body language, Qui-Gon thought that after the escape from the *Leverage*, it was possible their relationship had progressed past "business partners." It was none of his affair—but it was good to see them happy.

"As insufferable as I found your behavior on multiple occasions," Pax said, "I find I shall miss you."

"From you, Pax, I suspect that's a great compliment." Qui-Gon turned to Rahara. "Governor Orth tells me the 'refugees' from the *Leverage* have begun traveling offplanet."

She nodded, leaning against the *Meryx* door. "Some of them have home planets to go to. Others have been offered funds to help settle newly inhabited worlds, and are taking the Republic up on it. At least a couple of them want to stay here on Pijal. Despite the bad memories they must have, it's beautiful here."

"Beautiful or not, we've tarried here too long already." Pax sighed. "The money we earned selling 'fools' kyber' will only just cover the repairs to the *Facet*. Important as this trip has been for us, it has utterly failed to be profitable."

"About that." Qui-Gon reached toward his belt and opened a small pouch he always kept there. "I thought this might help make up for, shall we say, sunk costs."

When he held it out in his palm to catch the light, both Pax and Rahara gasped. It was Rahara who said, "Is that—a Mustafar fire diamond?"

Qui-Gon nodded. "Not as valuable as a piece of meryx, surely, but it ought to more than cover your time here on Pijal."

"And would if we remained here another three years." Pax looked at Qui-Gon in consternation. "And you're just *giving* it to us? Are you sure?"

For one moment, Qui-Gon remembered when it had been given to him—twenty years ago, on Felucia. What it had meant, why it had been so precious that he'd kept it close every day since.

But he didn't need the diamond to preserve that within his heart. In the end, the memories were what mattered.

Qui-Gon dropped the diamond into Rahara's hand. "Yes, I'm sure."

Finally, he went to bid farewell to Rael Averross.

Rael still lived in the regent's quarters, mostly because nobody else had expressed any need for them yet. It looked as though he was packing to leave—though, given the mess, it was hard to tell.

"Figured I'd see you soon." Rael stubbed out a death stick. "Your Padawan came by earlier. He's a good kid. Someday he'll be a great Jedi Knight."

"Yes, he will." Qui-Gon put one hand on Rael's shoulder. "Have you spoken to Fanry?"

Shaking his head, Rael said, "Maybe someday. Not anytime soon." He sighed. "I guess the Council was right after all."

Qui-Gon didn't follow. "About what?"

Rael sat atop a pile of not-quite-folded clothes on the unmade bed. "About how love warps our judgment. I cared so damn much about that little girl—but the way I went about it convinced her I didn't care at all. That all of it was about Nim, and none of it was about her." He sighed heavily. "Maybe someday she'll see it clearer. Maybe I will, too."

"When are you traveling back to Coruscant?" Qui-Gon asked. The sooner Rael had a new mission, the better, he thought.

Rael shrugged. "Not sure. I'm not even sure I *am* going back. Maybe this path—maybe it's not for me."

It had been shocking when Dooku left the Order. But as good a Jedi

Knight as Rael was, in some ways, being a Jedi had never been an easy fit. It would be a shame to lose him, but not a surprise. "What would you do?"

"Still thinkin' it over. Talkin' to some old friends. You know." Rael looked up at Qui-Gon with a sad smile. "When you're on the Jedi Council, don't forget me?"

"Impossible," Qui-Gon said, before hugging Rael goodbye.

Obi-Wan sat in the stable, scratching his varactyl's head. He'd only ridden it once, but would miss it all the same.

When his Master appeared, Obi-Wan patted the varactyl goodbye and went to Qui-Gon's side. "Are we ready to leave, then?"

"We are."

They walked together across the grounds, listening to the ocean, as they returned to the corvette. Obi-Wan spoke first. "I suppose you're eager to return to Coruscant. To accept the Council's offer."

"If it still holds." Qui-Gon shook his head ruefully. "After my refusal to sign the treaty, I'm not sure it does."

"It does," Obi-Wan said. When Qui-Gon looked at him in confusion, he explained, "When I called the Council to tell them what was going on, one of the Masters asked whether they should rethink your invitation. Yoda said they wouldn't, that the invitation wouldn't be undone. And everyone always says, as Yoda goes, so goes the Council."

"That's not invariably true," Qui-Gon said. "But you've given me much to think about."

What was there to think about? Then Obi-Wan had a thought. "Are you trying to choose my future Master?"

Qui-Gon nodded. "As a matter of fact, I am."

Coruscant, hectic as it could be, was still home. Qui-Gon felt refreshed, even comfortable, by the time he presented himself to the Council.

"Hasty, you were, to risk so much on the strength of a dream," said Yoda. "But a true future it revealed."

"Not exactly," said Eeth Koth. "If I understand Padawan Kenobi's report correctly, Qui-Gon believed Fanry would be the victim in the incident, not the perpetrator—"

"That's the most interesting thing about this, to me," Qui-Gon said. "Because I've come to realize that I was not only meant to have the vision—I was also meant to misinterpret it."

The Council members traded glances. It was Mace Windu who said, "What do you mean?"

"I mean, had I been on the dais with Fanry and Deren, they would've tried to sabotage my lightsaber instead of Obi-Wan's. But Fanry only knew how Obi-Wan's works. Mine has a very different inner mechanism. If she'd done to my lightsaber what she did to his, I wouldn't have wound up with a modified weapon. I wouldn't have had any weapon at all. Deren would've cut me down, Obi-Wan would almost certainly have remained on the planet's surface, and the conflict above Pijal—rather than being swiftly defused, with no loss of life—could well have sparked a war."

Yoda's ears swiveled. "Sure you are of this?"

"As certain as the Force allows," said Qui-Gon.

He knew, now, that the prophecies were real. What he had seen, the ancient mystics had seen. The Force meant for him to understand this. He knew also that he had seen the kyber that wasn't kyber—which meant the days of prophecy were at hand. Everything would change. It might even be in Qui-Gon's lifetime. In those days, slaves could be freed. Peace could be won. Qui-Gon knew that was less certain, but . . . he chose to believe.

Mace Windu seemed ready to move on from the topic. "The time has come to address your invitation to the Jedi Council. That invitation stands. While some felt your behavior to be rash, others recognize that you perceived something extraordinary through the Force. That ability is one that can only enhance this Council's deliberations."

"You honor me," Qui-Gon said. "I have only the greatest respect for every one of you. So I hope you'll understand that this isn't a repudiation of you. But I must decline to join the Jedi Council."

Silence. Qui-Gon wasn't sure anyone had turned down an invitation before, at least not in the past several centuries. Several of the Council members stared at him, and Poli Dapatian kept blinking hard, as though he wasn't sure he was seeing correctly.

Mace regained his aplomb before most of the others. "May we ask why?"

Qui-Gon knew the Council to be wrong about many things. He felt they'd allowed the Jedi Order to become a sort of chancellor's police, rather than concentrating on knowing the Force. Yes, they were wise to refuse to rule—but unwise to simply accept the status quo. Short-sighted, to lose touch with the living Force by spending so much of their time and energy on enforcing laws that could as easily be left to civilian authorities. Immoral, to refuse to act against evils such as slavery.

But none of those were the reasons he'd chosen to decline.

"My relationship to the Force has changed," Qui-Gon said. "I wish to . . . be silent for a while. To surrender to it. To accept whatever the Force brings. Joining the Council would take me far away from that goal. But this is the path I must follow."

That, in the end, was why the prophecies weren't dangerous to him, not the same way they'd been to others who'd been led to darkness. The danger came in thinking that knowing the future became a form of control over it. Finally Qui-Gon understood it was the exact opposite. Knowing the future meant surrendering to fate. Surrendering to the ebb and flow of life. Only through that surrender could the Force be truly known.

After the Council meeting, Qui-Gon set out to find Obi-Wan. Of all places, he turned out to be in the gardens. That gave them a quiet place to sit together while Qui-Gon explained what he had decided, and why. Obi-Wan was staggered at first, but he came to understand very quickly.

"I suppose in the end you couldn't agree with the Council even about your being on the Council!" he said. "But if this is the path you're called to, then this is the path you must follow."

"Which comes to the question of whether you'll follow it with me." Qui-Gon took a deep breath. "I realize we've had difficulties. But this mission changed things, I think, and for the better. If you would prefer another Master, I won't be offended. If it were up to me, though, we would continue on as we are."

Slowly, Obi-Wan began to smile. "You know, Master, I've realized— I wouldn't learn nearly as much from someone who always agreed with me."

Qui-Gon grinned back, and they clasped hands, more truly partners than ever before.

It was nearly midnight when Averross's comm unit chimed. He groaned, ready to yell at whoever thought this was a great time to call—then realized this was the communication he'd been waiting for.

Averross hit the holoprojector, and a beam of light took the form of Count Dooku.

"Rael," Dooku said, his voice deeper and graver than ever. "Have you thought more about my proposal?"

With a short laugh, Averross said, "Like I could've thought of anything else."

Dooku continued, "You would learn much here on Serenno with me. You have yet to even imagine the truth of the Force, but you could find the way. There are so many things I've learned, that I could teach you— far more than they ever told us at the Temple. You will gain more understanding, more power, than you can yet comprehend. If we stood together—we would be unconquerable."

"Glad you think so," Averross said. "But actually, I've decided. I'm goin' back to Coruscant. Not sure what the Council's gonna do with me, but I guess I'll find out."

Dooku drew himself up. Still stiff as a plank, Rael thought. "Why would you choose the path that leads to weakness? The path that is destined to fail?"

"We don't choose the light because we want to win." Averross smiled sadly. "We choose it because it is the light."

With that, he snapped the projector off, and Dooku disappeared.

AFTER

Queen Amidala entered the shrine, dipping her head so that her elaborate hairstyle wouldn't scrape the ceiling. When Obi-Wan looked up, she knelt carefully by his side. "It's nightfall." Her voice was gentle, patient, like a woman far older than her years. "Are you ready?"

Am I ready to see my Master consumed by the flames? To know I will never see him again? "Give me one more moment."

Amidala pressed her hand to his forearm, then went back outside.

Within minutes, Qui-Gon's pyre would be carried outside and burned. It was the proper end for a Jedi, and it would be accompanied by the greatest honors. Qui-Gon's death was the will of the Force. But Obi-Wan could reconcile himself to none of it.

Qui-Gon lay on a white cloth, his face as placid as it had once been in the depths of meditation. Obi-Wan had chosen not to dress him in a new tunic, but to allow those at the funeral to see the burned mark where the Sith Lord's lightsaber had pierced him through. It was the only hint of the violence of Qui-Gon's death.

The first Jedi killed by a Sith in a thousand years, he thought numbly. *That fate should never have fallen to anyone. But if it had to happen, why didn't it happen to me instead of you?*

Obi-Wan remembered that, for the first few years of his apprenticeship, he and Qui-Gon hadn't gotten along—but he remembered it the same way he remembered dates in Jedi history: as flat facts, with little life to them. Instead, when Obi-Wan thought on his time as Qui-Gon's Padawan, he always thought of the years after that mission to Pijal— the years when they had become both partners and friends. He'd expected to go through the trials, to be knighted in the proper ceremony with Qui-Gon at his side, and for the two of them to remain friends for the rest of their lives.

Instead, Obi-Wan had become a Jedi Knight that morning via a hasty field promotion. He would never again have Qui-Gon's advice, support, or companionship. In fact, his only inheritance from Qui-Gon was rather more complicated.

He glanced to the door of the shrine. Though night was falling, Obi-Wan could make out the silhouette of little Anakin Skywalker.

After Pijal, Qui-Gon's devotion to the prophecies had never faltered. Still, Obi-Wan would never have guessed that Qui-Gon would confidently identify the Chosen One as a small enslaved boy. Less would he have expected to be abruptly cast aside in favor of that same boy—a wound in his relationship with Qui-Gon that had only just begun to heal before his Master had died. Obi-Wan understood Qui-Gon's reasons, but he hadn't shared his Master's conviction that Anakin was the Chosen One.

And yet, Obi-Wan thought, *maybe this is as the Force wills it.* Qui-Gon came to believe in the prophesies again in Pijal, where he first began arguing that the Jedi should push the Republic harder on combating slavery. Never had Qui-Gon stopped arguing this to anyone who would listen—but he had never betrayed his mandate, not even on Tatooine. *If Anakin is the Chosen One, and he keeps his promise to free the slaves, it will fulfill all of Qui-Gon's hopes.*

With his dying breath, Qui-Gon had asked Obi-Wan to train Anakin as a Jedi. Most Jedi Knights didn't become Masters until years after they'd passed their own trials, the years during which they got to forge their own path. For Obi-Wan to take a Padawan after having been a Jedi Knight for a few hours was—unprecedented, surely. Possibly also unwise.

But Obi-Wan had promised. It was the last thing he'd ever said to Qui-Gon. So it had to be true.

"I will train him, Master," he said, bowing his head low until it almost touched Qui-Gon's still hand. "I will do everything for him that you would've done."

Qui-Gon had faith that Anakin Skywalker was the Chosen One. Obi-Wan would have to find faith in it, too.

Looking at Qui-Gon's face for the last time, Obi-Wan whispered, "I choose to believe."

ACKNOWLEDGMENTS

I owe significant thanks to everyone in the entire publishing process—in particular Michael Siglain, Elizabeth Schaefer, Jennifer Heddle, Pablo Hidalgo, Matt Martin, and the long-suffering copy editors whose names I do not know. Also, I owe a debt to the many friends and fellow writers who helped me stay focused through the process, in particular Cavan Scott, Daniel José Older, Stephanie Stoecker, Marti Dumas, Sarah Tolscer, Alys Arden, and Brittany Williams. Certainly none of this could've been accomplished without the tireless help of my assistant, Sarah Simpson Weiss, and the support of my agent, Diana Fox. Above all, I'd like to thank Paul Christian, who supported the writing of this book in every way possible—from researching various ancient theories about prophecy to doing the laundry. I am so grateful to every single one of you.

ABOUT THE AUTHOR

Claudia Gray is the author of *Star Wars: Lost Stars* and *Star Wars: Bloodline,* as well as the Firebird, Evernight, and Spellcaster series. She has worked as a lawyer, a journalist, a disc jockey, and a particularly ineffective waitress. Her lifelong interests include old houses, classic movies, vintage style, and history. She lives in New Orleans.

claudiagray.com
Facebook.com/authorclaudiagray
Twitter: @claudiagray

ABOUT THE TYPE

This book was set in Minion, a 1990 Adobe Originals typeface by Robert Slimbach (b. 1956). Minion is inspired by classical, old-style typefaces of the late Renaissance, a period of elegant, beautiful, and highly readable type designs. Created primarily for text setting, Minion combines the aesthetic and functional qualities that make text type highly readable with the versatility of digital technology.